LINDA HOWARD

THE MACKENZIE FAMILY

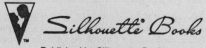

Published by Silhouette Books

America's Publisher of Contemporary Romance

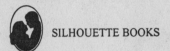 SILHOUETTE BOOKS

ISBN 0-373-48376-7

THE MACKENZIE FAMILY

Copyright © 1998 by Harlequin Books S.A.

MACKENZIE'S PLEASURE
Copyright © 1996 by Linda Howington

MACKENZIE'S MAGIC
Copyright © 1996 by Linda Howington

Printed in U.S.A.

CONTENTS

Dear Reader,

From the time *Mackenzie's Mountain* hit the stands nine years ago (good heavens, has it been that long?) I've felt as if I had a tiger by the tail and there was no way to turn loose. I never intended this to be a continuing series, but in the first book I fell in love with Wolf's son, Joe, and just *had* to write his story, *Mackenzie's Mission*. In that book I fell in love with two of his younger siblings, Zane and Maris, so of course I had to write their stories, too.

In *Mackenzie's Pleasure*, Zane, a SEAL team commander, is called upon to rescue an ambassador's kidnapped daughter. The rescue doesn't go according to plan; Barrie Lovejoy is much more than he expected, and rescuing her doesn't end the danger. But during their short time together Barrie becomes *his* woman, and Zane is the most dangerous of the Mackenzies, a man who will stop at nothing to protect those he loves.

Maris, the only Mackenzie daughter, is magic. She's fey, almost psychic, and can charm the wildest horse— as well as other dangerous animals, such as the undercover FBI agent who's on the trail of a killer, and in whose bed Maris lands. The only problem is, she was banged on the head, and she doesn't remember what happened or how she got there.

I hope you enjoy these two installments of the Mackenzie saga. Happy reading!

Linda Howard

The Mackenzie Family is dedicated to all the wonderful fans who fell as much in love with the Mackenzies as I did.

MACKENZIE'S PLEASURE

Prologue

Wolf Mackenzie slipped out of bed and restlessly paced over to the window, where he stood looking out at the stark, moonlit expanse of his land. A quick glance over his bare shoulder reassured him that Mary slept on undisturbed, though he knew it wouldn't be long before she sensed his absence and stirred, reaching out for him. When her hand didn't encounter his warmth, she would wake, sitting up in bed and drowsily pushing her silky hair out of her face. When she saw him by the window she would slide out of bed and come to him, nestling against his naked body, sleepily resting her head on his chest.

A slight smile touched his hard mouth. Like as not, if he stayed out of bed long enough for her to awaken, when they returned to the bed it wouldn't be to sleep but to make love. As he remembered, Maris had been conceived on just such an occasion, when he had been restless because Joe's fighter wing had just been deployed overseas during some flare-up. It had been Joe's first action, and Wolf had been as tense as he'd been during his own days in Vietnam.

Luckily, he and Mary were past the days when spontaneous passion could result in a new baby. Nowadays they had grandkids, not kids of their own. Ten at the last count, as a matter of fact.

But he was restless tonight, and he knew why.

The wolf always slept better when all of his cubs were accounted for.

Never mind that the cubs were adults, some of them with children of their own. Never mind that they were, one and all, supremely capable of taking care of themselves. They were *his,* and he was there if they needed him. He also liked to know, within reason, where they were bedding down for the night. It wasn't necessary for him to be able to pinpoint their location—some things a parent was better off not knowing—but if he knew what *state* they were in, that was usually enough. Hell, sometimes he would have been glad just to know which *country* they were roaming.

His concern wasn't for Joe, this time. He knew where Joe was— the Pentagon. Joe wore four stars now, and sat on the Joint Chiefs of Staff.

Joe would still rather strap on a metal bird and fly at twice the speed of sound, but those days were behind him. If he had to fly a desk, then he would damn sure fly it the best it could be flown. Besides, as he'd once said, being married to Caroline was more challenging than being in a dogfight and outnumbered four to one.

Wolf grinned when he thought of his daughter-in-law. Genius IQ, doctorates in both physics and computer sciences, a bit arrogant, a bit quirky. She'd gotten her pilot's license just after the birth of their first son, on the basis that the wife of a fighter pilot should know something about flying. She had received her certification on small jet aircraft around the time the third son had made his appearance. After the birth of her fifth son, she had grumpily told Joe that she was calling it quits with that one, because she'd given him five chances and obviously he wasn't up to the job of fathering a daughter.

It had once been gently suggested to Joe that Caroline should quit her job. The company that employed her was heavily engaged in government contract work, and the appearance of any favoritism could hurt his career. Joe had turned his cool, blue laser gaze on his superiors and said, "Gentlemen, if I have to choose between my wife and my career, I'll give you my resignation immediately." That was *not* the answer that had been expected, and nothing else was said about Caroline's work in research and development.

Wolf wasn't worried about Michael, either. Mike was the most settled of all his children, though just as focused. He had decided at an early age that he wanted to be a rancher, and that's exactly what he was. He owned a sizable spread down toward Laramie, and he and his wife were happily raising cattle and two sons.

The only uproar Mike had ever caused was when he decided to marry Shea Colvin. Wolf and Mary had given him their blessing, but the problem was that Shea's mother was Pam Hearst Colvin, one of Joe's old girlfriends—and Pam's father, Ralph Hearst, was as adamantly opposed to his beloved granddaughter marrying Michael Mackenzie as he had been to his daughter dating Joe Mackenzie.

Michael, with his typical tunnel vision, had ignored the whole tempest. His only concern was marrying Shea, and to hell with the storm erupting in the Hearst family. Quiet, gentle Shea had been torn, but she wanted Michael and refused to call off the wedding as her grandfather demanded. Pam herself had finally put an end to it, standing nose to nose with her father in the middle of his store.

"Shea *will* marry Michael," she'd stormed, when Ralph had threatened to take Shea out of his will if she married one of those damn breeds. "You didn't want me to date Joe, when he was one of the most decent men I've ever met. Now Shea wants Michael, and she's going to have him. Change your will, if you like. Hug your hate real close, because you won't be hugging your granddaughter—or your great-grandchildren. Think about that!"

So Michael had married Shea, and despite his growling and grumping, old Hearst was nuts about his two great-grandsons. Shea's second pregnancy had been difficult, and both she and the baby had nearly died. The doctor had advised them not to have any more children, but they had already decided to have only two, anyway. The two boys were growing up immersed in cattle ranching and horses. Wolf was amused that Ralph Hearst's great-grandchildren bore the Mackenzie name. Who in hell ever would have thought?

Josh, his third son, lived in Seattle with his wife, Loren, and their three sons. Josh was as jet-mad as Joe, but he had opted for the Navy rather than the Air Force, perhaps because he wanted to succeed on his own, not because his older brother was a general.

Josh was cheerful and openhearted, the most outgoing of the bunch, but he, too, had that streak of iron determination. He'd barely survived the crash that left him with a stiffened right knee and ended his naval career, but in typical Josh fashion, he had put that behind him and concentrated on what was before him. At the time, that had been his doctor—Dr. Loren Page. Never one to dither around, Josh had taken one look at tall, lovely Loren and begun his courtship from his hospital bed. He'd still been on crutches when they married. Now, three sons later, he worked for an aeronautics firm, developing new fighter aircraft, and Loren practiced her orthopedic specialty at a Seattle hospital.

Wolf knew where Maris was, too. His only daughter was currently in Montana, working as a trainer for a horse rancher. She was considering taking a job in Kentucky, working with Thoroughbreds. From the time she'd been old enough to sit unaided on a horse, her ambitions had all centered around the big, elegant animals. She had his touch with horses, able to gentle even the most contrary or vicious beast. Privately Wolf thought that she probably surpassed his skill. What she could do with a horse was pure magic.

Wolf's hard mouth softened as he thought of Maris. She had wrapped his heart around her tiny finger the moment she had been placed in his arms, when she was mere minutes old, and had looked up at him with sleepy dark eyes. Of all his children, she was the only one who had his dark eyes. His sons all looked like him, except for their blue eyes, but Maris, who resembled Mary in every other way, had her father's eyes. His daughter had light, silvery brown hair, skin so fine it was almost translucent, and her mother's determination. She was all of five foot three and weighed about a hundred pounds, but Maris never paid any attention to her slightness; when she made up her mind to do something, she persisted with bulldog stubbornness until she succeeded. She could more than hold her own with her older, much larger and domineering brothers.

Her chosen career hadn't been easy for her. People tended to think two things. One was that she was merely trading on the Mackenzie name, and the other was that she was too delicate for the job. They soon found out how wrong they were on both counts, but it was a battle Maris had fought over and over. She kept at it, though, slowly winning respect for her individual talents.

The mental rundown of his kids next brought him to Chance. Hell, he even knew where Chance was, and that was saying something. Chance roamed the world, though he always came back to Wyoming, to the mountain that was his only home. He had happened to call earlier that day, from Belize. He'd told Mary that he was going to rest for a few days before moving on. When Wolf had taken his turn on the phone, he had moved out of Mary's hearing and quietly asked Chance how bad he was hurt.

"Not too bad," Chance had laconically replied. "A few stitches and a couple of cracked ribs. This last job went a little sour on me."

Wolf didn't ask what the last job had entailed. His soldier-of-fortune son occasionally did some delicate work for the government, so Chance seldom volunteered details. The two men had an unspoken agreement to keep Mary in the dark about the danger Chance faced on a regular basis. Not only did they not want her to worry, but if she knew he was wounded, she was likely to hop on a plane and fetch him home.

When Wolf hung up the phone and turned, it was to find Mary's slate blue gaze pinned on him. "How bad is he hurt?" she demanded fiercely, hands planted on her hips.

Wolf knew better than to try lying to her. Instead he crossed the room to her and pulled her into his arms, stroking her silky hair and cradling her slight body against the solid muscularity of his. Sometimes the force of his love for this woman almost drove him to his knees. He couldn't protect her from worry, though, so he gave her the respect of honesty. "Not too bad, to use his own words."

Her response was instant. "I want him here."

"I know, sweetheart. But he's okay. He doesn't lie to us. Besides, you know Chance."

She nodded, sighing, and turned her lips against his chest. Chance was like a sleek panther, wild and intolerant of fetters. They had brought him into their home and made him one of the family, binding him to them with love when no other restraint would have held him. And like a wild creature that had been only half-tamed, he accepted the boundaries of civilization, but lightly. He roamed far and wide, and yet he always came back to them.

From the first, though, he had been helpless against Mary. She had instantly surrounded him with so much love and care that he hadn't been able to resist her, even though his light hazel eyes had reflected his consternation, even embarrassment, at her attention. If Mary went down to fetch Chance, he would come home without protest, but he would walk into the house wearing a helpless, slightly panicked "Oh, God, get me out of this" expression. And then he would meekly let her tend his wounds, pamper him and generally smother him with motherly concern.

Watching Mary fuss over Chance was one of Wolf's greatest amusements. She fussed over all of her kids, but the others had grown up with it and took it as a matter of course. Chance, though...he had been fourteen and half wild when Mary had found him. If he'd ever had a home, he didn't remember it. If he had a name, he didn't know it. He'd evaded well-meaning social authorities by staying on the move, stealing whatever he needed, food, clothes, money. He was highly intelligent and had taught himself to read from newspapers and magazines that had been thrown away. Libraries had become a favorite place for him to hang out, maybe even spend the night if he could manage it, but never two nights in a row. From what he read and what little television he saw, he understood the concept of a family, but that was all it was to him—a concept. He trusted no one but himself.

He might have grown to adulthood that way if he hadn't contracted a monster case of influenza. While driving home from work, Mary had found him lying on the side of a road, incoherent and burning up with fever. Though he was half a foot taller than she and some fifty pounds heavier, somehow she had wrestled and bullied the boy into her truck and taken him to the local clinic, where Doc Nowacki discovered that the flu had progressed into pneumonia and quickly transferred Chance to the nearest hospital, eighty miles away.

Mary had driven home and insisted that Wolf take her to the hospital—immediately.

Chance was in intensive care when they arrived. At first the nursing staff hadn't wanted to let them see him, since they weren't family and in fact didn't know anything about him. Child services had been notified, and someone was on the way to take care of the paperwork. They had been reasonable, even kind, but they hadn't reckoned with Mary. She was relentless. She wanted to see the boy, and a bulldozer couldn't have budged her until she saw him. Eventually the nurses, overworked and outclassed by a will far stronger than their own, gave in and let Wolf and Mary into the small cubicle.

As soon as he saw the boy, Wolf knew why Mary was so taken with him. It wasn't just that he was deathly ill; he was obviously part American Indian. He would have reminded Mary so forcibly of her own children that she could no more have forgotten about him than she could one of them.

Wolf's expert eye swept over the boy as he lay there so still and silent, his eyes closed, his breathing labored. The hectic color of fever stained his high cheekbones. Four different bags dripped an IV solution into his muscular right arm, which was taped to the bed. Another bag hung at the side of the bed, measuring the output of his kidneys.

Not a half-breed, Wolf had thought. A quarter, maybe. No more than that. But still, there was no doubting his heritage. His fingernails were light against the tanned skin of his fingers, where an Anglo's nails would have been pinker. His thick, dark brown hair, so long it brushed his shoulders, was straight. There were those high cheekbones, the clear-cut lips, the high-bridged nose. He was the most handsome boy Wolf had ever seen.

Mary went up to the bed, all her attention focused on the boy who lay so ill and helpless on the snowy sheets. She laid her cool hand lightly against his forehead, then stroked it over his hair. "You'll be all right," she murmured. "I'll make sure you are."

He had lifted his heavy lids, struggling with the effort. For the first time Wolf saw the light hazel eyes, almost golden, and circled with a brown rim so dark it was almost black. Confused, the boy had focused first on Mary; then his gaze had wandered to Wolf, and belated alarm flared in his eyes. He tried to heave himself up, but he was too weak even to tug his taped arm free.

Wolf moved to the boy's other side. "Don't be afraid," he said quietly. "You have pneumonia, and you're in a hospital." Then, guessing what lay at the bottom of the boy's panic, he added, "We won't let them take you."

Those light eyes had rested on his face, and perhaps Wolf's appearance had calmed him. Like a wild animal on guard, he slowly relaxed and drifted back to sleep.

Over the next week, the boy's condition improved, and Mary swung into action. She was determined that the boy, who still had not given them a name, not be taken into state custody for even one day. She pulled strings, harangued people, even called on Joe to use his influence, and her tenacity worked. When the boy was released from the hospital, he went home with Wolf and Mary.

He had gradually become accustomed to them, though by no stretch of the imagination had he been friendly, or even trustful. He would answer their questions, in one word if possible, but he never actually *talked* with them. Mary hadn't been discouraged. From the first, she simply treated the boy as if he was hers—and soon he was.

The boy who had always been alone was suddenly plunged into the middle of a large, volatile family. For the first time he had a roof over his head every night, a room all to himself, ample food in his belly. He had clothing hanging in the closet and new boots on his feet. He was still too weak to share in the chores everyone did, but Mary immediately began tutoring him to bring him up to Zane's level academically, since the two boys were the same age, as near as they could tell. Chance took to the books like a starving pup to its mother's teat, but in every other way he determinedly remained at arm's length. Those shrewd, guarded eyes took note of every nuance of their family relationships, weighing what he saw now against what he had known before.

Finally he unbent enough to tell them that he was called Sooner. He didn't have a real name.

Maris had looked at him blankly. "Sooner?"

His mouth had twisted, and he'd looked far too old for his fourteen years. "Yeah, like a mongrel dog."

"No," Wolf had said, because the name was a clue. "You know

you're part Indian. More than likely you were called Sooner because you were originally from Oklahoma—and that means you're probably Cherokee.''

The boy merely looked at him, his expression guarded, but still something about him had lightened at the possibility that he hadn't been likened to a dog of unknown heritage.

His relationships with everyone in the family were complicated. With Mary, he wanted to hold himself away, but he simply couldn't. She mothered him the way she did the rest of her brood, and it terrified him even though he delighted in it, soaking up her loving concern. He was wary of Wolf, as if he expected the big man to turn on him with fists and boots. Wise in the ways of wild things, Wolf gradually gentled the boy the same way he did horses, letting him get accustomed, letting him realize he had nothing to fear, then offering respect and friendship and, finally, love.

Michael had already been away at college, but when he did come home he simply made room in his family circle for the newcomer. Sooner was relaxed with Mike from the start, sensing that quiet acceptance.

He got along with Josh, too, but Josh was so cheerful it was impossible not to get along with him. Josh took it on himself to be the one who taught Sooner how to handle the multitude of chores on a horse ranch. Josh was the one who taught him how to ride, though Josh was unarguably the worst horseman in the family. That wasn't to say he wasn't good, but the others were better, especially Maris. Josh didn't care, because his heart was wrapped up in planes just the way Joe's had been, so perhaps he had been more patient with Sooner's mistakes than anyone else would have been.

Maris was like Mary. She had taken one look at the boy and immediately taken him under her fiercely protective wing, never mind that Sooner was easily twice her size. At twelve, Maris had been not quite five feet tall and weighed all of seventy-four pounds. It didn't matter to her; Sooner became hers the same way her older brothers were hers. She chattered to him, teased him, played jokes on him—in short, drove him crazy, the way little sisters were supposed to do. Sooner hadn't had any idea how to handle the way she treated him, any more than he had with Mary. Sometimes he had watched Maris as if she was a ticking time bomb, but it was Maris who won his first smile with her teasing. It was Maris who actually got him to enter the family conversations: slowly, at first, as he learned how families worked, how the give-and-take of talking melded them together, then with more ease. Maris could still tease him into a rage, or coax a laugh out of him, faster than anyone else. For a while Wolf had wondered if the two might become romantically interested in each other as they grew older, but it hadn't happened. It was a testament to how fully Sooner had become a part of their family; to both of them, they were simply brother and sister.

Things with Zane had been complicated, though.

Zane was, in his own way, as guarded as Sooner. Wolf knew warriors, having been one himself, and what he saw in his youngest son was almost frightening. Zane was quiet, intense, watchful. He moved like a cat, gracefully, soundlessly. Wolf had trained all his children, including Maris, in self-defense, but with Zane it was something more. The boy took to it with the ease of someone putting on a well-worn shoe; it was as if it had been made for him. When it came to marksmanship, he had the eye of a sniper, and the deadly patience.

Zane had the instinct of a warrior: to protect. He was immediately on guard against this intruder into the sanctity of his family's home turf.

He hadn't been nasty to Sooner. He hadn't made fun of him or been overtly unfriendly, which wasn't in his nature. Rather, he had held himself away from the newcomer, not rejecting, but certainly not welcoming, either. But because they were the same age, Zane's acceptance was the most crucial, and Sooner had reacted to Zane's coolness by adopting the same tactics. They had ignored each other.

While the kids were working out their relationships, Wolf and Mary had been pushing hard to legally adopt Sooner. They had asked him if that was what he wanted and, typically, he had responded with a shrug and an expressionless, "Sure." Taking that for the impassioned plea it was, Mary redoubled her efforts to get the adoption pushed through.

As things worked out, they got the word that the adoption could go forward on the same day Zane and Sooner settled things between them.

The dust was what had caught Wolf's attention.

At first he hadn't thought anything of it, because when he glanced over he saw Maris sitting on the top rail of the fence, calmly watching the commotion. Figuring one of the horses was rolling in the dirt, Wolf went back to work. Two seconds later, however, his sharp ears caught the sound of grunts and what sounded suspiciously like blows.

He walked across the yard to the other corral. Zane and Sooner had gotten into the corner, where they couldn't be seen from the house, and were ferociously battering each other. Wolf saw at once that both boys, despite the force of their blows, were restraining themselves to the more conventional fisticuffs rather than the faster, nastier ways he'd also taught them. He leaned his arms on the top rail beside Maris. "What's this about?"

"They're fighting it out," she said matter-of-factly, without taking her eyes from the action.

Josh soon joined them at the fence, and they watched the battle. Zane and Sooner were both tall, muscular boys, very strong for their ages. They stood toe to toe, taking turns driving their fists into each other's faces. When one of them got knocked down, he got to his feet and waded back into the fray. They were almost eerily silent, except for the involuntary grunts and the sounds of hard fists hitting flesh.

Mary saw them standing at the fence and came out to investigate. She stood beside Wolf and slipped her small hand into his. He felt her flinch every time a blow landed, but when he looked at her, he saw that she was wearing her prim schoolteacher's expression, and he knew that Mary Elizabeth Mackenzie was about to call the class to order.

She gave it five minutes. Evidently deciding this could go on for hours, and that both boys were too stubborn to give in, she settled the matter herself. In her crisp, clear teaching voice she called out, "All right, boys, let's get this wrapped up. Supper will be on the table in ten minutes." Then she calmly walked back to the house, fully confident that she had brought detente to the corral.

She had, too. She had reduced the fight to the level of a chore or a project, given them a time limit and a reason for ending it.

Both boys' eyes had flickered to that slight retreating figure with the ramrod spine. Then Zane had turned to Sooner, the coolness of his blue gaze somewhat marred by the swelling of his eyes. "One more," he said grimly, and slammed his fist into Sooner's face.

Sooner picked himself up off the dirt, squared up again and returned the favor.

Zane got up, slapped the dirt from his clothes and held out his hand. Sooner gripped it, though they had both winced at the pain in their knuckles. They shook hands, eyed each other as equals, then returned to the house to clean up. After all, supper was almost on the table.

At supper, Mary told Sooner that the adoption had been given the green light. His pale hazel eyes had glittered in his battered face, but he hadn't said anything.

"You're a Mackenzie now," Maris had pronounced with great satisfaction. "You'll have to have a real name, so choose one."

It hadn't occurred to her that choosing a name might require some thought, but as it happened, Sooner had looked around the table at the family that pure blind luck had sent him, and a wry little smile twisted up one side of his bruised, swollen mouth. "Chance," he said, and the unknown, unnamed boy became Chance Mackenzie.

Zane and Chance hadn't become immediate best friends after the fight. What they had found, instead, was mutual respect, but friendship grew out of it. Over the years, they became so close that they could well have been born twins. There were other fights between them, but it was well known around Ruth, Wyoming, that if anyone decided to take on either of the boys, he would find himself facing both of them. They could batter each other into the ground, but by God, no one else was going to.

They had entered the Navy together, Zane becoming a SEAL, while Chance had gone into Naval Intelligence. Chance had since left the Navy, though, and gone out on his own, while Zane was a SEAL team leader.

And that brought Wolf to the reason for his restlessness.

Zane.

There had been a lot of times in Zane's career when he had been out of touch, when they hadn't known where he was or what he was doing. Wolf hadn't slept well then, either. He knew too much about the SEALs, having seen them in action in Vietnam during his tours of duty. They were the most highly trained and skilled of the special forces, their stamina and teamwork proven by grueling tests that broke lesser men. Zane was particularly well-suited for the work, but in the final analysis, the SEALs were still human. They could be killed. And because of the nature of their work, they were often in dangerous situations.

The SEAL training had merely accentuated the already existing facets of Zane's nature. He had been honed to a perfect fighting machine, a warrior who was in top condition, but who used his brain more than his brawn. He was even more lethal and intense now, but he had learned to temper that deadliness with an easier manner, so that most people were unaware they were dealing with a man who could kill them in a dozen different ways with his bare hands. With that kind of knowledge and skill at his disposal, Zane had learned a calm control that kept him in command of himself. Of all Wolf's offspring, Zane was the most capable of taking care of himself, but he was also the one in the most danger.

Where in hell *was* he?

There was a whisper of movement from the bed, and Wolf looked around as Mary slipped from between the sheets and joined him at the window, looping her arms around his hard, trim waist and nestling her head on his bare chest.

"Zane?" she asked quietly, in the darkness.

"Yeah." No more explanation was needed.

"He's all right," she said with a mother's confidence. "I'd know if he wasn't."

Wolf tipped her head up and kissed her, lightly at first, then with growing intensity. He turned her slight body more fully into his embrace and felt her quiver as she pressed to him, pushing her hips against his, cradling the rise of his male flesh against her softness. There had been passion between them from their first meeting, all those years ago, and time hadn't taken it from them.

He lifted her in his arms and carried her back to bed, losing himself in the welcome and warmth of her soft body. Afterward, though, lying in the drowsy aftermath, he turned his face toward the window. Before sleep claimed him, the thought came again. Where was Zane?

Chapter 1

Zane Mackenzie wasn't happy.

No one aboard the aircraft carrier USS *Montgomery* was happy; well, maybe the cooks were, but even that was iffy, because the men they were serving were sullen and defensive. The seamen weren't happy, the radar men weren't happy, the gunners weren't happy, the Marines weren't happy, the wing commander wasn't happy, the pilots weren't happy, the air boss wasn't happy, the executive officer wasn't happy, and Captain Udaka sure as hell wasn't happy.

The combined unhappiness of the five thousand sailors on board the carrier didn't begin to approach Lieutenant-Commander Mackenzie's level of unhappiness.

The captain outranked him. The executive officer outranked him. Lieutenant-Commander Mackenzie addressed them with all the respect due their rank, but both men were uncomfortably aware that their asses were in a sling and their careers on the line. Actually, their careers were probably in the toilet. There wouldn't be any court-martials, but neither would be there any more promotions, and they would be given the unpopular commands from now until they either retired or resigned, their choice depending on how clearly they could read the writing on the wall.

Captain Udaka's broad, pleasant face was one that wore responsibility easily, but now his expression was set in lines of unhappy acceptance as he met the icy gaze of the lieutenant-commander. SEALs in general made the captain nervous; he didn't quite trust them or the way they operated outside normal regulations. This one in particular made him seriously want to be somewhere—anywhere—else.

He had met Mackenzie before, when both he and Boyd, the XO, had been briefed on the security exercise. The SEAL team under Mackenzie's command would try to breach the carrier's security, probing for weaknesses that could be exploited by any of the myriad terrorist groups so common these days. It was a version of the exercises once conducted by the SEAL Team Six Red Cell, which had been so notorious and so far outside the regulations that it had been disbanded after seven years of operation. The concept, however, had lived on, in a more controlled manner. SEAL Team Six was a covert, counterterrorism unit, and one of the best ways to counter terrorism was to prevent it from happening in the first place, rather than reacting to it after people were dead. To this end, the security of naval installations and carrier battle groups was tested by the SEALs, who then recommended changes to correct the weaknesses they had discovered. There were always weaknesses, soft spots—the SEALs had never yet been completely thwarted, even though the base commanders and ships' captains were always notified in advance.

At the briefing, Mackenzie had been remote but pleasant. Controlled. Most SEALs had a wild, hard edge to them, but Mackenzie had seemed more regular Navy, recruiting-poster perfect in his crisp whites and with his coolly courteous manner. Captain Udaka had felt comfortable with him, certain that Lieutenant-Commander Mackenzie was the administrative type rather than a true part of those wild-ass SEALs.

He'd been wrong.

The courtesy remained, and the control. The white uniform looked as perfect as it had before. But there was nothing at all pleasant in the deep voice, or in the cold fury that lit the pale blue gray eyes so they glittered like moonlight on a knife blade. The aura of danger surrounding him was so strong it was almost palpable, and Captain Udaka knew that he had been drastically wrong in his assessment of

Mackenzie. This was no desk jockey; this was a man around whom others should walk very lightly indeed. The captain felt as if his skin was being flayed from his body, strip by strip, by that icy gaze. He had also never felt closer to death than he had the moment Mackenzie had entered his quarters after learning what had happened.

"Captain, you were briefed on the exercise," Zane said coldly. "Everyone on this ship was advised, as well as notified that my men wouldn't be carrying weapons of any sort. Explain, then, *why in hell two of my men were shot!*"

The XO, Mr. Boyd, looked at his hands. Captain Udaka's collar felt too tight, except that it was already unbuttoned, and the only thing choking him was the look in Mackenzie's eyes.

"There's no excuse," he said rawly. "Maybe the guards were startled and fired without thinking. Maybe it was a stupid, macho turf thing, wanting to show the big bad SEALs that they couldn't penetrate our security, after all. It doesn't matter. There's no excuse." Everything that happened on board his ship was, ultimately, his responsibility. The trigger-happy guards would pay for their mistake—and so would he.

"My men had *already* penetrated your security," Zane said softly, his tone making the hairs stand up on the back of the captain's neck.

"I'm aware of that." The breach of his ship's security was salt in the captain's wounds, but nothing at all compared to the enormous mistake that had been made when men under his command had opened fire on the unarmed SEALs. His men, his responsibility. Nor did it help his feelings that, when two of their team had gone down, the remainder of the SEAL team, *unarmed,* had swiftly taken control and secured the area. Translated, that meant the guards who had done the shooting had been roughly handled and were now in sick bay with the two men they had shot. In reality, the phrase "roughly handled" was a euphemism for the fact that the SEALS had beaten the hell out of his men.

The most seriously wounded SEAL was Lieutenant Higgins, who had taken a bullet in the chest and would be evacuated by air to Germany as soon as he was stabilized. The other SEAL, Warrant Officer Odessa, had been shot in the thigh; the bullet had broken his femur. He, too, would be taken to Germany, but his condition was stable, even if his temper was not. The ship's doctor had been forced to sedate him to keep him from wreaking vengeance on the battered guards, two of whom were still unconscious.

The five remaining members of the SEAL team were in Mission Planning, prowling around like angry tigers looking for someone to maul just to make themselves feel better. They were restricted to the area by Mackenzie's order, and the ship's crew was giving them a wide berth. Captain Udaka wished he could do the same with Mackenzie. He had the impression of cold savagery lurking just beneath the surface of the man's control. There would be hell to pay for this night's fiasco.

The phone on his desk emitted a harsh *brr.* Though he was relieved by the interruption, Captain Udaka snatched up the receiver and barked, "I gave orders I wasn't to be—" He stopped, listening, and his expression changed. His gaze shifted to Mackenzie. "We'll be right there," he said, and hung up.

"There's a scrambled transmission coming in for you," he said to Mackenzie, rising to his feet. "Urgent." Whatever message the transmission contained, Captain Udaka looked on it as a much-welcomed reprieve.

Zane listened intently to the secure satellite transmission, his mind racing as he began planning the logistics of the mission. "My team is two men short, sir," he said. "Higgins and Odessa were injured in the security exercise." He didn't say *how* they'd been injured; that would be handled through other channels.

"Damn it," Admiral Lindley muttered. He was in an office in the U.S. Embassy in Athens. He looked up at the others in the office: Ambassador Lovejoy, tall and spare, with the smoothness bequeathed by a lifetime of privilege and wealth, though now there was a stark, panicked expression in his hazel eyes; the CIA station chief, Art Sandefer, a nondescript man with short gray hair and tired, intelligent eyes; and, finally, Mack Prewett, second only to Sandefer in the local CIA hierarchy. Mack was known in some circles as Mack the Knife; Admiral Lindley knew Mack was generally considered a man who got things done, a man whom it was dangerous to cross. For all his decisiveness, though, he wasn't a cowboy who was likely to endanger people by going off half-cocked. He was as thorough as he was decisive, and it was through his contacts that they had obtained such good, prompt information in this case.

The admiral had put Zane on the speakerphone, so the other three in the room had heard the bad news about the SEAL team on which they had all been pinning their hopes. Ambassador Lovejoy looked even more haggard.

"We'll have to use another team," Art Sandefer said.

"That'll take too much time!" the ambassador said with stifled violence. "My God, already she could be—" He stopped, anguish twisting his face. He wasn't able to complete the sentence.

"I'll take the team in," Zane said. His amplified voice was clear in the soundproofed room. "We're the closest, and we can be ready to go in an hour."

"You?" the admiral asked, startled. "Zane, you haven't seen live action since—"

"My last promotion," Zane finished dryly. He hadn't liked trading action for administration, and he was seriously considering resigning his commission. He was thirty-one, and it was beginning to look as if his success in his chosen field was going to prevent him from practicing it; the higher-ranking the officer, the less likely that officer was to be in the thick of the action. He'd been thinking about something in law enforcement, or maybe even throwing in with Chance. There was nonstop action there, for sure.

For now, though, a mission had been dumped in his lap, and he was going to take it.

"I train with my men, Admiral," he said. "I'm not rusty, or out of shape."

"I didn't think you were," Admiral Lindley replied, and sighed. He met the ambassador's anguished gaze, read the silent plea for help. "Can six men handle the mission?" he asked Zane.

"Sir, I wouldn't risk my men if I didn't think we could do the job."

This time the admiral looked at both Art Sandefer and Mack Prew-

ett. Art's expression was noncommittal, the Company man refusing
to stick his neck out, but Mack gave the admiral a tiny nod. Admiral
Lindley swiftly weighed all the factors. Granted, the SEAL team
would be two members short, and the leader would be an officer who
hadn't been on an active mission in over a year, but that officer happened to be Zane Mackenzie. All things considered, the admiral
couldn't think of any other man he would rather have on this mission.
He'd known Zane for several years now, and there was no better
warrior, no one he trusted more. If Zane said he was ready, then he
was ready. "All right. Go in and get her out."

As the admiral hung up, Ambassador Lindley blurted, "Shouldn't
you send in someone else? My daughter's life is at stake! This man
hasn't been in the field, he's out of shape, out of practice—"

"Waiting until we could get another team into position would drastically lower our chances of finding her," the admiral pointed out as
kindly as possible. Ambassador Lindley wasn't one of his favorite
people. For the most part, he was a horse's ass and a snob, but there
was no doubt he doted on his daughter. "And as far as Zane Mackenzie is concerned, there's no better man for the job."

"The admiral's right," Mack Prewett said quietly, with the authority that came so naturally to him. "Mackenzie is so good at what
he does it's almost eerie. I would feel comfortable sending him in
alone. If you want your daughter back, don't throw obstacles in his
way."

Ambassador Lindley shoved his hand through his hair, an unchar-
acteristic gesture for so fastidious a man; it was a measure of his
agitation. "If anything goes wrong..."

It wasn't clear whether he was about to voice a threat or was simply
worrying aloud, but he couldn't complete the sentence. Mack Prewett
gave a thin smile. "Something always goes wrong. If anyone can
handle it, Mackenzie can."

After Zane terminated the secure transmission he made his way
through the network of corridors to Mission Planning. Already he
could feel the rush of adrenaline pumping through his muscles as he
began preparing, mentally and physically, for the job before him.

When he entered the room with its maps and charts and communication systems, and the comfortable chairs grouped around a large table, five hostile faces turned immediately toward him, and he felt the surge of renewed energy and anger from his men.

Only one of them, Santos, was seated at the table, but Santos was the team medic, and he was usually the calmest of the bunch. Ensign Peter "Rocky" Greenberg, second in command of the team and a controlled, detail-oriented kind of guy, leaned against the bulkhead with his arms crossed and murder in his narrowed brown eyes. Antonio Withrock, nicknamed Bunny because he never ran out of energy, was prowling the confines of the room like a mean, hungry cat, his dark skin pulled tight across his high cheekbones. Paul Drexler, the team sniper, sat cross-legged on top of the table while he wiped an oiled cloth lovingly over the disassembled parts of his beloved Remington bolt-action 7.62 rifle. Zane didn't even lift his eyebrows at the sight. His men were supposed to be unarmed, and they had been during the security exercise that had gone so damn sour, but *keeping* Drexler unarmed was another story.

"Planning on taking over the ship?" Zane inquired mildly of the sniper.

His blue eyes cold, Drexler cocked his head as if considering the idea. "I might."

Winstead "Spooky" Jones had been sitting on the deck, his back resting against the bulkhead, but at Zane's entrance he rose effortlessly to his feet. He didn't say anything, but his gaze fastened on Zane's face, and a spark of interest replaced some of the anger in his eyes.

Spook never missed much, and the other team members had gotten in the habit of watching him, picking up cues from his body language. No more than three seconds passed before all five men were watching Zane with complete concentration.

Greenberg was the one who finally spoke. "How's Bobcat doing, boss?"

They had read Spooky's tension, but misread the cause, Zane realized. They thought Higgins had died from his wounds. Drexler began assembling his rifle with sharp, economical motions. "He's stabilized," Zane reassured them. He knew his men, knew how tight they were. A SEAL team had to be tight. Their trust in each other had to be absolute, and if something happened to one of them, they all felt it. "They're transferring him now. It's touchy, but I'll put my money on Bobcat. Odie's gonna be okay, too." He hitched one hip on the edge of the table, his pale eyes glittering with the intensity that had caught Spooky's attention. "Listen up, children. An ambassador's daughter was snatched a few hours ago, and we're going into Libya to get her."

Six black-clad figures slipped silently along the narrow, deserted street in Benghazi, Libya. They communicated by hand signals, or by whispers into the Motorola headsets they all wore under their black knit balaclava hoods. Zane was in his battle mode; he was utterly calm as they worked their way toward the four-story stone building where Barrie Lovejoy was being held on the top floor, if their intelligence was good, and if she hadn't been moved within the past few hours.

Action always affected him this way, as if every cell in his body had settled into its true purpose of existence. He had missed this, missed it to the point that he knew he wouldn't be able to stay in the Navy without it. On a mission, all his senses became more acute, even as a deep center of calm radiated outward. The more intense the action, the calmer he became, as time stretched out into slow motion. At those times he could see and hear every detail, analyze and predict the outcome, then make his decision and act—all within a split second that felt like minutes. Adrenaline would flood his body—he would feel the blood racing through his veins—but his mind would remain detached and calm. He had been told that the look on his face during those times was frighteningly remote, jarring in its total lack of expression.

The team moved forward in well-orchestrated silence. They each knew what to do, and what the others would do. That was the purpose of the trust and teamwork that had been drilled into them through the twenty-six weeks of hell that was formally known as BUD/S training. The bond between them enabled them to do more together than could be accomplished if each worked on his own. Teamwork wasn't just a word to the SEALs, it was their center.

Spooky Jones was point man. Zane preferred using the wiry Southerner for that job because he had unfrayable nerves and could ghost around like a lynx. Bunny Withrock, who almost reverberated with nervous energy, was bringing up the rear. No one sneaked up on Bunny—except the Spook. Zane was right behind Jones, with Drexler, Greenberg and Santos ranging between him and Bunny. Greenberg was quiet, steady, totally dependable. Drexler was uncanny with that rifle, and Santos, besides being a damn good SEAL, also had the skill to patch them up and keep them going, if they were patchable. Overall, Zane had never worked with a better group of men.

Their presence in Benghazi was pure luck, and Zane knew it. Good luck for them and, he hoped, for Miss Lovejoy, but bad luck for the terrorists who had snatched her off the street in Athens fifteen hours ago. If the *Montgomery* hadn't been just south of Crete and in perfect position for launching a rescue, if the SEALs hadn't been on the carrier to practice special insertions as well as the security exercise, then there would have been a delay of precious hours, perhaps even as long as a day, while another team got supplied and into position. As it was, the special insertion into hostile territory they had just accomplished had been the real thing instead of just a practice.

Miss Lovejoy was not only the ambassador's daughter, she was an employee at the embassy, as well. The ambassador was apparently very strict and obsessive about his daughter, having lost his wife and son in a terrorist attack in Rome fifteen years before, when Miss Lovejoy had been a child of ten. After that, he had kept her secluded in private schools, and since she had finished college, she had been acting as his hostess as well as performing her "work" at the embassy. Zane suspected her job was more window dressing than anything else, something to keep her busy. She had never really worked a day in her life, never been out from under her father's protection—until today.

She and a friend had left the embassy to do some shopping. Three men had grabbed her, shoved her into a car and driven off. The friend had immediately reported the abduction. Despite efforts to secure the airport and ports—cynically, Zane suspected deliberate foot-dragging by the Greek authorities—a private plane had taken off from Athens and flown straight to Benghazi.

Thanks to the friend's prompt action, sources on the ground in Benghazi had been alerted. It had been verified that a young woman of Miss Lovejoy's description had been taken off the plane and hustled into the city, into the very building Zane and his team were about to enter.

It had to be her; there weren't that many red-haired Western women in Benghazi. In fact, he would bet there was only one—Barrie Lovejoy.

They were betting her life or it

Chapter 2

Barrie lay in almost total darkness, heavy curtains at the single window blocking out most of whatever light would have entered. She could tell that it was night; the level of street noise outside had slowly diminished, until now there was mostly silence. The men who had kidnapped her had finally gone away, probably to sleep. They had no worries about her being able to escape; she was naked, and tied tightly to the cot on which she lay. Her wrists were bound together, her arms drawn over her head and tied to the frame of the cot. Her ankles were also tied together, then secured to the frame. She could barely move; every muscle in her body ached, but those in her shoulders burned with agony. She would have screamed, she would have begged for someone to come and release the ropes that held her arms over her head, but she knew that the only people who would come would be the very ones who had tied her in this position, and she would do anything, give anything, to keep from ever seeing them again.

She was cold. They hadn't even bothered to throw a blanket over her naked body, and long, convulsive shivers kept shaking her, though she couldn't tell if she was chilled from the night air or from shock. She didn't suppose it mattered. Cold was cold.

She tried to think, tried to ignore the pain, tried not to give in to shock and terror. She didn't know where she was, didn't know how she could escape, but if the slightest opportunity presented itself, she would have to be ready to take it. She wouldn't be able to escape tonight; her bonds were too tight, her movements too restricted. But tomorrow—oh, God, tomorrow.

Terror tightened her throat, almost choking off her breath. Tomorrow they would be back, and there would be another one with them, the one for whom they waited. A violent shiver racked her as she thought of their rough hands on her bare body, the pinches and slaps and crude probings, and her stomach heaved. She would have vomited, if there had been anything to vomit, but they hadn't bothered to feed her.

She couldn't go through that again.

Somehow, she had to get away.

Desperately she fought down her panic. Her thoughts darted around like crazed squirrels as she tried to plan, to think of something, anything, that she could do to protect herself. But what *could* she do, lying there like a turkey all trussed up for Thanksgiving dinner?

Humiliation burned through her. They hadn't raped her, but they had done other things to her, things to shame and terrorize her and break her spirit. Tomorrow, when the leader arrived, she was sure her reprieve would be over. The threat of rape, and then the act of it, would shatter her and leave her malleable in their hands, desperate to do anything to avoid being violated again. At least that was what they planned, she thought. But she would be damned if she would go along with their plan.

She had been in a fog of terror and shock since they had grabbed her and thrown her into a car, but as she lay there in the darkness, cold and miserable and achingly vulnerable in her nakedness, she felt as if the fog was lifting, or maybe it was being burned away. No one who knew Barrie would ever have described her as hot-tempered, but then, what she felt building in her now wasn't as volatile and fleeting as mere temper. It was rage, as pure and forceful as lava forcing its way upward from the bowels of the earth until it exploded outward and swept away everything in its path.

Nothing in her life had prepared her for these past hours. After her mother and brother had died, she had been pampered and protected as few children ever were. She had seen some—most, actually—of her schoolmates as they struggled with the misery of broken parental promises, of rare, stressful visits, of being ignored and shunted out of the way, but she hadn't been like them. Her father adored her, and she knew it. He was intensely interested in her safety, her friends, her schoolwork. If he said he would call, then the call came exactly when he'd said it would. Every week had brought some small gift in the mail, inexpensive but thoughtful. She'd understood why he worried so much about her safety, why he wanted her to attend the exclusive girls' school in Switzerland, with its cloistered security, rather than a public school, with its attendant hurly-burly.

She was all he had left.

He was all she had left, too. When she'd been a child, after the incident that had halved the family, she had clung fearfully to her father for months, dogging his footsteps when she could, weeping inconsolably when his work took him away from her. Eventually the dread that he, too, would disappear from her life had faded, but the pattern of overprotectiveness had been set.

She was twenty-five now, a grown woman, and though in the past few years his protectiveness had begun to chafe, she had enjoyed the even tenor of her life too much to really protest. She liked her job at the embassy, so much that she was considering a full-time career in the foreign service. She enjoyed being her father's hostess. She had the duties and protocol down cold, and there were more and more female ambassadors on the international scene. It was a moneyed and insular community, but by both temperament and pedigree she was suited to the task. She was calm, even serene, and blessed with a considerate and tactful nature.

But now, lying naked and helpless on a cot, with bruises mottling her pale skin, the rage that consumed her was so deep and primal she felt as if it had altered something basic inside her, a sea change of her very nature. She would *not* endure what they—nameless, malevolent "they"—had planned for her. If they killed her, so be it. She was prepared for death; no matter what, she would not submit.

The heavy curtains fluttered.

The movement caught her eye, and she glanced at the window, but the action was automatic, without curiosity. She was already so cold that even a wind strong enough to move those heavy curtains couldn't chill her more.

The wind was black, and had a shape.

Her breath stopped in her chest.

Mutely she watched the big black shape, as silent as a shadow, slip through the window. It couldn't be human; people made *some* sound when they moved. Surely, in the total silence of the room, she would have been able to hear the whisper of the curtains as the fabric moved, or the faint, rhythmic sigh of breathing. A shoe scraping on the floor, the rustle of clothing, anything—if it was human.

After the black shape had passed between them, the curtains didn't fall back into the perfect alignment that had blocked the light; there was a small opening in them, a slit that allowed a shaft of moonlight, starlight, street light—whatever it was—to relieve the thick darkness. Barrie strained to focus on the dark shape, her eyes burning as she watched it move silently across the floor. She didn't scream; whoever or whatever approached her, it couldn't be worse than the only men likely to come to her rescue.

Perhaps she was really asleep and this was only a dream. It certainly didn't feel real. But nothing in the long, horrible hours since she had been kidnapped had felt real, and she was too cold to be asleep. No, this was real, all right.

Noiselessly the black shape glided to a halt beside the cot. It towered over her, tall and powerful, and it seemed to be examining the naked feast she presented.

Then it moved once again, lifting its hand to its head, and it peeled off its face, pulling the dark skin up as if it was no more than the skin of a banana.

It was a mask. As exhausted as she was, it was a moment before she could find a logical explanation for the nightmarish image. She blinked up at him. A man wearing a mask. Neither an animal, nor a phantom, but a flesh-and-blood man. She could see the gleam of his eyes, make out the shape of his head and the relative paleness of his face, though there was an odd bulkiness to him that in no way affected the eerily silent grace of his movements.

Just another man.

She didn't panic. She had gone beyond fear, beyond everything but rage. She simply waited—waited to fight, waited to die. Her teeth were the only weapon she had, so she would use them, if she could. She would tear at her attacker's flesh, try to damage him as much as possible before she died. If she was lucky, she would be able to get him by the throat with her teeth and take at least one of these bastards with her into death.

He was taking his time, staring at her. Her bound hands clenched into fists. Damn him. Damn them all.

Then he squatted beside the cot and leaned forward, his head very close to hers. Startled, Barrie wondered if he meant to *kiss* her—odd that the notion struck her as so unbearable—and she braced herself, preparing to lunge upward when he got close enough that she had a good chance for his throat.

"Mackenzie, United States Navy," he said in a toneless whisper that barely reached her ear, only a few inches away.

He'd spoken in *English,* with a definitely American accent. She jerked, so stunned that it was a moment before the words made sense. *Navy. United States Navy.* She had been silent for hours, refusing to speak to her captors or respond in any way, but now a small, helpless sound spilled from her throat.

"Shh, don't make any noise," he cautioned, still in that toneless whisper. Even as he spoke he was reaching over her head, and the tension on her arms suddenly relaxed. The small movement sent agony screaming through her shoulder joints, and she sucked in her breath with a sharp, gasping cry.

She quickly choked off the sound, holding it inside as she ground her teeth against the pain. "Sorry," she whispered, when she was able to speak.

She hadn't seen the knife in his hand, but she felt the chill of the blade against her skin as he deftly inserted the blade under the cords and sliced upward, felt the slight tug that freed her hands. She tried to move her arms and found that she couldn't; they remained stretched above her head, unresponsive to her commands.

He knew, without being told. He slipped the knife into its scabbard and placed his gloved hands on her shoulders, firmly kneading for a moment before he clasped her forearms and gently drew her arms down. Fire burned in her joints; it felt as if her arms were being torn from her shoulders, even though he carefully drew them straight down, keeping them aligned with her body to lessen the pain. Barrie set her teeth again, refusing to let another sound break past the barrier. Cold sweat beaded her forehead, and nausea burned in her throat once more, but she rode the swell of pain in silence.

He dug his thumbs into the balls of her shoulders, massaging the sore, swollen ligaments and tendons, intensifying the agony. Her bare body drew into a taut, pale arch of suffering, lifting from the cot. He held her down, ruthlessly pushing her traumatized joints and muscles through the recovery process. She was so cold that the heat emanating from his hands, from the closeness of his body as he bent over her, was searingly hot on her bare skin. The pain rolled through her in great shudders, blurring her sight and thought, and through the haze she realized that now, when she definitely needed to stay conscious, she was finally going to faint.

She couldn't pass out. She refused to. Grimly she hung on, and in only a few moments, moments that felt much longer, the pain began to ebb. He continued the strong kneading, taking her through the agony and into relief. She went limp, relaxing on the cot as she breathed through her mouth in the long, deep drafts of someone who has just run a race.

"Good girl," he whispered as he released her. The brief praise felt like balm to her lacerated emotions. He straightened and drew the knife again, then bent over the foot of the cot. Again there was the chill of the blade, this time against her ankles, and another small tug, then her feet were free, and involuntarily she curled into a protective ball, her body moving without direction from her brain in a belated, useless effort at modesty and self-protection. Her thighs squeezed tightly together, her arms crossed over and hid her breasts, and she buried her face against the musty ticking of the bare mattress. She couldn't look up at him, she couldn't. Tears burned her eyes, clogged her throat.

"Have you been injured?" he asked, the ghostly whisper rasping over her bare skin like an actual touch. "Can you walk?"

Now wasn't the time to let her raw nerves take over. They still had to get out undetected, and a fit of hysteria would ruin everything. She gulped twice, fighting for control of her emotions as grimly as she had fought to control the pain. The tears spilled over, but she forced herself to straighten from the defensive curl, to swing her legs over the edge of the cot. Shakily she sat up and forced herself to look at him. She hadn't done anything to be ashamed of; she would get through this. "I'm okay," she replied, and was grateful that the obligatory whisper disguised the weakness of her voice.

He crouched in front of her and silently began removing the web gear that held and secured all his equipment. The room was too dark for her to make out exactly what each item was, but she recognized the shape of an automatic weapon as he placed it on the floor between them. She watched him, uncomprehending, until he began shrugging out of his shirt. Sick terror hit her then, slamming into her like a sledgehammer. My God, surely *he* wasn't—

Gently he put the shirt around her, tucking her arms into the sleeves as if she was a child, then buttoning each button, taking care to hold the fabric away from her body so his fingers wouldn't brush against her breasts. The cloth still held his body heat; it wrapped around her like a blanket, warming her, covering her. The sudden feeling of security unnerved her almost as much as being stripped naked. Her heart lurched inside her chest, and the bottom dropped out of her stomach. Hesitantly she reached out her hand in an apology, and a plea. Tears dripped slowly down her face, leaving salty tracks in their wake. She had been the recipient of so much male brutality in the past day that his gentleness almost destroyed her control, where their blows and crudeness had only made her more determined to resist them. She had expected the same from him and instead had received a tender care that shattered her with its simplicity.

A second ticked past, two: then, with great care, he folded his gloved fingers around her hand.

His hand was much bigger than hers. She felt the size and heat of it engulf her cold fingers and sensed the control of a man who exactly knew his own strength. He squeezed gently, then released her.

She stared at him, trying to pierce the veil of darkness and see his features, but his face was barely distinguishable and blurred even more by her tears. She could make out some details, though, and discern his movements. He wore a black T-shirt, and as silently as he had removed his gear, he now put it on again. He peeled back a flap on his wrist, and she caught the faint gleam of a luminous watch. "We have exactly two and a half minutes to get out of here," he murmured. "Do *what* I say, *when* I say it."

Before, she couldn't have done it, but that brief moment of understanding, of connection, had buoyed her. Barrie nodded and got to her feet. Her knees wobbled. She stiffened them and shoved her hair out of her face. "I'm ready."

She had taken exactly two steps when, below them, a staccato burst of gunfire shattered the night.

He spun instantly, silently, slipping away from her so fast that she blinked, unable to follow him. Behind her, the door opened. A harsh, piercing flood of light blinded her, and an ominous form loomed in the doorway. The guard—of course there was a guard. Then there was a blur of movement, a grunt, and the guard sagged into supporting arms. As silently as her rescuer seemed to do everything else, he dragged the guard inside and lowered him to the floor. Her rescuer stepped over the body, snagged her wrist in an unbreakable grip and towed her from the room.

The hallway was narrow, dirty and cluttered. The light that had seemed so bright came from a single naked bulb. More gunfire was erupting downstairs and out in the street. From the left came the sound of pounding feet. To the right was a closed door, and past it she could see the first step of an unlit stairway.

He closed the door of the room they had just left and lifted her off her feet, slinging her under his left arm as if she was no more than a sack of flour. Barrie clutched dizzily at his leg as he strode swiftly to the next room and slipped into the sheltering darkness. He had barely shut the door when a barrage of shouts and curses in the hallway made her bury her face against the black material of his pants leg.

He righted her and set her on her feet, pushing her behind him as he unslung the weapon from his shoulder. They stood at the door, unmoving, listening to the commotion just on the other side of the wooden panel. She could discern three different voices and recognized them all. There were more shouts and curses, in the language she had heard off and on all day long but couldn't understand. The curses turned vicious as the guard's body, and her absence, were discovered. Something thudded against the wall as one of her kidnappers gave vent to his temper.

"This is One. Go to B."

That toneless whisper startled her. Confused, she stared at him, trying to make sense of the words. She was so tired that it took her a moment to realize he must be speaking a coded message into a radio. Of course he wasn't alone; there would be an entire team of rescuers. All they had to do was get out of the building, and there would be a helicopter waiting somewhere, or a truck, or a ship. She didn't care if they'd infiltrated on bicycles; she would gladly walk out—barefoot, if necessary.

But first they had to get out of the building. Obviously the plan had been to spirit her out the window without her kidnappers being any the wiser until morning, but something had gone wrong, and the others had been spotted. Now they were trapped in this room, with no way of rejoining the rest of his team.

Her body began to revolt against the stress it had endured for so many long hours, the terror and pain, the hunger, the effort. With a sort of distant interest she felt each muscle begin quivering, the shudders working their way up her legs, her torso, until she was shaking uncontrollably.

She wanted to lean against him but was afraid she would hinder his movements. Her life—and his—depended completely on his expertise. She couldn't help him, so the least she could do was stay out of his way. But she was desperately in need of support, so she fumbled her way a couple of steps to the wall. She was careful not to make any noise, but he sensed her movement and half turned, reaching behind himself with his left hand and catching her. Without speaking he pulled her up against his back, keeping her within reach should he have to change locations in a hurry.

His closeness was oddly, fundamentally reassuring. Her captors had filled her with such fear and disgust that every feminine instinct had been outraged, and after they had finally left her alone in the cold and the dark, she had wondered with a sort of grief if she would ever again be able to trust a man. The answer, at least with *this* man, was yes.

She leaned gratefully against his back, so tired and weak that, just for a moment, she had to rest her head on him. The heat of his body penetrated the rough fabric of the web vest, warming her cheek. He even smelled hot, she noticed through a sort of haze; his scent was a mixture of clean, fresh sweat and musky maleness, exertion and tension heating it to an aroma as heady as that of the finest whiskey. *Mackenzie.* He'd said his name was Mackenzie, whispered it to her when he crouched to identify himself.

Oh, God, he was so warm, and she was still cold. The gritty stone floor beneath her bare feet seemed to be wafting cold waves of air up her legs. His shirt was so big it dwarfed her, hanging almost to her knees, but still she was naked beneath it. Her entire body was shaking.

They stood motionless in the silent darkness of the empty room for an eternity, listening to the gunfire as it tapered off in the distance, listening to the shouts and curses as they, too, diminished, listened for so long that Barrie drifted into a light doze, leaning against him with her head resting on his back. He was like a rock, unmoving, his patience beyond anything she had ever imagined. There were no nervous little adjustments of position, no hint that his muscles got tired. The slow, even rhythm of his breathing was the only movement she could discern, and resting against him as she was, the sensation was like being on a raft in a pool, gently rising, falling....

She woke when he reached back and lightly shook her. "They think we got away," he whispered. "Don't move or make any sound while I check things out."

Obediently she straightened away from him, though she almost cried at the loss of his body heat. He switched on a flashlight that gave off only a slender beam; black tape had been placed across most of the lens. He flicked the light around the room, revealing that it was empty except for some old boxes piled along one wall. Cobwebs festooned all of the corners, and the floor was covered with a thick layer of dust. She could make out a single window in the far wall, but he was careful not to let the thin beam of light get close to it and possibly betray their presence. The room seemed to have been unused for a very long time.

He leaned close and put his mouth against her ear. His warm breath washed across her flesh with every word. "We have to get out of this building. My men have made it look as if we escaped, but we probably won't be able to hook up with them again until tomorrow night. We need someplace safe to wait. What do you know about the interior layout?"

She shook her head and followed his example, lifting herself on tiptoe to put her lips to his ear. "Nothing," she whispered. "I was blindfolded when they brought me here."

He gave a brief nod and straightened away from her. Once again Barrie felt bereft, abandoned, without his physical nearness. She knew it was just a temporary weakness, this urge to cling to him and the security he represented, but she needed him now with an urgency that was close to pain in its intensity. She wanted nothing more than to press close to him again, to feel the animal heat that told her she wasn't alone; she wanted to be in touch with the steely strength that stood between her and those bastards who had kidnapped her.

Temporary or not, Barrie hated this neediness on her part; it reminded her too sharply of the way she had clung to her father when her mother and brother had died. Granted, she had been just a child then, and the closeness that had developed between her and her father had, for the most part, been good. But she had seen how stifling it could be, too, and quietly, as was her way, she had begun placing increments of distance between them. Now this had happened, and her first instinct was to cling. Was she going to turn into a vine every time there was some trauma in her life? She didn't want to be like that, didn't want to be a weakling. This nightmare had shown her too vividly that all security, no matter how solid it seemed, had its weak points. Instead of depending on others, she would do better to develop her own strengths, strengths she knew were there but that had lain dormant for most of her life. From now on, though, things were going to change.

Perhaps they already had. The incandescent anger that had taken hold of her when she'd lain naked and trussed on that bare cot still burned within her, a small, white-hot core that even her mind-numbing fatigue couldn't extinguish. Because of it, she refused to give in to her weakness, refused to do anything that might hinder Mackenzie in any way. Instead she braced herself, forcing her knees to lock and her shoulders to square. "What are we going to do?" she whispered. "What can I do to help?"

Because there were no heavy blackout curtains on this grimy window, she was able to see part of his features as he looked at her. Half his face was in shadow, but the scant light gleamed on the slant of one high, chiseled cheekbone, revealed the strong cut of his jaw, played along a mouth that was as clearly defined as that of an ancient Greek statue.

"I'll have to leave you here alone for a little while," he said. "Will you be all right?"

Panic exploded in her stomach, her chest. She barely choked back the scream of protest that would have betrayed them. Grinding her teeth together and electing not to speak, because the scream would escape if she did, she nodded her head.

He hesitated, and Barrie could feel his attention focusing on her, as if he sensed her distress and was trying to decide whether or not it was safe to leave her. After a few moments he gave a curt nod that acknowledged her determination, or at least gave her the benefit of the doubt. "I'll be back in half an hour," he said. "I promise."

He pulled something from a pocket on his vest. He unfolded it, revealing a thin blanket of sorts. Barrie stood still as he snugly wrapped it around her. Though it was very thin, the blanket immediately began reflecting her meager body heat. When he let go of the edges they fell open, and Barrie clutched frantically at them in an effort to retain that fragile warmth. By the time she had managed to pull the blanket around her, he was gone, opening the door a narrow crack and slipping through as silently as he had come through the window in the room where she had been held. Then the door closed, and once again she was alone in the darkness.

Her nerves shrieked in protest, but she ignored them. Instead she concentrated on being as quiet as she could, listening for any sounds in the building that could tell her what was going on. There was still some noise from the street, the result of the gunfire that had alarmed the nearby citizenry, but that, too, was fading. The thick stone walls of the building dulled any sound, anyway. From within the building, there was only silence. Had her captors abandoned the site after her supposed escape? Were they in pursuit of Mackenzie's team, thinking she was with them?

She swayed on her feet, and only then did she realize that she could sit down on the floor and wrap the blanket around her, conserving even more warmth. Her feet and legs were almost numb with cold. Carefully she eased down onto the floor, terrified she would inadvertently make some noise. She sat on the thin blanket and pulled it around herself as best she could. Whatever fabric it was made from, the blanket blocked the chill of the stone floor. Drawing up her legs, Barrie hugged her knees and rested her head on them. She was more comfortable now than she had been in many long hours of terror and, inevitably, her eyelids began to droop heavily. Sitting there alone in the dark, dirty, empty room, she went to sleep.

Chapter 3

Pistol in hand, Zane moved silently through the decrepit old building, avoiding the piles of debris and crumbled stone. They were already on the top floor, so, except for the roof, the only way he could go was down. He already knew where the exits were, but what he didn't know was the location of the bad guys. Had they chosen this building as only a temporary hiding place and abandoned it when their victim seemingly escaped? Or was this their regular meeting place? If so, how many were there, and *where* were they? He had to know all that before he risked moving Miss Lovejoy. There was only another hour or so until dawn; he had to get her to a secure location before then.

He stopped at a turn in the corridor, flattening himself against the wall and easing his head around the corner just enough that he could see. Empty. Noiselessly, he moved down the hallway, just as cautiously checking the few rooms that opened off it.

He had pulled the black balaclava into place and smeared dust over his bare arms to dull the sheen of his skin and decrease his visibility. Giving his shirt to Miss Lovejoy and leaving his arms bare had increased his visibility somewhat, but he judged that his darkly tanned arms weren't nearly as likely to be spotted as her naked body. Even in the darkness of the room where they had been keeping her, he had been able to clearly make out the pale shimmer of her skin. Since none of her clothes had been in evidence, giving her his shirt was the only thing he could have done. She'd been shaking with cold—evidence of shock because the night was warm—and she likely would have gone into hysterics if he'd tried to take her out of there while she was stark naked. He had been prepared, if necessary, to knock her out. But she'd been a little trooper so far, not even screaming when he had suddenly loomed over her in the darkness. With his senses so acute, though, Zane could feel how fragile her control was, how tightly she was strung.

It was understandable. She had likely been raped, not once but many times, since she had been kidnapped. She might fall apart when the crisis was over and she was safe, but for now she was holding together. Her gutsiness made his heart clench with a mixture of tenderness and a lethal determination to protect her. His first priority was to get her out of Libya, not wreak vengeance on her kidnappers—but if any of the bastards happened to get in his way, so be it.

The dark maw of a stairwell yawned before him. The darkness was reassuring; it not only signaled the absence of a guard, it would shield him. Humans still clung to the primitive instincts of cave dwellers. If they were awake, they wanted the comfort of light around them, so they could see the approach of any enemies. Darkness was a weapon that torturers used to break the spirit of their captives, because it emphasized their helplessness, grated on their nerves. But he was a SEAL, and darkness was merely a circumstance he could use. He stepped carefully into the stairwell, keeping his back to the wall to avoid any crumbling edges of the stone. He was fairly certain the stairs were safe, otherwise the kidnappers wouldn't have been using them, but he didn't take chances. Like idiots, people stacked things on stair steps, blocking their own escape routes.

A faint lessening of the darkness just ahead told him that he was nearing the bottom of the steps. He paused while he was still within the protective shadow, listening for the slightest sound. There. He heard what he'd been searching for, the distant sound of voices, angry voices tripping over each other with curses and excuses. Though Zane spoke Arabic, he was too far away to make out what they were saying. It didn't matter; he'd wanted to know their location, and now he did.

Grimly he stifled the urge to exact revenge on Miss Lovejoy's behalf. His mission was to rescue her, not endanger her further.

There was a stairwell at each end of the building. Knowing now that the kidnappers were on the ground floor at the east end, Zane began making his way to the west staircase. He didn't meet up with any guards; as he had hoped, they thought the rescue had been effected, so they didn't see any point now in posting guards.

In his experience, perfect missions were few and far between, so rare that he could count on one hand the number of missions he'd been on where everything had gone like clockwork. He tried to be prepared for mechanical breakdowns, accidents, forces of nature, but there was no way to plan for the human factor. He didn't know how the kidnappers had been alerted to the SEALs' presence, but he had considered that possibility from the beginning and made an alternate plan in case something went wrong. Something had—exactly what, he would find out later: except for that brief communication with his men, telling them to withdraw and switch to the alternate plan, they had maintained radio silence.

Probably it was pure bad luck, some late-night citizen unexpectedly stumbling over one of his men. Things happened. So he had formulated Plan B, his just-in-case plan, because as they had worked their way toward the building, he'd had an uneasy feeling. When his gut told him something, Zane listened. Bunny Withrock had once given him a narrow-eyed look and said, "Boss, you're even spookier than the Spook." But they trusted his instincts, to the point that mentally they had probably switched to Plan B as soon as he'd voiced it, before he had even gone into the building.

With Miss Lovejoy to consider, he'd opted for safety. That was why he had gone in alone, through the window, after Spook's reconnaissance had reported that the kidnappers had set guards at intervals throughout the first floor. There were no lights in any of the rooms on the fourth floor, where Miss Lovejoy was reportedly being held, so it was likely there was no guard actually in the room with her; a guard wouldn't want to sit in the darkness.

The kidnappers had inadvertently pinpointed the room for him: only one window had been covered with curtains. When Zane had reached that room, he had carefully parted the heavy curtains to make certain they hadn't shielded an interior light, but the room beyond had been totally dark. And Miss Lovejoy had been there, just as he had expected.

Now, ostensibly with nothing left to guard, the kidnappers all seemed to be grouped together. Zane cat-footed through the lower rooms until he reached the other staircase, then climbed silently upward. Thanks to Spooky, he knew of a fairly secure place to take Miss Lovejoy while they waited for another opportunity for extraction; all he had to do was get her there undetected. That meant he had to do it before dawn, because a half-naked, red-haired Western woman would definitely be noticeable in this Islamic country. He wouldn't exactly blend in himself, despite his black hair and tanned skin, because of his dark cammies, web gear and weaponry. Most people noticed a man with camouflage paint on his face and an automatic rifle slung over his shoulder.

He reached the room where he'd left Miss Lovejoy and entered as quietly as he'd left. The room was empty. Alarm roared through him, every muscle tightening, and then he saw the small, dark hump on the floor and realized that she had curled up with the thin survival blanket over her. She wasn't moving. Zane listened to the light, almost inaudible evenness of her breathing and realized she had gone to sleep. Again he felt that subtle inner clenching. She had been on edge and terrified for hours, obviously worn out but unable to sleep; the slight measure of security he'd been able to give her, consisting of his shirt, a blanket and a temporary, precarious hiding place, had been enough for her to rest. He hated to disturb her, but they had to move.

Gently he put his hand on her back, lightly rubbing, not shaking her awake but easing her into consciousness so she wouldn't be alarmed. After a moment she began stirring under his touch, and he felt the moment when she woke, felt her instant of panic, then her quietly determined reach for control.

"We're moving to someplace safer," he whispered, removing his hand as soon as he saw she was alert. After what she had been through, she wouldn't want to endure a man's touch any more than necessary. The thought infuriated him, because his instinct was to comfort her; the women in his family, mother, sister and sisters-in-law, were adored and treasured by the men. He wanted to cradle Barrie Lovejoy against him, whisper promises to her that he would personally dismember every bastard who had hurt her, but he didn't want to do anything that would undermine her fragile control. They didn't have time for any comforting, anyway.

She clambered to her feet, still clutching the blanket around her. Zane reached for it, and her fingers tightened on the fabric, then slowly loosened. She didn't have to explain her reluctance to release the protective cloth. Zane knew she was still both extrasensitive to cold and painfully embarrassed by her near nudity.

"Wear it this way," he whispered, wrapping the blanket around her waist sarong-style so that it draped to her feet. He tied the ends securely over her left hipbone, then bent down to check that the fabric wasn't too tight around her feet, so she would have sufficient freedom of movement if they had to run.

When he straightened, she touched his arm, then swiftly lifted her hand away, as if even that brief touch had been too much. "Thank you," she whispered.

"Watch me closely," he instructed. "Obey my hand signals." He explained the most basic signals to her, the raised clenched fist that meant "Stop!" and the open hand that meant merely "halt," the signal to proceed and the signal to hide. Considering her state of mind, plus her obvious fatigue, he doubted she would be able to absorb more than those four simple commands. They didn't have far to go, anyway; if he needed more commands than that, they were in deep ca-ca.

She followed him out of the room and down the west staircase, though he felt her reluctance to step into the Stygian depths. He showed her how to keep her back to the wall, how to feel with her foot for the edge of the step. He felt her stumble once, heard her sharply indrawn breath. He whirled to steady her; his pistol was in his right hand, but his left arm snaked out, wrapping around her hips to steady her as she teetered two steps above him. The action lifted her off her feet, hauling her against his left side. She felt soft in his grip, her hips narrow but nicely curved, and his nostrils flared as he scented the warm sweetness of her skin.

She was all but sitting on his encircling arm, her hands braced on his shoulders. Reluctantly he bent and set her on her feet, and she immediately straightened away from him. "Sorry," she whispered in the darkness.

Zane's admiration for her grew. She hadn't squealed in alarm, despite nearly falling, despite the way he'd grabbed her. She was holding herself together, narrowing her focus to the achievement of one goal: freedom.

She was even more cautious in her movements after that one misstep, letting more distance grow between them than he liked. On the last flight of steps he stopped, waiting for her to catch up with him. Knowing that she couldn't see him, he said, "Here," when she was near, so she wouldn't bump into him.

He eased his way down the last couple of steps into the faint light. There was no one in sight. With a brief wave of his hand he signaled her forward, and she slipped out of the darkness of the stairwell to stand beside him.

There was a set of huge wooden double doors that opened onto the street, but Zane was aware of increased noise outside as dawn neared, and it was too risky to use that exit. From their left came a raised voice, shouting in Arabic, and he felt her tense. Quickly, before the sound of one of her kidnappers unnerved her, he shepherded her into a cluttered storage room, where a small, single window shone high on the wall. "We'll go out this window," he murmured. "There'll be a drop of about four feet to the ground, nothing drastic. I'll boost you up. When you hit the ground, move away from the street but stay against the side of the building. Crouch down so you'll present the smallest possible silhouette. Okay?"

She nodded her understanding, and they picked their way over the jumbled boxes and debris until they were standing under the window. Zane stretched to reach the sill, hooked his fingers on the plaster and boosted himself up until he was balanced with one knee on the sill and one booted foot braced against a rickety stack of boxes. The window evidently hadn't been used in a long time; the glass was opaque with dust, the hinges rusty and stiff. He wrestled it open, wincing at the scraping noise, even though he knew it wouldn't carry to where the kidnappers were. Fresh air poured into the musty room. Like a cat he dropped to the floor, then turned to her.

"You can put your foot in my hand, or you can climb on my shoulders. Which do you prefer?"

With the window open, more light was coming through. He could see her doubtful expression as she stared at the window, and for the first time he appreciated the evenness of her features. He already knew how sweetly her body was shaped, but now he knew that Miss Lovejoy didn't hurt his eyes at all.

"Can you get through there?" she whispered, ignoring his question as she eyed first the expanse of his shoulders and then the narrowness of the window.

Zane had already made those mental measurements. "It'll be a tight fit, but I've been through tighter ones."

She gazed at his darkened face, then gave one of her sturdy nods, the one that said she was ready to go on. Now he could see her calculating the difficulty of maneuvering through the window with the blanket tied around her waist, and he saw the exact moment when she made her decision. Her shoulders squared and her chin came up as she untied the blanket and draped it around her like a long scarf, winding it around her neck and tossing the ends over her shoulders to dangle rakishly down her back.

"I think I'd better climb on your shoulders," she said. "I'll have more leverage that way."

He knelt on the floor and held his hands up for her to catch and brace herself. She went around behind him and daintily placed her right foot on his right shoulder, then lifted herself into a half crouch. As soon as her left foot had settled into place and her hands were securely in his, he rose steadily until he was standing erect. Her weight was negligible compared to what he handled during training. He moved closer to the wall, and she released his right hand to brace her hand against the sill. "Here I go," she whispered, and boosted herself through the window.

She went through it headfirst. It was the fastest way, but not the easiest, because she had no way of breaking her fall on the other side. He looked up and saw the gleam of pale, bare legs and the naked curves of her buttocks; then she vanished from sight, and there was a thump as she hit the ground.

Quickly Zane boosted himself up again. "Are you all right?" he whispered harshly.

There was silence for a moment, then a shaky, whispered answer. "I think so."

"Take the rifle." He handed the weapon to her, then dropped to the floor while he removed his web gear. That, too, went through the window. Then he followed, feet first, twisting his shoulders at an angle to fit through the narrow opening and landing in a crouch. Obediently, she had moved to the side and was sitting against the wall with the blanket once more clutched around her and his rifle cradled in her arms.

Dawn was coming fast, the remnants of darkness no more than a deep twilight. "Hurry," he said as he shrugged into the web vest and took the rifle from her. He slid it into position, then drew the pistol again. The heavy butt felt reassuring and infinitely familiar in his palm. With the weapon in his right hand and her hand clasped in his left, he pulled her into the nearest alley.

Benghazi was a modern city, fairly Westernized, and Libya's chief port. They were near the docks, and the smell of the sea was strong in his nostrils. Like the vast majority of waterfronts, it was one of the rougher areas of the city. From what he'd been able to tell, no authorities had shown up to investigate the gunfire, even supposing it had been reported. The Libyan government wasn't friendly—there were no diplomatic relations between the United States and Libya—but that didn't mean the government would necessarily turn a blind eye to the kidnapping of an ambassador's daughter. Of course, it was just as likely that it would, which was why diplomatic channels hadn't been considered. The best option had seemed to go in and get Miss Lovejoy out as quickly as possible.

There were plenty of ramshackle, abandoned buildings in the waterfront area. The rest of the team had withdrawn to one, drawing any pursuers away from Zane and Miss Lovejoy, while they holed up in another. They would rendezvous at oh-one-hundred hours the next morning.

Spooky had chosen the sites, so Zane trusted their relative safety. Now he and Miss Lovejoy wended their way through a rat's nest of alleyways. She made a stifled sound of disgust once, and he knew she'd stepped on something objectionable, but other than that she soldiered on in silence.

It took only a few minutes to reach the designated safe area. The building looked more down than up, but Spooky had investigated and reported an intact inner room. One outer wall was crumbled to little more than rubble. Zane straddled it, then caught Miss Lovejoy around the waist and effortlessly lifted her over the heap, twisting his torso to set her on the other side. Then he joined her, leading her under half-fallen timbers and around spiderwebs that he wanted left undisturbed. The fact that he could see those webs meant they had to get under cover, fast.

The door to the interior room hung haphazardly on one hinge, and the wood was rotting away at the top. He pulled her inside the protective walls. "Stay here while I take care of our tracks," he whispered, then dropped to a crouch and moved to where they had crossed the remnants of the outer wall. He worked backward from there, scattering dirt to hide the signs of their passage. There were dark, wet places on the broken pieces of stone that were all that remained of the floor. He frowned, knowing what those dark patches meant. Damn it, why hadn't she said something? Had she left a trail of blood straight to their hiding place?

Carefully he obliterated the marks. It wasn't completely her fault; he should have given more thought to her bare feet. The truth was, his mind had been more on her bare butt and the other details of her body that he'd already seen. He was far too aware of her sexually; the proof of it was heavy in his loins. After what she had been through that was the last thing she needed, so he would ignore his desire, but that didn't make it go away.

When he had worked his way to the room, he silently lifted the door and reset it in the frame, bracing it so it wouldn't sag again. Only then did he turn to face her. "Why didn't you tell me you'd cut your foot? When did it happen?" His voice was low and very even.

She was still standing where he'd left her, her face colorless in the half light coming through the open shutters of the window, her eyes so huge with fatigue and strain that she looked like a forlorn, bedraggled little owl. A puzzled frown knit her brows as she looked at her feet. "Oh," she said in dazed discovery as she examined the dark stains on her left foot. "I didn't realize it was cut. It must have happened when I stepped in that...what- ever...in the alley. I remember that it hurt, but I thought there was just a sharp rock under the... stuff."

At least it hadn't happened any sooner than that. Their position should still be safe. He keyed the radio, giving the prearranged one click that told the team he was in the safe area and receiving two clicks in return, meaning his men were secure in their position, too. They would check in with each other at set intervals, but for the most part they would spend the day resting. Relieved, Zane turned his mind to other matters.

"Sit down and let me see your foot," he ordered. The last thing he needed was for her to be hobbled, though from what he'd seen of her so far, she wouldn't breathe a word of complaint, merely limp along as fast as she could.

There was nothing to sit on except the broken stones of the floor, so that was where she sat, carefully keeping the blanket wrapped around her waist. Her feet were filthy, caked with the same mess that caked his boots. Blood oozed sullenly from a cut on the instep of her left foot.

Zane shucked off his black hood and headset, took off his web vest and removed his gloves; then he unpacked his survival gear, which included a small and very basic first-aid kit. He sat cross-legged in front of her and lifted her foot to rest on his thigh. After tearing open a small packet containing a premoistened antiseptic pad, he thoroughly cleaned the cut and the area around it, pretending not to notice her involuntary flinches of pain, which she quickly tried to control.

The cut was deep enough that it probably needed a couple of stitches. He took out another antiseptic pad and pressed it hard over the wound until the bleeding stopped. "How long has it been since your last tetanus vaccination?" he asked.

Barrie thought that she had never heard anything as calm as his voice. She could see him clearly now; it was probably a good thing she hadn't been able to do so before, because her nerves likely couldn't have stood the pressure. She cleared her throat and managed to say, "I don't remember. Years," but her mind wasn't on what she was saying.

His thick black hair was matted with sweat, and his face was streaked with black and green paint. The black T-shirt he wore was grimy with mingled dust and sweat, not that the shirt she had on was in much better shape. The material strained over shoulders that looked a yard wide, clung to a broad chest and flat stomach, stretched over powerful biceps. His arms were corded with long, steely muscles, his wrists almost twice as thick as hers; his long-fingered hands were well-shaped, callused, harder than any human hands should be—and immensely gentle as he cleansed the wound on her foot.

His head was bent over the task. She saw the dense black eyelashes, the bold sweep of his eyebrows, the thin and arrogantly high bridge of his nose, the chiseled plane of his cheekbones. She saw his mouth, so clear-cut and stern, as if he seldom smiled. Beard stubble darkened his jaw beneath the camouflage paint. Then his gaze flicked up to her for a moment, cool and assessing, as if he was gauging her reaction to the sting of the antiseptic, and she was stunned by the clear, pale beauty of his blue gray eyes. He had silently and efficiently killed that guard, then stepped over the body as if it didn't exist. A wicked, ten-inch black blade rode in a scabbard strapped to his thigh, and he handled both pistol and rifle with an ease that bespoke a familiarity that went far beyond the normal. He was the most savage, dangerous, lethal thing, man or beast, that she had ever seen—and she felt utterly safe with him.

He had given her the shirt off his back, treating her with a courtesy and tenderness that had eased her shock, calmed her fears. He had seen her naked; she had been able to ignore that while they were still trapped in the same building with her kidnappers, but now they were relatively safe, and alone, and she was burningly aware of both his intense masculinity and of her nakedness beneath his shirt. Her skin felt unusually sensitive, as if it was too hot and tight, and the rasp of the fabric against her nipples was almost painfully acute.

Her foot looked small and fragile in his big hands. He frowned in concentration as he applied an antibiotic ointment to the cut, then fashioned a butterfly bandage to close the wound. He worked with a swift, sure dexterity, and it was only a moment before the bandaging was complete. Gently he lifted her foot off his leg. "There. You should be able to walk with no problem, but as soon as we get you to the ship, get the doc to put in a couple of stitches and give you an injection for tetanus."

"Yes, sir," she said softly.

He looked up with a swift, faint smile. "I'm Navy. That's, 'Aye, aye, sir.'"

The smile nearly took her breath. If he ever truly smiled, she thought, she might have heart failure. To hide her reaction, she held out her hand to him. "Barrie Lovejoy. I'm pleased to make your acquaintance."

He folded his fingers around hers and solemnly shook hands. "Lieutenant-Commander Zane Mackenzie, United States Navy SEALs."

A SEAL. Her heart jumped in her chest. That explained it, then. SEALs were known as the most dangerous men alive, men so skilled in the arts of warfare that they were in a class by themselves. He didn't just look lethal; he *was* lethal.

"Thank you," she whispered.

"My pleasure, ma'am."

Hot color flooded her face as she looked at her blanket-covered lap. "Please, call me Barrie. After all, your shirt is the only thing I..." Her voice trailed off, and she bit her lip. "I mean, formality at this point is—"

"I understand," he said gently, breaking into her stumbling explanation. "I don't want you to be embarrassed, so the circumstances are strictly between us, if you prefer. But I advise you to tell the ship's surgeon, or your own doctor, for the sake of your health."

Barrie blinked at him in confusion, wondering what on earth her health had to do with the fact that he'd seen her naked. Then comprehension dawned; if she hadn't been so tired, she would have realized immediately what conclusion he had drawn from the situation.

"They didn't rape me," she whispered. Her face flushed even hotter. "They—they touched me, they hurt me and did some...other things, but they didn't actually rape me. They were saving that for today. Some important guy in their organization was supposed to arrive, and I suppose they were planning a sort of p-party."

Zane's expression remained calm and grave, and she knew he didn't believe her. Why should he? He'd found her tied up and naked, and she'd already been in the kidnappers' hands for most of a day. Chivalry wasn't part of their code; they had refrained from rape only on orders from their leader, because he wanted to be there to enjoy her himself before the others had their turn on her.

He didn't say anything, and Barrie busied herself with the used antiseptic pads, which were still damp enough to clean the rest of the disgusting muck from her feet. She longed for a bath, but that was so far out of the question that she didn't even voice the wish.

While she busied herself with tidying up, he explored the small room, which didn't take long, because there was nothing in it. He closed the broken shutters over the window; the wooden slats were rotted away at the top, allowing some light through but preventing any passersby from seeing inside.

With the room mostly dark once more, it was like being in a snug, private cave. Barrie smothered a yawn, fighting the fatigue that dragged on her like lead weights. The only sleep she'd had was that brief nap while Zane had been finding a way out of the building, and she was so tired that even her hunger paled in comparison.

He noticed, of course; he didn't miss anything. "Why don't you go to sleep?" he suggested. "In a couple of hours, when more people are moving around and I won't be as noticeable, I'll go scrounge up something for us to eat and liberate some clothes for you."

Barrie eyed the paint streaking his face. "With makeup like that, I don't believe you're going to go unnoticed no matter how crowded the streets are."

That faint smile touched his lips again, then was gone. "I'll take it off first."

The smile almost kept her awake. Almost. She felt her muscles slowly loosening, as if his permission to sleep was all her body needed to hear. Her eyelids were too heavy for her to hold open anymore; it was like a veil of darkness descending. With her last fraction of consciousness, she was aware of his arms around her, gently lowering her to the floor.

Chapter 4

She had gone to sleep like a baby, Zane thought, watching her. He'd seen it often enough in his ten nephews, the way little children had of dropping off so abruptly, their bodies looking almost boneless as they toppled over into waiting arms. His gaze drifted over her face. Now that dawn was here, even with the shutters closed, he could plainly see the exhaustion etched on her face; the wonder was that she had held up so well, rather than that she'd gone to sleep now.

He could use some rest himself. He stretched out beside her, keeping a slight distance between them; not touching, but close enough that he could reach her immediately if their hiding place was discovered. He was still wired, too full of adrenaline to sleep yet, but it felt good to relax and let himself wind down while he waited for the city to come completely awake.

Now he could also see the fire in her hair, the dark auburn shade that, when she stood in the sun, would glint with gold and bronze. Her eyes were a deep, soft green, her brows and lashes like brown mink. He wouldn't have been surprised by freckles, but her skin was clear and creamy, except for the bruise that mottled one cheek. There were bruises on her arms, and though he couldn't see them, he knew the shirt covered other marks left by brutal men. She'd insisted they hadn't raped her, but probably she was ashamed for anyone else to know, as if she'd had any choice in the matter. Maybe she wanted to keep it quiet for her father's sake. Zane didn't care about her reasons; he just hoped she would get the proper medical care.

He thought dispassionately about slipping to the building where they'd held her and killing any and all of the bastards who were still there. God knew they deserved it, and he wouldn't lose a minute's worth of sleep over any of them. But his mission was to rescue Miss Lovejoy—Barrie—and he hadn't accomplished that yet. If he went back, there was the chance that he would be killed, and that would endanger her, as well as his men. He'd long ago learned how to divorce his emotions from the action so he could think clearly, and he wasn't about to compromise a mission now... But *damn,* he wanted to kill them.

He liked the way she looked. She wasn't drop-dead gorgeous or anything like that, but her features were regular, and asleep, with her woes put aside for the moment, her expression was sweetly serene. She was a pretty little thing, as finely made as an expensive porcelain figurine. Oh, he supposed she was probably of middle height for a woman, about five feet five, but he was six-three and outweighed her by at least a hundred pounds, so to him she was little. Not as little as his mother and sister, but they were truly slight, as delicate as fairies. Barrie Lovejoy, for all her aristocratic bloodlines, had the sturdiness of a pioneer. Most women, with good reason, would have broken down long before now.

He was surprised to feel himself getting a little drowsy. Despite their situation, there was something calming about lying here beside her, watching her sleep. Though he was solitary by nature and had always preferred sleeping alone after his sexual appetite had been satisfied, it felt elementally right, somehow, to guard her with his body as they slept. Had cavemen done this, putting themselves between the mouth of the cave and the sleeping forms of their women and children, drowsily watching the gentle movements of their breathing as the fires died down and night claimed the land? If it was an ancient instinct, Zane mused, he sure as hell hadn't felt it before now.

But he wanted to touch her, to feel the softness of her flesh beneath his hand. He wanted to fold her within the warm protection of his body, tuck her in close, curl around her and keep her there with an arm draped around her waist. Only the knowledge that the last thing in the world she would want now was a man's touch kept him from doing just that.

He wanted to hold her. He ached to hold her.

She was dwarfed by his shirt, but he'd seen the body hidden by the folds of cloth. His night vision was very good; he'd been able to discern her high, round breasts, not very big, but definitely mouth-watering, and tipped with small, tight nipples. She was curvy, wom-anly, with a small waist and rounded hips and a neat little triangle of pubic hair. He'd seen her buttocks. Just thinking about it made him feel hollowed out with desire; her butt was fine indeed. He would like to feel it snuggled up against his thighs.

He wasn't going to be able to sleep, after all. He was fully aroused, desire pulsing through his swollen and rigid flesh. Wincing, he turned onto his back and adjusted himself to a more comfortable position, but the comfort was relative. The only way he would truly find ease was within the soft, hot clasp of her body, and that wasn't likely to happen.

The small room grew brighter and warmer as dawn developed into full morning. The stone walls would protect them from most of the day's heat, but soon they would need water. Water, food, and clothes for her. A robe would be better than Western-style clothing, because the traditional Muslim attire would cover her hair, and there were enough traditionalists in Benghazi that a robe wouldn't draw a second glance.

The streets were noisy now, the waterfront humming with activity. Zane figured it was time for him to do some foraging. He wiped the camouflage paint from his skin as best he could and disguised what was left by smearing dirt on his face. He wasn't about to go unarmed, so he pulled the tail of his T-shirt free from his pants and tucked the pistol into the waistband at the small of his back, then let the shirt fall over it. Anyone who paid attention would know the bulge for what it was, but what the hell, it wasn't unusual for people to go armed in this part of the world. Thanks to his one-quarter Comanche heritage, his skin had a rich bronze hue, and in addition he was darkly tanned from countless hours of training in the sun and sea and wind. There was nothing about his appearance that would attract undue notice, not even his eyes, because there were plenty of Libyans with a European parent.

He checked Barrie, reassuring himself that she was still sleeping soundly. He'd told her that he would be slipping out for a while, so she shouldn't be alarmed if she woke while he was gone. He left their crumbling sanctuary as silently as he had entered it.

It was over two hours before he returned, almost time for the designated check-in time with his men. He had a definite talent for scavenging, he thought, though outright thievery would probably be a better term. He carried a woman's black robe and head covering, and wrapped up in it was a selection of fruit, cheese and bread, as well as a pair of slippers he hoped would fit Barrie. The water had been the hardest to come by, because he'd lacked a container. He'd solved that by stealing a stoppered gallon jug of wine, forbidden by the Koran but readily available anyway. He had poured out the cheap, sour wine and filled the jug with water. The water would have a definite wine taste to it, but it would be wet, and that was all they required.

While he had the opportunity, he disguised the entrance to their lair a bit, piling some stones in front of it, arranging a rotted timber so that it looked as if it blocked the door. The door was still visible, but looked much less accessible. He tested his handiwork to make certain they could still get out easily enough, then slipped inside and once again braced the door in its sagging frame.

He turned to check on Barrie. She was still asleep. The room was considerably warmer, and she had kicked the blanket aside. His shirt was up around her waist.

The kick of desire was like taking a blow to the chest. He almost staggered from it, his heart racing, his breath strangling in his throat. Sweat beaded on his forehead, ran down his temple. *God*.

He should turn away. He should put the blanket over her. He should put sex completely out of his mind. There were any number of things he should do, but instead he stared at her with a hunger so intense he ached with it, quivered with it. Greedily his gaze moved over every female inch of her. His sex was throbbing like a toothache. He wanted her more intensely than he'd ever wanted a woman before. His famous cool remoteness had failed him—there wasn't a cool inch on him, and his desire was so damn strong and immediate, he was shaking from the effort of resisting it.

Moving slowly, stiffly, he set his purloined goodies on the floor. His breath hissed between his clenched teeth. He hadn't known sexual frustration could be this painful. He'd never had any trouble getting a woman whenever he'd wanted one. This woman was off-limits, though, from even an attempt at seduction. She'd been through enough without having to fend off her rescuer, too.

As warm as the room was now, if he spread the blanket over her she would only kick it off again. Gingerly he went down on one knee beside her and with shaking hands pulled the shirt tail down to cover her. With slight disbelief he eyed the fine tremor of his fingers. He never trembled. He was rock steady during the most tense and dangerous situations, icily controlled in combat. He had parachuted out of a burning plane, swum with sharks and sewn up his own flesh. He had ridden unbroken horses and even bulls a time or two. He had killed. He had done all of that with perfect control, but this sleeping, red-haired woman made him shake.

Grimly he forced himself to turn aside and pick up the radio headset. Holding the earpiece in place, he clicked once and immediately heard two clicks in response. Everything was okay.

Maybe some water would cool him down. At least thinking about it was better than thinking about Barrie. He dropped a couple of purification tablets into the jug, in case the small amount of wine that had remained in it wasn't enough to kill all the invisible little critters. The tablets didn't improve the taste any—just the opposite—but they were better than a case of the runs.

He drank just enough to relieve his thirst, then settled down with his back to a wall. There was nothing to do but wait and contemplate the walls, because he sure as hell didn't trust himself to look at Barrie.

Voices woke her. They were loud, and close by. Barrie bolted upright, her eyes huge with alarm. Hard arms grabbed her, and an even harder hand clamped itself over her mouth, stifling any sound she might have made. Confused, disoriented, in sheer terror she began to fight as much as she could. Teeth. She should use her teeth. But his fingers were biting hard into her jaw, and she couldn't open her mouth. Desperately she tried to shake her head, and he merely gathered her in tighter, tucking her against him in a way that was oddly protective.

"Shh" came that toneless whisper, and the familiarity of it cut through the panic and fog of sleep. Zane.

Instantly she relaxed, weak with relief. Feeling the tension leave her muscles, he tilted her face, still keeping his hand over her mouth. Their eyes met in the shadowed light, and he gave a brief nod as he saw that she was awake now, and aware. He released her jaw, his hard fingers trailing briefly over her skin in apology for the tightness of his grip. The barely there caress went through her like lightning. She shivered as it seared a path along nerve endings throughout her body and instinctively turned her face into the warm hollow created by the curve of his shoulder.

The arm around her had loosened immediately when she shivered, but at her action she felt him hesitate a fraction of a second, then gather her snugly against him once more.

The voices were closer, and added to them were some thuds and the sound of crumbling rock. She listened to the rapid, rolling syllables of Arabic, straining to concentrate on the voices. Were they the same voices she had heard through yesterday's long nightmare? It was difficult to tell.

She didn't understand the language; hers had been a finishing-school education, suited to an ambassador's daughter. She spoke French and Italian fluently, Spanish a little less so. After her father's posting in Athens she had made it a point to study Greek, too, and had learned enough that she could carry on a simple conversation, though she understood more than she spoke.

Fiercely she wished she had insisted on lessons in Arabic, too. She had hated every moment she'd spent in the kidnappers' hands, but not speaking the language had made her feel even more helpless, more isolated.

She would rather die than let them get their hands on her again

She must have tensed, because Zane gave her a light squeeze of reassurance. Swiftly she glanced at his face. He wasn't looking at her; instead he was concentrating on the fragile, half-rotted door that protected the entrance to their sanctuary, and on the voices beyond. His expression was utterly calm and distant. Abruptly she realized that he *did* understand Arabic, and whatever was being said by the people picking through the ruins of the building, he wasn't alarmed by it. He was alert, because their hiding place could be compromised at any moment, but evidently he felt confident of being able to handle that problem.

With reason, no doubt. From what she'd seen, she thought he was capable of handling just about any situation. She would trust him with her life—and had.

The voices went on for a long time, sometimes coming so close to their hiding place that Zane palmed that big pistol and held it aimed unwaveringly at the door. Barrie stared at that hand, so lean and powerful and capable. There wasn't the slightest tremor visible; it was almost unreal, almost inhuman, for any man to be that calm and have such perfect control over his body.

They sat silently in the warm, shadowy little room, their breathing for the most part their only movements. Barrie noticed that the blanket no longer covered her legs, but the shirt, thank God, kept her reasonably decent. It was too hot to lie under the blanket, anyway.

Time crept by at a sloth's pace. The warmth and silence were hypnotic, lulling her into a half dream state of both awareness and distance. She was ferociously hungry, but unaffected by it, as if she was merely aware of someone else's hunger. After a while her muscles began to ache from being in one position for so long, but that didn't matter, either. Thirst, though, was different. In the increasing heat, her need for water began to gnaw at her. The kidnappers had given her some water a couple of times, but she'd had nothing to drink in hours—since she had learned they expected her to relieve herself in their presence, in fact. She had chosen to do without water rather than provide them with such amusement again.

Sweat streaked down Zane's face and dampened his shirt. She was perfectly content to remain where she was, nestled against his side.

The arm around her made her feel safer than if their hiding place had been constructed of steel, rather than crumbling stone and plaster, and rotting wood.

She had never been exposed to a man like him before. Her only contact with the military had been with the senior officers who attended functions at the embassy, colonels and generals, admirals, the upper brass; there were also the Marine guards at the embassy, with their perfect uniforms and perfect manners. Though she supposed the Marine guards had to be exemplary soldiers or they wouldn't have been chosen as embassy guards, still, they were nothing like the man who held her so protectively. They were soldiers; he was a warrior. He was as different from them as the lethal, ten-inch black blade strapped to his thigh was from a pocketknife. He was a finely honed weapon.

For all that, he wasn't immortal, and they weren't safe. Their hiding place could be discovered. He could be killed; she could be recaptured. The hard reality of that was something she couldn't ignore as she could hunger and cramped muscles.

After a long, long time, the voices went away. Zane released her and walked noiselessly to the door to look out. She had never before seen anyone move with such silent grace, like a big jungle cat on velvet paws instead of a battle-hardened warrior in boots.

She didn't move until he turned around, the faint relaxation of his expression telling her the danger was past. "What were they doing?" she asked, taking care to keep her voice low.

"Scavenging building materials, picking up blocks, any pieces of wood that hadn't rotted. If they'd had a sledgehammer, they probably would have dismantled these walls. They carted the stuff off in a wheelbarrow. If they need more, they'll probably be back."

"What will we do?"

"The same thing we did this time—hunker down and keep quiet."

"But if they come in here—"

"I'll handle it." He cut her worry short before she could completely voice it, but he did it with a tone of reassurance. "I brought some food and water. Interested?"

Barrie scrambled to her knees, eagerness in every line of her body.

"Water! I'm so thirsty!" Then she halted, her recent experience fresh in her mind. "But if I drink anything, where will I go to...you know."

He regarded her with faint bemusement, and she blushed a little as she realized that wasn't a problem he normally encountered. When he and his men were on a mission, they would relieve themselves wherever and whenever they needed.

"I'll find a place for you to go," he finally said. "Don't let that stop you from drinking the water you need. I also found some clothes for you, but as hot as it's getting in here, you'll probably want to wait until night before you put them on."

He indicated the black bundle beside his gear, and she realized it was a robe. She thought of the modesty it would provide, and gratitude flooded her; at least she wouldn't have to face his men wearing nothing more than his shirt. But he was right; in the heat of day, and in the privacy of this small room, she would prefer wearing his shirt. They both knew she was bare beneath it; he'd already seen her stark naked, and demonstrated his decency by giving her the shirt and ignoring her nakedness, so there was no point now in swathing herself in an ankle-length robe.

He produced a big jug and unstoppered it. "It'll taste funny," he warned as he passed the jug to her. "Purification tablets."

It did taste funny—warm, with a chemical flavor. But it was wonderful. She drank a few swallows, not wanting to make her stomach cramp after being empty for so long. While she was drinking, he unwrapped the bits of food he'd procured—a loaf of hard bread, a hunk of cheese and several oranges, plums and dates. It looked like a feast.

He straightened the blanket for her to sit on, then took out his knife and cut small portions of both the loaf and cheese and gave them to her. She started to protest that she was hungry enough to eat much more than that, but realized that what he had would have to last them all day, and perhaps longer than that. She wasn't about to complain about the amount of food she *did* have.

She had never been particularly fond of cheese, and she suspected that if she hadn't been so hungry she wouldn't have been fond of this cheese, either, but at the moment it was delicious. She nibbled at both bread and cheese, finding satisfaction in the simple act of chewing. As it happened, she had overestimated her appetite. The small portion he had given her was more than enough.

He ate more heartily, and polished off one of the oranges. He insisted that she eat a couple of the juicy slices and drink a bit more water. Feeling replete, Barrie yawned and refused the offer of another orange slice.

"No, thanks, I'm full."

"Would you like to freshen up now?"

Her head whipped around, sending her red hair flying. Amusement twinkled in his pale eyes at her eager, pleading expression. "There's enough water?"

"Enough to dampen a bandana."

She didn't have a bandana, of course, but he did. Carefully he poured just enough water from the jug to wet the square cloth, then politely turned his back and busied himself with his gear.

Slowly Barrie smoothed the wet cloth over her face, sighing in pleasure at the freshness of the sensation. She hadn't realized how grimy she felt until now, when she was able to rectify the situation. She found a sore place on her cheek, where one of the men had hit her, and other tender bruises on her arms. Glancing at Zane's broad back, she quickly unbuttoned the shirt just enough that she could slide the handkerchief inside and rub it over her torso and under her arms. After she fastened the garment, her dusty legs got the same attention. The dampness was wonderfully cooling, almost voluptuous in the sensual delight it gave her.

"I'm finished," she said, and returned the dark bandana to him when he turned around. "It felt wonderful. Thank you."

Then her heart leaped in her chest, because he evidently felt the same need to cool off as she had, but unlike her, he didn't keep his shirt on. He peeled the snug black T-shirt off over his head and dropped it on the blanket, then sat on his heels while he moistened the bandana and began scrubbing it over his face.

Oh, my. Helplessly she stared at the rippling muscles of his chest and stomach, the way they flexed and relaxed with the flow of his movements. The dim light caught the deep bronze of his skin, gleamed on the smooth, powerful curve of his shoulder. Her fascinated gaze wandered over the slant of his shoulder blades, the diamond of black hair that stretched from nipple to nipple on his chest. He twisted around to reach for something, and she found his back equally fascinating, with the deep furrow of his spine bisecting two muscular planes.

There was an inch-long scar on his left cheekbone. She hadn't noticed it before because his face had been so dirty, but now she could plainly see the silvery line of it. It wasn't a disfiguring scar at all, just a straight little slash, as precise as a surgeon's cut. The scar along his rib cage was different, easily eight or nine inches in length, jagged, the scar tissue thick and ridged. Then there were the two round, puckered scars, one just above his waist, the other just below his right shoulder blade. Bullet wounds. She'd never seen one before, but she recognized them for what they were. There was another slash running along his right bicep, and God only knew how many other scars there were on the rest of his body. The warrior hadn't led a charmed life; his body bore the signs of battle.

He squatted half-naked, unconcernedly rubbing the damp handkerchief across his sweaty chest, lifting his arms to wash under them, exposing the smooth undersides and intriguing patches of hair. He was so fundamentally, elementally male, and so purely a warrior, that her breath strangled in her lungs as she watched him.

The rush of warmth through her body told her that she was more female than she'd ever imagined.

A little dazed, she sat back, resting against the wall. Absently she made certain the shirt tail preserved her modesty, but thoughts were tumbling through her mind, dizzyingly fast yet very clear.

They weren't out of danger yet.

During the past twenty-four horrific hours, she hadn't spent a lot of time wondering about the motive behind her kidnapping. She'd had too much to deal with as it was, the sheer terror, the confusion, the pain of the blows they'd given her.

She'd been blindfolded much of the time, and disoriented. She'd been humiliated, stripped naked and roughly fondled, taunted with the prospect of rape, and yet they had stopped short of rape—for a reason.

Sheer psychological torture had undoubtedly played a role, but most of all they'd had orders to save her for the man who was to arrive today.

Who was he? He was the one behind her kidnapping; he had to be. But why?

Ransom? When she thought about it now, coolly and clearly, she didn't think so. Yes, her father was rich. Many a diplomat came from a moneyed background; it wasn't unusual. But if money had been the motive, there were others who were richer, though perhaps she had been chosen specifically because it was well known that her father would beggar himself to keep her safe. Perhaps.

But why would they have taken her out of the country? Wouldn't they have wanted to keep her close by, to make the exchange for money easier? No, the very fact that they'd taken her out of the country meant they'd kidnapped her for another reason. Maybe they would have asked for money anyway; since they already had her, why not? But money wasn't the primary object. So what was?

She didn't know, and since she didn't know who the leader was, she had no way of guessing what he truly wanted.

Not herself. She dismissed that notion out of hand. She wasn't the object of obsession, because no man so obsessed with a woman that he was driven to such lengths would let his men maul her. Nor was she the type to inspire obsession, she thought wryly. Certainly none of the men she'd dated had shown any signs of obsessive behavior.

So…there was something else, some piece of puzzle she was missing. Was it someone she knew? Something she'd read or seen?

Nothing came to mind. She wasn't involved in intrigue, though of course she knew which employees at the embassy were employed by the CIA. That was standard, nothing unusual. Her father often spoke privately with Art Sandefer and, lately, Mack Prewett, too. She'd often thought that Art was more bureaucrat than spy, though the intelligence in his tired gaze said he'd done his time in the field, too. She didn't know about Mack Prewett. There was something restless and hard about him, something that made her uneasy.

Her father said Mack was a good man. She wasn't certain about that, but neither did he seem like a villain. Still, there had been that time a couple of weeks ago when she hadn't known anyone was with her father and had breezily walked in without knocking. Her father had been handing a thick manila envelope to Mack; both of them had looked startled and uncomfortable, but her father wasn't a diplomat for nothing. He'd efficiently smoothed over the slight awkwardness, and Mack had left the office almost immediately, taking the envelope with him. Barrie hadn't asked any questions about it, because if it was CIA business, then it wasn't her business.

Now she wondered what had been in that envelope.

That small incident was the only thing the slightest bit untoward that she could remember. Art Sandefer had once said that there was no such thing as coincidence, but could that moment be linked to her kidnapping? Could it be the *cause* of it? That was a reach.

She didn't know what was in the envelope, hadn't shown any interest in it. But she had seen her father giving it to Mack Prewett. That meant...what?

She felt as if she was feeling her way through a mental maze, taking wrong turns, stumbling into dead ends, then groping her way back to logic. Her father would never, in any way, do anything that would harm her. Therefore, that envelope had no significance—unless he was involved in something dangerous and wanted out. Her kidnapping made sense only if someone was using her as a weapon to make her father do something he didn't want to do.

She couldn't accept the idea of her father doing anything traitorous—at least, not voluntarily. She wasn't blind to his weaknesses. He was a bit of a snob, he didn't at all like even the idea that someday she might fall in love and get married, he was protective to the point of smothering her. But he was an honorable man, and a truly patriotic man. It could be that the kidnappers were trying to force her father to do something, give them some information, perhaps, and he had resisted; she could be the means they were using to force him to do what they wanted.

That felt logical. The envelope probably had nothing at all to do with her kidnapping, and Art Sandefer was wrong about coincidence.

But what if he wasn't?

Then, despite her instincts about him, her father was involved in something he shouldn't be. The thought made her sick to her stomach, but she had to face the possibility, had to think of every angle. She had to face it, then put it aside, because there was nothing she could do about it now

If the kidnappers had been going to use her as a weapon against her father, then they wouldn't give up. If it had just been ransom, they would have thrown up their hands at her supposed escape and said the Arabic equivalent of, "Ah, to hell with it."

The leader hadn't been here. She didn't even know where "here" was; she'd had too much on her mind to ask questions about her geographic location.

"Where are we?" she murmured, thinking she really should know.

Zane lifted his eyebrows. He was sitting down, lounging against the wall at a right angle to her, having finished cleaning up, and she wondered how long she'd been lost in thought. "The waterfront district," he said. "It's a rough section of town."

"I meant, what town?" she clarified.

Realization dawned in his crystal clear eyes. "Benghazi," he said softly. "Libya."

Libya. Stunned, she absorbed the news, then went back to the mental path she'd been following.

The leader had been flying in today. From where? Athens? If he'd been in contact with his men, he would know she'd somehow escaped. But if he had access to the embassy, and to her father, then he would also know that she hadn't been returned to the embassy. Therefore, she would logically still be in Libya. Also logically, they would be actively searching for her.

She looked at Zane again. His eyes were half-closed, he looked almost asleep. Because of the heat, he hadn't put his T-shirt back on. But despite the drowsy look on his face, she sensed that he was vitally aware of everything going on around them, that he was merely letting his body rest while his mind remained on guard.

After the humiliation and pain her guards had dealt her, Zane's concern and consideration had been like a balm, soothing her, helping to heal her bruised emotions before she even had time to know how deep the damage went. Almost before she knew it, she had been responding to him as a woman does to a man, and somehow that was all right.

He was the exact opposite of the thugs who had so delighted in humiliating her. Those thugs were probably searching all over the city for her, and until she was out of this country, the possibility existed that they would recapture her. And if they did, this time there would be no respite.

No. It was intolerable. But if the unthinkable happened, she would be damned if she would give them the satisfaction they'd been anticipating. She would be damned if she would let them take her virginity.

She had never thought of her virginity as anything other than a lack of experience and inclination. At school in Switzerland there had been precious few opportunities for meeting boys, and she hadn't been particularly interested in those she had met. After she left school, her father's protective possessiveness, as well as her duties at the embassy, had restricted any social life she might have developed. The men she met hadn't seemed any more interesting than the few boys she had met while in school. With AIDS added in as a threat, it simply hadn't seemed worth the risk to have sex simply for the experience.

But she had dreamed. She had dreamed of meeting a man, growing to love him, making love with him. Simple, universal dreams.

The kidnappers had almost taken all that from her, almost wrecked her dream of loving a man by abusing her so severely that, if she had remained in their hands much longer, she knew she would have been so severely traumatized that she might never have been able to love a man or tolerate his touch. If Zane hadn't taken her out of there, her first sexual experience would have been one of rape.

No. A thousand times no.

Even if they managed to recapture her, she wouldn't let them murder that dream.

Scrambling to her feet, Barrie took the few steps to where Zane lounged against the wall. She saw his muscled body come to alertness at her action, though he didn't move. She stood over him, staring at him with green eyes burning in the dim light. The look he gave her was hooded, unreadable.

"Make love to me," she said in a raw voice.

Chapter 5

"Barrie..." he began, his tone kind, and she knew he was going to refuse.

"No!" she said fiercely. "Don't tell me I should think about it, or that I really don't want to do it. I know what I went through with those bastards. I know you don't believe it, but they *didn't* rape me. But they looked at me, they touched me, and I couldn't stop them." She stopped and drew a deep breath, steadying herself. "I'm not stupid. I know we're still in danger, that you and your men could be wounded or even killed trying to rescue me and that I could end up back in their hands anyway. I've never made love before, with anyone. I don't want my first time to be rape, do you understand? I don't want them to have that satisfaction. *I want the first time to be with you.*"

She had surprised him, she saw, and she had already noticed that Zane Mackenzie wasn't a man whose expression revealed much of what he was thinking. He sat up straight, his pale eyes narrowed as he examined her with a piercing gaze.

He was still going to refuse, and she didn't think she could bear it. "I promise," she blurted desperately. "They didn't do that to me. I can't have any disease, if that's what you're worried about."

"No," he said, his voice suddenly sounding strained. "That isn't what I'm worried about."

"Don't make me beg," she pleaded, wringing her hands together, aware that she was already doing exactly that.

Then the expression in those pale eyes softened, grew warmer. "I won't," he said softly, and rose to his feet with that powerful, feline grace of his. He towered over her, and for a moment Barrie felt the difference in their sizes so sharply that she wondered wildly what she thought she was doing. Then he moved past her to the blanket; he knelt and smoothed it, then dropped down on it, stretching out on his back, and watched her with a world of knowledge in his slightly remote, too-old eyes.

He knew. And until she read that knowledge in his eyes, she hadn't even been aware of what she really needed. But watching him lie down and put himself at her service, something inside her shattered. *He knew.* He understood the emotions roiling deep inside her, understood what had brought her to him with her fierce, startling demand. It wasn't just that she wanted her first time to be of her own volition, with the man of her choice; the kidnappers had taken something from her, and he was giving it back. They had tied her down, stripped her, humiliated her, and she had been helpless to stop them. Zane was giving control back to her, reassuring her and at the same time subtly letting her exact her vengeance against the male of the species.

She didn't want to lie helpless beneath him. She wanted to control this giving of her body, wanted things to move at her pace instead of his, wanted to be the one who decided how much, how far, how fast.

And he was going to let her do it.

He was giving control of his body to her.

She could barely breathe as she sank to her knees beside him. The warm, bare, richly tanned flesh lured her hands closer, closer, until the urge overcame her nervousness and her fingers lightly skimmed over his stomach, his chest. Her heart hammered wildly. It was like petting a tiger, knowing how dangerous the animal was but fascinated beyond resistance by the rich pelt. She wanted to feel all of that power under her hands. Carefully she flattened her hands along his ribs, molding his flesh beneath her palms, feeling the resilience of skin over the powerful bands of muscle and, beneath that, the strong solidity of bone. She could feel the rhythmic thud of his heartbeat, the expansion of his ribs as he breathed.

Both heartbeat and breathing seemed fast. Swiftly she glanced at his face and blushed at what she saw there, the heat in his heavy-lidded eyes, the deepened color of his lips. She knew what lust looked like; she'd seen the cruel side of it on the faces of her captors, and now she saw the pleasurable side of it in Zane. It startled her, because somehow she hadn't considered lust in the proposition she'd made to him, and her hands fell away from his body.

His lips parted in a curl of amusement that revealed the gleam of white teeth, and she felt her heart almost stop. His smile was even more potent than she'd expected. "Yeah, I'm turned on," he said softly. "I have to be, or this won't work."

He was right, of course, and her blush deepened. That was the trouble with inexperience. Though she knew the mechanics of love-making, and once or twice her escort for the evening had kissed her with unexpected ardor and held her close enough for her to tell that he was aroused, still, she'd never had to deal directly with an erection—until now.

This particular one was there for her bidding. Furtively she glanced at the front of his pants, at the ridge pushing against the cloth.

"We don't have to do this," he offered once again, and Barrie flared from hesitance to determination.

"Yes, I do."

He moved his hands to his belt. "Then I'd better—"

Instantly she stopped him, pushing his hands up and away, forcing them down on each side of his head. "I'll do it," she said, more fiercely than she'd intended. This was her show.

"All right," he murmured, and again she knew that he understood. Her show, her control, every step of the way. He relaxed against the blanket, closing his eyes as if he was going to take a nap.

It was easier, knowing he wasn't watching her, which of course had been his intention. Barrie didn't want to fumble, didn't want to underline her inexperience any more than she already had, so before she reached for his belt she studied the release mechanism for a moment to make certain she understood it. She didn't give herself time to lose her nerve. She simply reached out, opened the belt and unfastened his pants. Under the pants were black swim trunks. Puzzled, Barrie stared at them. Swim trunks?

Then she understood. He was a SEAL; the acronym stood for Sea, Air and Land. He was at home in all three elements, capable of swimming for miles. Since Benghazi was a seaport, that was probably how his team had infiltrated, from the sea. Maybe they'd used some sort of boat to reach land, but it was possible they'd been dropped off some distance from the port and had swum the rest of the way.

He had risked his life to save her, was still doing so, and now he was giving her his body. Everything inside her squeezed tight, and she trembled from the rush of emotion. Oh, God. She had learned more about herself in the past twenty-four hours than in the entire past twenty-five years of her life. Perhaps the experience had changed her. Either way, something had happened inside her, something momentous, and she was learning how to deal with it.

She had let her father wrap her in a suffocating blanket of protection for fifteen years; she couldn't blame him for it, because she'd *needed* that blanket. But that time was past. Fate had pitched her headlong into life, ripped her out of her protective cocoon, and like a butterfly, she couldn't draw the silken threads back around her. All she could do was reach out for the unknown.

She slipped her hands under the waistband of the swim trunks and began working them, and his pants, down his hips. He levered his pelvis off the ground to aid her. "Don't take them all the way off," he murmured, still keeping his eyes closed and his hands resting beside his head. "I can handle things if I get caught with my pants down, but if they're completely off, it would slow me down some."

Despite her nervousness, Barrie smiled at that supreme self-confidence, the wry humor. If he wasn't so controlled, he could be described as cocky. He had no doubt whatsoever about his fighting ability.

Her hands stroked down his buttocks as she slipped her hands inside his garments. An unexpected frisson of pleasure rippled through her at the feel of his butt, cool and smooth, hard with muscle. Tush connoisseurs would envy her the moment, and she wished she had the nerve to linger, to fully appreciate this male perfection. Instead she tugged at his clothes, pulling them down to the middle of his thighs. He relaxed, letting his hips settle on the blanket again, and Barrie studied the startling reality of a naked man. She'd read books that described sexual arousal, but seeing it firsthand, and at close range, was far more impressive and wondrous.

Blindly she reached out, her hand drawn as if by a magnet. She touched him, stroking one fingertip down the length of his swollen sex. It pulsed and jerked upward, as if following the caress. He inhaled sharply. His reaction warmed her, and the tightness in her chest, her body, clenched once more, then began to loosen with that rush of warmth. Bolder now, she folded her fingers around him, gently sighing with pleasure as she felt the heat beneath the coolness, iron beneath silk, the urgent throbbing.

And she felt her own desire, rushing like a heated river through her flesh, turning angry determination into lovemaking. *This is how it should be,* she thought with relief; they should come together in pleasure, not in anger. And she didn't want to wait, didn't want to give herself time to reconsider, or she would lose her nerve.

Swiftly she straddled him, mounted him. No longer in anger at other men, no longer in desperation. *Pleasure,* warm and sweet. With her knees clasping his hips, acting on instinct, she held the thick shaft in position and slowly sank down on him, guiding their bodies together.

The first brush of his flesh against hers was hot, startling, and she instinctively jerked herself upright, away from the alien touch. Zane quivered, the barest ripple of reaction, then once more lay motionless between her legs, his eyes still closed, letting her proceed at her own pace.

Her chest was so constricted she could barely breathe; she sucked in air in quick little gasps. That contact, brief as it had been, had touched off an insistent throbbing between her legs, as if her body, after its initial startled rejection, had paused in instinctive recognition of female for male. Her breasts felt tight and feverish beneath the black fabric of his shirt. Alien, yes…but infinitely exciting. Desire wound through her, the river rising.

She told herself that she was prepared for the sudden acute sense of vulnerability, for her body's panic at the threat of penetration, even though desire was urging her on to that very conclusion. More gingerly, she settled onto him again, holding herself steady as she placed him against the entrance to her body and let her weight begin to impale her on the throbbing column of flesh.

The discomfort began immediately and was worse than she'd expected. She halted her movement, gulping as she tried to control her instinctive flinching away from the source of pain. He was breathing deeply, too, she noticed, though that was the only motion he made. She pushed harder, gritting her teeth against the burning sensation of being stretched, and then she couldn't bear any more and jerked herself off him. This time the discomfort between her legs didn't go away but continued to burn.

It wasn't going to get any better, she told herself. She might as well go ahead and do it. Breathing raggedly, once more she lowered herself onto him. Tears burned in her eyes as she struggled to complete the act. Why wouldn't it just go *in?* The pressure between her legs was enormous, intolerable, and a sob caught in her throat as she surged upward.

"Help me," she begged, her voice almost inaudible.

Slowly his eyes opened, and she almost flinched at the pale fire that burned there. He moved just one hand, the right one. Gently he touched her cheek, his callused fingertips rough and infinitely tender; then he trailed them down her throat and lightly over the shirt to her left breast, where they lingered for a heart-stopping moment at her nipple, then finally down to the juncture of her legs.

The caress was as light as a whisper. It lingered between her legs, teasing, brushing, stroking. She went very still, her body poised as she concentrated on this new sensation. Her eyes closed as all her senses focused on his hand and what it was doing, the way he was touching her. It was delicious, but not...quite... enough. He tantalized her with the promise of something more, something that was richer, more powerful, and yet that lightly stroking finger never quite touched her where she wanted. Barrie inhaled deeply, her nipples rising in response. Her entire body hung in suspense. She waited, waited for the gentle touch to brush her with ecstasy, waited.... Her hips moved, her body instinctively seeking, following his finger.

Ah. There. Just for a moment, *there.* A low moan bubbled up in her throat as pleasure shot through her. She waited for him to repeat the caress, but instead his fingers moved maddeningly close, teasing and retreating. Again her hips followed, and again she was rewarded by that lightning flash of pure sensation.

A subtle, sensual dance began. He led, and she followed. The just-right touches came more often, the pleasure became more shattering as the intensity built with each repetition. Between her legs, his male shaft still probed for entrance, and somehow each movement of her hips seemed to ease him a bit closer to that goal. Her body rocked, swaying in the ancient rhythm of desire, surging and retreating like the tides. She could feel him stretching her, feel the discomfort sharpened by her movements...and yet the desire lured her onward like a Lorelei, and somehow she began to need him inside her, need him to the point that the pain no longer mattered. She braced her hands on his chest, and her movements changed, lifting and falling rather than swaying side to side. His touch changed, too, suddenly pressing directly on the place where she most wanted it.

She bit her lip to keep from crying out. His thumb rubbed insistently, releasing a torrent, turning the warm river into something wild and totally beyond her control. She was so hot that she was burning up with desire, aching with emptiness. The pain no longer mattered; she had to have what his body promised, what hers needed. With a low moan she pressed downward, forcing her soft flesh to admit the intruder. She felt the resistance, the inner giving; then suddenly his hot, swollen sex pushed up inside her.

It hurt. It hurt a lot. She froze in place, and her eyes flew open, huge with distress. Their gazes locked, hers dark with pain, his burning with ruthlessly restrained desire. Suddenly she became aware of how taut the muscled body beneath her was, how much his control was costing him. But he had promised to let her set the pace, and he had kept that promise, moving only when she had asked for help.

Part of her wanted to stop, but a deeper, more powerful instinct kept her astride him. She could feel him throbbing inside her, feel the answering tightening of her body, as if the flesh knew more than the mind, and perhaps it did. He tensed even more. His skin gleamed with sweat, his heartbeat hammered beneath her palm. She felt a jolt of excitement at having this supremely male, incredibly dangerous warrior as hers to command, just for this time suspended from reality. They had met only hours ago; they had only hours left before they would likely never see each other again. But for now he was hers, embedded inside her, and she wasn't going to forgo a moment of the experience.

"What do I do now?" she whispered.

"Just keep moving," he whispered in return, and she did.

Rising. Falling. Lifting herself almost off him, then sinking down. Over and over, until she forgot about the pain and lost herself in the primeval joy. His hand remained between her legs, continuing the caress that urged her onward, even though she no longer needed to be urged. She moved on him, faster and faster, taking him deeper and deeper. His powerful body flexed between her thighs, arching, and a growl rumbled in his throat. Immediately he forced himself to lie flat again, chained by his promise.

Up. Down. Again. And again, the crescendo building inside her, the heat rising to an unbearable fever, the tension coiling tighter and tighter, until she felt as if she would shatter if she moved another muscle. She froze in place over him, whimpering, unable to push herself over the final hurdle.

The growl rumbled in his throat again. No, deeper than a growl; it was the sound of a human volcano exploding from the forces pent up inside. His control broke, and he moved, fiercely clamping both hands on her hips and pulling her down hard even as he arched once more and thrust himself in her to the hilt. He hadn't gone so deep before; she hadn't taken that much of him. The sensation was electric. She stifled a scream as he convulsed beneath her, heaving upward between her thighs, lifting her so that her knees left the ground. His head was thrown back, his neck corded with the force of his release, his teeth bared. Barrie felt the hot spurting of his release, felt him so deep inside her that he was touching the very center of her being, and it was enough to push her over the edge.

Pure lightning speared through her. She heard herself cry out, a thin cry of ecstasy that nothing could stifle. All her inner muscles contracted around him, relaxed, squeezed again, over and over, as if her body was drinking from his.

Finally the storm subsided, leaving her weak and shaking. Her bones had turned to jelly, and she could no longer sit upright. Helplessly she collapsed forward, folding on him like a house of cards caught in an earthquake. He caught her, easing her down so that she lay on his chest, and he wrapped his arms around her as she lay there gasping and sobbing. She hadn't meant to cry, didn't understand why the tears kept streaming down her face. "Zane," she whispered, and couldn't say anything more.

His big, hard hands stroked soothingly up and down her back. "Are you okay?" he murmured, and there was something infinitely male and intimate in his deep voice, an undertone of satisfaction and possessiveness.

Barrie gulped back the tears, forcing herself to coherency. "Yes," she said in a thin, waterlogged tone. "I didn't know it would hurt so much. Or feel so good," she added, because she was crying for both reasons. Odd, that she should have been as unprepared for the pleasure as she had been for the pain. She felt overwhelmed, unbalanced. Had she truly been so foolish as to think she could perform such an intimate act and remain untouched emotionally? If she had been capable of that kind of mental distance she wouldn't have remained a virgin until now. She would have found a way around her father's obsessive protectiveness if she had wanted to, if any man had ever elicited onetenth the response in her this warrior had aroused within two minutes of their meeting. If her rescuer had been any other man, she wouldn't have asked such an intimate favor of him.

Their lovemaking had forged a link between them, a bond of the flesh that was far stronger and went far deeper than she'd imagined. Despite her chastity, had she believed the modern, permissive notion that making love could have no more lasting meaning than simple fun, like riding a roller coaster? Maybe, for some people, *sex* could be as trivial as a carnival ride, but she would never again think of lovemaking as anything that shallow. True lovemaking was deep and elemental, and she knew she would never be the same. She hadn't been from the moment he had given her his shirt and she had fallen in love with him. Without even seeing his face, she had fallen in love with the essence of the man, his strength and decency. It wouldn't have mattered if, when morning came, his features had been ugly or twisted with scars. In the darkness of that barren room, and the darkness of her heart, she had already seen beneath whatever lay on the surface, and she had loved him. It was that simple, and that difficult.

Just because she felt that way didn't mean he did. Barrie knew what a psychologist would say. It was the white-knight syndrome, the projection of larger-than-life characteristics onto a person because of the circumstances. Patients fell in love with their doctors and nurses all the time. Zane had simply been doing his job in rescuing her, while to her it had meant her life, because she hadn't for a moment supposed that her captors would let her live. She owed him her life, would have been grateful to him for the rest of that life—but she didn't think she would have loved just any man who had crawled through that window. She loved *Zane.*

She lay silently on him, her head nestled against his throat, their bodies still linked. She could feel the strong rhythm of his heartbeat thudding against her breasts, could feel his chest expand with each breath. His hot, musky scent excited her more than the most expensive cologne. She felt more at home here, lying with him on a blanket in the midst of a shattered building, than she ever had in the most luxurious and protected environment.

She knew none of the details of his life. She didn't know how old he was, where he was from, what he liked to eat or read or what programs he watched on television. She didn't know if he'd ever been married.

Married. My God, she hadn't even asked. She felt suddenly sick to her stomach. If he was married, then he wouldn't be the man she had thought he was, and she had just made the biggest mistake of her life.

But neither would the fault be entirely his. She had begged him, and he had given her more than one chance to change her mind. She didn't think she could bear it if he'd made love to her out of pity.

She drew a deep breath, knowing she had to ask. Ignorance might be bliss, but she couldn't allow herself that comfort. If she had done something so monumentally wrong, she wanted to know.

"Are you married?" she blurted.

He didn't even tense but lay utterly relaxed beneath her. One hand slid up her back and curled itself around her neck. "No," he said in that low voice of his. "You can take your claws out of me now." The words were lazily amused.

She realized she was digging her fingernails into his chest and hastily relaxed her fingers. Distressed, she said, "I'm sorry, I didn't mean to hurt you."

"There's pain, and there's pain," he said comfortably. "Bullets and knives hurt like hell. In comparison, a little she-cat's scratching doesn't do much damage."

"She-cat?" Barrie didn't know if she should be affronted or amused. After a brief struggle, amusement won. None of her friends or associates would ever have described her in such terms. She'd heard herself described as ladylike, calm, circumspect, conscientious, but certainly never as a she-cat.

"Mmm." The sound was almost like a purr in his throat. His hard fingers lazily massaged her neck, while his other hand slipped down her back to burrow under the shirt and curl possessively over her bottom. His palm burned her flesh like a brand. "Dainty. And you like being stroked."

She couldn't deny that, not when he was the one doing the stroking. The feel of his hand on her bottom was startlingly erotic. She couldn't help wiggling a little, and then gasped as she felt the surge of his flesh inside her. His breath caught, too, and his fingers dug into the cleft of her buttocks.

"I need to ask you a couple of questions," he said, and his voice sounded strained.

Barrie closed her eyes, once again feeling the warm loosening deep inside that signaled the return of desire. That had been a remarkable sensation, when his sex had expanded inside her, both lengthening and getting thicker. Oh, dear. She wanted to do it again, but she didn't think she had the strength. "What?" she murmured, distracted by what was happening between her legs.

"Did you get rid of the ghosts?"

Ghosts. He meant her lingering horror at the way those men had touched her. She thought about it and realized, with some surprise, that she had. She was still angry at the way she'd been treated, and she would dearly love to have Zane's pistol in her hands and those men in her sights, even though she'd never held a pistol before in her life. But the wounded, feminine part of her had triumphed by finding pleasure in making love with Zane, and in doing so she had healed herself. Pleasure... somehow the word fell far short of what she had experienced. Even ecstasy didn't quite describe the intensity, the sensation of imploding, melting, becoming utterly lost in her physical self.

"Yes," she whispered. "The ghosts are gone."

"Okay." His voice still sounded strained. "Second question. Will that damn shirt have to be surgically removed?"

She was startled into sitting upright. The action drove him deeper inside her and wrenched a sharp gasp from her, a groan from him. Panting, she stared at him. They had just made love—were, in fact, *still* making love—but the shirt she wore was what had kept her from going to pieces when he'd first found her, had given her the nerve to run barefoot down dark alleys, had become the symbol of a lot more than just modesty. Maybe she wasn't as recovered as she'd thought. The kidnappers had stripped her, forced her to be naked in front of them, and when Zane had first entered the room and seen her that way, she had been mortified. She didn't know if she could be naked with him now, if she could let him see the body that had been pinched and bruised by other men.

His crystal clear gaze was calm, patient. Again he understood. He knew what he was asking of her. He could have left things as they were, but he wanted more. He wanted her trust, her openness, with no dark secrets between them.

He wanted them to become lovers.

The realization was sharp, almost painful. They had loved each other physically, but with restraint like a wall between them. He had done what she had asked of him, had held himself back until the last moment, when his climax had shattered his control. Now he was asking something of her, asking her to give as he had given.

Almost desperately she clutched the front of the shirt. "I—they left marks on me."

"I've seen bruises before." He reached up and gently touched her cheek. "You have one right here, as a matter of fact."

Instinctively she reached up to the cheek he'd touched, feeling the tenderness. As soon as she released the front of the shirt, he moved his hands to the buttons and slowly began unfastening them, giving her time to protest. She bit her lip, fighting the urge to grab the widening edges of the cloth and hold them together.

When the garment was open all the way down, he slid his hands inside and cupped her breasts, his palms hot as they covered the cool mounds. Her nipples tingled as they hardened, reaching out for the contact. "The bruises shame *them,*" he murmured. "Not you."

She closed her eyes as she sat astride him, feeling him hard and hot inside her, his hands just as hard and hot on her breasts. She didn't protest when his hands left her breasts, left them feeling oddly tight and aching, while he pushed the black shirt off her shoulders. The fabric puddled around her arms, and he lifted each in turn, slipping them free.

She was naked. The warm air brushed against her bare skin with the lightest of touches, and then she felt his fingertips doing the same, trailing so gently over each of the dark marks on her shoulders, her arms and breasts, her stomach, that she barely felt him. "Lean down," he said.

Slowly she obeyed, guided by his hands, down, down—and he lifted his head, meeting her mouth with his.

Their first kiss...and they'd already made love. Barrie was shocked at how she could have been so foolish as to forgo the pleasure of his kisses. His lips were firm, warm, hungry. She sank against him with a little sound of mingled surprise and delight humming in her throat. Her breasts flattened against him, the crisp hair on his chest rasping her ultrasensitive nipples, another joy she had unknowingly skipped.

Oh, this was delicious. His tongue probed for entrance, and she immediately gave it.

Several minutes later he let his head drop to the blanket. He was panting slightly, his eyes heavy-lidded. "I have another question."

"What?" She didn't want to give up the delights of his mouth. She'd never enjoyed kissing so much before, but he was diabolically good at it. She followed him down, nipping at his lower lip, depositing hot little kisses.

He chuckled beneath her mouth. The deep, rusty sound charmed her. She sensed that his laughter was even rarer than his smiles, therefore doubly precious.

"Will you let me be on top this time?"

The question surprised her into laughter. She stifled it as best she could, burying her head against his neck, but her body shook with giggles. He slipped out of her, making her laugh even harder. She was still laughing when he wrapped one strong arm around her and rolled, lifting her so they didn't roll off the blanket, efficiently tucking her beneath him and settling between her legs. Her laughter caught on a gasp as he surged heavily into her.

Her senses swam as she was bombarded by new feelings, when she had already experienced so much. She'd known he was a big man, but lying beneath him sharply brought home the difference in their sizes. Though he propped his weight on his forearms to keep from crushing her, she still felt the heaviness of that iron-muscled body. His shoulders were so broad that he dwarfed her, wrapped around her, shielded her. When she had been on top, she had controlled the depth of his penetration. The control was his now, her thighs spread wide by his hips. He felt bigger, harder than he had before.

He waited a moment to see how she would accept the vulnerability of her position. But she didn't feel vulnerable, she realized. She felt utterly secure, buffered by his strength. Tremulously she smiled at him and lifted her arms to wind them around his neck.

He smiled in return. And then Zane Mackenzie made love to her.

Chapter 6

There seemed to be scarcely a moment for the rest of the day when they weren't making love, resting from making love or about to make love. The sounds of the waterfront surrounded them, the low bellow of ships, truck horns, the sounds of chains and cranes, but inside that small, dim room there seemed to be nothing else in the world but each other. Barrie lost herself in the force of his unbridled sensuality and discovered within herself a passion that matched his. The need to be quiet only added to the intensity.

He kissed the bruises on her breasts and sucked her nipples until they throbbed with pleasure. His beard-stubbled chin rasped against her breasts, her belly, but he was always careful not to cause her pain as he searched for all the other bruises on her body and paid them the same tender homage.

"Tell me how they hurt you," he murmured, "and I'll make it better."

At first Barrie shied away from divulging the details, even to him, but as the hot afternoon wore on and he pleasured her so often she was drunk with the overload on her senses, it began to seem pointless to keep anything from him. Haltingly she began to whisper things to him.

"Like this?" he asked, repeating the action that had so upset her—

except it wasn't the same. What had been meant to punish at the hands of the kidnappers became purest pleasure in Zane Mackenzie's hands. He caressed her until her body forgot those other touches, until it remembered only him.

She whispered another detail, and he wiped out that memory, too, replacing the bad with caresses that lifted her to peak after sensual peak. She couldn't imagine being handled more tenderly than he handled her, or with such delight. He didn't try to hide how much he enjoyed looking at her, touching her, making love to her. He reveled in her body, in the contrast between her soft curves and his hard muscularity. It aroused her to be the focus of such intense masculine pleasure, to feel his absorption with the texture of her skin, the curve of her breast, the snug sheathing between her legs. He explored her; he petted her, he drowned her in sexuality. The area around them was still so busy they didn't dare converse much, so they communicated with their bodies.

Three times, while they were lying drowsily in the aftermath of loving, he checked his watch and reached for the headset radio. He would click it once, listen, then put it aside.

"Your men?" she asked, after the first time.

He nodded. "They're hiding out, waiting until it's safe to rendezvous."

Then the chatter of voices outside became louder as some people approached, and they fell silent.

The afternoon wore on, and the light began to dim. She wasn't particularly hungry, but Zane insisted that she eat. He pulled up his pants; she once more donned his shirt. More formally attired now, they sat close together on the blanket and finished off the bread and fruit, but neither of them wanted any of the cheese. The water was warm and still tasted of chemicals. Barrie sat within the curve of his arm and dreaded leaving.

She wanted to be safe and comfortable again, but she hated to lose this closeness with Zane, this utter reliance and companionship and intimacy. She wouldn't push him to continue their relationship; under the circumstances, he might feel responsible and think he would have to let her down gradually, and she didn't want to put him in that position. If he indicated that he wanted to see her afterward, then...why, then her heart would fly.

But even if he did, it would be difficult for them to see each other regularly. He was more than just a military man; he was a SEAL. Much of what he did couldn't be discussed. He would have a home base, duties, missions. If they escaped safely, the danger to him didn't end there. A chill settled around her heart when she thought of the times in the future when, because it was his job, he would calmly and deliberately walk into a deadly situation. While they were hidden in this small room might be the only time she could ever be certain he was safe and unharmed.

The fear and uncertainty would almost drive her mad, but she would endure them, she would endure anything, for the opportunity to see him, to grow closer to him. Their relationship, if there was to be one, would have to grow in reverse. Usually people came to know each other, grew to trust and care, and then became lovers; they had become lovers almost immediately, and now they would have to get to know each other, find out all the quirks and personal history and tastes that made them individuals.

When she got back, she would have to deal with her father. He must be frantic, and once she was safely home, he would be even more paranoid and obsessive. But if Zane wanted her, she would have to deliberately hurt her father's feelings for the first time in her life; he would be supplanted as number one in her life. Most parents handled the change in their offsprings' lives with happiness, assuming the chosen mate was decent, but Barrie knew it wouldn't matter who she fell in love with, her father would be opposed to him. No man, to him, was good enough for her. Even more, he would bitterly resent anything that would take her out of his protection. She was all he had left of his family, and it didn't help that she greatly resembled her mother. As ambassador, her father had a very active social life, but he'd only ever loved one woman, and that was her mother.

She would never turn her back on her father, because she loved him dearly, but if the chance for a relationship, possibly a lifetime, with Zane was in the balance, she would put as much distance between herself and her father as necessary until he accepted the situation.

She was planning her life around dreams, she thought wryly as she brushed the bread crumbs from the blanket. She would do better to let the future take care of itself and concern herself with how they were going to get out of Benghazi.

"What time do we leave?"

"After midnight. We'll give most people time to get settled down for the night." He turned to her with the heavy-lidded gaze she had already learned signaled arousal and, reaching out, he began to unbutton her shirt. "Hours," he whispered.

Afterward they lay close together, despite the heat, and dozed. She didn't know how long it was before she woke, but when she did it was to almost total darkness. Unlike the night before, though, when she had lain in cold, lonely terror, now she was pressed against Zane's side, and his arms securely held her. Her head was pillowed on his shoulder, one bare leg was hooked over his hips. She stretched a bit and yawned, and his arms tightened, letting her know that he was awake. Perhaps he had never slept at all, but had held her and safeguarded her. The noise beyond the ruined building had died down; even the sounds from the docks were muted, as if the darkness smothered them.

"How much longer?" she asked, sitting up to fumble for the jug of water. She found it and drank; the taste wasn't too bad, she decided. Maybe she was becoming used to the chemicals, whatever they were.

He peeled the cover from his watch so he could see the luminous dial. "Another few hours. I need to check in with the guys in a couple of minutes."

She passed the water jug to him, and he drank. They lay back down, and she cuddled close. She put her right hand on his chest and felt the strong, healthy thudding of his heart. Idly she twirled her fingers in the crisp hairs, delighting in the textures of his body.

"What happens then? When we leave, I mean."

"We get out of the city, make our rendezvous point just at sunrise, and we're picked up."

He made it sound so simple, so easy. She remembered the swim trunks he wore and lifted her head to frown at him, even though she knew he couldn't see her. "Is our rendezvous point on dry land?"

"Not exactly."

"I see. I hope you have a boat?" It was a question, not a statement.

"Not exactly."

She caught his chest hairs and gave them a tug. "*Exactly* what do you have?"

"Ouch!" Snagging her hand, he disentangled it and lifted it to his mouth, lightly brushing his lips across her knuckles. "*Exactly*, we have a Zodiac, a seven-man, motorized inflatable craft. My team came in short two men, so there are only six of us. We'll be able to fit you in."

"I'm so glad." She yawned and snuggled her head more securely into the hollow of his shoulder. "Did you leave someone behind so there would be room for me?"

"No," he said shortly. "We're undermanned because of a problem I'll have to take care of when we get back. If there had been any other team available, we wouldn't be here, but we were the closest, and we needed to get you out in a hurry, before they moved you."

His tone dissuaded her from asking about the problem that put him in such a black mood, but she'd seen him in action; she knew she wouldn't want to be on the receiving end of his anger when he got back. She waited while he picked up the headset and checked in with his men, then returned to her questions.

"Where do we go in the Zodiac?"

"Out to sea," he said simply. "We radio ahead, and we'll be picked up by a helicopter from the *Montgomery,* an aircraft carrier. You'll be flown home from the carrier."

"What about you?" she whispered. "Where will you go?" That was as close as she would allow herself to get to asking him about his future plans.

"I don't know. My team was performing exercises on the *Montgomery*, but that's blown to hell now, with two of them injured. I'll have to clean up that mess, and I don't know how long it will take."

He didn't know where he would be, or if he did, he wasn't saying. Neither was he saying that he would call her, though he *did* know where *she* would be. Barrie closed her eyes and listened painfully to all that he wasn't saying. The hurt was worse than she'd anticipated.

but she closed it off in a place deep inside. Later it would come out, but if she only had a few hours left with him, she didn't intend to waste them crying about what might have been. Few women would have a chance to even know a man like Zane Mackenzie, much less love him. She was greedy; she wanted it all, wanted everything, but even this little bit was more than a lot of people experienced, and she would have to be grateful for that.

Whatever happened, she could never return to the safe little cocoon her father had fashioned for her. She couldn't let herself forget the kidnapping and the unknown *why* of it. Of course, her father would know why; the kidnapper would already have made his demands. But Barrie wanted to know the reason, too; after all, she had been more directly affected than anyone else.

Lightly Zane touched her nipple, circling it with his callused fingertips and bringing it erect. "I know you have to be sore," he said, sliding his hand down her belly to nestle it between her legs. "But can you take me again?" With the utmost care he eased one long finger into her; Barrie winced, but didn't flinch away from him. Yes, she was sore; she had been sore since the first time. She had discovered that the discomfort was easily discounted when the rewards were so great.

"I could be persuaded," she whispered, sliding her hand down his belly to measure his immediate seriousness. She found that he was very serious. Granted, she had no experience against which to compare this, but she had read magazine articles and knew that usually only teenage boys and very young men could maintain this pace. Maybe it was because he was in such superb physical condition. Maybe she was just lucky, though twenty-four hours before she hadn't thought so. But circumstances had changed, and so had she.

Fate had given her this man for now, and for a few more hours, she thought as he leaned over her and his mouth captured hers. She would make the most of it.

Once more he led her through the maze of alleys, but this time she was clad in the enveloping black robe, and a chador covered her hair. Her feet were protected by slippers, which were a little too big and kept slipping up and down on her heels, but at least she wasn't barefoot. It felt strange to have on clothes, especially so many, even though she was bare underneath the robe.

Zane was once more rigged out with his gear and weaponry, and with the donning of those things he had become subtly more remote, almost icily controlled, the way he'd been the night before when he'd first found her. Barrie sensed his acute alertness and guessed that he was concentrating totally on the job at hand. She silently followed him, keeping her head a little bowed as a traditional Muslim woman would do.

He halted at the corner of a building and sank to his haunches, motioning for her to do the same. Barrie copied him and took the extra precaution of drawing the chador across her face.

"Two, this is One. How's it looking?" Once more he was speaking in that toneless whisper that barely carried to her, though she was right behind him. After a moment he said, "See you in ten."

He glanced around at Barrie. "It's a go. We don't have to shift to Plan C."

"What was Plan C?" she whispered.

"Run like hell for Egypt," he said calmly. "It's about two hundred miles due east."

He would do it, too, she realized. He would steal some kind of vehicle and go for it. His nerves must be made of solid iron. Hers weren't; she was shaking inside with nervousness, but she was holding up. Or maybe it wasn't nervousness; maybe it was exhilaration at the danger and excitement of action, of *escaping*. As long as they were still in Benghazi, in Libya, they hadn't really gotten free.

Ten minutes later he stopped in the shadow of a dilapidated warehouse. Perhaps he clicked his radio; in the dark, she couldn't tell. But suddenly five black shapes materialized out of the darkness, and they were surrounded before she could blink.

"Gentlemen, this is Miss Lovejoy," Zane said. "Now let's get the hell out of Dodge."

"With pleasure, boss." One of the men bowed to Barrie and held out his hand. "This way, Miss Lovejoy."

There was a certain rough élan about them that she found charming, though they didn't let it interfere with the business at hand. The six men immediately began moving out in choreographed order, and Barrie smiled at the man who'd spoken as she took the place he had indicated in line. She was behind Zane, who was second in line behind a man who moved so silently, and blended so well into the shadows, that even knowing he was there, sometimes she couldn't see him. The other four men ranged behind her at varying distances, and she realized that she couldn't hear them, either. In fact, she was the only one of the group who was making any noise, and she tried to place her slippered feet more carefully.

They wound their way through the alleys and finally stopped beside a battered minibus. Even in the darkness Barrie could see the huge dents and dark patches of rust that decorated the vehicle. They stopped beside it, and Zane opened the sliding side door for her. "Your chariot," he murmured.

Barrie almost laughed as he handed her into the little bus: if she hadn't had experience navigating long evening gowns, she would have found the ankle-length robe awkward, but she managed it as if she was a nineteenth-century lady being handed into a carriage. The men climbed in around her. There were only two bench seats; if there had ever been a third one in the back, it had long since been removed, perhaps to make room for cargo. A wiry young black man got behind the steering wheel, and Zane took the other seat in front. The eerily silent man who had been on point squeezed in on her left side, and another SEAL sat on her right, carefully placing her in a human security box. The other two SEALs knelt on the floorboard behind them, their muscular bodies and their gear filling the limited space.

"Let's go, Bunny Rabbit," Zane said, and the young black man grinned as he started the engine. The minibus looked as though it was on its last wheels, but the motor purred.

"You shoulda been there last night," the black guy said. "It was tight for a minute, real tight." He sounded as enthusiastic as if he was describing the best party he'd ever attended.

"What happened?" Zane asked.

"Just one of those things, boss," the man on Barrie's right said with a shrug evident in his voice "A bad guy stepped on Spook, and the situation went straight into fubar."

Barrie had been around enough military men to know what fubar meant. She sat very still and didn't comment.

"Stepped right *on* me," the SEAL on her left said in an aggrieved tone. "He started squalling like a scalded cat, shooting at everything that moved and most things that didn't. Aggravated me some." He paused. "I'm not staying for the funeral."

"When we got your signal we pulled back and ran like hell," the man on her right continued. "You must've already had her out, because they came after us like hound dogs. We laid low, but a couple of times I thought we were going to have to fight our way out. Man, they were walking all over us, and they kept hunting all night long."

"No, we were still inside," Zane said calmly. "We just stepped into the next room. They never thought to check it."

The men snorted with mirth; even the eerie guy on her left managed a chuckle, though it didn't sound as if he did it often enough to be good at it.

Zane turned around in the seat and gave Barrie that brief twitch of a smile. "Would you like some introductions, or would you rather not know these raunchy-smelling bums?"

The atmosphere in the bus *did* smell like a locker room, only worse. "The introductions, please," she said, and her smile was plain in her voice.

He indicated the driver. "Antonio Withrock, Seaman Second Class. He's driving because he grew up wrecking cars on dirt tracks down South, so we figure he can handle any situation."

"Ma'am," said Seaman Withrock politely.

"On your right is Ensign Rocky Greenberg, second in command."

"Ma'am," said Ensign Greenberg.

"On your left is Seaman Second Class Winstead Jones."

Seaman Winstead Jones growled something unintelligible. "Call him Spooky or Spook, not Winstead," Zane added.

"Ma'am," said Seaman Jones.

"Behind you are Seamen First Class Eddie Santos, our medic, and Paul Drexler, the team sniper."

"Ma'am," said two voices behind her.

"I'm glad to meet you all," Barrie said, her sincerity plain. She had trained her memory at countless official functions, so she had their names down cold. She hadn't yet put a face to Santos or Drexler, but from his name she figured Santos would be Hispanic, so that would be an easy distinction to make.

Greenberg began to tell Zane the details of everything that had happened. Barrie listened and didn't intrude. The fact was, this midnight drive through Benghazi felt a little surreal. She was surrounded by men armed to their eyeteeth, but they were traveling through an area that was still fairly active for so late at night. There were other vehicles in the streets, pedestrians on the sidewalks. They even stopped at a traffic light, with other vehicles around them. The driver, Withrock, hummed under his breath. No one else seemed concerned. The traffic light changed, the battered little minibus moved forward, and no one paid them any attention at all.

Several minutes later they left the city. Occasionally she could see the gleam of the Mediterranean on their right, which meant they were traveling west, toward the center of Libya's coast. As the lights faded behind them, she began to feel lightheaded with fatigue. The sleep she had gotten during the day, between bouts of lovemaking, hadn't been enough to offset the toll stress had taken on her. She couldn't see herself leaning on either of the men beside her, however, so she forced herself to sit upright and keep her eyes open.

She suspected that she was more than a little punch-drunk.

After a while Zane said, "Red goggles."

She was tired enough that she wondered if that was some kind of code, or if she'd misunderstood him. Neither, evidently. Each man took a pair of goggles from his pack and donned them. Zane glanced at her and said in explanation, "Red protects your night vision. We're going to let our vision adjust now, before Bunny kills the headlights."

She nodded, and closed her eyes to help her own vision adjust. She realized at once that, if she wanted to stay awake, closing her eyes for whatever reason wasn't the smartest thing to do, but her eyelids were so heavy that she couldn't manage to open them again. The next thing she knew, the minibus was lurching heavily from side to side, throwing her against first Greenberg, then Spooky. Dazed with sleep, she tried to hold herself erect, but she couldn't seem to find her balance or anything to hold on to. She was about to slide to the floorboard when Spooky's forearm shot out in front of her like an iron bar, anchoring her in the seat.

"Thank you," she said groggily.

"Anytime, ma'am."

Sometime while she had been asleep, Bunny had indeed killed the headlights, and they were plunging down an embankment in the dark. She blinked at something shiny looming in front of them; she had a split second of panic and confusion before she recognized the sea, gleaming in the starlight.

The minibus lurched to a halt. "End of the line," Bunny cheerfully announced. "We have now reached the hidey-hole for one IBS. That's military talk for inflatable boat, small," he said over his shoulder to Barrie. "These things are too fancy to be called plain old rafts."

Zane snorted. Barrie remembered that he'd described it as exactly that, a raft.

Watching them exit the minibus was like watching quicksilver slip through cracks. If there had been a working overhead light when the SEALs had commandeered the vehicle, they had taken care of that detail, because no light came on when the doors were cracked open. Spooky slipped past her, no mean feat given the equipment he was carrying, and when Greenberg slid the side door open a few inches, Spooky wiggled on his stomach through the small opening. One second he was there, the next he was gone. Barrie stared at the door with widened eyes in full appreciation of how he'd acquired his nickname. He was definitely spooky.

The others exited the minibus in the same manner; it was as if they were made of water, and when the doors opened they simply leaked out. They were that fluid, that silent. Only Bunny, the driver, remained behind with Barrie. He sat in absolute silence, pistol in hand, as he methodically surveyed the night-shrouded coast. Because he was silent, she was too. The best way not to be any trouble to them, she thought, was to follow their example.

There was one quick little tap on the window, and Bunny whispered, "It's clear. Let's go, Miss Lovejoy."

She scooted over the seat to the door while Bunny eeled out on the driver's side. Zane was there, opening the door wider, reaching in to steady her as she slid out onto the ground. "Are you holding up okay?" he asked quietly.

She nodded, not trusting herself to speak, because she was so tired her speech was bound to be slurred.

As usual, he seemed to understand without being told. "Just hold on for another hour or so, and we'll have you safe on board the carrier. You can sleep then."

Without him, though; that fact didn't need stating. Even if he intended to continue their relationship, and he hadn't given any indication of it, he wouldn't do so on board the ship. She would put off sleeping forever if it would postpone the moment when she had to admit, once and for all, that their relationship had been a temporary thing for him, prompted by both the hothouse of intimacy in which they'd spent the day, and her own demands.

She wouldn't cry; she wouldn't even protest, she told herself. She'd had him for a day, for one incredibly sensual day.

He led her down to the small, rocky strip of beach, where the dark bulk of the IBS had been positioned. The other five men were gathered around it in specific positions, each standing with his back to the raft while he held his weapon at the ready, edgily surveying the surroundings.

Zane lifted her into the IBS and showed her where to sit. The IBS bobbed in the water as the men eased it away from the shore. When the water was chest deep on Santos, the shortest one, they all swung aboard in a maneuver they had practiced so many times it looked effortless. Spooky started the almost soundless motor and aimed the IBS for the open sea.

Then a roar erupted behind them, and all hell broke loose.

She recognized the sharp *rat-tat-tat* of automatic weapons and half turned to look behind them. Zane put his hand on her head and shoved her down to the bottom of the boat, whirling, already bringing his automatic rifle around as he did so. The IBS shot forward as Spooky gave it full throttle. The SEALs returned fire, lightning flashing from the weapons, spent cartridges splattering down on her as she curled into a ball and drew the chador over her face to keep the hot brass from burning her.

"Drexler!" Zane roared. "Hit those bastards with explosives!"

"Got it, boss!"

Barrie heard a grunt, and something heavy and human fell across her. One of the men had been hit. Desperately she tried to wriggle out from under the crushing weight so she could help him, but she was effectively pinned, and he groaned every time she moved.

She knew that groan.

Terror such as she had never felt before raced through her veins. With a hoarse cry she heaved at the heavy weight, managing to roll him to the side. She fought her way free of the enveloping chador and didn't even notice the hot cartridge shell that immediately skimmed her right cheek.

An explosion shattered the night, lighting up the sea like fireworks, the percussion knocking her to the bottom of the boat again. She scrambled to her knees, reaching for Zane. "No," she said hoarsely. "No!"

The light from the explosion had sharply delineated every detail in stark white. Zane lay sprawled half on his side, writhing in pain as he pressed his hands to his abdomen. His face was a colorless blur, his eyes closed, his teeth exposed in a grimace. A huge wet patch glistened on the left side of his black shirt, and more blood was pooling beneath him.

Barrie grabbed the chador and wadded it up, pressing it hard to the wound. A low animal howl rattled in his throat, and he arched in pain. "Santos!" she screamed, trying to hold him down while still holding the chador in place. "*Santos!*"

With a muttered curse the stocky medic shouldered her aside. He lifted the chador for a second, then quickly pressed it into place and grabbed her hand, guiding it into position. "Hold it," he rapped out. "Press down—hard."

There was no more gunfire, only the hum of the motor. Salt spray lashed her face as the boat shot through the waves. The team maintained their discipline, holding their assigned positions. "How bad is it?" Greenberg yelled.

Santos was working feverishly. "I need light!"

Almost instantly Greenberg had a flashlight shining down on them. Barrie bit her lip as she saw how much blood had puddled around them. Zane's face was pasty white, his eyes half-shut as he gasped for breath.

"He's losing blood fast," Santos said. "Looks like the bullet got a kidney, or maybe his spleen. Get that damn helicopter on the way. We don't have time to get into international waters." He popped the cap off a syringe, straightened Zane's arm and deftly jabbed the needle into a vein. "Hang on, boss. We're gonna get you airlifted outta here."

Zane didn't reply. He was breathing noisily through his clenched teeth, but when Barrie glanced at him she could see the gleam of his eyes. His hand lifted briefly, touched her arm, then fell heavily to his side.

"Damn you, Zane Mackenzie," she said fiercely. "Don't you *dare*—" She broke off. She couldn't say the word, couldn't even admit to the possibility that he might die.

Santos was checking Zane's pulse. His eyes met hers, and she knew it was too fast, too weak. Zane was going into shock, despite the injection Santos had given him.

"I don't give a damn how close in we still are!" Greenberg was yelling into the radio. "We need a helo *now*. Just get the boss out of here and we'll wait for another ride!"

Despite the pitching of the boat, Santos got an IV line started and began squeezing a bag of clear plasma into Zane's veins. "Don't let up on the pressure," he muttered to Barrie.

"I won't." She didn't take her gaze off Zane's face. He was still aware, still looking at her. As long as that connection was maintained, he would be all right. He had to be.

The nightmare ride in the speeding boat seemed to take forever. Santos emptied the first bag of plasma and connected a second one to the IV. He was cursing under his breath, his invectives varied and explicit.

Zane lay quietly, though she knew he was in terrible pain. His eyes were dull with pain and shock, but she could sense his concentration, his determination. Perhaps the only way he could remain conscious was by focusing so intently on her face, but he managed it.

But if that helicopter didn't get there soon, not even his superhuman determination would be able to hold out against continued blood loss. She wanted to curse, too, wanted to glare at the night sky as if she could conjure a helicopter out of thin air, but she didn't dare look away from Zane. As long as their gazes held, he would hold on.

She heard the distinctive *whap-whap-whap* only a moment before the Sea King helicopter roared over them, blinding lights picking them out. Spooky throttled back, and the boat settled gently onto the water. The helicopter circled to them and hovered directly overhead, the powerful rotors whipping the sea into a frenzy. A basket dropped almost on their heads. Working swiftly, Santos and Greenberg lifted Zane into the basket and strapped him in, maneuvering around Barrie as she maintained pressure on the wound.

Santos hesitated, then indicated for her to let go and move back. Reluctantly she did. He lifted the chador, then immediately jammed it back into place. Without a word he straddled the basket, leaning hard on the wound. "Let's go!" he yelled. Greenberg stepped back and gave the thumbs-up to the winch operator in the helicopter. The basket rose toward the hovering monster, with Santos perched precariously on top of Zane. As the basket drew even with the open bay, several pairs of hands reached out and drew them inward. The helicopter immediately lifted away, banking hard, roaring toward the carrier.

There was an eerie silence left behind. Barrie slumped against one of the seats, her face rigid with the effort of maintaining control. No one said a word. Spooky started the motor again, and the little craft shot through the darkness, following the rapidly disappearing lights of the helicopter.

It was over an hour before the second helicopter settled onto the deck of the huge carrier. The remaining four members of the team leaped to the deck almost before the helicopter had touched down.

Barrie clambered after them, ran with them. Greenberg had one hand clamped on her arm to make certain she didn't get left behind.

Someone in a uniform stepped in front of them. "Miss Lovejoy, are you all right?"

Barrie gave him a distracted glance and dodged around him. Another uniform popped up, but this one was subtly different, as if the wearer belonged on board this gigantic ship. The first man had worn a dress uniform, marking him as a non-crew member. Greenberg skidded to a halt. "Captain—"

"Lieutenant-Commander Mackenzie is in surgery," the captain said. "Doc didn't think he'd make it to a base with such a high rate of blood loss. If they can't get the bleeding stopped, they'll have to remove his spleen."

The first uniformed officer had reached them. "Miss Lovejoy," he said firmly, taking her arm. "I'm Major Hodson. I'll escort you home."

The military moved at its own pace, to its own rules. She was to be taken home immediately; the ambassador wanted his daughter back. Barrie protested. She yelled, she cried, she even swore at the harried major. None of it did any good. She was hustled aboard another aircraft, this time a cargo transport plane. Her last glimpse of the *Montgomery* was as the sun's first rays glistened on the blue waters of the Mediterranean, and the sight was blurred by her tears.

Chapter 7

By the time the transport touched down in Athens, Barrie had cried so hard and for so long that her eyes were swollen almost shut. Major Hodson had tried everything to pacify her, then to console her; he assured her that he was just following orders, and that she would be able to find out how the SEAL was doing later. It was understandable that she was upset. She'd been through a lot, but she would have the best medical care—

At that, Barrie shot out of the uncomfortable web seat, which was all the transport plane afforded. "*I'm* not the one who was shot!" she yelled furiously. "I don't need medical care, best, worst or mediocre! I want to be taken to wherever Zane Mackenzie is taken. I don't care what your orders are!"

Major Hodson looked acutely uncomfortable. He tugged at the collar of his uniform. "Miss Lovejoy, I'm sorry. I can't do anything about this situation. After we're on the ground and your father is satisfied that you're okay, then where you go is up to you."

His expression plainly said that as far as he was concerned, she could go to hell. Barrie sat down, breathing hard and wiping away tears. She'd never acted like that before in her life. She'd always been such a lady, a perfect hostess for her father.

She didn't feel at all ladylike now; she felt like a ferocious tigress, ready to shred anyone who got in her way. Zane was severely wounded, perhaps dying, and these *fools* wouldn't let her be with him. Damn military procedure, and damn her father's influence, for they had both wrenched her away from him.

As much as she loved her father, she knew she would never forgive him if Zane died and she wasn't there. It didn't matter that he didn't know about Zane; nothing mattered compared to the enormous horror that loomed before her. *God, don't let him die!* She couldn't bear it. She would rather have died herself at her kidnappers' hands than for Zane to be killed while rescuing her.

The flight took less than an hour and a half. The transport landed with a hard thump that jerked her in the web seat, then taxied for what seemed like an interminable length of time. Finally it rolled to a stop, and Major Hodson stood, plainly relieved to be free of his unpleasant burden.

A door was slid open, and a flight of steps rolled up to it. Clutching the black robe around her, Barrie stepped out into the bright Athens sunlight. It was full morning now, the heat already building. She blinked and lifted a hand to shield her eyes. It felt like forever since she'd been in the sunshine.

A gray limousine with darkly tinted windows was waiting on the tarmac. The door was shoved open, and her father bounded out, dignity forgotten as he ran forward. "Barrie!" Two days of worry and fear lined his face, but there was an almost desperate relief in his expression as he hurried up the steps to fold her in his arms.

She started crying again, or maybe she had never stopped. She buried her face against his suit, clutching him with desperate hands. "I've got to go back," she sobbed, the words barely intelligible.

He tightened his arms around her. "There, there, baby," he breathed. "You're safe now, and I won't let anything else happen to you, I swear. I'll take you home—"

Wildly she shook her head, trying to pull away from him. "No," she choked out. "I've got to get back to the *Montgomery*. Zane—he was shot. He might die. Oh, God, I've got to go back *now!*"

"Everything will be all right," he crooned, hustling her down the steps with an arm locked around her shoulders. "I have a doctor waiting—"

"I don't need a doctor!" she said fiercely, jerking away from him. She'd never done that before, and his face went blank with shock. She shoved her hair out of her face. The tangled mass hadn't been combed in two days, and it was matted with sweat and sea spray. "Listen to me! The man who rescued me was shot. *He might die.* He was still in surgery when Major Hodson forced me on board this plane. I want to go back to the ship. I want to make sure Zane is okay."

William Lovejoy firmly took hold of his daughter's shoulders again, leading her across the tarmac to the waiting limo. "You don't have to go back to the ship, sweetheart," he said soothingly. "I'll ask Admiral Lindley to find out how his man is doing. He *is* one of the SEAL team, I presume?"

Numbly she nodded.

"There wouldn't be any point in going back to the ship, I'm sure you can see that. If he survived surgery, he'll be airlifted to a military hospital."

If he survived surgery. The words were like a knife, hot and slicing, going through her. She balled her hands into fists, every cell in her body screaming for her to ignore logic, ignore the attempts to soothe her. She needed to get to Zane.

Three days later, she stood in her father's office with her chin high and her eyes colder than he'd ever seen them. "You told Admiral Lindley to block my requests," she accused.

The ambassador sighed. He removed his reading glasses and carefully placed them on the inlaid walnut desk. "Barrie, you know I've denied you very little that you've asked for, but you're being unreasonable about this man. You know that he's recovering, and that's all you need to know. What point would there be in rushing to his bedside? Some tabloid might find out about it, and then your ordeal would be plastered in sleazy newspapers all over the world. Is that what you want?"

"My ordeal?" she echoed. "*My* ordeal? What about his? He nearly died! That's assuming Admiral Lindley told me the truth, and he really is still alive!''

"Of course he is. I only asked Joshua to block any inquiries you made about his location." He unfolded his tall form from the chair and came around to lean against the desk and take her resistant hands in his. "Barrie, give yourself time to get over the trauma. I know you've invested this…this guerrilla fighter with all sorts of heroic characteristics, and that's only normal. After a while, when you've regained your perspective, you'll be glad you didn't embarrass yourself by chasing after him.''

It was almost impossible to contain the volcanic fury rising in her. Nobody was listening; no one wanted to listen. They kept going on and on about her ordeal, how she would heal in time, until she wanted to pull her hair out. She had insisted over and over that she hadn't been raped, but she had fiercely refused to be examined by a doctor, which of course had only fueled speculation that the kidnappers had indeed raped her. But she'd known her body bore the marks of Zane's lovemaking, marks and traces that were precious and private, for no one else's eyes. Everyone was treating her as if she was made of crystal, carefully not mentioning the kidnapping, until she thought she would go mad.

She wanted to see Zane. That was all. Just see him, assure herself that he would be all right. But when she'd asked one of the Marine officers stationed at the embassy to make some inquiries about Zane, it was Admiral Lindley who had gotten back to her instead of the captain.

The dignified, distinguished admiral had come to the ambassador's private quarters less than an hour before. Barrie hadn't yet returned to her minor job in the embassy, feeling that she couldn't keep her mind on paperwork, so she had received the admiral in the beautifully appointed parlor.

After polite conversation about her health and the weather, the admiral came to the point of his visit. "You've been making some inquiries about Zane Mackenzie," he said kindly. "I've kept abreast of his condition, and I can tell you now with complete confidence that he'll fully recover. The ship's surgeon was able to stop the bleeding, and it wasn't necessary to remove his spleen. His condition was stabilized, and he was transferred to a hospital. When he's able, he'll be sent Stateside for the remainder of his convalescence."

"Where is he?" Barrie had demanded, her eyes burning. She'd scarcely slept in three days. Though she was once more impeccably clothed and coifed, the strain she'd been under had left huge dark circles under her eyes, and she was losing weight fast, because her nerves wouldn't let her eat.

Admiral Lindley sighed. "William asked me to keep that information from you, Barrie, and I have to say, I think he's right. I've known Zane a long time. He's an extraordinary warrior. But SEALs are a breed apart, and the characteristics that make them such great warriors don't, as a whole, make them model citizens. They're trained weapons, to put it bluntly. They don't keep high profiles, and most information about them is restricted."

"I don't want to know about his training," she said, her voice strained. "I don't want to know about his missions. I just want to see him."

The admiral shook his head. "I'm sorry."

Nothing she said budged him. He refused to give her even one more iota of information. Still, Zane was alive; he would be all right. Just knowing that made her feel weak inside, as the unbearable tension finally relaxed.

That didn't mean she would forgive her father for interfering.

"I love him," she now said deliberately. "You have no right to keep me from seeing him."

"Love?" Her father gave her a pitying look. "Barrie, what you feel isn't love, it's hero-worship. It will fade, I promise you."

"Do you think I haven't considered that?" she fired back. "I'm not a teenager with a crush on a rock star. Yes, I met him under dangerous, stressful circumstances. Yes, he saved my life—and he nearly died doing it. I know what infatuation is, and I know what love is, but even if I didn't, the decision isn't yours to make."

"You've always been reasonable," he argued. "At least concede that your judgment may not be at its sharpest right now. What if you acted impulsively, married this man—I'm sure he'd jump at the chance—and then realized that you really didn't love him? Think what a mess it would be. I know it sounds snobbish, but he isn't our kind. He's a sailor, and a trained killer. You've dined with kings and danced with princes. What could the two of you have in common?"

"First, that doesn't just *sound* snobbish, it *is* snobbish. Second, you must not think much of me as a person if you consider your money my only attraction."

"You know that isn't what I meant," he said, genuinely shocked. "You're a wonderful person. But how could someone like that appreciate the life you live? How do you know he wouldn't have his eye on the main chance?"

"Because I know him," she declared. "I know him in a way I never would have if I'd met him at an embassy party. According to you, a SEAL couldn't be kind and considerate, but he was. They all were, for that matter. Dad, I've told you over and over that I wasn't raped. I know you don't believe me, and I know you've suffered, worrying about me. But I swear to you—I *swear*—that I wasn't. They were planning to, the next day, but they were waiting for someone. So, though I was terrified and upset, I haven't been through the trauma of a gang rape the way you keep thinking. Seeing Zane lying in a pool of blood was a hell of a lot more traumatic than anything those kidnappers did!"

"Barrie!" It was the first time her father had ever heard her curse. Come to think of it, she had never cursed at all, until rough men had grabbed her off the street and subjected her to hours of terror. She had cursed them, and meant it. She had cursed Major Hodson, and meant that, too.

With an effort, she regulated her tone. "You know that the first attempt to get me out didn't quite work."

He gave an abrupt nod. He'd suffered agonies, thinking their only hope of rescuing her had failed and imagining what she must be suffering. That was when he'd given up hope of ever seeing her alive again. Admiral Lindley hadn't been as pessimistic; the SEALs hadn't checked in, and though there were reports of gunfire in Benghazi, if a team of SEALs had been killed or captured, the Libyan government would have trumpeted it all over the world. That meant they were still there, still working to free her. Until they heard from the team that the rescue had failed, there was still hope.

"Well, it did work, in a way. Zane came in alone to get me, while the rest of the team was a diversion, I guess, in case things went wrong. He had a backup plan, what to do if they were spotted, because you can't control the human factor." She realized she was repeating things Zane had said to her during those long hours when they had lain drowsily together, and she missed him so much that pain knotted her insides. "The team was so well-hidden that one of the guards didn't see Spooky until he actually stepped on him. That's what gave the alarm and started the shooting. A guard had been posted in the corridor outside the room where they had me tied up, and he ran in. Zane killed him," she said simply. "Then, while the others were chasing the team, he got me out of the building. We were separated from the team and had to hide for a day, but I was safe."

The ambassador listened gravely, soaking up these details of how she had been returned to him. They hadn't talked before, not about the actual rescue. She had been too distraught about Zane, almost violent in her despair. Now that she knew he was alive, even though she was still so angry she could barely contain it, she was able to tell her father how she had been returned to him alive.

"While I stayed in our hiding place, Zane risked his life by going out and stealing food and water for us, as well as the robe and chador for me. He took care of the cut on my foot. When scavengers were practically dismantling the place around us, he kept himself between me and any danger. That's the man I fell in love with, that's the man you say isn't 'our kind.' He may not be yours, but he's definitely mine!"

The expression in her father's eyes was stunned, almost panicked. Too late, Barrie saw that she had chosen the wrong tack in her argument. If she had presented her concern for Zane as merely for someone who had done so much for her, if she had insisted that it was only right she thank him in person, her father could have been convinced. He was very big on preserving the niceties, on behaving properly. Instead, she had convinced him that she truly loved Zane Mackenzie, and too late she saw how much he had feared exactly that. He didn't want to lose her, and now Zane presented a far bigger threat than before.

"Barrie, I..." He fumbled to a stop, her urbane, sophisticated father who was never at a loss for words. He swallowed hard. It was true that he'd seldom denied her anything, and those times he had refused had been because he thought the activity she planned or the object she wanted—once it had been a motorcycle—wasn't safe. Keeping her safe was his obsession, that and holding tightly to his only remaining family, his beloved child, who so closely resembled the wife he'd lost.

She saw it in his eyes as his instinct to pamper her with anything she desired warred with the knowledge that this time, if he did, he would probably lose her from his life. He didn't want occasional visits from her; they had both endured that kind of separation during her school years. He wanted her *there,* in his everyday life. She knew part of his obsession was selfish, because she made domestic matters very easy for him, but she had never doubted his love for her.

Pure panic flashed in his expression. He said stiffly, "I still think you need to give yourself time for your emotions to calm. And surely you realize that the conditions you describe are what that man is *used* to. How could he ever fit into your life?"

"That's a moot question, since marriage or even a relationship was never discussed. I want to see him. I don't want him to think that I didn't care enough even to check on his condition."

"If any sort of relationship was never discussed, why would he expect you to visit him? It was a mission for him, nothing more."

Barrie's shoulders were military straight, her jaw set, her green eyes dark with emotion. "It was more," she said flatly, and that was as much of what had happened between her and Zane as she was willing to discuss. She took a deep breath and pulled out the heavy artillery. "You owe it to me," she said, her gaze locked with his. "I haven't asked any details about what happened here, but I'm an intelligent, logical person—"

"Of course you are," he interrupted, "but I don't see—"

"Was there a ransom demanded?" She cut across his interruption. He was a trained diplomat; he seldom lost control of his expression.

But now, startled, the look he gave her was blank with puzzlement. "A ransom?" he echoed.

A new despair knotted itself in her stomach, etched itself in her face. "Yes, ransom," she said softly. "There wasn't one, was there? Because money wasn't what *he* wanted. He wants something from you, doesn't he? Information. He's either trying to force you to give it to him, or you're already in it up to your eyebrows and you've had a falling out with him. Which is it?"

Again his training failed him; for a split second his face revealed panicked guilt and consternation before his expression smoothed into diplomatic blandness. "What a ridiculous charge," he said calmly.

She stood there, sick with knowledge. If the kidnapper had been using her as a weapon to force her father into betraying his country, the ambassador most likely would have denied it, because he wouldn't want her to be worried, but that wasn't what she'd read in his face. It was guilt.

She didn't bother responding to his denial. "You owe me," she repeated. "You owe Zane."

He flinched at the condemnation in her eyes. "I don't see it that way at all."

"You're the reason I was kidnapped."

"You know there are things I can't tell you," he said, releasing her hands and walking around the desk to resume his seat, symbolically leaving the role of father and entering that of ambassador. "But your supposition is wrong, and, of course, an indication of how off-balance you still are."

She started to ask if Art Sandefer would think her supposition was so wrong, but she couldn't bring herself to threaten her father. Feeling sick, she wondered if that made her a traitor, too. She loved her country; living in Europe as much as she had, she had seen and appreciated the dramatic differences between the United States and every other country on earth. Though she liked Europe and had a fondness for French wine, German architecture, English orderliness, Spanish music and Italy in general, whenever she set foot in the States she was struck by the energy, the richness of life where even people who were considered poor lived well compared to everywhere else. The United

States wasn't perfect, far from it, but it had something special, and she loved it.

By her silence, she could be betraying it.

By staying here, she remained in danger. Kidnapping her had failed once, but that didn't mean *he*, the unknown, faceless enemy, wouldn't try again. Her father knew who *he* was, she was certain of it. Immediately she saw how it would be. She would be confined to the embassy grounds, or allowed out only with an armed escort. She would be a prisoner of her father's fear.

There was really no place she would be entirely safe, but remaining here only made the danger more acute. And once she was away from the enclave of the embassy, she would have a better chance of locating Zane, because Admiral Lindley's influence couldn't cover every nook and cranny of the globe. The farther away from Athens she was, the thinner that influence would be.

She faced her father, knowing that she was deliberately breaking the close ties that had bound them together for the past fifteen years. "I'm going home," she said calmly. "To Virginia."

Two weeks later, Zane sat on the front porch of his parents' house, perched on top of Mackenzie's Mountain, just outside Ruth, Wyoming. The view was breathtaking, an endless vista of majestic mountains and green valleys. Everything here was as familiar to him as his own hands. Saddles, boots, some cattle but mostly horses. Books in every room of the sprawling house, cats prowling through the barns and stables, his mother's sweet, bossy coddling, his father's concern and understanding.

He'd been shot before; he'd been sliced up in a knife fight. He'd had his collarbone broken, ribs cracked, a lung punctured. He had been seriously injured before, but this was the closest he'd ever come to dying. He'd been bleeding to death, lying there in the bottom of the raft with Barrie crouched over him, pressing the chador over the wound with every ounce of her weight. Her quickness, her determination, had made the difference. Santos squeezing the plasma from the bags into his veins had made the difference. He had been so close that he could pick out a dozen details that had made the difference; if any one of them hadn't happened, he would have died.

He'd been unusually quiet since leaving the naval hospital and returning home for convalescence. It wasn't that he was in low spirits, but rather that he had a lot of thinking to do, something that hadn't been easy when practically the entire family had felt compelled to visit and reassure themselves of his relative well-being. Joe had flown in from Washington for a quick check on his baby brother; Michael and Shea had visited several times, bringing their two rapscallion sons with them; Josh and Loren and their three had descended for a weekend visit, which was all the time Loren's job at the hospital in Seattle had allowed. Maris had driven all night to be there when he was brought home. At least he'd been able to walk on his own by then, even if very slowly, or likely she would still be here. She had pulled up a chair directly in front of him and sat for hours, her black eyes locked on his face as if she was willing vitality from her body into his. Maybe she had been. His little sister was fey, magical; she operated on a different level than other people did.

Hell, even Chance had shown up. He'd done so warily, eyeing their mother and sister as if they were bombs that might go off in his face, but he was here, sitting beside Zane on the porch.

"You're thinking of resigning."

Zane didn't have to wonder how Chance had known what was on his mind. After nearly battering each other to death when they were fourteen, they had reached an unusual communion. Maybe it was because they'd shared so much, from classes to girls to military training. Even after all this time, Chance was as wary as a wounded wolf and didn't like people to get close to him, but even though he resisted, he was helpless against family. Chance had never in his life been loved until Mary had brought him home with her and the sprawling, brawling Mackenzies had knocked him flat. It was fun to watch him still struggle against the family intimacy each time he was drawn into the circle, because within an hour he always surrendered. Mary wouldn't let him do anything else; nor would Maris. After accepting him as a brother, Zane had never even acknowledged Chance's wariness. Only

Wolf was willing to give his adopted son time to adjust—but there was still a limit on how much time he would allow.

"Yeah," he finally said.

"Because you nearly bought it this time?"

Zane snorted. "When has that ever made any difference to either of us?" He alone of the family knew the exact details of Chance's work. It was a toss-up which of them was in the most danger.

"Then it's this last promotion that did it."

"It took me out of the field," Zane said quietly. Carefully he leaned back in the chair and propped his booted feet on the porch railing. Though he was a fast healer, two and a half weeks wasn't quite long enough to let him ignore the wound. "If two of my men hadn't been wounded in that screwup on the *Montgomery,* I wouldn't have been able to go on this last mission."

Chance knew about the screwup. Zane had told him about it, and screwup was the most polite description he'd used. As soon as he'd regained consciousness in the naval hospital, he'd been on the phone, starting and directing the investigation. Though Odessa would fully recover, it was likely Higgins would have to retire on disability. The guards who had shot the two SEALs might escape court-martial if their counsel was really slick, but at the very least they would be cashiered out of the service. The extent of the damage to the careers of Captain Udaka and Executive Officer Boyd remained to be seen; Zane had targeted the shooters, but the ripple effect would go all the way up to the captain.

"I'm thirty-one," Zane said. "That's just about the upper limit for active missions. I'm too damn good at my job, too. The Navy keeps promoting me for it, then they say I'm too highly ranked to go on missions."

"You want to throw in with me?" Chance asked casually.

He'd considered it. Very seriously. But something kept nagging at him, something he couldn't quite bring into focus.

"I want to. If things were different, I would, but..."

"What things?"

Zane shrugged. At least part of his uneasy feeling could be nailed down. "A woman," he said.

"Oh, hell." Chance kicked back and surveyed the world over the toes of his boots. "If it's a woman, you won't be able to concentrate on anything until you've gotten her out of your system. Damn their sweet little hides," he said fondly. Chance generally had women crawling all over him. It didn't hurt that he was drop-dead handsome, but he had a raffish, daredevil quality to him that brought them out of the woodwork.

Zane wasn't certain he could get Barrie out of his system. He wasn't certain he wanted to. He didn't wonder why she had disappeared without even saying goodbye, hope you're feeling better. Bunny and Spook had told him how she'd been dragged, kicking and yelling and swearing, aboard a plane and taken back to Athens. He figured her father, combined with the Navy's policy of secrecy concerning the SEALs, had prevented her from finding out to which hospital they'd taken him.

He missed her. He missed her courage, her sturdy willingness to do whatever needed doing. He missed the serenity of her expression, and the heat of her lovemaking.

God, yes.

The one memory, more than any of the others, that was branded in his brain was the moment when she had reached for his belt and said in that fierce whisper, "I'll do it!"

He'd understood. Not just why she needed to be in control, but the courage it took her to wipe out the bad memories and replace them with good ones. She'd been a virgin; she had told the truth about that. She hadn't known what to do, and she hadn't expected the pain. But she had taken him anyway, sweetly, hotly, sliding her tight little body down on him and shattering his control the way no other woman had ever done.

She could have been a spoiled, helpless little socialite; she *should* have been exactly that. Instead she had made the best of a tense, dangerous situation, done what she could to help and hadn't voiced a single complaint.

He liked being with her, liked talking to her. He was too much of a loner to easily accept the word love in connection with anyone other than family, but with Barrie...maybe. He wanted to spend more time with her, get to know her better, let whatever would develop get to developing.

He wanted her.

First things first, though. He had to get his strength back; right now he could walk from room to room without aid, but he would think twice about heading down to the stables by himself. He had to decide whether or not he was going to stay in the Navy; it felt like time to be moving on, since the reason he'd joined in the first place was being taken away from him as he moved up the ranks. If he wasn't going to remain a SEAL, then what would he do for a living? He had to decide, had to get his life settled.

Barrie might not be interested in any kind of relationship with him, though from the way Spook and Bunny had described her departure, he didn't think that was the case. The day of lovemaking they had shared had been more than propinquity for both of them.

Getting in touch with her could take some doing, though. That morning he had placed a call to the embassy in Athens. He'd given his name and asked to speak to Barrie Lovejoy. It had been Ambassador William Lovejoy who had come on the line, however, and the conversation hadn't been cordial.

"It isn't that Barrie doesn't appreciate what you did, but I'm sure you understand that she wants to put all of that behind her. Talking with you would bring it all back and needlessly upset her," the ambassador had said in a cool, well-bred voice, his diction the best money could buy.

"Is that her opinion, or yours?" Zane had asked, his tone arctic.

"I don't see that it matters," the ambassador had replied, and hung up.

Zane decided he would let it rest for now. He wasn't in any shape to do much about it, so he would wait. When he had his mind made up about what he was going to do, there would be plenty of time to get in touch with Barrie, and now that he knew the ambassador had given orders for his calls not to be routed to her, the next time he would be prepared to do an end run around her father.

"Zane," his mother called from inside the house, pulling his thoughts to the present. "Are you getting tired?"

"I feel fine," he called back. It was an exaggeration, but he wasn't unduly tired. He glanced at Chance and saw the smirk on his brother's face.

"With all the worry about you, she forgot about my cracked ribs," Chance whispered.

"Glad to be of service," Zane drawled. "Just don't expect me to get shot every time you bang yourself up a little." The entire family thought it was hilarious the way Chance reacted to Mary's coddling and fussing, as if the attention terrified him, even though he was never able to resist her. Chance was putty in Mary's hands, but then, they all were. They'd grown up with the fine example of their father to emulate, and Wolf Mackenzie might growl and stomp, but Mary usually got her way.

"Chance?"

Zane controlled a grin as Chance stiffened, the smirk disappearing from his face as if it had never been.

"Ma'am?" he answered cautiously.

"Are you still keeping a pressure wrap on your ribs?"

That familiar panicked expression was in his eyes now. "Ah...no, ma'am." He could have lied; Mary would have believed him. But none of them ever lied to her, even when it was in their best interests. It would hurt the little tyrant's feelings too much if she ever discovered any of her kids had lied to her.

"You know you're supposed to wrap them for another week," said the voice from inside the house. It was almost like hearing God speak, except this voice was light and sweet and liquidly Southern.

"Yes, ma'am."

"Come inside and let me take care of that."

"Yes, ma'am," Chance said again, resignation in his voice. He got up from his rocking chair and went into the house. As he passed Zane, he muttered, "Getting shot didn't work. Try something else."

Chapter 8

Two months later, Sheriff Zane Mackenzie stood naked at the window of the pleasant two-bedroom Spanish-style house he had bought in southern Arizona. He was staring out over the moonlit desert, something wild and hot running through him at the sight. His SEAL training had taught him how to adapt to any environment, and the hot, dry climate didn't bother him.

Once he'd made up his mind to resign his commission, things had rapidly fallen into place. Upon hearing that he was leaving the Navy, a former SEAL team member who was now on the governor's staff in Phoenix had called and asked if he would be interested in serving the remaining two years of the term of a sheriff who had died in office.

At first Zane had been taken aback; he'd never considered going into law enforcement. Moreover, he didn't know anything about Arizona state laws.

"Don't worry about it," his friend had said breezily. "Sheriff is a political position, and most of the time it's more administrative than anything else. The situation you'd be going into is more hands-on, though. A couple of the deputies have quit, so you'd be shorthanded until some more can be hired, and the ones still there will resent the hell out of you because one of them wasn't appointed to finish out the sheriff's term."

"Why not?" Zane asked bluntly. "What's wrong with the chief deputy?"

"She's one of the ones who quit. She left a couple of months before the sheriff died, took a job on the force in Prescott."

"None of the others are qualified?"

"I wouldn't say that."

"Then what would you say?"

"You gotta understand, there's not a lot of selection here. A couple of the young deputies are good, real good, but they're *too* young, not enough experience. The one twenty-year guy isn't interested. A fifteen-year guy is a jerk, and the rest of the deputies hate his guts."

Sheriff. Zane thought about it, growing more intrigued with the idea. He had no illusions about it being a cakewalk. He would have difficulties with the fifteen-year veteran, at least, and likely all the other deputies would have some reservations and resistance about someone from the outside being brought in. Hell, he liked it better that way. Cakewalks didn't interest him. He'd rather have a challenging job any day. "Okay, I'm interested. What does it involve?"

"A lot of headache, mostly. The pay's decent, the hours are lousy. A reservation sits on part of the county, so you'll have to deal with the BIA. There's a big problem with illegal immigrants, but that's for the INS to worry about. Generally, this isn't a high crime area. Not enough people."

So here he was, his strength back, the owner of a house and a hundred acres of land, newly sworn in as sheriff. He'd brought in a few of his horses from his parents' place in Wyoming. It was a hell of a change from the Navy.

It was time to see about Barrie. He'd thought about her a lot over the past few months, but lately he couldn't think about anything else. The uneasy feeling was persisting, growing stronger. He'd put his resources to work, and to his surprise found that she'd left Athens within a week of being returned there. She was currently living at the Lovejoy private residence in Arlington, Virginia. Moreover, last month the ambassador had abruptly asked to be replaced, and he, too, had returned to Virginia. Zane wished Mr. Lovejoy had remained in Athens, but his presence was a problem that could be handled.

No matter what her father did or said, Zane was determined to see Barrie. There was unfinished business between them, a connection that had been abruptly cut when he'd been shot and she had been forced aboard a flight to Athens. He knew the hot intimacy of those long hours together could have been a product of stress and propinquity, but at this point, he didn't give a damn. There were other considerations, ones he couldn't ignore. That was why he had a flight out of Tucson to Washington in the morning. He needed to be sleeping, but one thought kept going around and around in his head. She was pregnant.

He couldn't say why he was so convinced of it. It was a gut feeling, an intuition, even a logical conclusion. There hadn't been any means of birth control available; they had made love several times. Put the two facts together, and the possibility of pregnancy existed. He didn't think it was a mere possibility, though; he thought it was a fact.

Barrie was going to have his baby.

The rush of fierce possessiveness he felt was like a tidal wave, sweeping away all his cautious plans. There wouldn't be any gradual getting-to-know-each-other stage, no easing into the idea of a serious relationship. If she was pregnant, they would get married immediately. If she didn't like the idea, he would convince her. It was as simple as that.

She was pregnant. Barrie hugged the precious knowledge to herself, not ready yet to let anyone else know, certainly not her father. The kidnapping and the aftermath had driven a wedge between them that neither of them could remove. He was desperate to restore their former relationship; nothing else could have induced him to resign from a post, an action that could have had serious repercussions for his career if it hadn't generally been thought that he had resigned because she had been so traumatized by the kidnapping that she couldn't remain in Athens and he wanted to be with her.

She tried not to think about whatever he might be involved in, because it hurt. It hurt horribly that he might be a traitor. Part of her simply couldn't believe it; he was an old-fashioned man, a man to whom honor wasn't just a word but a way of life. She had no proof, only logic and her own deductions...that, and the expression he hadn't quite been able to hide when she had asked him directly if he was involved in anything that might have resulted in her being kidnapped.

It also hurt horribly that he had kept her from Zane. She had made inquiries once she reached Virginia, but once again she had collided with a stone wall. No one would give her any information at all about him. She had even contacted SEAL headquarters and been politely stonewalled again. At least with the SEALs it was probably policy to safeguard the team members' identities and location, given the sensitive nature of the antiterrorism unit.

She was having his baby. She wanted him to know about it. She wouldn't expect anything of him that he didn't want to give, but she wanted him to know about his child. And she desperately wanted to see him again. She was adrift and lonely and frightened, her emotions in turmoil, and she needed some security in that part of her life, at least. He wasn't the kind of man who would blithely walk away from his offspring and ignore their existence. This baby would be a permanent link between them, something she could count on.

She doubted her father would relent concerning Zane even if he knew about the baby; his possessiveness would probably extend to a grandchild, even an illegitimate one. He would take steps to keep her pregnancy quiet, and even when the news got around, as it inevitably would, people would assume it was a child of rape, and they would look at her pityingly and talk about how brave she was.

She thought she would go mad. She had escaped to Virginia only to have her father follow. He panicked if she went anywhere unescorted. She had her own car, but he didn't want her driving it; he wanted his driver to take her wherever she wanted to go. She had had to sneak to a pharmacy to buy a home pregnancy test, though she had been sure fairly early on that she was pregnant. The test had merely confirmed what her body had already told her.

Barrie knew she should be worried and upset about this unplanned pregnancy, but it was the only thing in her life right now that made her happy. She was intensely lonely; the kidnapping and the long hours alone with Zane had set her apart from the other people in her life. She had memories they couldn't share, thoughts and needs no one could understand. Zane had been there with her; he would have understood her occasional pensiveness, her reticence in talking about it. It wasn't that she was secretive, for she would have liked to talk to someone who understood. But what she had shared with Zane was like a combat experience, forming a unique bond between the people who had lived it.

She wouldn't be able to keep her pregnancy secret much longer; she had to arrange prenatal care, and all telephone calls were now recorded. She supposed she could sneak out again and set up a doctor's appointment from a pay phone, but she would be damned if she would.

Enough was enough. She was an adult, and soon to be a mother. She hated the fact that her relationship with her father had deteriorated to the point where they barely spoke, but she couldn't find a way to mend it. As long as the possibility of his involvement in treasonous activities remained, she was helpless. She wanted him to explain, to give her a plausible reason why she had been kidnapped. She wanted to stop looking over her shoulder every time she went out; she didn't want to feel as if she truly *needed* to be guarded. She wanted to live a normal life. She didn't want to raise her baby in an atmosphere of fear.

But that was exactly the atmosphere that permeated the house. It was stifling her. She had to get away, had to remove herself from the haunting fear that, as long as her father was involved in whatever had given him such a guilty expression, she could be kidnapped again. The very thought made her want to vomit, and she didn't have just herself to worry about now. She had her baby to protect.

The fatigue of early pregnancy had gotten her into the habit of sleeping late, but one morning she woke early, disturbed by a pair of raucous birds fighting for territory in the tree outside her window. Once she was awake, nausea soon followed, and she made her usual morning dash to the bathroom. Also as usual, when the bout of morning sickness had passed, she felt fine. She looked out the window at the bright morning and realized she was inordinately hungry, the first time in weeks that the idea of food was appealing.

It was barely six o'clock, too early for Adele, the cook, to have arrived. Breakfast was normally at eight, and she had been sleeping past that. Her stomach growled. She couldn't wait another two hours for something to eat.

She put on her robe and slippers and quietly left her room; her father's bedroom was at the top of the stairs, and she didn't want to disturb him. Even more, she didn't want him to join her for an awkward tête-à-tête. He tried so hard to carry on as if nothing had happened, and she couldn't respond as she had before.

He should still be asleep, she thought, but when she reached the top of the stairs she heard him saying something she couldn't understand. She paused, wondering if he'd heard her after all and had been calling out to her. Then she heard him say *Mack* in a sharp tone, and she froze.

A chill roughened her entire body, and the bottom dropped out of her stomach. The only Mack she knew was Mack Prewett, but why would her father be talking to him? Mack Prewett was still stationed in Athens, as far as she knew, and since her father had resigned, he shouldn't have had any reason to be talking to him.

Then her heart leaped wildly as another possibility occurred to her. Perhaps he had been saying *Mackenzie* and she'd heard only the first syllable. Maybe he was talking about Zane. If she listened, she might find out where he was, or at least *how* he was. With no additional information about his condition, it had been hard to believe Admiral Lindley's assurance that he would fully recover. Belief required trust, and she no longer trusted the admiral, or her father.

She crept closer to his door and put her ear against it.

"—finished soon," he was saying sharply, then he was silent for a moment. "I didn't bargain on this. Barrie wasn't supposed to be involved. Get it wrapped up, Mack."

Barrie closed her eyes in despair. The chill was back, even colder than before. She shook with it, and swallowed hard against the return of nausea. So he *was* involved, he and Mack Prewett both. Mack was CIA. Was he a double agent, and if so, for whom? The world situation wasn't like it had been back in the old days of the Cold War, when the lines had been clearly drawn. Nations had died since then, and new ones taken their place. Religion or money seemed to be the driving force behind most differences these days; how would her father and Mack Prewett fit into that? What information would her father have that Mack wouldn't?

The answer eluded her. It could be anything. Her father had friends in every country in Europe, and any variety of confidential information could come his way. What didn't make sense was why he would sell that information; he was already a wealthy man. But money, to some people, was as addictive as a narcotic. No amount was ever enough; they had to have more, then still more, always looking for the next hit in the form of cash and the power that went with it.

Could she have been so wrong in her judgment of him? Had she still been looking at him with a child's eyes, seeing only her father, the man who had been the security in her life, instead of a man whose ambitions had tainted his honor?

Blindly she stumbled to her bedroom, not caring if he heard her. He must still have been engrossed in his conversation, though, or she didn't make as much noise as she thought she had, because his door remained closed.

She curled up on the bed, protectively folding herself around the tiny embryo in her womb.

What was it he hadn't bargained on? The kidnapping? That was over two months in the past. Had there been a new threat to use her as a means of ensuring he did something?

She was helplessly fumbling around in the dark with these wild conjectures, and she hated it. It was like being in alien territory, with no signs to guide her. What was she supposed to do? Take her suspicions to the FBI? She had nothing concrete to go on, and over the years her father had made a lot of contacts in the FBI; who could she trust there?

Even more important, if she stayed here, was she in danger? Maybe her wild conjectures weren't wild at all. She had seen a lot during her father's years in foreign service and noticed even more when she had started working at the embassy. Things happened, skulduggery went on, dangerous situations developed. Given the kidnapping, her father's reaction and now his unreasonable attitude about her safety, she didn't think she could afford to assume everything would be okay.

She had to leave.

Feverishly she began trying to think of someplace she could go where it wouldn't be easy to find her, and how she could get there without leaving a paper trail that would lead a halfway competent terrorist straight to her. Meanwhile, Mack Prewett wasn't a halfway competent bureaucrat, he was frighteningly efficient; he was like a spider, with webs of contacts spreading out in all directions. If she booked a flight using her real name, or paid for it with a credit card, he would know.

To truly hide, she had to have cash, a lot of it. That meant emptying her bank account, but how could she get there without her father knowing? It had reached the point where she would have to climb out the window and walk to the nearest pay phone to call a cab.

Maybe the house was already being watched.

She moaned and covered her face with her hands. Oh, God, this was making her paranoid, but did she dare *not* suspect anything? As some wit had observed, even paranoids had enemies.

She had to think of the baby. No matter how paranoid an action seemed, she had to err on the side of safety. If she had to dress in dark clothing, slither out a window in the wee hours of the morning and crawl across the ground until she was well away from this house...as ridiculous as it sounded, she would do it. Tonight? The sooner she got away, the better.

Tonight.

That decision made, she took a deep breath and tried to think of the details. She would have to carry some clothing. She would take her checkbook and bank book, so she could close out both her checking and savings accounts. She would take her credit cards and get as much cash as she could on them; everything together would give her a hefty amount, close to half a million dollars. How would she carry that much money? She would need an empty bag.

This was beginning to sound ludicrous, even to her. How was she supposed to crawl across the lawn in the darkness, dragging two suit-cases behind her?

Think! she fiercely admonished herself. Okay, she wouldn't have to carry either clothes or suitcases with her. All she would need to carry was her available cash, which was several hundred dollars, her checkbook and savings account book, and her credit cards, which she would destroy after they had served their purpose. She could buy new clothes and makeup, as well as what luggage she would immediately need, as soon as a discount store opened. She could buy do-it-yourself hair coloring and dye her red hair brown, though not until after she had been to the bank. She didn't want the teller to be able to describe her disguise.

With cash in her possession, she would have several options. She could hop on Amtrak and go in any direction, then get off the train before her ticketed destination. Then she could buy a cheap used car, pay cash for it, and no one would know where she went from there To be on the safe side, she would drive that car for only one day, then trade it in on a better car, again paying cash.

These were drastic measures, but doable. She still wasn't certain she wasn't being ridiculous, but did she dare bet that way, when her life, and that of her child, could hang in the balance? *Desperate times call for desperate measures.* Who had said that? Perhaps an eigh-teenth-century revolutionary; if so, she knew how he had felt. She had to disappear as completely as possible. She would mail her father a postcard before she left town, letting him know that she was all right but that she thought it would be better to get away for a while, oth-erwise he would think she had indeed been kidnapped again, and he would go mad with grief and terror. She couldn't do that to him. She still loved him very much, even after all he had done. Again a wave of disbelief and uncertainty hit her. It seemed so impossible that he would sell information to terrorists, so opposite to the man she had always known him to be. She was aware that he wasn't universally well liked, but the worst accusation she had ever heard leveled against him was that he was a snob, which even she admitted was accurate. He was very effective as a diplomat and ambassador, working with the CIA, which was of course set up in every embassy, using his social standing and contacts to smooth the way whenever a problem cropped up. He had personally been acquainted with the last six presidents, and prime ministers called him a friend. This man was a traitor?

It couldn't be. If she had only herself to consider, she would give him the benefit of the doubt.

But there was the baby, the tiny presence undetectable to any but herself. She could feel it in her breasts, which had become so tender she was always aware of them, and in the increased sensitivity and pressure low down in her abdomen, as her womb began to swell with amniotic fluid and increased blood flow. It was almost a hot feeling, as if the new life forming within her was generating heat with the effort of development.

Zane's baby.

She would do anything, no matter how Draconian, to keep it safe. She had to find some secure place where she could get the prenatal care she needed. She would have to change her name, get a new driver's license and a new social security card; she didn't know how these last two would be accomplished, but she would find out. There were always shady characters who could tell her. The driver's license could be forged, but the social security card would have to come through the regular administration. Even though social security was being phased out, until it was completely gone, everyone still had to have a number in order to get a legitimate job.

There was something else to consider. It would be stupid of her to live off her cash until it was all gone. She would need a job, anything that paid enough to keep a roof over their heads and food in their stomachs. She had degrees in art and history, but she wouldn't be able to use her own name, so she wouldn't be able to use those degrees to get a teaching job.

She didn't know what the job situation would be wherever she settled; she would simply have to wait and see. It didn't matter what she did, waiting tables or office work, she would take whatever was available.

She glanced at the clock: seven-thirty. Nerves notwithstanding, she was acutely hungry now, to the point of being sick with it. Her pregnant body had its own agenda, ignoring upset emotions and concentrating only on the business at hand.

The thought brought a smile to her face. It was almost as if the baby was already stomping a tiny foot and demanding what it wanted.

Tenderly she pressed her hand over her belly, feeling a slight firmness that surely hadn't been there before. "All right," she whispered to it. "I'll feed you."

She showered and dressed, mentally preparing herself to face her father without giving anything away. When she entered the breakfast room, he looked up with an expression of delight, quickly tempered by caution. "Well, it's a pleasure to have your company," he said, folding the newspaper and laying it aside.

"Some birds woke me up," she said, going to the buffet to help herself to toast and eggs. She fought a brief spell of nausea at the sight of sausage and changed her mind about the eggs, settling on toast and fruit. She hoped that would be enough to satisfy the demanding little creature.

"Coffee?" her father asked as she sat down. He already had the silver carafe in his hand, poised to pour.

"No, not today," she said hastily, as her stomach again clenched warningly. "I've been drinking too much caffeine lately, so I'm trying to cut down." That was a direct lie. She had stopped drinking anything with caffeine in it as soon as she suspected she might be pregnant, but it was as if her system was still warning her against it. "I'll drink orange juice." So far, that hadn't turned her stomach.

She applied herself to her food, replying civilly to his conversational gambits, but she couldn't bring herself to wholeheartedly enter into a discussion with him the way she once would have done. She could barely look at him, afraid her feelings would be plain on her face. She didn't want him any more alert than he already was.

"I'm having lunch with Congressman Garth," he told her. "What are your plans for the day?"

"None," she replied. Her plans were all for the night.

He looked relieved. "I'll see you this afternoon, then. I'll drive myself, so Poole will be available to drive you if you do decide to go anywhere."

"All right," she said, agreeing with him because she wasn't going anywhere.

Once he'd left the house, she spent the day reading and occasionally napping. Now that she had made up her mind to go, she felt more peaceful. Tomorrow would be an exhausting day, so she needed to rest while she could.

Her father returned in the middle of the afternoon. Barrie was sitting in the living room, curled up with a book. She looked up as he entered and immediately noticed how the drawn look of worry eased when he saw her. "Did you have a nice lunch?" she asked, because that was what she would have done before.

"You know how these political things are," he said. Once he would have sat down and told her all about it, but this time he smoothly evaded talking specifics. Senator Garth was on several important committees concerning national security and foreign affairs. Before she could ask any more questions, he went into his study, closing the door behind him. Before, he had always kept it open as an invitation to her to visit whenever she wanted. Sadly Barrie looked at the closed door, then returned to her book.

The doorbell startled her. She put the book aside and went to answer it, cautiously looking through the peephole before opening the door. A tall, black-haired man was standing there.

Her heart jumped wildly, and a wave of dizziness swept over her. Behind her, she heard her father coming out of his study. "Who is it?" he asked sharply. "Let me get it."

Barrie didn't reply. She jerked the door open and stared up into Zane's cool, blue gray eyes. Her heart was pounding so hard she could barely breathe.

That sharp gaze swept down her body, then came up to her face. "Are you pregnant?" he asked quietly, his voice pitched low so her father couldn't hear, even though he was rapidly approaching.

"Yes," she whispered.

He nodded, a terse movement of his head as if that settled that. "Then we'll get married."

Chapter 9

Her father reached them then, and shouldered Barrie aside. "Who are you?" he demanded, still in that sharp tone.

Zane coolly surveyed the man who would be his father-in-law. "Zane Mackenzie," he finally replied, when he had finished his appraisal. His darkly tanned face was impassive, but there was a piercing quality to his pale eyes that made Barrie suddenly aware of how dangerous this man could be. It didn't frighten her; under the circumstances, this quality was exactly what she needed.

William Lovejoy had been alarmed, but now his complexion turned pasty, and his expression froze. He said stiffly, "I'm sure you realize it isn't good for Barrie to see you again. She's trying to put that episode behind her—"

Zane looked past Lovejoy to where Barrie stood, visibly trembling as she stared at him with pleading green eyes. He hadn't realized how green her eyes were, a deep forest green, or how expressive. He got the impression that she wasn't pleading for him to be nice to her father, but rather that she was asking for help in some way, with something. His battle instincts stirred, his senses lifting to the next level of acuity. He didn't know exactly what she was asking of him, but he would find out, as soon as he dealt with the present situation. It was time to let the former ambassador know exactly where he stood.

"We're getting married," he said, still looking at Barrie, as he cut through the ambassador's continuing explanation on why it would be best if he left immediately. His steely voice, which had instantly commanded the attention of the deadliest guerrilla fighters in the world, cut through Lovejoy's stuffy, patronizing explanation.

The ambassador broke off, and a look of panic flashed across his face. Then he said, "Don't be ridiculous," in a strained tone. "Barrie isn't going to marry a sailor who thinks he's something special because he's a trained assassin."

Zane's cool gaze switched from Barrie to her father and went arctic cold, the blue fading to a gray that glinted like shards of ice. Lovejoy took an involuntary step back, his complexion going from pasty to white.

"Barrie, will you marry me?" Zane asked deliberately, keeping his gaze focused on Lovejoy.

She glanced from him to her father, who tensed as he waited for her answer.

"Yes," she said, her mind racing. Zane. She wouldn't question the miracle that had brought him here, but she was so desperate that she would have married him even if she hadn't loved him. Zane was a SEAL; if anyone could keep her safe from the unknown enemy who had her father so on edge, he could. She was carrying his child, and evidently that possibility was what had brought him to Virginia in search of her. He was a man who took his responsibilities seriously. She would have preferred that he cared for her as deeply as she did for him, but she would take what she could get. She knew he was attracted to her; if he wasn't, she wouldn't be pregnant.

She would marry him, and perhaps with time he would come to love her.

Her father flinched at her answer. Half turning to her, he said imploringly, "Baby, you don't want to marry someone like him. You've always had the best, and he can't give it to you."

Squaring her shoulders, she said, "I'm going to marry him—as soon as possible."

Seeing the intractability in her expression, her father looked at Zane. "You won't get a penny of her inheritance," he said with real venom.

"Dad!" she cried, shocked. She had her own money, inheritances from her mother and grandparents, so she wasn't worried about being destitute even if he carried through on his threat; it was the fact that he'd made the threat at all, that he would try to sabotage her future with Zane in such a blatant, hurtful manner, that hurt.

Zane shrugged. "Fine," he said with deceptive mildness. Barrie heard the pure iron underlying the calm, even tone. "Do what you want with your money, I don't give a damn. But you're a fool if you thought you could keep her with you for the rest of your life. You can act like an ass and cheat yourself out of your grandchildren if you want, but nothing you say is going to change a damn thing."

Lovejoy hung there, his face drawn with pain. Anguish darkened his eyes as he looked at his daughter. "Don't do it," he pleaded, his voice shaking.

Now it was her turn to wince, because in spite of everything, she hated to hurt him. "I'm pregnant," she whispered, straightening her shoulders against any other hurtful thing he might say. "And we're getting married."

He swayed on his feet, stunned by her announcement. She hadn't thought it possible he could turn any whiter, but he did. "What?" he croaked. "But—but you said you weren't raped!"

"She wasn't," Zane said. There was a soft, drawling, very masculine undertone in his voice.

Their eyes met. Barrie gave him a soft, wry smile. "I wasn't," she verified, and despite everything, a sudden, subtle glow lit her face.

Her father couldn't think of anything else to say. He gaped at them for a moment, unable to handle this turn of events. Then a red tide of anger ran up his face, chasing away the pallor. "You bastard!" he choked out. "You took advantage of her when she was vulnerable—"

Barrie grabbed his arm and jerked him around. "Stop it!" she yelled, her slender body tense with fury. Her nerves had been shredded since that morning, and this confrontation was only making them worse. Zane's sudden appearance, though it made her almost giddy with happiness, was another shock to her system, and she'd had enough. "If anyone took advantage, *I* did. If you want the details I'll give them to you, but I don't think you really want to know!"

It was on the tip of her tongue to ask him if he'd thought he could keep her a virgin forever, but she bit the bitter words off unspoken. That would be too hurtful, and once said, she would never be able to take the words back. He loved her, perhaps too much; his fear of losing her was why he was lashing out. And, despite everything, she loved him, too. Pain congealed inside her as she stared starkly at him, all pretense gone. "I know," she whispered. "Do you understand? I *know*. I know why you've been so paranoid every time I've left the house. *I have to leave.*"

He inhaled sharply, shock ripping away his last vestige of control. He couldn't sustain her burning gaze, and he looked away. "Keep her safe," he said to Zane in a stifled voice, then walked stiffly toward his study.

"I intend to." That difficulty solved, he spared no more than a glance for his departing foe. His gaze switched to Barrie, and a slow, heart-stopping smile touched his lips. "Go get packed," he said.

They were on their way within the hour.

She hurried up to her bedroom and filled her suitcases, bypassing the evening gowns and designer suits in favor of more practical clothing. The ankle-length cotton skirt she was already wearing was comfortable enough for travel; she pulled on a silk shirt over the sleeveless blouse she wore and let it go at that. Every instinct she had was screaming at her to hurry.

She dragged the bags to the top of the stairs. It didn't require a lot of effort, they all had wheeled bottoms, but when Zane saw her, he left his post by the door and took the stairs two at a time. "Don't lift those," he ordered, taking the bags from her hands. "You should have called me."

His tone was the same one he had used in commanding his men, but Barrie was too nervous to fight that battle with him right now. He lifted all three cases with an ease that made her blink and started down the stairs with them. She rushed after him. "Where are we going? Are we flying or driving?"

"Las Vegas. Flying."

"You already have the tickets?" she asked in surprise.

He paused and glanced over his shoulder at her, the dark wings of his eyebrows lifting fractionally. "Of course," he said, and resumed his trip down the stairs.

Such certainty and self-assurance were daunting. Briefly she wondered what on earth she was getting herself into. More and more she was becoming aware of just how much in control Zane Mackenzie was, of himself and everything around him. She might never be able to break through that barrier. *Except in bed.* The memory zinged through her, bringing a flush to her cheeks that wasn't caused by rushing around. He had lost control there, and it had been... breathtaking.

"What time is the flight?" Once more she hurried to catch up to him. "Will we have time to go to my bank? I need to close out my accounts—"

"You can transfer them to a local bank when we get home."

While he carried her bags out to the rental car he was driving, Barrie went to the study and knocked softly on the door. There was no answer; after a moment she opened the door anyway. Her father was sitting at the desk, his elbows propped on top of it and his face buried in his hands.

"Bye, Dad," she said softly.

He didn't answer, but she saw his Adam's apple bob as he swallowed.

"I'll let you know where I am."

"No," he said, his voice strangled. "Don't." He lifted his head. His eyes were anguished. "Not yet. Wait...wait a while."

"All right," she whispered, understanding slicing through her. It was safer for her that way. He must suspect the phone line was tapped.

"Baby, I—" He broke off and swallowed hard again. "I only want you to be happy—and safe."

"I know." She felt dampness on her cheeks and wiped away the tears that were wetting them.

"He isn't the kind of man I wanted for you. The SEALs are—well, never mind." He sighed. "Maybe he *can* keep you safe. I hope so. I love you, baby. You've been the center of my life. You know I never meant—" He halted, unable to go on.

"I know," she said again. "I love you, too."

She quietly closed the door and stood with her head bowed. She didn't hear him approach, but suddenly Zane was there, his arm hard around her waist as he drew her with him out to the car. He didn't ask any questions, just opened the door for her and helped her inside, then closed the door with a finality that was unmistakable.

She sat tensely during the drive to the airport, watching the traffic buzz around them.

"This is the most privacy we'll have for a while," Zane said as he competently threaded the car through the insanity of rush hour. "Why don't you tell me what's going on?" He had slipped on a pair of sunglasses, and his eyes were hidden from her view, but she didn't have to see them to know how cool and remote the expression in them was.

She lifted her chin and stared straight ahead, considering the way his suggestions sounded like orders. This wasn't going to be easy, but he had to know everything. She needed his protection, at least while she still carried his child. He wouldn't be on guard unless he knew there was a threat. She had to be honest with him. "I want you to know—one of the reasons I agreed to marry you is that I need protection, and you're a SEAL. If anything... dangerous...happens, you'll know how to handle it."

"Dangerous, how?" He sounded very matter-of-fact, almost disinterested. She supposed that, given his job, danger was so common to him that it was more the rule than the exception.

"I think the kidnappers may try again. And now I have more than just myself to worry about." Briefly, unconsciously, her hand moved to her lower belly in the instinctive way a pregnant woman touched the growing child within, as if reassuring it of its safety.

He glanced in the rearview mirror, calmly studying the traffic behind and around them. After a moment of consideration, he went straight to the heart of the matter. "Have you notified the FBI? The police?"

"No."

"Why not?"

"Because I think Dad may be involved," she said, almost strangling on the words.

Once again he checked the rearview mirror. "In what way?"

He sounded so damn remote. She clenched her hands into fists, determined to hold on to her control. If he could be self-contained, then so could she. She forced her voice to evenness. "The reason for the kidnapping wasn't ransom, so they must want information from him. I can't think of anything else it *could* be."

He was silent for a moment, deftly weaving in and out of the tangle of vehicles. She could almost hear that cool, logical brain sorting through the ramifications. Finally he said, "Your father must be in it up to his neck, or he'd have gone to the FBI himself. You would have been taken to a safe place and surrounded by a wall of agents."

He'd reached exactly the same conclusion she had. That didn't make her feel any better. "Since we've been back in Virginia, he's been impossible. He doesn't want me to leave the house by myself, and he's monitoring all telephone calls. He was always protective, but not like this. At first I thought he was overreacting because of what happened in Athens, but when I thought it through, I realized the threat still existed." She swallowed. "I'd made up my mind to sneak out tonight and disappear for a while."

If Zane had waited another day, she would have been gone. He wouldn't have had any idea where to find her, and she had no way of contacting him. Tears burned her eyes at the thought. Dear God, it had been so close.

"Hold on," he said, then jerked the steering wheel to the right, cutting across a lane of traffic and throwing the car into a sharp turn into another street. The tires squealed, and horns blared. Even with his warning, she barely had time to brace herself, and the seat belt tightened with a jerk.

"What's wrong?" she cried, struggling to right herself and ease the strangling grip of the seat belt.

"There's a possibility we had company. I didn't want to take any chances."

Alarmed, Barrie twisted around in the seat, staring at the cars passing through the intersection behind them, vainly trying to see anyone who looked familiar or any vehicle making an obvious effort to cut across traffic and follow them. The traffic pattern looked normal.

"Two Caucasian men, in their thirties or forties, both wearing sunglasses," Zane said with no more emphasis than if he'd been observing the clouds in the sky. She remembered this almost supernatural calmness from before. In Benghazi, the more tense the situation, the cooler he had become, totally devoid of emotion. For him to take the action he had, he'd been certain they were being followed. The bottom dropped out of her stomach, and she fought a sudden rise of nausea. To suspect she was in danger was one thing, having it confirmed was something else entirely.

Then what he'd said registered in her brain. "Caucasian?" she echoed. "But—" She stopped, because of course it made sense. While she had subconsciously been looking for Libyans, she had to remember that this Gordian knot of intrigue involved both Libyans and Mack Prewett's cohorts; given his resources, she had to be suspicious of everyone, not just Middle Easterners. Black, white or Oriental, she couldn't trust anyone—except Zane.

"Since they know what I'm driving, we're going to ditch the car." Zane took another turn, this time without the dramatics, but also without signaling or slowing down more than was necessary. "I'll make a phone call and have the car taken care of. We'll get a ride to the airport."

She didn't ask who he would call; the area was crawling with military personnel from all the branches of service. Someone in dress whites would collect the car and return it to the rental company, and that would be that. By then, she and Zane would be on their way to Las Vegas.

"They'll be able to find me anyway," she said suddenly, thinking of the airline ticket in her name.

"Eventually. It'll take a while, though. We have a substantial grace period."

"Maybe not." She bit her lip. "I overheard Dad talking to Mack Prewett this morning. Mack's CIA, deputy station chief in Athens. Dad told him that he wanted this finished, that he never meant for me to be involved."

Zane lifted his eyebrows. "I see."

She supposed he did. If her father was working with the CIA in anything legitimate, he would have been able to protect her through legal channels. Mack Prewett's involvement changed the rules. He would have access to records that ordinary people wouldn't have. Even though the CIA didn't operate within the United States, the tentacles of influence were far-reaching. If Mack wanted to know if she'd taken a flight out of either of the major area airports, he would have that information within minutes.

"If they were sharp enough to get the license plate number on the car, they'll have my name very shortly," he said. "If they didn't get the number, then they won't have a clue about my identity. Either way, it's too late to worry about it now. They either have it or they don't, and there's no need to change our immediate plans. We'll take the flight to Las Vegas and lose them there, at least for a while."

"How will we lose them? If Mack can get access to your records..."

"I resigned my commission. I'm not a SEAL anymore."

"Oh," she said blankly. She struggled to adjust to yet another change. She had already been imagining and mentally preparing for life as the wife of a military officer, with the frequent moves, the politics of rank. It wouldn't have been much different from life in the embassy, just on a different level. Now she realized she had no idea what kind of life they would have.

"What will we do, then?" she asked.

"I've taken the job of sheriff in a county in southern Arizona. The sheriff died in office, so the governor appointed me to complete his term. There are two years left until new elections, so we'll be in Arizona for at least two years, maybe more."

A sheriff! That was a definite surprise, and the offhand manner with which he had announced it only deepened her sense of unreality. She struggled to focus on the important things. "What your job is doesn't matter," she said as evenly as possible. "It's your training that counts."

He shrugged and wheeled the car into the entrance of a parking garage. "I understand." His voice was flat, emotionless. "You agreed to marry me because you think I'll be able to protect you.'' He let down the window and leaned out to get the ticket from the automatic dispenser. The red barrier lifted, and he drove through.

Barrie wound her fingers together. Her initial flush of happiness had given way to worry. Zane had come after her, yes, and asked her to marry him, but perhaps she'd been wrong about the attraction between them. She felt uprooted and off-balance. Zane didn't seem particularly happy to see her, but then, she had certainly tossed a huge problem into his lap. He would become a husband and a father in very short order, and on top of that, he had to protect them from an unknown enemy. He hadn't even kissed her, she thought, feeling close to tears, and she was a little surprised at herself for even thinking of such a thing right now. If he was right and someone had been following them, then the danger had been more immediate than she had feared. How could she worry about his reasons for marrying her? After all, the baby's safety was one of the reasons she was marrying *him*. "I want you to protect our baby," she said quietly. "There are other reasons, but that's the main one." Her feelings for him were something she could have handled on her own; she wouldn't take that chance with her baby's safety.

"A damn important one. You're right, too." He gave her a brief glance as he pulled the car into a parking slot on the third level. "I won't let anything hurt you or the baby."

He pulled off his sunglasses and got out of the car with a brief "Wait here," and strode off toward a pay phone. When he reached it, he punched in a series of numbers, then turned so he could watch her and the car while he talked.

Barrie felt her nerves jolt and her stomach muscles tighten as she stared across the parking deck at him. She was actually marrying this man. He looked taller than she remembered, a little leaner, though his shoulders were so wide they strained the seams of his white cotton shirt. His black hair was a bit longer, she thought, but his tan was just as dark. Except for the slight weight loss, he didn't show any sign of having been shot only a little over two months earlier. His physical toughness was intimidating; *he* was intimidating. How could she have forgotten? She had remembered only his consideration, his passion, the tender care he'd given her, but he'd used no weapon other than his bare hands to kill that guard. While she had remembered his lethal competency and planned to use it on her own behalf, she had somehow forgotten that it was a prominent part of him, not a quality she could call up when she needed it and tuck away into a corner when the need was over. She would have to deal with this part of him on a regular basis and accept the man he was. He wasn't, and never would be, a tame house cat.

She liked house cats, but she didn't want him to be one, she realized.

She felt another jolt, this time of self-discovery. She needed to be safe now, because of the baby, but she didn't want to be permanently cossetted and protected. The grueling episode in Benghazi had taught her that she was tougher and more competent than she'd ever thought, in ways she hadn't realized. Her father would have approved if she'd married some up-and-coming ambassador-to-be, but that wasn't what she wanted. She wanted some wildness in her life, and Zane Mackenzie was it. For all that maddening control of his, he was fierce and untamed. He didn't have a streak of wildness; he had a core of it.

The strain between them unnerved her. She had dreamed of him finding her and holding out his arms, of falling into them, and when she had opened the door to him today she had expected, like a fool, for her dream to be enacted. Reality was much more complicated than dreams.

The truth was, they had known each other for about twenty-four hours total, and most of those hours had been over two months earlier. In those hours they had made love with raw, scorching passion, and he had made her pregnant, but the amount of time remained the same.

Perhaps he had been involved with someone else, but a sense of responsibility had driven him to locate her and find out if their lovemaking had had any consequences. He would do that, she thought; he would turn his back on a girlfriend, perhaps even a fiancée, to assume the responsibility for his child.

Again she was crashing into the brick wall of ignorance; she didn't know anything about his personal life. If she had known anything about his family, where he was from, she would have been able to find him. Instead, he must think she hadn't cared enough even to ask about his condition, to find out if he had lived or died.

He was coming back to the car now, his stride as smooth and effortlessly powerful as she remembered, the silent walk of a predator. His dark face was as impassive as before, defying her efforts to read his expression.

He opened the door and slid behind the wheel. "Transport will be here in a few minutes."

She nodded, but her mind was still occupied with their personal tangle. Before she lost her nerve, she said evenly, "I tried to find you. They took me back to Athens immediately, while you were still in surgery. I tried to get in touch with you, find out if you were still alive, how you were doing, what hospital you were in—anything. Dad had Admiral Lindley block every inquiry I made. He did tell me you were going to be okay, but that's all I was able to find out."

"I guessed as much. I tried to call you at the embassy a couple of weeks after the mission. The call was routed to your father."

"He didn't tell me you'd called," she said, the familiar anger and pain twisting her insides. Since she'd been forced off the *Montgomery,* those had been her two main emotions. So he *had* tried to contact her. Her heart lifted a little. "After I came home, I tried again to find you, but the Navy wouldn't tell me anything."

"The antiterrorism unit is classified." His tone was absent; he was watching in the mirrors as another car drove slowly past them, looking for an empty slot.

She sat quietly, nerves quivering, until the car had disappeared up the ramp to the next level.

"I'm sorry," she said, after several minutes of silence. "I know this is a lot to dump in your lap."

He gave her an unreadable glance, his eyes very clear and blue. "I wouldn't be here if I didn't want to be."

"Do you have a girlfriend?"

This time the look he gave her was so long that she blushed and concentrated her attention on her hands, which were twisting together in her lap.

"If I did, I wouldn't have made love to you," he finally said.

Oh, dear. She bit her lip. This was going from bad to worse. He was getting more and more remote, as if the fleeting moment of silent communication between them when he'd asked her to marry him had never existed. Her stomach clenched, and suddenly a familiar sensation of being too hot washed over her.

She swallowed hard, praying that the nausea that had so far confined itself to the mornings wasn't about to put in an unexpected appearance. A second later she was scrambling out of the car and frantically looking around for a bathroom. God, did parking decks *have* bathrooms?

"Barrie!" Zane was out of the car, striding toward her, his dark face alert. She had the impression that he intended to head her off, though she hadn't yet chosen a direction in which to dash.

The stairwell? The elevator? She thought of the people who would use them and discarded both options. The most sensible place was right there on the concrete, and everything fastidious in her rebelled at the idea. Her stomach had different ideas, however, and she clamped a desperate hand over her mouth just as Zane reached her.

Those sharp, pale eyes softened with comprehension. "Here," he said, putting a supporting arm around her. The outside barriers of the parking deck were waist-high concrete walls, and that was where he swiftly guided her. She resisted momentarily, appalled at the possibility of throwing up on some unsuspecting passerby below, but his grip was inexorable, and her stomach wasn't waiting any longer. He held her as she leaned over the wall and helplessly gave in to the spasm of nausea.

She was shaking when it was over. The only comfort she could find was that, when she opened her eyes, she saw there was nothing three stories below but an alley. Zane held her, leaning her against his supporting body while he blotted her perspiring face with his handkerchief, then gave it to her so she could wipe her mouth. She felt scorched with humiliation. The strict teachings of her school in Switzerland hadn't covered what a lady should do after vomiting in public.

And then she realized he was crooning to her, his deep voice an almost inaudible murmur as he brushed his lips against her temple, her hair. One strong hand was splayed over her lower belly, spanning her from hipbone to hipbone, covering his child. Her knees felt like noodles, so she let herself continue leaning against him, let her head fall into the curve of his shoulder.

"Easy, sweetheart," he whispered, once again pressing his lips to her temple. "Can you make it back to the car, or do you want me to carry you?"

She couldn't gather her thoughts enough to give him a coherent answer. After no more than a second, he evidently thought he'd given her enough time to decide, so he made the decision for her by scooping her up into his arms. A few quick strides brought them to the car. He bent down and carefully placed her on the seat, lifting her legs into the car, arranging her skirt over them. "Do you want something to drink? A soft drink?"

Something cold and tart sounded wonderful. "No caffeine," she managed to say.

"You won't be out of my sight for more than twenty seconds, but keep an eye out for passing cars, and blow the horn if anything scares you."

She nodded, and he hit the door lock, then closed the door, shutting her inside a cocoon of silence. She preferred the fresh air but understood why she shouldn't be standing outside the car, exposed to view—and an easy target. She leaned her head against the headrest and closed her eyes. The nausea was gone as swiftly as it had come, though her insides felt like jelly. She was weak, and sleepy, and a bit bemused by his sudden tenderness.

Though she shouldn't be surprised, she thought. She was pregnant with his child, and the possibility of exactly that was what had brought him in search of her. As soon as he'd realized she was nauseated, a condition directly related to her condition, so to speak, he'd shown nothing but tender concern and demonstrated once again his ability to make snap decisions in urgent situations.

His tap on the window startled her, because in her sleepy state she hadn't thought he'd been gone nearly long enough to accomplish his mission. But a green can, frosty with condensation, was in his hand, and suddenly she ferociously wanted that drink. She unlocked the door and all but snatched the can from him before he could slide into the seat. She had it popped open and was drinking greedily by the time he closed the door.

When the can was empty, she leaned back with a sigh of contentment. She heard a low, strained laugh and turned her head to find Zane looking at her with both amusement and something hot and feral mingled in his gaze. "That's the first time watching a woman drink a soft drink has made me hard. Do you want another? I'll try to control myself, but a second one might be more than I can stand."

Barrie's eyes widened. A blush warmed her cheeks, but that didn't stop her from looking at his lap. He was telling the truth. Good heavens, was he ever telling the truth! Her hand clenched with the sudden need to reach out and stroke him. "I'm not thirsty now," she said, her voice huskier than usual. "But I'm willing to go for a second one if you are."

The amusement faded out of his eyes, leaving only the heat behind. He was reaching out for her when his head suddenly snapped around, his attention caught by an approaching vehicle. "Here's our ride," he said, and once again his voice was cool and emotionless.

Chapter 10

She was marrying him because she wanted his protection. The thought gnawed at Zane during the long flight to Las Vegas. She sat quietly beside him, sometimes dozing, talking only if he asked her a question. She had the drained look of someone who had been under a lot of pressure, and now that it had eased, her body was giving in to fatigue. Finally she fell soundly asleep, her head resting against his shoulder.

The pregnancy would be taking a toll on her, too. He couldn't see any physical change in her yet, but his three older brothers had produced enough children that he knew how tired women always got the first few months—at least, how tired Shea and Loren had been. Nothing ever slowed Caroline down, not even five sons.

At the thought of the baby, fierce possessiveness jolted through him again. His baby was inside her. He wanted to scoop her onto his lap and hold her, but a crowded plane wasn't the place for what he had in mind. That would have to wait until after the marriage ceremony, when they were in a private hotel room.

He wanted her even more than he had before.

When she had opened the door and he'd looked down into her stunned green eyes, his arousal had been so strong and immediate that he'd had to restrain himself from reaching for her. Only the sight of her father bearing down on them had held him back.

He shouldn't have waited as long as he had. As soon as he'd been able to get around okay, he should have come after her. She had been living in fear, and handling it the same way she had in Benghazi, with calm determination.

He didn't want her ever to be afraid again.

Bunny's and Spooky's arrival at the parking deck, in Bunny's personally customized 1969 Oldsmobile 442, had been like a reunion. Barrie had tumbled out of the rental car with a happy cry and been enthusiastically hugged and twirled around by both SEALs. They were both discreetly armed, he'd noticed approvingly. They were wearing civilian clothes, with their shirts left loose outside their pants to conceal the firepower tucked under their arms and in the smalls of their backs. Normally, when they were off-duty, they didn't carry firearms, but Zane had explained the situation to them and left their preparations to their own discretion, since he wasn't their commanding officer any longer. In typical fashion, they had prepared for anything. His own weapon was still resting in a holster under his left armpit, covered by a lightweight summer jacket.

"Don't you worry none, ma'am," Spooky had reassuringly told Barrie. "We'll get you and the boss to the airport safe and sound. There's nothing outside of NASCAR that can keep up with Bunny's wheels."

"I'm sure there isn't," she'd replied, eyeing the car. It looked unremarkable enough; Bunny had painted it a light gray, and there wasn't any more chrome than would be on a factory job. But the deep-throated rumble from the idling engine didn't sound like any sound a factory engine would make, and the tires were wide, with a soft-looking tread.

"Bulletproof glass, reinforced metal," Bunny said proudly as he helped Zane transfer her luggage to the trunk of his car. "Plate steel would be too heavy for the speed I want, so I went with the new generation of body armor material, lighter and stronger than Kevlar. I'm still working on the fireproofing."

"I'll feel perfectly safe," she assured him.

As she and Zane crawled into the back seat of the two-door car, she whispered to him, "Where's Nascar?"

Spooky could hear a pin drop at forty paces. Slowly he turned around in the front seat, his face mirroring his incredulity. "Not where, ma'am," he said, struggling with shock. "*What.* NASCAR. Stock car racing." A good Southerner, he'd grown up with stock car racing and was always stunned when he encountered someone who hadn't enjoyed the same contact with the sport.

"Oh," Barrie said, giving him an apologetic smile. "I've spent a lot of time in Europe. I don't know anything about racing except for the Grand Prix races."

Bunny snorted in derision. "Play cars," he said dismissively. "You can't run them on the streets. Stock car racing, now that's real racing." As he was speaking, he was wheeling his deceptive monster out of the parking deck, his restless gaze touching on every surrounding detail.

"I've been to horse races," Barrie offered, evidently in an attempt to redeem herself.

Zane controlled a smile at the earnestness of her tone. "Do you ride?" he asked.

Her attention swung to him. "Why, yes. I love horses."

"You'll make a good Mackenzie, then," Spooky drawled. "Boss raises horses in his spare time." There was a bit of irony in his tone, because SEALs had about as much spare time as albinos had color.

"Do you really?" Barrie asked, her eyes shining.

"I own a few. Thirty or so."

"Thirty!" She sat back, a slight look of confusion on her face. He knew what she was thinking: one horse was expensive to own and keep, let alone thirty. Horses needed a lot of land and care, not something she associated with an ex-Naval officer who had been a member of an elite antiterrorism group.

"It's a family business," he explained, swiveling his head to examine the traffic around them.

"Everything's clear, boss," Bunny said. "Unless they've tagged us with a relay, but I don't see how that's possible."

Zane didn't, either, so he relaxed. A moving relay surveillance took a lot of time and coordination to set up, and the route had to be known. Bunny was taking such a circuitous route to the airport that any tail would long since have been revealed or shaken. Things were under control—for now.

They made it to National without incident, though to be on the safe side Bunny and Spooky had escorted them as far as the security check. While Zane quietly handled his own armed passage through security, his two former team members had taken themselves off to collect the rental car and turn it in, though to the agency office at Dulles, not National, where he had rented it. Just another little twist to delay anyone who was looking for them.

Now that they were safely on the plane, he began planning what he would do to put an end to the situation.

The first part of it was easy. He would put Chance on the job of finding out what kind of mess her father was involved in; for her sake, he hoped it wasn't anything treasonous, but whatever was going on, he intended to put a stop to it. Chance had access to information that put national security agencies to shame. If William Lovejoy was selling out his country, then he would go down. There was no other option. Zane had spent his adult years offering his life in protection of his country, and now he was a peace officer sworn to uphold the law; it was impossible for him to look the other way, even for Barrie. He didn't want her to be hurt, but he damn sure wanted her to be safe.

Barrie slept until the airliner's wheels bounced on the pavement. She sat upright, pushing her hair away from her face, looking about with a slight sense of disorientation. She had never before been able to sleep on a plane; this sleepiness was just one more of the many changes her pregnancy was making in her body, and her lack of control over the process was disconcerting, even frightening.

On the other hand, the rest had given her additional energy, something she needed to face the immense change she was about to make in her life. This change was deliberate, but no less frightening.

"I want to shower and change clothes first," she said firmly. This marriage might be hasty, without any resemblance to the type of wedding ceremony she had always envisioned for herself, but while she was willing to forgo the pomp and expensive trappings, she wasn't willing—outside of a life-and-death situation—to get married wearing wrinkled clothes and still blinking sleep from her eyes.

"Okay. We'll check in to a hotel first." He rubbed his jaw, his callused fingers rasping over his beard stubble. "I need to have a shave anyway."

He had needed to shave that day in Benghazi, too. In a flash of memory she felt again the scrape of his rough chin against her naked breasts, and a wave of heat washed over her, leaving her weak and flushed. The cool air blowing from the tiny vent overhead was suddenly not cool enough.

She hoped he wouldn't notice, but it was a faint hope, because he was trained to take note of every detail around him. She imagined he could describe every passenger within ten rows of them in either direction, and when she'd been awake she had noticed that he'd shown an uncanny awareness of anyone approaching them from the rear on the way to the lavatories.

"Are you feeling sick?" he asked, eyeing the color in her cheeks.

"No, I'm just a little warm," she said with perfect truth, while her blush deepened.

He continued to watch her, and the concern in his eyes changed to a heated awareness. She couldn't even hide that from him, damn it. From the beginning it had been as if he could see beneath her skin; he sensed her reactions almost as soon as she felt them.

Slowly his heavy-lidded gaze moved down to her breasts, studying the slope and thrust of them. She inhaled sharply as her nipples tightened in response to his blatant interest, a response that shot all the way to her loins.

"Are they more sensitive?" he murmured.

Oh, God, he shouldn't do this to her, she thought wildly. They were in the middle of a plane full of people, taxiing toward an empty gate, and he was asking questions about her breasts and looking as if he would start undressing her any minute now.

"Are they?"

"Yes," she whispered. Her entire body felt more sensitive, from both her pregnancy and her acute awareness of him. Soon he would be her husband, and once again she would be lying in his arms.

"Ceremony first," he said, his thoughts echoing hers in that eerie way he had. "Otherwise we won't get out of the hotel until tomorrow."

"Are you psychic?" she accused under her breath.

A slow smile curved his beautiful mouth. "It doesn't take a psychic to know what those puckered nipples mean."

She glanced down and saw her nipples plainly beaded under the lace and silk of her bra and blouse. Her face red, she hastily drew her shirt over the betraying little nubs, and he gave a low laugh. At least no one else was likely to have heard him, she thought with scant comfort. He'd pitched his voice low, and the noise on board made it difficult to overhear conversations, anyway.

The flight attendants were telling them to remain in their seats until the plane was secured and the doors opened, and as usual the instructions were ignored as passengers surged into the aisles, opening the overhead bins and dragging down their carry-on luggage or hauling it out from under the seats. Zane stepped deftly into the aisle, and the movement briefly pulled his jacket open. She saw the holster under his left arm and the polished metal butt of the pistol tucked snugly inside it. Then he automatically shrugged one shoulder, and the jacket fell into place, a movement he'd performed so many times he didn't have to think about it.

She'd known he was armed, of course, because he'd informed the airport and airline security before they'd boarded the plane. During the boredom and enforced inactivity of the flight, however, she had managed to push the recent events from her mind, but the sight of that big automatic brought them all back.

He extended his hand to steady her as she stepped into the aisle ahead of him. Standing pressed like sardines in the line, she felt him like a warm and solid wall at her back, his arms slightly extended so that his hands rested on the seat backs, enveloping her in security. His breath stirred the hair on top of her head, making her realize anew exactly how big he was. She was of average height, but if she leaned back, her head would fit perfectly into the curve of his shoulder.

The man in front of her shifted, forcing her backward, and Zane curved one arm around her as he gathered her against his body, his big hand settling protectively over her lower belly. Barrie bit her lip as her mind bounced from worry to the pleasure of his touch. This couldn't go on much longer—either this exquisite frustration or the sharp darts of terror—or she would lose her mind.

The line of passengers began to shuffle forward as the doors were opened and they were released from the plane. Zane's hand dropped from her belly. As she began to move forward, Barrie caught the eye of an older woman who had chosen to remain in her seat until the stampede was over, and the woman gave her a knowing smile, her gaze flicking to Zane.

"Ma'am," Zane said smoothly in acknowledgment, and Barrie knew he'd caught the little byplay. His acute awareness of his surroundings was beginning to spook her. What if she didn't want him to notice everything? Most women would be thrilled to death with a husband who actually took note of details, but probably not to the extent that Zane Mackenzie did.

On the other hand, if the alternative was living without him, she would learn how to cope, she thought wryly. She'd spent over two months pining for him, and now that she had him, she wasn't about to get cold feet because he was alert. He was a trained warrior—an assassin, her father had called him. He wouldn't have survived if he hadn't been aware of everything going on around him, and neither would she.

That alertness was evident as they followed the signs to the baggage claim area. The airport was a shifting, flowing beehive, and Zane's cool gaze was constantly assessing the people around them, As he had more than once before, he kept himself between her and everybody else, steering her close to the wall and protecting her other side with his body. He'd already taken one bullet while doing that, she thought, and had to fight the sudden terrified impulse to grab him and shove *him* against the wall.

Before they reached the baggage claim, however, he pulled her to a halt. "Let's wait here a minute," he said.

She strove for calm, for mastery over the butterflies that suddenly took flight in her stomach. "Did you see anything suspicious?" she asked.

"No, we're waiting for someone." He looked at her, his cool gaze warming as he studied her face. "You're a gutsy little broad, Miss Lovejoy. No matter what, you hold it together and try to do the best you can. Not bad for a pampered society babe."

Barrie was taken aback. She'd never been called a broad before, or a society babe. If it hadn't been for the teasing glint in his eyes, she might have taken exception to the terms. Instead, she considered them for a moment, then gave a brief nod of agreement. "You're right," she said serenely. "I *am* gutsy for a pampered society babe."

He was surprised into a chuckle, a deliciously rich sound that was cut short when they were approached by a middle-aged man who wore a suit and carried a radio set in his hand. "Sheriff Mackenzie?" he asked.

"Yes."

"Travis Hulsey, airport security." Mr. Hulsey flashed his identification. "We have your luggage waiting for you in a secure area, as requested. This way, please."

So he'd even thought of that, Barrie marveled as they followed Mr. Hulsey through an unmarked door. An attempt to grab her inside the airport would be tricky, given the security, so the most logical thing to do would be to wait at the ground transportation area, where everyone went after collecting luggage, then follow them to their destination and wait for a better opportunity. Zane had thwarted that; he must have made the arrangements when he'd gone forward to the lavatory.

The dry desert heat slapped them in the face as soon as they stepped through the door. Her three suitcases and his one garment bag, which he had collected from a locker at National, were waiting for them at a discreet entrance well away from the main ground transportation area. Also waiting for them was a car, beside which stood a young man with the distinctive austere military haircut, even though he wore civilian clothes.

The young man all but snapped to attention. "Sir," he said. "Airman Zaharias at your service, sir."

Zane's dark face lit with amusement. "At ease," he said. "I'm not my brother."

Airman Zaharias relaxed with a grin. "When I first saw you, sir, I wasn't sure."

"If he pulled rank and this is messing up your leave time, I'll get other transport."

"I volunteered, sir. The general did me a personal favor when I was fresh out of basic. Giving his brother a ride downtown is the least I can do."

Brother? *General?* Barrie raised some mental eyebrows. First horses, now this. She realized she didn't know anything about her soon-to-be husband's background, but the details she'd gleaned so far were startling, to say the least.

Zane introduced her with grave courtesy. "Barrie, Airman Zaharias is our safe transport, and he has donated his personal vehicle and time off for the service. Airman Zaharias, my fiancée, Barrie Lovejoy."

She solemnly shook hands with the young airman, who was almost beside himself in his eagerness to please.

"Glad to meet you, ma'am." He unlocked the trunk and swiftly began loading their luggage, protesting when Zane lifted two of the bags and stowed them himself. "Let me do that, sir!"

"I'm a civilian now," Zane said, amusement still bright in his eyes. "And I was Navy, anyway."

Airman Zaharias shrugged. "Yes, sir, but you're still the general's brother." He paused, then asked, "Were you really a SEAL?"

"Guilty."

"Damn," Airman Zaharias breathed.

They climbed into the air-conditioned relief of the airman's Chevrolet and were off. Their young driver evidently knew Las Vegas well, and without asking for instructions he ignored the main routes. Instead he circled around and took Paradise Road north out of the airport. He chattered cheerfully the entire time, but Barrie noticed that he didn't mention the exact nature of the favor Zane's general brother had done for him, nor did he venture into personal realms. He talked about the weather, the traffic, the tourists, the hotels. Zane directed him to a hotel off the main drag, and soon Airman Zaharias was on his way and they were checking in to the hotel.

Barrie bided her time, standing quietly to one side while Zane arranged for them to be listed in the hotel's computer as Glen and Alice Temple—how he arrived at those names she had no idea—and ignoring the clerk's knowing smirk. He probably thought they were adulterous lovers on a tryst, which suited her just fine; it would keep him from being curious about them.

They weren't alone in the elevator, so she held her tongue then, too. She held it until they were in the suite Zane had booked, and the bellman had been properly tipped and dismissed. The suite was as luxurious as any she had stayed in in Europe. A few hours before, she might have worried that the cost was more than Zane could afford, that he'd chosen it because he thought she would expect it. Now, however, she had no such illusion. As soon as he had closed and locked the door behind the bellman, she crossed her arms and stared levelly at him. "Horses?" she inquired politely. "Family business? A brother who happens to be an Air Force general?"

He shrugged out of his jacket, then his shoulder holster. "All of that," he said.

"I don't know you at all, do I?" She was calm, even a little bemused, as she watched him wrap the straps around the holster and deposit the weapon on the bedside table.

He unzipped his garment bag and removed a suit from it, then began unpacking other items. His pale glance flashed briefly at her. "You know *me*," he said. "You just don't know all the details of my family yet, but we haven't had much time for casual chatting. I'm not deliberately hiding anything from you. Ask any question you want."

"I don't want to conduct a catechism," she said, though she needed to do exactly that. "It's just..." She spread her hands in frustration, because she was marrying him and she didn't already know all this.

He began unbuttoning his shirt. "I promise I'll give you a complete briefing when we have time. Right now, sweetheart, I'd rather you got your sweet little butt in one shower while I get in the other, so we can get married and into this bed as fast as possible. About an hour after *that,* we'll talk."

She looked at the bed, a bigger-than-king-size. Priorities, priorities, she mused. "Are we safe here?"

"Safe enough for me to concentrate on other things."

She didn't have to ask what those other things were. She looked at the bed again and took a deep breath. "We could rearrange the order of these things," she proposed. "What do you think about bed, talk and then wedding? Say, tomorrow morning?"

He froze in the act of removing his shirt. She saw his eyes darken, saw the sexual tension harden his face. After a moment he pulled the garment free and dropped it to the floor, his movements deliberate. "I haven't kissed you yet," he said.

She swallowed. "I noticed. I've wondered—"

"Don't," he said harshly. "Don't wonder. The reason I haven't kissed you is that, once I start, I won't stop. I know we're doing things out of order—hell, everything's been out of order from the beginning, when you were naked the first time I saw you. I wanted you then, sweetheart, and I want you now, so damn bad I'm aching with it. But trouble is still following you around, and my job is to make damn sure it doesn't get close to you and our baby. I might get killed—"

She made a choked sound of protest, but he cut her off. "It's a possibility, one I accept. I've accepted it for years. I want us married as soon as possible, because I don't know what might happen tomorrow. In case I miscalculate or get unlucky, I want our baby to be legitimate, to be born with the Mackenzie name. A certain amount of protection goes with that name, and I want you to have it. Now."

Tears swam in her eyes as she stared at him, at this man who had already taken one bullet for her and was prepared to take another. He was right—she knew *him*, knew the man he was, even if she didn't know what his favorite color was or what kind of grades he'd made in school. She knew the basics, and it was the basics she had so swiftly and fiercely learned to love. So he wasn't as forthcoming as she might have wished; she would deal with it. So what if he was so controlled it was scary, and so what if those uncanny eyes noticed everything, which would make it difficult to surprise him on Christmas and his birthday? She would deal with that, too, very happily.

If he was willing to die for her, the least she could do was be completely honest with him.

"There's another reason I agreed to marry you," she said.

His dark brows lifted in silent question.

"I love you."

Chapter 11

He wore a dark gray suit with black boots and a black hat. Barrie wore white. It was a simple dress, ankle length and sleeveless, classic in its lines and lack of adornment. She loosely twisted up her dark auburn hair, leaving a few wisps hanging about her face to soften the effect. Her only jewelry was a pair of pearl studs in her ears. She got ready in the bath off the bedroom, he showered in the bath off the parlor. They met at the door between the two rooms, ready to take the step that would make them husband and wife.

At her blunt declaration of love, an equally blunt expression of satisfaction had crossed his face, and for once he didn't hide anything he was feeling. "I don't know about love," he'd said, his voice so even she wanted to shake him. "But I do know I've never wanted another woman the way I want you. I know this marriage is forever. I'll take care of you and our children, I'll come home to you every night, and I'll try my damnedest to make you happy."

It wasn't a declaration of love, but it was certainly one of devotion, and the tears that came so easily to her these days swam in her eyes. Her self-contained warrior *would* love her, when he lowered his guard enough to let himself. He had spent years with his emotions locked down, while he operated in tense, life-and-death situations that demanded cool, precise thoughts and decisions. Love was neither cool nor concise; it was turbulent, unpredictable, and it left one vulnerable. He would approach love as cautiously as if it was a bomb.

"Don't cry," he said softly. "I swear I'll be a good husband."

"I know," she replied, and then they had both gone to their separate bathrooms to prepare for their wedding.

They took a taxi to a chapel, one of the smaller ones that didn't get as much business and didn't have a drive-through service. Getting married in Las Vegas didn't take a great deal of effort, though Zane took steps to make it special. He bought her a small bouquet of flowers and gave her a bracelet of dainty gold links, which he fastened around her right wrist. Her heart beat heavily as they stood before the justice of the peace, and the bracelet seemed to burn around her wrist. Zane held her left hand securely in his right, his grip warm and gentle, but unbreakable.

Outwardly it was all very civilized, but from the first moment they'd met, Barrie had been acutely attuned to him, and she sensed the primal possessiveness of his actions. He had already claimed her physically, and now he was doing it legally. She already carried his child inside her. His air of masculine satisfaction was almost visible, it was so strong. She felt it, too, as she calmly spoke her vows, this linkage of their lives. During a long, hot day in Benghazi they had forged a bond that still held, despite the events that had forced them apart.

He had one more surprise for her. She hadn't expected a ring, not on such short notice, but at the proper moment he reached into the inside pocket of his jacket and produced two plain gold bands, one for her and one for him. Hers was a little loose when he slipped it over her knuckle, but their eyes met in a moment of perfect understanding. She would be gaining weight, and soon the ring would fit. She took the bigger, wider band and slid it onto the ring finger of his left hand, and she felt her own thrill of primal satisfaction. He was hers, by God!

Their marriage duly registered, the certificate signed and witnessed, they took another taxi to the hotel. "Supper," he said, steering her toward one of the hotel's dining rooms. "You didn't eat anything on the plane, and it's after midnight eastern time."

"We could order room service," she suggested.

His eyes took on that heavy-lidded look. "No, we couldn't." His tone was definite, a little strained. His hand was warm and heavy on the small of her back. "You need to eat, and I don't trust my self-control to last that long unless we're in a public place."

Perhaps feeding her was his only concern, or perhaps he knew more about seduction than most men, she thought as they watched each other over a progression of courses. Knowing that he was going to make love to her as soon as they reached the suite, anticipating the heaviness of his weight on her, the hard thrust of his turgid length into her...the frustration readied her for him as surely as if he was stroking her flesh. Her breasts lifted hard and swollen against the bodice of her dress. Her insides tightened with desire, so that she had to press her legs together to ease the throbbing. His gaze kept dropping to her breasts, and as before, she couldn't temper her response. She could feel her own moisture, feel the heaviness in her womb.

She was scarcely aware of what she ate—something bland, to reduce the chances of early-pregnancy nausea. She drank only water. But turnabout was fair play, so she lingered over each bite while she stared at his mouth, or in the direction of his lap. She delicately licked her lips, shivering with delight as his face darkened and his jaw set. She stroked the rim of her water glass with one fingertip, drawing his gaze, making his breath come harder and faster. Beneath the table, she rubbed her foot against the muscled calf of his leg.

He turned to snare their waiter with a laser glare. "Check!" he barked, and the waiter hurried to obey that voice of command. Zane scribbled their room number and his fictitious name on the check, and Barrie stared at him in amazement. It was hard to believe he could remember something like that when she could barely manage to walk.

For revenge, when he pulled her chair back so she could stand, she allowed the knuckles of one hand to brush, oh, so very lightly, against his crotch. He went absolutely rigid for a moment, and his breath hissed out between his teeth. All innocence, Barrie turned to give him a sweetly inquiring What's-wrong? look.

His darkly tanned face was even darker with the flush running under the browned skin. His expression was set, giving away little, but his eyes were glittering like shards of diamond. His big hand closed firmly around her elbow. "Let's go," he said in the soundless whisper she'd first heard in a dark room in Benghazi. "And don't do that again, or I swear I'll have you in the elevator."

"Really." She smiled at him over her shoulder. "How...uplifting."

A faint but visible shudder racked him, and the look he gave her promised retribution. "Here I've been thinking you were so sweet."

"I am sweet," she declared as they marched toward the elevator. "But I'm not a pushover."

"We'll see about that. I'm going to push you over." They reached the bank of elevators, and he jabbed the call button with more force than necessary.

"You won't have to push hard. As a matter of fact, you can just blow me over." She gave him another sweet smile and pursed her lips, blowing a tiny puff of air against his chest to demonstrate.

The bell chimed, the doors opened, and they stood back to allow the car's passengers to exit. They stepped inside alone, and even though people were hurrying toward them to catch that car, Zane ruthlessly punched their floor number and then the door close button. When the car began to rise, he turned on her like a tiger on fresh meat.

She stepped gracefully out of his reach, staring at the numbers flashing on the digital display. "We're almost there."

"You're damn right about that," he growled, coming after her. In the small confines of the elevator she didn't have a chance of evading him, not that she wanted to. What she wanted was to drive him as crazy as he was driving her. His hard hands closed around her waist and lifted her; his muscled body pinned her to the wall. His hips pushed insistently at hers, and she gasped at how hard he was. Automatically her legs opened, allowing him access to the tender recesses of her body. He thrust against her, his hips moving rhythmically, and his mouth came down on hers, smothering, fiercely hungry.

The bell chimed softly, and the elevator gave a slight lurch as it stopped. Zane didn't release her. He simply turned with her still in his grasp and left the elevator, striding rapidly down the hall to their suite. Barrie twined her arms around his neck and her legs around his hips, biting back little moans as each stride he took rubbed his swollen sex against the aching softness of her loins. Pleasure arced through her like lightning with every step, and helplessly she felt her hips undulate against him in a mindless search for a deeper pleasure. A low curse hissed out from between his clenched teeth.

She didn't know if they passed anyone in the hall. She buried her face against his neck and gave in to the soaring hunger. She had needed him for so long, missed him, worried herself sick about him. Now he was here, vitally alive, about to take her with the same uncomplicated fierceness as before, and she didn't care about anything else.

He pushed her against a wall, and for one terrified, delirious moment she thought she had tempted him too much. Instead he unhooked her legs from around his waist and let her slide to the floor. He was breathing hard, his eyes dilated with a sexual hunger that wouldn't be denied much longer, but on one level he was still very much in control. Lifting one finger to his lips to indicate silence, he slipped his right hand inside his jacket. When his hand emerged, it was filled with the butt of that big automatic. He thumbed off the safety, dealt with the electronic lock on the door to their suite, depressed the door handle and slipped noiselessly inside. The door closed as silently as it had opened.

Barrie stood frozen in the hallway, sudden terror chasing away her desire as she waited with her eyes closed and her hands clenched into fists, all her concentration focused on trying to hear anything from inside the suite. She heard nothing. Absolutely nothing. Zane moved like a cat, but so did other men, men like him, men who worked best under cover of night and who could kill as silently as he had dispatched that guard in Benghazi. Her kidnappers hadn't possessed the same expertise, but whoever was behind her abduction wouldn't use Middle Eastern men here in the middle of the glitter and flash of Las Vegas. Perhaps this time he would hire someone more deadly, someone more interested in getting the job done than in terrifying a bound and helpless woman. Any thump, any whisper, might signal the end of Zane's life, and she thought she would shatter under the strain.

She didn't hear the door open again. All she heard was Zane saying,

"All clear," in a calm, normal tone, and then she was in his arms again. She didn't think she moved; she thought he simply gathered her in, pulling her into the security of his embrace.

"I'm sorry," he murmured against her hair as he carried her inside. He paused to lock and chain the door. "But I won't take chances with your safety."

Fury roared through her like a brushfire. She lifted her head from the sanctuary of his shoulder and glared at him. "What about yours?" she demanded violently. "Do you have any idea what it does to me when you do things like that? Do you think I don't notice when you put yourself between me and other people, so if anyone shoots at me, you'll be the one with the bullet hole?" She hit him on the chest with a clenched fist, amazing even herself; she had never struck anyone before. She hit him again. "Damn it, I want you healthy and whole! I want our baby to have its daddy! I want to have more of your babies, so that means you have to stay alive, do you hear me?"

"I hear," he rumbled, his tone soothing as he caught her pounding fists and pressed them against his chest, stilling them. "I'd like the same things myself. That means I have to do whatever's necessary to keep you and Junior safe."

She relaxed against him, her lips trembling as she fought back tears. She wasn't a weepy person; it was just the hormonal roller coaster of pregnancy that was making her so, but still, she didn't want to cry all over him. He had enough to handle without having to deal with a sobbing wife every time he turned around.

When she could manage a steady tone, she said in a small voice, "Junior, is it?"

She saw the flash of his grin as he lifted her in his arms. "I'm afraid so," he said as he carried her to the bed. "My sister Maris is the only female the Mackenzies have managed to produce, and that was twenty-nine years and ten boys ago."

He bent and gently placed her on the bed and sat down beside her. His dark face was intent as he reached beneath her for the zipper of her dress. "Now let's see if I can get you back to where you were before you got scared, and we'll introduce Junior to his daddy," he whispered.

Barrie was seized by a mixture of shyness and uneasiness as he stripped the dress down her hips and legs, then tossed it aside. Since her kidnappers had stripped her in a deliberate attempt to terrorize her, to break her spirit, she hadn't been comfortable with being naked. Except for those hours hidden in the ruins in Benghazi, when Zane had finally coaxed her out of his shirt and she had lost herself in his lovemaking, she had hurried through any times of necessary nudity, such as when she showered, pulling on clothes or a robe as soon as possible. Once upon a time she had lingered after her bath, enjoying the wash of air over her damp skin as she pampered herself with perfumed oils and lotions, but for the past two months that luxury had fallen beneath her urgent need to be covered.

Zane wanted her naked.

Her dress was already gone, and the silk and lace of her matching bra and underpants weren't much protection. Deftly he thumbed open the front fastening of her bra, and the cups loosened, sliding apart to reveal the inner curves of her breasts. Barrie couldn't help herself; she protectively crossed her arms over her breasts, holding the bra in place.

Zane paused, his face still as his pale gaze lifted to her face, examining the helpless, embarrassed expression she wore. She didn't have to explain. He'd been there; he knew. "Still having problems with that shirt?" he asked gently, referring to the way she'd clung so desperately to his garment.

He'd switched on a single lamp. She lay exposed in the small circle of light, while his face was shadowed. She moistened her lips and nodded once, a slight acknowledgment that was all he needed.

"We can't undo things," he said, his face and tone serious. Using one finger, he lightly stroked the upper curves of her breasts, where they plumped above the protection of her crossed arms. "We can put them behind us and move on, but we can't undo them. They stay part of us, they change us inside, but as other things happen, we change still more. I remember the face of the first man I killed. I don't regret doing it, because he was a bomb-happy piece of scum who had left his calling card on a cruise ship, killing nine old people who were just trying to enjoy their retirement. Right then he was trying like hell to kill *me*...but I always carry his face with me, deep inside.''

He paused, thinking, remembering. ''He's a part of me now, because killing him changed me. He made me stronger. I know that I can do whatever has to be done, and I know how to go on. I've killed others,'' he said, as calmly as if he was discussing the weather, ''but I don't remember their faces. Only his. And I'm glad I won.''

Barrie stared at him, the shadows emphasizing the planes and hollows of his somber face, deepening the oldness in his eyes. Deep inside she understood, the realization going past thought into the center of instinct. Being kidnapped had changed her; she'd faced that before Zane had rescued her. She *was* stronger, more decisive, more willing to take action. When he'd shown up that afternoon, she had been preparing to take extraordinary measures to protect herself and the child she carried by disappearing from the comfortable life she'd always known. She'd been naked with Zane before—and enjoyed it. She would again.

Slowly she lifted one hand and stroked the precise line of the small scar on his left cheekbone. He turned his head a little, rubbing his cheek against her fingers.

''Take off *your* clothes,'' she suggested softly. Balance. If her nudity was balanced by his, she would be more comfortable.

His eyebrows quirked upward. ''All right.''

She didn't have to explain, but then, she'd known she wouldn't. She lay on the bed and watched him peel out of his jacket, then remove the shoulder holster, which once more carried its lethal cargo. This last was carefully placed on the bedside table, where it would be within reach. Then his shirt came off, and he dropped it on the floor, along with her dress and his jacket.

The new scar on his upper abdomen was red and puckered, and bisected by a long surgical scar where the ship's surgeon had sliced into him to stop the bleeding and save his life. She had seen the scar before, when he had removed his shirt before showering, but she had been under orders not to touch him then lest she make him forget his priorities. There was no such restriction now.

Her fingers moved over the scar, feeling the heat and vitality of the man, and she thought how easily all of that could have been snuffed out. She had come so close to losing him....

"Don't think about it," he murmured, catching her hand and lifting it to his lips. "It didn't happen."

"It could have."

"It didn't." His tone was final as he bent over to tug off his boots. They dropped to the floor with twin thuds, then he stood to unfasten his pants.

He was right. It hadn't happened. Pick yourself up, learn something, and go on. It was in the past. The future was their marriage, their child. The present was *now,* and as Zane swiftly stripped off his remaining clothes, a lot more urgent.

He sat beside her again, comfortable in his own skin. It was such wonderful skin, she thought a little dreamily, reaching out to stroke his gleaming shoulders and furry chest and rub the tiny nipples hidden among the hair until they stood stiffly erect. She knew she was inviting him to reciprocate, and her breath caught in her chest as she waited for him to accept.

He wasn't slow about it. His hands went to the parted cups of her bra, and his gaze lifted to hers. "Ready?" he asked with a slight smile.

She didn't reply, just shrugged one shoulder so that her breast slid free of the cup, and that was answer enough.

He glanced downward as he pushed the other cup aside, and she saw his pupils flare with arousal as he looked at her. His breath hissed out through parted lips. "I see our baby here," he whispered, gently touching one nipple with a single fingertip. "You haven't gained any weight, your stomach's still flat, but he's changed you here. Your nipples are darker, and swollen." Ever so lightly, his touch circled the aureola, making it pucker and stand upright. Barrie whimpered with the rush of desire, the familiar lightning strike from breast to loin.

He rubbed his thumb over the tip, then gently curved his hand beneath her breast, lifting it so that it plumped in his palm. "How much more sensitive are they?" he asked, never looking up from his absorption with these new details in her body.

"Some—sometimes I can't bear the touch of my bra." she breathed.

"Your veins are bluer, too," he murmured. "They look like rivers running under a layer of white satin." He leaned down and kissed her, taking possession of her mouth while he continued to fondle her breasts with exquisite care. She melted with a purring little hum of pleasure, lifting herself so she could taste him more deeply. His lips were as hot and forceful as she remembered, as delicious. He took his time; the kiss was slow and deep, his tongue probing. Her pregnancy-sensitive breasts hardened into almost painful arousal, her loins becoming warm and liquid.

He bore her down onto the pillows, his hands slipping over her body, completely removing the bra and then disposing of her underpants. His eyes glittered hotly as he leaned over her. "I'm going to do everything to you I couldn't do before," he whispered. "We don't have to worry about being on guard, or making noise, or what time it is. I'm going to eat you up, Little Red."

She should have been alarmed, because his expression was so fierce and hungry she could almost take him literally. Instead, she reached out for him, almost frantic with the need to feel him covering her, taking her.

He had other ideas. He caught her hands and pressed them to the bed, as she had once done to him. He had trusted her with control, and now she returned the gift, arching her body up for whatever was his pleasure.

His pleasure was her breasts, with their fascinating changes. He took one distended nipple into his mouth, carefully, lightly. That was enough to make her moan, though not with pain; the prickles of sensation were incredibly intense. His tongue batted at her nipple, swirled around it, then pushed it hard against the roof of his mouth as he began suckling.

Her cry was thin, wild. Her breath exploded out of her lungs, and she couldn't seem to draw in any replacement air. Oh, God, she hadn't realized her breasts were *that* sensitive, or that he would so abruptly push her past both pleasure and pain into a realm so raw and powerful she couldn't bear it. She surged upward, and he controlled the motion, holding her down, transferring his mouth to her other nipple, which received the same tender care and enticement, then the sudden, deliberate pressure that made her cry out again.

He wouldn't stop. She screamed for him to, begged him, but he wouldn't stop. She heard her voice, frantic, pleading: "Zane—please. Oh, God, please. Don't—more. *More*." And then, sobbing, *"Harder!"* And she realized she wasn't begging him to stop, but to continue. She writhed in his arms as he pushed her higher and higher, harder and harder, his mouth voracious on her breasts, and suddenly all her senses coalesced into a huge single throb that centered in her loins, and she came apart with pleasure.

When she could breathe again, think again, her limbs were weak and useless in the aftermath. She lay limply on the bed, her eyes closed, and wondered how she had survived the implosion.

"Just from sucking your breasts?" he murmured incredulously as he kissed his way down her stomach. "Oh, damn, are we going to have fun for the next seven months!"

"Zane...wait," she whispered, lifting one hand to his head. It was the only movement she had enough energy to make. "I can't—I need to rest."

He slid down between her legs and lifted her thighs onto his shoulders. "You don't have to move," he promised her in a deep, rich voice. "All you have to do is lie there." Then he kissed her, slowly, deeply, and her body arched as it began all over again, and he showed her all the things he hadn't been able to do to her before.

He brought her to completion once more before finally crawling forward and settling his hips between her thighs. She moaned when he filled her with a smooth, powerful thrust. She quivered beneath him, shocked by the thickness and depth of his penetration. How could she have forgotten? The discomfort took her by surprise, and she clung to him as she tried to adjust, to accept. He soothed her, whispering hot, soft words in her ear, stroking her flesh, which was already so sensitive that even the smooth sheet beneath her felt abrasive.

But, oh, how she had wanted this. *This*. Not just pleasure, but the sense of being joined together, the deep and intimate linkage of their bodies. This fed a craving within her that the climaxes he'd given her hadn't begun to touch. Her hips lifted. She wanted all of him, wanted him so deep that he touched her womb, ripening with his seed. He tried to moderate the thrusts that were rapidly pushing her toward yet another climax, but she dug her nails into his back, insisting without words on everything he had to give.

He shuddered, and with a deep-throated groan, gave her what she asked.

She slept then. It was long after midnight on the east coast, and she was exhausted. She was disturbed by the presence of the big, muscled man beside her in the bed, though, his body radiating heat like a furnace, and she kept waking from a restless doze.

He must sleep like a cat, she thought, because every time she woke and changed positions, he woke up, too. Finally he pulled her on top of him, settling her with her face tucked against his neck and her legs straddling his hips. "Maybe now you can rest," he murmured, kissing her hair. "You slept this way in Benghazi."

She remembered that, remembered the long day of making love, how he had sometimes been on top when they dozed, and sometimes she had. Or perhaps she had been the only one who dozed while he had remained alert.

"I've never slept with a man before," she murmured in sleepy explanation, nestling against him. "*Slept* slept, that is."

"I know. I'm your first in both cases."

The room was dark; at some time he had turned off the lamp, though she didn't remember when. The heavy curtains were drawn against the neon of the Las Vegas night, with only thin strips of light penetrating around the edges. It reminded her briefly of that horrible room in Benghazi, before Zane had taken her away, but then she shut out the memory. That no longer had the power to frighten her. Zane was her husband now, and the pleasant ache in her body told her that the marriage had been well and truly consummated.

"Tell me about your family," she said, and yawned against his neck.

"Now?"

"Mmm. We're both awake, so you might as well."

There was a twitch of flesh against her inner thigh. "I can think of other things to do," he muttered.

"I'm not ruling anything out." She wriggled her hips and was rewarded by a more insistent movement. "But you can talk, too. Tell me about the Mackenzie clan."

She could feel his slight shrug. "My dad is a half-breed American Indian, my mom is a schoolteacher. They live on a mountain just outside Ruth, Wyoming. Dad raises and trains horses. He's the best I've ever seen, except for my sister. Maris is magic with horses."

"So the horses really are a family business."

"Yep. We were all raised on horseback, but Maris is the only one who went into the training aspect. Joe went to the Air Force Academy and became a jet jockey, Mike became a cattle rancher, Josh rode jets for the Navy, and Chance and I went to the Naval Academy and got our water wings. We can both fly various types of aircraft, but flying is just a means of getting us to where we're needed, nothing else. Chance got out of Naval Intelligence a couple of years ago."

Barrie's talent with names kicked in. She lifted her head, all sleepiness gone as she ran that list of names through her head. She settled on one, put the details together and gasped. "Your brother is General Joe Mackenzie on the Joint Chiefs of Staff?" Of course. How many Joe Mackenzies were Air Force generals?

"The one and only."

"Why, I've met him and his wife. I think it was the year before last, at a charity function in Washington. Her name is Caroline."

"You're right on target." He shifted a little, and she felt a nudging between her legs. She inhaled as he slipped inside her. Talk about right on target.

"Joe and Caroline have five sons, Michael and Shea have two boys, and Josh and Loren have three," Zane murmured, gently thrusting. "Junior will be the eleventh grandchild."

Barrie sank against him, her attention splintered by the pleasure building with each movement of his hips. "Don't talk," she said, and heard his quiet laughter as he rolled over and placed her beneath him...just where she wanted to be.

Chapter 12

Barrie awoke to nausea, sharp and urgent. She bolted out of bed and into the bathroom, barely reaching it in time. When the bout of vomiting was over, she sank weakly to the floor and closed her eyes, unable to work up enough energy to care that she was curled naked on the floor of a hotel bathroom, or that her husband of less than twelve hours was witness to it all. She heard Zane running water; then a wonderfully cool, wet washcloth was placed on her heated forehead. He flushed the toilet, something she hadn't been able to manage, and said, "I'll be right back."

As usual, she rapidly began to feel better after she had thrown up. Embarrassed, she got up and washed out her mouth and was standing in front of the mirror surveying her tousled appearance with some astonishment when Zane appeared with a familiar green can in his hand.

He had already popped the top. She snatched the can from him and began greedily drinking, tilting the can up like some college freshman guzzling beer. When it was empty, she sighed with repletion and slammed the can down on the countertop as if it was indeed an empty soldier of spirits. Then she looked at Zane, and her eyes widened.

"I hope you didn't go out to the drink machine like that," she said faintly. He was still naked. Wonderfully, impressively naked. And very aroused.

He looked amused. "I got it out of the minibar in the parlor." He glanced down at himself, and the amusement deepened. "There's another can. Want to go for it?"

Barrie drew herself up and folded a bold hand around his thrusting sex. "I'm not the kind of woman who loses her inhibitions after a couple of Seven-Ups," she informed him with careful dignity. She paused, then winked at him. "One will do."

Somehow she had expected they would make it back to the bed. They didn't. His hunger was particularly strong in the mornings, and after a tempestuous few moments she found herself on her knees, half bent over the edge of the bathtub while he crouched behind her. Their lovemaking was raw and fast and powerful, and left her once again lying weakly on the floor. She found some satisfaction in the fact that he was sprawled beside her, his long legs stretched under the vanity top.

After a long time he said lazily, "I'd thought I could wait until we were in the shower. I underestimated the effect of a soft drink on you, sweetheart...and what watching you drink it does to me."

"I think we're on to something," she reflected, curling nakedly against him and ignoring the chill of the floor. "We need to buy stock in the company."

"Good idea." He turned his head and began kissing her, and for a moment she wondered if the bathroom floor was going to get another workout. But he released her and rose lithely to his feet, then helped her up. "Do you want to have room service, or go down to a restaurant for breakfast?"

"Room service." She was already hungry, and with room service their breakfast should be there by the time she showered and dressed. She gave Zane her order, then, while he called it in, she selected the clothes she wanted. The silk dress was badly wrinkled, so she carried it into the bathroom with her to let the steam from her shower repair the damage.

She took her time in the shower, but even so, some wrinkles remained in the dress by the time she finished. She left the water running and turned it on hot to increase the amount of steam. On a hook behind the door hung a thick terry-cloth bathrobe with the hotel's logo stitched on the breast pocket. She pulled it on and belted it around her, smiling at the weight and size of the garment, and went out to see how long it would be before their breakfast arrived.

Zane wasn't in the bedroom; she could hear him talking in the parlor, and wondered if room service had been unusually quick. But she heard only his voice as she walked to the open door.

He was on the phone, half-turned away from her as he sat on the arm of the couch. She had the impression that he was listening to the shower running even as he carried on his conversation.

"Keep the tail on her father, as well as on *his* tail," he was saying. "I want to catch them all at one time, so I don't have to worry about any loose ends. When the dust settles, Justice and State can sort it out between them."

Barrie gasped, all the color washing out of her face. Zane's head jerked around, and he stared at her, the blue mostly gone from his eyes, leaving them as sharp and gray as frost.

"Yeah, ' he said into the receiver, his gaze never wavering from hers. "Everything's under control here. Keep the pressure on." He hung up and turned fully to face her.

He hadn't showered yet, she noticed dully. His hair wasn't wet; there was no betraying dampness to his skin. He must have gotten on the phone as soon as she had begun her shower, setting in motion the betrayal that could send her father to jail.

"What have you done?" she whispered, barely holding herself together against the pain that racked her. "Zane, *what have you done?*"

Coolly he stood and came toward her. Barrie backed up, clutching the lapels of the thick robe as if it could protect her.

He flicked a curious glance toward the bathroom, where billows of steam were escaping from the half-open door. "Why is the shower still running?"

"I'm steaming the wrinkles out of my dress," she answered automatically.

His eyebrows lifted wryly. Though she didn't find the pun amusing, she had the thought that this was evidently a wrinkle he hadn't anticipated.

"Who were you talking to?" she asked, her voice stiff with hurt and betrayal and the strain of holding it all under control.

"My brother Chance."

"What does he have to do with my father?"

Zane watched her steadily. "Chance does intelligence work for a government agency; not the FBI or CIA."

Barrie swallowed against the constriction in her throat. Maybe Zane hadn't betrayed her father; maybe he'd already been under surveillance. "How long has he been following my father?"

"Chance is directing the tails, not doing them himself," Zane corrected.

"How long?"

"Since last night. I called him while you were showering then, too."

At least he didn't try to lie or evade. "How could you?" she whispered, her eyes wide and stark.

"Very easily," he replied, his voice sharp. "I'm an officer of the law. Before that, I was an officer in the Navy, in service to this country. Did you think I would ignore a traitor, even if it's your father? You asked me to protect you and our baby, and that's exactly what I'm doing. When you clean out a nest of snakes, you don't pick out a few of them to kill and leave the others. You wipe them out."

The edges of her vision blurred, and she felt herself sway. Oh, God, how could she ever forgive him if her father went to prison? How could she ever forgive herself? She was the cause of this. She had known the kind of man Zane was, but she had allowed herself to ignore it because she'd wanted him so desperately. Of course he'd turned her father in; if she'd been thinking clearly, instead of with her emotions, her hormones, she would have known exactly what he would do, what he had done. It didn't take a genius to predict the actions of a man who had spent his life upholding the laws of his country, and only a fool would ignore the obvious conclusion.

She hadn't even thought about it, so she guessed that made her the biggest fool alive.

She heard him say her name, his tone insistent, and then her vision was blocked by his big body as he gripped her arms.

Desperately she hung on to consciousness, gulping in air and refusing to let herself faint. "Let go of me," she protested, and was shocked at how far away her voice sounded.

"Like hell I will." Instead he swung her off her feet and carried her to the bed, then bent to place her on the tumbled sheets.

As he had the night before, he sat beside her. Now that she was lying down, her head cleared rapidly. He was leaning over her, one arm braced on the other side of her hip, enclosing her in the iron circle of his embrace. His gaze never left her face.

Barrie wished she could find refuge in anger, but there was none. She understood Zane's motives, and his actions. All she could feel was a huge whirlpool of pain, sucking her down. Her father! As much as she loved Zane, she didn't know if she could bear it if he caused her father to be arrested. This wasn't anything like theft or drunken driving. Treason was heinous, unthinkable. No matter what conclusion her logic drew, she simply couldn't see her father doing anything like that, unless he was somehow being forced to do it. She knew *she* wasn't the weapon being used against him, although she had been drawn into it, probably when he had balked at something. No, she and Zane had both realized immediately that if she was being threatened and her father had nothing to hide, he would have had her whisked away by the FBI before she knew what was happening.

"Please," she begged, clutching his arm. "Can't you warn him somehow, get him out of it? I know you didn't like him, but you don't know him the way I do. He's always done what he thought was best for me. He was always there when I needed him, and b-before I left he gave me his blessing." Her voice broke on a sob, and she quickly controlled it. "I know he's a snob, but he isn't a bad person! If he's gotten involved in something he shouldn't, it was by accident, and now he doesn't know how to get out without endangering me! That *has* to be it. Zane, please!"

He caught her hand, folding it warmly within his. "I can't do that," he said quietly. "If he hasn't done anything wrong, he'll be all right. If he's a traitor—" He shrugged, indicating the lack of options. He wouldn't lift a finger to help a traitor, period. "I didn't want you to know anything about it because I didn't want you to be upset any more than necessary. I knew I wouldn't be able to protect you from worry if he's arrested, but I didn't want you to find out about it beforehand. You've had enough to deal with these past couple of months. My first priority is keeping you and the baby safe, and I'll do that, Barrie, no matter what."

She stared at him through tear-blurred eyes, knowing she had collided with the steel wall of his convictions. Honor wasn't just a concept to him, but a way of life. Still, there was one way she might reach him. "What if it was *your* father?" she asked.

A brief spasm touched his face, telling her that she'd struck a nerve. "I don't know," he admitted. "I hope I'd be able to do what's right...but I don't know."

There was nothing more she could say.

The only thing she could do was warn her father herself.

She moved away from him, sliding off the bed. He lifted his arm and let her go, though he watched her closely, as if waiting for her to faint or throw up or slap him in the face. Considering her pregnancy and her state of mind, she realized, all three were possible, if she relaxed her control just a fraction. But she wasn't going to do any of them, because she couldn't afford to waste the time.

She hugged the oversize robe about her, as she had once hugged his shirt. "What exactly is your brother doing?" She needed as much information as possible if she was going to help her father. Maybe it was wrong, but she would worry about that, and face the consequences, later. She knew she was operating on love and blind trust, but that was all she had to go on. When she thought of her father as the man she knew him to be, she knew she had to trust both that knowledge and his honor. Despite their enormous differences, in that respect he was very like Zane, the man he'd scorned as a son-in-law: honor was a part of his code, his life, his very being.

Zane stood. "You don't need to know, exactly."

For the first time she felt the flush of anger redden her cheeks. "Don't throw my words back at me," she snapped. "You can say no without being sarcastic."

He studied her, then gave a curt nod. "You're right. I'm sorry."

She stalked into the bathroom and slammed the door. The small room was hot and damp with steam, the air thick with it. Barrie turned off the shower and turned on the exhaust fan. There wasn't a wrinkle left in the silk dress. Hurriedly she shed the robe and pulled on the underwear she'd carried into the bathroom, then pulled the dress on over her head. The silk stuck to her damp skin; she had to jerk the fabric to get it into place. The need to hurry beat through her like wings. How much time did she have before room service arrived with their breakfast?

The mirror was fogged over. She grabbed a towel and rubbed a clear spot on the glass, then swiftly combed her hair and began applying a minimum of makeup. The air was so steamy that it would be a wasted effort to apply very much, but she wanted to appear as normal as possible.

Oh, God, the exhaust fan was making so much noise she might not have heard their breakfast arriving. Hastily she cut it off. Zane would have knocked if their food was here, she assured herself. It hadn't arrived yet.

She tried to remember where her purse was, and think how she could get it and get out the door without Zane knowing. His hearing was acute, and he would be watching for her. But the room service waiter would bring their breakfast to the parlor, and Zane, being as cautious as he was, would watch the man's every move. That was the only time he would be distracted, and the only chance she would have to get out of the room undetected. Her window of opportunity would be brief, because he would call her as soon as the waiter left. If she had to wait for an elevator, she was sunk. She could always try the stairs, but all Zane would have to do was take the elevator down to the lobby and wait for her there. With his hearing, he probably heard the elevator every time it chimed, and that would give him an idea of whether she had been able to get one of the cars or had taken the stairs.

She opened the bathroom door a little, so he wouldn't be able to catch the click of the latch.

"What are you doing?" he called. It sounded as if he was standing just inside the double doors that connected the bedroom to the parlor, waiting for her.

"Putting on makeup," she snapped, with perfect truth. She blotted the sweat off her forehead and began again with the powder. Her brief flash of anger was over, but she didn't want him to know it. Let him think she was furious; a woman who was both pregnant and angry deserved a lot of space.

There was a brief knock on the parlor door, and a Spanish-accented voice called out, "Room service."

Quickly Barrie switched on the faucet, so the sound of running water would once again mask her movements. Peering through the small opening by the door, she saw Zane cross her field of vision, going to answer the knock. He was wearing his shoulder holster, which meant, as she had hoped, that he was on guard.

She slipped out of the bathroom, carefully pulled the door back to leave the same small opening, then darted to the other side of the bedroom, out of his line of sight if he glanced inside when he passed by the double doors. Her purse was lying on one of the chairs, and she snatched it up, then slipped her feet into her shoes.

The room service cart clattered as it was rolled into the room. Through the open parlor doors she could hear the waiter casually chatting as he set up the table. Zane's pistol made the waiter nervous; she could hear it in his voice. And his nervousness made Zane that much more wary of him. Zane was probably watching him like a hawk, those pale eyes remote and glacier-cold.

Now was the tricky part. She eased up to the open double doors, peeking through the crack to locate her husband. Relief made her knees wobble; he was standing with his back to the doors while he watched the waiter. The running faucet was doing its job; he was listening to it, rather than positioning himself on the other side of the table so he could watch both the waiter and the bathroom door. He probably did it deliberately, dividing his senses rather than diluting the visual attention he was paying to the waiter.

Her husband was not an ordinary man. Escaping him, even for five minutes, wouldn't be easy.

Taking a deep breath, she silently crossed the open expanse, every nerve in her body drawn tight as she waited for his hard hand to clamp down on her shoulder. She reached the bedroom door to the hallway and held the chain so it wouldn't clink when she slipped it free. That done, her next obstacle was the lock. She moved her body as close to the door as possible, using her flesh to muffle the sound, and slowly turned the latch. The dead bolt slid open with smooth precision and a snick that was barely audible even to her.

She closed her eyes and turned the handle then, concentrating on keeping the movement smooth and silent. If it made any noise, she was caught. If anyone was walking by in the hallway and talking, the change in noise level would alert Zane, and she was caught. If the elevator was slow, she was caught. Everything had to be perfect, or she didn't have a chance.

How much longer did she have? It felt as if she had already taken ten minutes, but it was probably no more than one. Crockery was still rattling in the parlor as the waiter arranged their plates and saucers and water glasses. The door opened, and she slipped through, then spent the same agonizing amount of time making sure it closed as silently as it opened. She released the handle and ran.

She reached the elevators without hearing him shout her name and jabbed the down button. It obediently lit, and remained lit. There was no welcoming chime to signal the arrival of the elevator. Barrie restrained herself from punching the button over and over again in a futile attempt to convey her urgency to a piece of machinery.

"Please," she whispered under her breath. *"Hurry."*

She would have tried calling her father from the hotel room, but she knew Zane would stop her if he heard her on the phone. She also knew her father's phone was tapped, which meant that incoming calls were automatically recorded. She would try to protect her father, but she refused to do anything that might endanger either Zane or their baby by leading the kidnappers straight to the hotel. She would have to call her father from a pay phone on the street, and a different street, at that.

Down the hall, she heard the room service cart clatter again as the waiter left their suite. Her heart pounding, she stared at the closed elevator doors, willing them to open. Her time was down to mere seconds.

The melodic chime sounded overhead.

The doors slid open.

She looked back as she stepped inside, and her heart nearly stopped. Zane hadn't yelled, hadn't called her name. He was running full speed down the hall, his motion as fluid and powerful as a linebacker's, and pure fury was blazing in his eyes.

He was almost there.

Panicked, she simultaneously pushed the buttons for the lobby and for the door to close. She stepped back from the closing gap as Zane lunged forward, trying to get his hand in the door, which would trigger the automatic opening sensor.

He didn't quite make it. The doors slid shut, and the box began to move downward. "God *damn* it," he roared in frustration, and Barrie flinched as his fist thudded against the doors.

Weakly she leaned against the wall and covered her face with her hands while she shook with reaction. Dear God, she'd never imagined anyone could be so angry. He'd been almost incandescent with it, his eyes all but glowing.

He was probably racing down the stairs, but he had twenty-one floors to cover, and he was no match for the elevator—unless it stopped to pick up passengers on other floors. This possibility nearly brought her to her knees. She watched the numbers change, unable to breathe. If it stopped even once, he might catch her in the street. If it stopped twice, he would catch her in the lobby. Three times, and he would be waiting for her at the elevator.

She would have to face that rage, and she'd never dreaded anything more. Leaving Zane had never been her intention. After she'd warned her father, she would go back to the suite. She didn't fear Zane physically; she knew instinctively that he would never hit her, but somehow that wasn't much comfort.

She had wanted to see him lose control, outside of that final moment in lovemaking when his body took charge and he gave himself over to orgasm. Nausea roiled in her stomach, and she shuddered. Why had she ever wished for such a stupid thing? Oh, God, she never wanted to see him lose his temper again.

He might never forgive her. She might be forsaking forever any chance that he could love her. The full knowledge of what she was risking to warn her father rode her shoulders all the way to the lobby, one long, smooth descent, without any stops.

The rattle and clink of the slot machines never stopped, no matter how early or how late. The din surrounded her as she hurried through the lobby and out to the street. The desert sun was blindingly white, the temperature already edging past ninety, though the morning was only half gone. Barrie joined the tourists thronging the sidewalk, walking quickly despite the heat. She reached the corner, crossed the street and kept walking, not daring to look back. Her red hair would be fairly easy to spot at a distance, even in a crowd, unless she was hidden by someone taller. Zane would have reached the lobby by now. He would quickly scan the slot machine crowd, then erupt onto the street.

Her chest ached, and she realized she was holding her breath again. She gulped in air and hurried to put a building between herself and the hotel entrance. She was afraid to look back, afraid she would see her big, black-haired husband bearing down on her like a thunderstorm, and she knew she would never be able to outrun him.

She crossed one more street and began looking for a pay phone. They were easy to find, but getting an available one was something else again. Why were so many tourists using pay phones at this time of the morning? Barrie stood patiently, the hot sun beating down on her head, while a blue-haired elderly lady in support stockings gave detailed instructions to someone on when to feed her cat, when to feed her fish and when to feed her plants. Finally she hung up with a cheerful, "Bye-bye, dearie," and she gave Barrie a sweet smile as she hobbled past. The smile was so unexpected that Barrie almost burst into tears. Instead she managed a smile of her own and stepped up to the phone before anyone could squeeze ahead of her.

She used her calling card number because it was faster, and since she was calling from a pay phone, it didn't matter how she placed the call. *Please, God, let him be there*, she silently prayed as she listened to the tones, then the ringing. It was lunchtime on the east coast; he could be having lunch with someone, or playing golf—he could be anywhere. She tried to remember his schedule, but nothing came to mind. Their relationship had been so strained for the past two months that she had disassociated herself from his social and political appointments.

"Hello?"

The answer was so cautious, so wary sounding, that at first she didn't recognize her father's voice.

"Hello?" he said again, sounding even more wary, if possible.

Barrie pressed the handset hard to her ear, trying to keep her hand from shaking. "Daddy," she said, her voice strangled. She hadn't called him Daddy in years, but the old name slipped out past the barrier of her adulthood.

"Barrie? Sweetheart?" Life zinged into his voice, and she could picture him in her mind, sitting up straighter at his desk.

"Daddy, I can't say much." She fought to keep her voice even, so he would be able to understand her. "You have to be careful. You have to protect yourself. People *know*. Do you hear me?"

He was silent a moment, then he said with a calmness that was beyond her, "I understand. Are you safe?"

"Yes," she said, though she wasn't sure. She still had to face her husband.

"Then take care, sweetheart, and I'll talk to you soon."

"Bye," she whispered, then carefully hung the receiver in its cradle and turned to go to the hotel. She had taken about ten steps when she was captured in the hard grip she had been dreading. She didn't see him coming, so she couldn't brace herself. One second he wasn't there, the next second he was, surfacing out of the crowd like a shark.

Despite everything, she was glad to see him, glad to get it over with instead of dreading the first meeting during every dragging step to the hotel. The tension and effort had drained her. She leaned weakly against him, and he clamped his arm around her waist to support her. "You shouldn't be out in the sun without something on your head," was all he said. "Especially since you haven't eaten anything today."

He was in control, that incandescent fury cooled and conquered.

She wasn't foolish enough to believe it was gone, however. "I had to warn him," she said tiredly. "And I didn't want the call traced to the hotel."

"I know." The words were brief to the point of curtness. "It might not make any difference. Las Vegas is crawling with a certain group of people this morning, and you may have been spotted. Your hair." Those two words were enough. Redheads were always distinctive, because there were so few of them. She felt like apologizing for the deep, rich luster of her hair.

"They're here?" she asked in a small voice. "The kidnappers?"

"Not the original ones. There's a deep game going on, baby, and I'm afraid you just jumped into the middle of it."

The sun beat down on her unprotected head, the heat increasing by the minute. Every step seemed more and more of an effort. Her thoughts scattered. She might have plunged Zane and herself into the very danger she'd wanted to avoid. "Maybe I *am* a pampered society babe with more hair than brains," she said aloud. "I didn't mean—"

"I know," he said again, and unbelievably, he squeezed her waist. "And I never said you have more hair than brains. If anything, you're too damn smart, and it seems you have a natural talent for sneaking around. Not many people could have gotten out of that suite without me hearing them. Spook, maybe. And Chance. No one else."

Barrie leaned more of her weight against him. She was on his left side, and she felt the hard lump of the holster beneath his jacket. When he'd grabbed her, he'd instinctively kept his right hand free, in case he needed his pistol. What he *didn't* need, she thought tiredly, was having to support her weight and keep his balance in a firefight. She forced herself to straighten away from him, despite the way his arm tightened around her waist. He gave her a questioning look.

"I don't want to impede you," she explained.

His mouth curved wryly. "See what I mean? Now you're thinking of combat stuff. If you weren't so sweet, Mrs. Mackenzie, you'd be a dangerous woman."

Why wasn't he lambasting her? She couldn't imagine he'd gotten over his fury so fast; Zane struck her as the type of man who seldom lost his temper, but when he did, it was undoubtedly a memorable occasion—one that could last for years. Maybe he was saving it for when they were in the privacy of the suite, remaining on guard while they were in the street. He could do that, compartmentalize his anger, shove it aside until it was safe to bring it out.

She found herself studying the surging, milling, strolling crowd of tourists that surrounded them, looking for any betraying sign of interest. It helped take her mind off how incredibly weak she felt. This pregnancy was making itself felt with increasing force; though it had been foolish of her to come out into the sun without eating breakfast, and without a hat, normally she wouldn't have had any problem with the heat in this short amount of time.

How much farther was it to the hotel? She concentrated on her steps, on the faces around her. Zane maintained a slow, steady pace, and when he could, he put himself between her and the sun. The human shade helped, marginally.

"Here we are," he said, ushering her into the cool, dim cavern of the lobby. She closed her eyes to help them adjust from the bright sunlight and sighed with relief as the blast of air-conditioning washed over her.

The elevator was crowded on the ride up. Zane pulled her against the back wall, so he would have one less side to protect, and also to set up a human wall of protection between them and the open doors. She felt a faint spurt of surprise as she realized she knew what he was thinking, the motives behind his actions. He would do what he could to keep anything from happening, and to protect these people, but if push came to shove, he would ruthlessly sacrifice the other people in this elevator to keep her safe.

They got off on the twenty-first floor, the ride uneventful. A man and woman got off at the same time, a middle-aged couple with Rochester accents. They turned down the hallway leading away from the suite. Zane guided Barrie after them, following the couple until they reached their room around the corner. As they walked past, Barrie glanced inside the room as the couple entered it; it was untidy, piled with shopping bags and the dirty clothes they'd worn the day before.

"Safe," Zane murmured as they wound their way to the suite.

"They wouldn't have had all the tourist stuff if they'd just arrived?"

He slanted an unreadable look at her. "Yeah."

The suite was blessedly cool. She stumbled inside, and Zane locked and chained the door. Their breakfast still sat on the table, untouched and cold. He all but pushed her into a chair anyway. "Eat," he ordered. "Just the toast, if nothing else. Put jelly on it. And drink all the water." He sat down on the arm of the couch, picked up the phone and began dialing.

Just to be safe, she ate half a slice of dry toast first, eschewing the balls of butter, which wouldn't melt on the cold toast anyway. Her stomach was peaceful at the moment, but she didn't want to do anything to upset it. She smeared the second half slice with jelly.

As she methodically ate and drank, she began to feel better. Zane was making no effort to keep her from hearing his conversation, and she gathered he was talking to his brother Chance again.

"If she was spotted, we have maybe half an hour," he was saying. "Get everyone on alert." He listened a moment, then said, "Yeah, I know. I'm slipping." He said goodbye with a cryptic, "Keep it cool."

"Keep what cool?" Barrie asked, turning in her chair to face him.

A flicker of amusement lightened his remote eyes. "Chance has a habit of sticking his nose, along with another part of his anatomy, into hot spots. He gets burned occasionally."

"And you don't, I suppose?"

He shrugged. "Occasionally," he admitted.

He was very calm, unusually so, even for him. It was like waiting for a storm to break. Barrie took a deep breath and braced herself. "All right, I'm feeling better," she said, more evenly than she felt. "Let me have it."

He regarded her for a moment, then shook his head— regretfully, she thought. "It'll have to wait. Chance said there's a lot of activity going on all of a sudden. It's all about to hit the fan."

Chapter 13

They didn't have even the half hour Zane had hoped for.

The phone rang, and he picked it up. "Roger," he said, and placed the receiver into its cradle. He stood and strode over to Barrie. "They're moving in," he said, lifting her from the chair with an implacable hand. "And you're going to a different floor."

He was shoving her out of harm's way. She stiffened against the pressure of his hand, digging in her heels. He stopped and turned to face her, then placed his hand over her belly. "You have to go," he said, without a flicker of emotion. He was in combat mode, his face impassive, his eyes cold and distant.

He was right. Because of the baby, she had to go. She put her hand over his. "All right. But do you have an extra pistol I could have— just in case?"

He hesitated briefly, then strode into the bedroom to his garment bag. The weapon he removed was a compact, five-shot revolver. "Do you know how to use it?"

She folded her hand around the butt, feeling the smoothness of the wood. "I've shot skeet, but I've never used a handgun. I'll manage."

"There's no empty chamber, and no safety," he said as he escorted her out the door. "You can pull the hammer back before you fire, or you can use a little more effort and just pull the trigger. Nothing to it but aiming and firing. It's a thirty-eight caliber, so it has stopping power." He was walking swiftly toward the stairs as he talked. He opened the stairwell door and began pushing her up the stairs, their steps echoing in the concrete silo. "I'm going to put you in an empty room on the twenty-third floor, and I want you to stay there until either Chance or I come for you. If anyone else opens the door, shoot them."

"I don't know what Chance looks like," she blurted.

"Black hair, hazel eyes. Tall. So good-looking you start drooling when you see him. That's what he says women do, anyway."

They reached the twenty-third floor. Barrie was only slightly winded, Zane not at all. As they stepped into the carpeted silence of the hallway, she asked, "How do you know which rooms are empty?"

He produced one of the electronic cards from his pocket. "Because one of Chance's people booked the room last night and slipped me the key card while we were eating supper. Just in case."

He always had an alternate plan—just in case. She should have guessed.

He opened the door to room 2334 and ushered her inside, but he didn't enter himself. "Lock and chain the door, and stay put," he said, then turned and walked swiftly toward the stairwell. Barrie stood in the doorway and watched him. He stopped and looked at her over his shoulder. "I'm waiting to hear the door being locked," he said softly.

She stepped back, turned the lock and slid the chain into place.

Then she stood in the middle of the neat, silent room and quietly went to pieces.

She couldn't stand it. Zane was deliberately walking into danger— *on her account*—and she couldn't join him. She couldn't be there with him, couldn't guard his back. Because of the baby growing inside her, she was relegated to this safe niche while the man she loved faced bullets for her.

She sat on the floor and rocked back and forth, her arms folded over her stomach, keening softly as tears rolled down her face. This terror for Zane's safety was worse than anything she'd ever felt before, far worse than what she'd known at the hands of her kidnappers, worse even than when he'd been shot. At least she'd *been* there then. She'd been able to help, able to touch him.

She couldn't do anything now.

A sharp, deep report that sounded like thunder made her jump. Except it wasn't thunder; the desert sky was bright and cloudless. She buried her face against her knees, weeping harder. More shots. Some lighter, flatter in tone. A peculiar cough. Another deep thundering, then several in quick succession.

Then silence.

She pulled herself together and scrambled to the far corner of the room, behind the bed. She sat with her back against the wall and her arms braced on her knees, the pistol steady as she held it trained on the door. She didn't see how anyone other than Zane or Chance could know where she was, but she wouldn't gamble on it. She didn't know what any of this was about, or who her enemies were, except for Mack Prewett, probably.

Time crawled past. She didn't have her wristwatch on, and the clock radio on the bedside table was turned away from her. She didn't get up to check the time. She simply sat there with the pistol in her hand and waited, and died a little more with each passing minute of Zane's absence.

He didn't come. She felt the coldness of despair grow in her heart, spreading until it filled her chest, the pressure of it almost stopping her lungs. Her heartbeat slowed to a heavy, painful rhythm. *Zane.* He would have come, if he'd been able. He'd been shot again. Wounded. She wouldn't let herself even think the word *dead,* but it was there, in her heart, her chest, and she didn't know how she could go on.

There was a brief knock on the door. "Barrie?" came a soft call, a voice that sounded tired and familiar. "It's Art Sandefer. It's over. Mack's in custody, and you can come out now."

Only Zane and Chance were supposed to know where she was. Zane had said that if anyone else opened the door, to shoot them. But she'd known Art Sandefer for years, known and respected both the man and the job he did. If Mack Prewett had been dirty, Art would have been on top of it. His presence here made sense.

"Barrie?" The door handle rattled.

She started to get up and let him in, then sank back to the floor. No. He wasn't Zane and he wasn't Chance. If she had lost Zane, the least she could do was follow his last instructions to the letter. His objective had been her safety, and she trusted him more than she had ever trusted anyone else in her life, including her father. She definitely trusted him more than she did Art Sandefer.

She was unprepared for the peculiar little coughing sound. Then the lock on the door exploded, and Art Sandefer pushed the door open and stepped inside. In his hand was a pistol with a thick silencer fitted onto the end of the barrel. Their eyes met across the room, his weary and cynical and acutely intelligent. And she knew.

Barrie pulled the trigger.

Zane was there only moments, seconds, later. Art had slumped to a sitting position against the open door, his hand pressed to the hole in his chest as his eyes glazed with shock. Zane kicked the weapon from Art's outstretched hand, but that was all the attention he paid to the wounded man. He stepped over him as if he wasn't there, rapidly crossing the room to where Barrie sat huddled in the corner, her face drawn and gray. Her gaze was oddly distant and unfocused. Panic roared through him, but a swift inspection didn't reveal any blood. She looked unharmed.

He hunkered down beside her, gently brushing her hair from her face. "Sweetheart?" he asked in a soft tone. "It's over now. Are you all right?"

She didn't answer. He sat down on the floor beside her and pulled her onto his lap, holding her close and tight against the warmth of his body. He kept up a reassuring murmur, a gentle sound of reassurance. He could feel the thud of her heartbeat against him, the rhythm hard and alarmingly slow. He held her tighter, his face buried against the richness of her hair.

"Is she all right?" Chance asked as he, too, stepped over Art Sandefer and approached his brother and new sister-in-law. Other people were coming into the room, people who tended to the wounded man. Mack Prewett was one of them, his eyes sharp and hard as he watched his former superior.

"She'll be fine," Zane murmured, lifting his head. "She shot Sandefer."

The brothers' eyes met in a moment of understanding. The first one was tough. With luck and good care, Sandefer would survive, but Barrie would always be one of those who knew what it was like to pull that trigger.

"How did he know which room?" Zane asked, keeping his voice calm.

Chance sat down on the bed and leaned forward, his forearms braced on his knees. His expression was pleasant enough, his eyes cool and thoughtful. "I must have a leak in my group," he said matter-of-factly. "And I know who it is, because only one person knew this room number. I'll take care of it."

"You do that."

Barrie stirred in Zane's grip, her arms lifting to twine around his neck. "Zane," she said, her voice faint and choked, shaking.

Because he'd felt the same way, he heard the panic in her voice, the despair. "I'm okay," he whispered, kissing her temple. "I'm okay."

A sob shook her, then was quickly controlled. She was soldiering on. Emotion swelled in his chest, a huge golden bubble of such force that it threatened to stop his breathing, his heartbeat. He closed his eyes to hold back the tears that burned his lids. "Oh, God," he said shakily. "I thought I was too late. I saw Sandefer walk in before I could get off a round at him, and then I heard the shot."

Her arms tightened convulsively around his neck, but she didn't say anything.

Zane put his hand on her belly, gulping in air as he fought for control. He was trembling, he noticed with distant surprise. Only Barrie could make mincemeat of his nerves. "I want the baby," he said, his voice still shaking. "But I didn't even think about it then. All I could think was that if I lost you—" He broke off, unable to continue.

"Baby?" Chance asked, politely inquiring.

Barrie nodded, her head moving against Zane's chest. Her face was still buried against him, and she didn't look up.

"Barrie, this is my brother Chance," Zane said. His tone was still rough, uneven.

Blindly Barrie held out her hand. Amused, Chance gently shook it, then returned it to Zane's neck. He had yet to see her face. "Glad to meet you," he said. "I'm happy about the baby, too. That should deflect Mom's attention for a while."

The room was filled to overflowing: hotel security, Las Vegas police, medics, not to mention Mack Prewett and the FBI, who were quietly controlling everything. Chance's people had pulled back, melting into the shadows where they belonged, where they operated best. Chance picked up the phone, made one brief call, then said to Zane, "It's taken care of."

Mack Prewett came over and sat down on the bed beside Chance. His face was troubled as he looked at Barrie, clutched so tightly in Zane's arms. "Is she all right?"

"Yes," she said, answering for herself.

'Art's critical, but he might make it. It would save us a lot of trouble if he didn't." Mack's voice was flat, emotionless.

Barrie shuddered.

"You were never meant to be involved, Barrie," Mack said. "I began to think Art was playing both sides, so I asked your father to help me set him up. The information had to be legitimate, and the ambassador knows more people, has access to more inside information, than can be believed. Art went for the bait like a hungry carp. But then he asked for something really critical, the ambassador stalled, and the next thing we knew, you'd been snatched. Your dad nearly came unglued."

"Then those bastards in Benghazi knew we were coming in," Zane said, his eyes going cold.

"Yeah. I managed to shuffle the time frame a little when I gave the information to Art, but that was the most I could do to help. They weren't expecting you as early as you got there."

"I couldn't believe it of him. Art Sandefer, of all people," Barrie said, lifting her head to look at Mack. "Until I saw his eyes. I thought *you* were the dirty one."

Mack smiled crookedly. "It rocked me that you figured out anything was going on at all."

"Dad tipped me off. He acted so frightened every time I left the house."

"Art wanted you," Mack explained. "He was playing it cool for a while, or we would have had this wrapped up weeks ago. But it wasn't just the information. Art wanted *you*."

Barrie was stunned by what Mack was saying. She glanced at Zane and saw his jaw tighten. So that was why she hadn't been raped in Benghazi; Art had been saving her for himself. He could never have released her, of course, if she had seen his face. Perhaps he would have drugged her, but more likely he would simply have raped her, kept her for himself for a while, then killed her. She shuddered, turning her face once more against Zane's throat. She was still having trouble believing he was safe and unharmed; it was difficult to drag herself out of the black pit of despair, even though she knew the worst hadn't happened. She felt numb, sick.

But then a thought occurred to her, one she would have had sooner if concern for Zane hadn't wiped everything else from her mind. She looked at Mack again. "Then my father's in the clear."

"Absolutely. He was working with me from the get-go." He met her gaze and shrugged. "Your dad can be a pain in the rear, but his loyalty was never in question."

"When I called him this morning—"

Mack grimaced. "He was relieved to know you loved him enough to call, despite the evidence against him. Your leaving the hotel stirred up a hornet's nest, though. I thought we had everything under control."

"How?"

"Me," Chance interjected, and for the first time Barrie looked at her brother-in-law. She didn't drool, but she had to admit that his good looks were startling. Viewed objectively, he was the most handsome man she'd ever seen. However, she far preferred Zane's scarred, somber face, with its ancient eyes.

"I checked into another hotel under Zane's name," Chance explained. "You weren't listed at all, but Art knew you were with Zane, because he'd checked the license plate on that rental car and traced the rental to Zane's credit card. We didn't want to make it too obvious for him, we wanted him to have to work to find us, so he wouldn't be suspicious. When he found out you'd married Zane, though, he stopped being so cautious." Chance grinned. "Then you went for a walk this morning, and fubar happened. The pay phone you chose was right across the street from the hotel where I'd checked in, and Art's people spotted you immediately."

Across the room, the medics finally had Art Sandefer ready for transport to a hospital. Zane watched the man being carried out, then cut his narrowed gaze to Mack. "If I'd known about you a little sooner, most of this could have been avoided."

Mack didn't back down from that glacial stare. "As far as that goes, Commander, I didn't expect you to have the contacts you have—" he glanced at Chance "—or to move as fast as you did. I'd been working on Art for months. You made things happen in one day."

Zane stood, effortlessly lifting Barrie in his arms as he did so. "It's over now," he said with finality. "If you gentlemen will excuse me, I need to take care of my wife."

Taking care of her involved getting a third room, because the suite was in bad shape and he didn't want her to see it. He placed her on the bed, locked the door, then stripped both her and himself and got into bed with her, holding their naked bodies as close together as possible. They both needed the reassurance of bare skin, no barriers between them. He got hard immediately, but now wasn't the time for lovemaking.

Barrie couldn't seem to stop trembling, and, to her astonishment, neither could Zane. They clung together, touching each other's faces, absorbing the smell and feel of each other in an effort to dispel the terror.

"I love you," he whispered, holding her so close her ribs ached from the pressure. "God, I was so scared! I can't keep it together where you're concerned, sweetheart. For the sake of my sanity, I hope the rest of our lives are as dull as dishwater."

"They will be," she promised, kissing his chest. "We'll work on it.'' And tears blurred her eyes, because she hadn't expected so much, so fast.

Then, finally, it was time for more. Gently he entered her, and they lay entwined, not moving, as if their nerves couldn't stand a sharp assault now, even one of pleasure. That, too, came in its own time... her pleasure, and his.

Epilogue

"Twins," Barrie said, her voice still full of stunned bewilderment as she and Zane drove along the road that wound up the side of Mackenzie's Mountain. "Boys."

"I told you how it would be," Zane said, glancing at the mound of her stomach, which was much too big for five months of pregnancy. "Boys."

She gave him a glassy stare of shock. "You didn't," she said carefully, "say they would come in pairs."

"There haven't been twins in our family before," Zane said, just as carefully. In truth, he felt as shaky as Barrie did. "This is a first."

She stared out the window, her gaze passing blindly over the breathtaking vista of craggy blue mountains. They lived in Wyoming now; with Zane's two-year tenure as sheriff in Arizona over, he had declined to run for election, and they had moved closer to the rest of the family. Chance had been after him for those two years to join his organization—though Barrie still wasn't certain exactly what that organization *was*—and Zane had finally relented. He wouldn't be doing fieldwork, because he didn't want to risk the life he had with Barrie and Nick and now these two new babies who were growing inside her, but he had a rare knack for planning for the unexpected, and that was the talent he was using.

The entire family, including her father, was gathered on the mountain to celebrate the Fourth of July, which was the next day. Zane, Barrie and Nick had driven up two days before for an extended visit, but today had been her scheduled checkup, and he'd driven her into town to the doctor's office. Given the way her waistline had been expanding, they should have expected the news, but Zane had simply figured she was further along in her pregnancy than they'd thought. Seeing those two little fetuses on the ultrasound had been quite a shock, but there hadn't been any doubt about it. Two heads, two tails, four arms and hands, four legs and feet—and both babies definitely male. Very definitely.

"I can't think of two names," Barrie said, sounding very near tears.

Zane reached over to pat her knee. "We have four more months to think of names."

She sniffed. "There's no way," she said, "that I can carry them for four more months. We'll have to come up with names before then."

They *were* big babies, both of them, much bigger than Nick had been at this stage.

"After Nick, it took a lot of courage just to think of having another baby," she continued. "I'd geared myself up for one. *One*. Zane, what if *they're both like Nick?*"

He blanched. Nick was a hellion. Nick had a good shot at turning the entire family gray-haired within another year. For a very short person with a limited vocabulary, their offspring could cause an unbelievable uproar in a remarkably short period of time.

They reached the crest of the mountain, and Zane slowed the car as they neared the large, sprawling ranch house. A variety of vehicles were parked around the yard—Wolf's truck, Mary's car, Mike and Shea's Suburban, Josh and Loren's rental, Ambassador Lovejoy's rental, Maris's snazzy truck, Chance's motorcycle. Joe and Caroline and their five hooligans had arrived by helicopter. Boys seemed to be everywhere, from Josh's youngest, age five, to John, who was Joe's oldest and was now in college and here with his current girlfriend.

They were adding two more to the gang.

They got out and walked up the steps to the porch. Zane put his arm around her and hugged her close, tilting her face up for a kiss that quickly grew heated. Barrie glowed with a special sexuality when she was pregnant, and the plain truth was he couldn't resist her. Their love play was often extended these days, now that pregnancy had once again made her breasts as sensitive as they had been when she'd carried Nick.

"Stop that!" Josh called cheerfully from inside the house. "That's what got her in that condition in the first place!"

Reluctantly Zane released his wife, and together they went into the house. "That isn't exactly right," he told Josh, who laughed.

The big television was on, and Maris, Josh and Chance were watching some show-jumping event. Wolf and Joe were discussing cattle with Mike. Caroline was arguing politics with the ambassador. Mary and Shea were organizing a game for the younger kids. Loren, who was often an oasis of calm in the middle of the Mackenzie hurricane, gave Barrie's rounded stomach a knowing look. "How did the checkup go?" she asked.

"Twins," Barrie said, still in that numb tone. She gave Zane a helpless, how-did-this-happen look.

The whirlwind of activity came to a sudden stop. Heads lifted and turned. Her father gasped. Mary's face suddenly glowed with radiance.

"Both boys," Zane announced, before anyone could ask.

A sigh almost of relief went around the room. "Thank God," Josh said weakly. "What if it was another one—or *two*—like Nick!"

Barrie's head swiveled around as she began searching for a particular little head. "Where *is* Nick?" she asked.

Chance bolted upright from his sprawled position on the couch. The adults looked around with growing panic. "She was right here," Chance said. "She was dragging one of Dad's boots around."

Zane and Barrie both began a rapid search of the house. "How long ago?" Barrie called.

"Two minutes, no more. Just before you drove up." Maris was on her knees, peering under beds.

"Two minutes!" Barrie almost moaned. In two minutes, Nick could almost single-handedly wreck the house. It was amazing how such a tiny little girl with such an angelic face could be such a demon.

"Nick!" she called. "Mary Nicole, come out, come out, wherever you are!" Sometimes that worked. Most times it didn't.

Everyone joined in the search, but their black-haired little terror was nowhere to be found. The entire family had been ecstatic at her birth, and she had been utterly doted on, with even the rough-and-tumble cousins fascinated by the daintiness and beauty of the newest Mackenzie. She really did look angelic, like Pebbles on the old *Flint-stones* cartoons. She was adorable. She had Zane's black hair; slanted, deceptively innocent blue eyes; and dimples on each side of her rose-bud mouth. She had sat up by herself at four months, crawled at six, walked at eight, and the entire family had been on guard ever since.

They found Wolf's boot beneath Mary's glassed-in collection of angels. From the scuff marks on the wall, Zane deduced his little darling had been trying to knock the collection down by heaving the boot at it. Luckily the boot had been too heavy for her to handle. Her throwing arm wasn't well developed yet, thank God.

She had a frightful temper for such a little thing, and an outsize will, too. Keeping her from doing something she was determined to do was like trying to hold back the tide with a bucket. She had also inherited her father's knack for planning, something that was eerie in a two-year-old. Nick was capable of plotting the downfall of anyone who crossed her.

Once, when Alex, Joe's second oldest, had seen her with a knife in her hand and swiftly snatched it away before she could harm anyone or anything, Nick had thrown a howling temper tantrum that had been halted only when Zane swatted her rear end. Discipline from her adored daddy made her sob so heartbrokenly that everyone else got a lump in their throats. That, and making her sit down in her punishment chair, were so far the only two things they'd discovered that could reduce her to tears.

When she had stopped sobbing, she had pouted in a corner for a while, all the time giving Alex threatening looks over one tiny shoulder. Then she had gone to Barrie for comfort, crawling into her mother's lap to be rocked. Her next stop had been Zane's lap, to show him that she forgave him. She'd wound her little arms around his neck and rubbed her chubby little cheek against his rough one. She'd even taken a brief nap, lying limply against his broad shoulder. She'd woken, climbed down and darted off to the kitchen, where she'd implored Mary, whom she called Gamma, for a "dink." She was allowed to have soft drinks without caffeine, so Mary had given her one of the green bottles they always kept in store especially for Nick. Zane and Barrie always shared a look of intimate amusement at their daughter's love for Seven-Up, but there was nothing unusual about seeing her clutching the familiar bottle in her tiny hands. She would take a few sips, then with great concentration screw the top onto the bottle and lug it around with her until it was finally empty, which usually took a couple of hours.

On this occasion, Zane had happened to be watching her, smiling at her blissful expression as her little hands closed on the bottle. She had strutted out of the kitchen without letting Mary open the bottle for her and stopped in the hallway, where she vigorously shook the bottle with so much vigor that her entire little body had been bouncing up and down. Then, with a meltingly sweet smile on her face, she had all but danced into the living room and handed the bottle to Alex with a flirtatious tilt of her head. "Ope' it, pees," she'd said in her adorable small voice...and then she'd backed up a few steps.

"No!" Zane had yelled, leaping up from his chair, but it was too late. Alex had already twisted the cap and broken the seal. The bottle spewed and spurted, the sticky liquid spraying the wall, the floor, the chair. It hit Alex full blast in the face. By the time he'd managed to get the cap securely back on the bottle, he was soaked.

Nick had clapped her hands and said, "Hee, hee, hee," and Zane wasn't certain if it was a laugh or a taunt. It didn't matter. He had collapsed on the floor in laughter, and there was an unbreakable law written in stone somewhere that you couldn't punish youngsters if you'd laughed at what they'd done.

"Nick!" he called now. "Do you want a Popsicle?" Next to Seven-Ups, Popsicles were her favorite treat.

There was no answer.

Sam tore into the house. He was ten, Josh and Loren's middle son. His blue eyes were wide. "Uncle Zane!" he cried. "Nick's on top of the house!"

"Oh, my God," Barrie gasped, and rushed out of the house as fast as she could. Zane tore past her, his heart in his throat, every instinct screaming for him to get to his child as fast as possible.

Everyone spilled into the yard, their faces pale with alarm, and looked up. Nick was sitting cross-legged on the edge of the roof, her little face blissful as she stared down at them. "Hi," she chirped.

Barrie's knees wobbled, and Mary put a supporting, protective arm around her.

It was no mystery how Nick had gotten on the roof—a ladder was leaning against the house, and Nick was as agile as a young goat. The ladder shouldn't have been there; in fact, Zane would have sworn it hadn't been when he and Barrie had arrived, no more than five minutes earlier.

He started up the ladder, his gaze glued on his daughter. A scowl screwed her small features together, and she scrambled to her feet, perilously close to the edge of the roof. "No!" she shrieked. "No, Daddy!"

He froze in place. She didn't want to come down, and she was absolutely fearless. She paid no more heed to her danger than if she'd been in her bed.

"Zane," Barrie whispered, her voice choked.

He was shaking. Nick stomped one little foot and pointed a dimpled finger at him. "Daddy down," she demanded.

He couldn't get to her in time. No matter how fast he moved, his baby was going to fall. There was only one thing to do. "Chance!" he barked.

Chance knew immediately. He ambled forward, not making any swift movements that would startle her. When he was directly below her, he grinned at his cherubic niece, and she grinned at him. He was her favorite uncle.

"Dance," she crowed, showing all her tiny white teeth.

"You little Antichrist," he said fondly. "I'm really going to miss you when you're in prison. I give you...oh, maybe to the age of six."

Benjy, Josh's youngest, piped up behind them, "Why did Uncle Chance call her Dannychrist? Her name's Nick."

Nick spread her arms wide, bouncing up and down on her tiptoes.

Chance held up his arms. "Come on, cupcake," he said, and laughed. "Jump!"

She did.

He deftly snagged her in midair, and hugged the precious little body to his chest. Barrie burst into tears of relief. Then Zane was there, taking his daughter in his arms, pressing his lips to her round little head, and Barrie rushed over to be enveloped in his embrace, too.

Caroline looked at Joe. "I forgive you for not having any female sperm," she announced, and Joe laughed.

Josh was frowning sternly at Sam. "How did the ladder get there?" he demanded.

Sam looked at his feet.

Mike and Joe began to frown at their boys.

"Whose bright idea was it to play on top of the house?" Mike asked of the seven boys who hadn't been inside, and thus absolved of blame.

Seven boys scuffed their shoes on the ground, unable to look up at the three fathers confronting them.

Josh took down the ladder, which was supposed to be in the barn. He pointed to the structure in question. "March," he said sternly, and two boys began their reluctant walk to the barn—and their retribution. Benjy clung to Loren's leg, blinking at his two older brothers.

Mike pointed to the barn. His two boys went.

Joe raised an eyebrow at his three youngest. They went.

The three tall, broad-shouldered brothers followed their sons to the barn.

Nick patted Barrie's face. "Mommy cwy?" she asked, and her lower lip quivered as she looked at Zane. "Fix, Daddy."

"I'll fix, all right," he muttered. "I'll fix some glue to your little butt and stick you on a chair."

Barrie giggled through her tears. "Everyone wished for a girl," she said, hiccuping as she laughed and cried at the same time. "Well, we got our wish!"

Wolf reached out and plucked his only granddaughter from his son's brawny arms. She beamed at him, and he said ruefully, "With luck, it'll be thirty years before there's another one. Unless..." His dark eyes narrowed as he looked at Chance.

"No way," Chance said firmly. "You can turn that look on Maris. I'm not getting married. I'm not reproducing. They're starting to come by the bunches now, so it's time to call a halt. I'm not getting into this daddy business."

Mary gave him her sweet smile. "We'll see," she said.

MACKENZIE'S MAGIC

Chapter 1

*H*er head hurt.

The pain thudded against the inside of her skull, pounded on her eyeballs. Her stomach stirred uneasily, as if awakened by all the commotion.

"My head hurts." Maris Mackenzie voiced the complaint in a low, vaguely puzzled tone. She never had headaches; despite her delicate appearance, she possessed in full the Mackenzie iron constitution. The oddity of her condition was what had startled her into speaking aloud.

She didn't open her eyes, didn't bother to look at the clock. The alarm hadn't gone off, so it wasn't time to get up. Perhaps if she went back to sleep the headache would go away.

"I'll get you some aspirin."

Maris's eyes snapped open, and the movement made her head give a sickening throb.

The voice was male, but even more startling, it had been right beside her; so close, in fact, that the man had only murmured the words and still his warm breath had stirred against her ear. The bed shifted as he sat up.

There was a soft click as he turned on the bedside lamp, and the light exploded in her head. Quickly she squeezed her eyes shut again, but not before she saw a man's broad, strongly muscled, naked back, and a well-shaped head covered with short, thick dark hair.

Confused panic seized her. Where *was* she? Even more important, who was *he?* She wasn't in her bedroom; one glance had told her that. The bed beneath her was firm, comfortable, but not hers.

An exhaust fan whirred to life when he turned on the bathroom light. She didn't risk opening her eyes again, but instead relied on her other senses to orient herself. A motel, then. That was it. And the strange whumping sound she had only now heard was the blower of the room's climate-control unit.

She had slept in plenty of motels, but never before with a man. Why was she in a motel, anyway, instead of her own comfortable little house close by the stables? The only time she stayed in motels was when she was traveling to or from a job, and since she had settled in Kentucky a couple of years ago the only traveling she'd done had been when she went home to visit the family.

It was an effort to think. She couldn't come up with any reason at all why she was in a motel with a strange man.

Sharp disappointment filled her, temporarily piercing the fogginess in her brain. She had never slept around before, and she was disgusted with herself for having done so now, an episode she didn't remember with a man she didn't know.

She knew she should leave, but she couldn't seem to muster the energy it would take to jump out of bed and escape. Escape? She wondered fuzzily at the strange choice of word. She was free to leave any time she wanted...if she could only manage to move. Her body felt heavily relaxed, content to do nothing more than lie there. She needed to do something, she was certain, but she couldn't quite grasp what that something was. Even aside from the pain in her head, her mind felt fuzzy, and her thoughts were vague and drifting.

The mattress shifted again as he sat down beside her, this time on the side of the bed closest to the wall, away from the hurtful light. Carefully Maris risked opening her eyes just a little; perhaps it was because she was prepared for the pain, but the resultant throb seemed to have lessened. She squinted up at the big man, who sat so close to her that his body heat penetrated the sheet that covered her.

He was facing her now; she could see more of him than just his back. Her eyes widened.

It was *him*.

"Here you go," he said, handing the aspirin to her. His voice was a smooth, quiet baritone, and though she didn't think she'd ever spoken to him before, something about that voice was strangely familiar.

She fumbled the aspirin from his hand and popped them into her mouth, making a face at both the bitter taste of the pills and her own idiocy. Of course his voice was familiar! After all, she'd been in bed with him, so she supposed she had talked to him beforehand, even if she couldn't remember meeting him, or how she'd gotten here.

He held out a glass of water. Maris tried to prop herself up on her elbow to take it, but her head throbbed so violently that she sank back against the pillow, wincing with pain as she put her hand to her forehead. What was wrong with her? She was never sick, never clumsy. This sudden uncooperativeness of her own body was alarming.

"Let me do it." He slipped his arm under her shoulders and effortlessly raised her to a sitting position, bracing her head in the curve of his arm and shoulder. He was warm and strong, his scent musky, and she wanted to press herself closer. The need surprised her, because she'd never before felt that way about a man. He held the glass to her lips, and she gulped thirstily, washing down the pills. When she was finished, he eased her down and removed his arm. She felt a pang of regret at the loss of his touch, astonishing herself.

Fuzzily she watched him walk around the bed. He was tall, muscular, his body showing the strength of a man who did physical work instead of sitting in an office all day. To her mingled relief and disappointment, he wasn't completely naked; he wore a pair of dark gray knit boxers, the fabric clinging snugly to his muscled butt and thighs. Dark hair covered his broad chest, and beard stubble darkened his jaw. He wasn't handsome, but he had a physical presence that drew the eye. It had drawn hers, anyway, since she'd first seen him two weeks ago, forking down hay in the barn.

Her reaction then had been so out of character that she had pushed it out of her mind and ignored it, or at least she had tried. She had deliberately not spoken to him whenever their paths crossed, she who had always taken pains to know everyone who worked with her horses. He threatened her, somehow, on some basic level that brought all her inner defenses screaming to alert. This man was dangerous.

He had watched her, too. She'd turned around occasionally and found his gaze on her, his expression guarded, but still, she'd felt the male heat of his attention. He was just temporary help, a drifter who needed a couple of weeks' pay in his pocket before he drifted away again, while she was the trainer at Solomon Green Horse Farms. It was a prestigious position for anyone, but for a woman to hold the job was a first. Her reputation in the horse world had made her a sort of celebrity, something she didn't particularly enjoy; she would rather be with the horses than putting on an expensive dress and adorning a party, but the Stonichers, who owned Solomon Green, often requested her presence. Maris wasn't a snob, but her position on the farm was worlds apart from that of a drifter hired to muck out the stables.

He knew his way around horses, though; she'd noticed that about him. He was comfortable with the big animals, and they liked him, which had drawn her helpless attention even more. She hadn't wanted to pay attention to the way his jeans stretched across his butt when he bent or squatted, something that he seemed to do a thousand times a day as he worked. She didn't want to notice the muscles that strained the shoulder seams of his shirts as he hefted loaded shovels or pitchforks. He had good hands, strong and lean; she hadn't wanted to notice them, either, or the intelligence in his blue eyes. He might be a drifter, but he drifted for his own reasons, not because he wasn't capable of making a more stable life for himself.

She'd never had time for a man in her life, hadn't particularly been interested. All her attention had been focused on horses, and building her career. In the privacy of her bed at night, when she wasn't able to sleep and her restless body felt too hot for comfort, she had admitted to herself the irony of her hormones finally being kicked into full gallop by a man who would likely be gone in a matter of weeks, if not days. The best thing to do, she'd decided, would be to continue ignoring him and the uncomfortable yearnings that made her want to be close to him.

Evidently she hadn't succeeded.

She lifted her hand to shield her eyes from the light as she watched him return the water glass to the bathroom, and only then did she notice what she herself was wearing. She wasn't naked; she was wearing her panties, and a big T-shirt that drooped off her shoulders. *His* T-shirt, specifically.

Had *he* undressed her, or had she done it herself? If she looked around, would she find their clothes haphazardly tossed together? The thought of him undressing her interfered with her lung function, constricting her chest and stifling her oxygen flow. She wanted to remember—she *needed* to remember—but the night was a blank. She should get up and put on her own clothes, she thought. She should, but she couldn't. All she could do was lie there and cope with the pain in her head while she tried to make sense of senseless things.

He was watching her as he came back to bed, his blue eyes narrowed, the color of his irises vivid even in the dim light. "Are you all right?"

She swallowed. "Yes." It was a lie, but for some reason she didn't want him to know she was as incapacitated as she really was. Her gaze drifted over his hairy chest and flat belly, down to the masculine bulge beneath those tight boxers. Had they really...? For what other reason would they be in a motel bed together? But if they had, why were they both wearing underwear?

Something about those sophisticated boxer shorts seemed a little out of place on a guy who did grunt work on a horse farm. She would have expected plain white briefs.

He turned off the lamp and stretched out beside her, the warmth of his body wrapping around her as he settled the sheet over them. He lay on his side, facing her, one arm curled under his pillow and the other resting across her belly, holding her close without actually wrapping her in his embrace. It struck her as a carefully measured position, close without being intimate.

She tried to remember his name, and couldn't.

She cleared her throat. She couldn't imagine what he would think of her, but she couldn't bear this fogginess in her mind any longer. She had to bring order to this confusion, and the best way to do that was to start with the basics. "I'm sorry," she said softly, almost whispering. "But I don't remember your name, or—or how we got here."

He went rigid, his arm tightening across her belly. For a long moment he didn't move. Then, with a muffled curse, he sat bolt upright, the action jarring her head and making her moan. He snapped on the bedside lamp again, and she closed her eyes against the stabbing light.

"Damn it," he muttered, bending over her. He sank his long fingers into her hair, sifting through the tousled silk as he stroked his fingertips over her skull. "Why didn't you tell me you were hurt?"

"I didn't know I was." It was the truth. What did he mean, hurt?

"I should have guessed." His voice was grim, his mouth set in a thin line. "I knew you were pale, and you didn't eat much, but I thought it was just stress." He continued probing, and his fingers brushed a place on the side of her head that made her suck in her breath as a sickening throb of pain sliced through her temples.

"Ah." Gently he turned her in to him, cradling her against his shoulder while he examined the injury. His fingers barely touched her scalp. "You have a nice goose egg here."

"Good," she mumbled. "I'd hate for it to be a bad goose egg."

He gave her another narrow-eyed look, something he had down to an art. "You have a concussion, damn it. Are you nauseated? How's your vision?"

"The light hurts," she admitted. "But my vision isn't blurred."

"What about nausea?"

"A little."

"And I've been letting you sleep," he growled to himself, half under his breath. "You need to be in a hospital."

"No," she said immediately, alarm jangling through her. The last thing she wanted was to go to a hospital. She didn't know why, but some instinct told her to stay away from public places. "It's safer here."

In a very controlled tone he said, "I can handle the safety. You need to see a doctor."

Again there was that nagging sense of familiarity, but she couldn't quite grasp what it was. There were other, more serious, things to worry about, however, so she let it go. She took stock of her physical condition, because a concussion could be serious, and she might indeed need to be in a hospital. There was the headache, the nausea... What else? Vision good, speech not slurred. Memory? Rapidly she ran through her family, remembering names and birthdays, thinking of her favorite horses through the years. Her memory was intact, except for... She tried to pinpoint her last memory. The last thing she could remember was eating lunch and walking down to the stables, but when had that been?

"I think I'm going to be okay," she said absently. "If you don't mind, answer a couple of questions for me. First, what's your name, and second, how did we wind up in bed together?"

"My name's MacNeil," he said, watching her closely.

MacNeil. MacNeil. Memory rushed back, bringing with it his first name, too. "I remember," she breathed. "Alex MacNeil." His name had struck her when she'd first heard it, because it was so similar to the name of one of her nephews, Alex Mackenzie, her brother Joe's second-oldest son. Not only were their first names the same, but their last names both indicated the same heritage.

"Right. As for your second question, I think what you're really asking is if we had sex. The answer is no."

She sighed with relief, then frowned a little. "Then why are we here?" she asked in bewilderment.

He shrugged. "We seem to have stolen a horse," he said.

Chapter 2

Stolen a horse? Maris blinked at him in total bewilderment, as if he'd said something in a foreign language. She'd asked him why they were in bed together, and he'd said they had stolen a horse. Not only was it ridiculous that she would steal a horse, but she couldn't see any connection at all between horse thievery and sleeping with Alex MacNeil.

Then a memory twinged in her aching head, and she went still as she tried to solidify the confused picture. She remembered moving rapidly, driven by an almost blinding sense of urgency, down the wide center aisle of the barn, toward the roomy, luxurious stall in the middle of the row. Sole Pleasure was a gregarious horse; he loved company, and that was why his stall was in the middle, so he would have companionship on both sides. She also remembered the fury that had gripped her; she'd never been so angry before in her life.

"What is it?" he asked, still watching her so intently that she imagined he knew every line of her face.

"The horse we 'seem' to have stolen—is it Sole Pleasure?"

"The one and only. If every cop in the country isn't already after us, they will be in a matter of hours." He paused. "What were you planning on doing with him?"

It was a good question. Sole Pleasure was the most famous horse in America right now, and very recognizable, with his sleek black coat, white star, and white stocking on the right foreleg. He'd been on the cover of *Sports Illustrated,* had been named their Athlete of the Year. He'd won over two million dollars in his short career and been retired at the grand old age of four to be syndicated at stud. The Stonichers were still weighing the offers, determined to make the best deal. The horse was black gold prancing around on four powerful, lightning-fast legs.

What *had* she been going to do with him? She stared at the ceiling, trying to bring the hours missing from her memory back to the surface of consciousness. Why would she steal Sole Pleasure? She wouldn't have sold him, or raced him—in disguise, of course—on her own. She rejected those possibilities out of hand. Stealing a horse was so foreign to her nature that she was at a loss to explain having apparently done exactly that. The only reason she could even imagine having for taking a horse would be the animal was in danger. She could see herself doing that, though she was more likely to take a whip to anyone mistreating one of her babies, or any horse at all, for that matter. She couldn't bear seeing them hurt.

Or *killed.*

The thought knifed through her, and suddenly she knew. Oh, God, she knew.

She jerked upright in bed. Instantly pain mushroomed inside her skull, the pressure almost blinding her for a second. She gave a gasping, almost soundless cry; a hard arm shot upward and closed around her, preventing her getting up, but it didn't matter anyway. She felt her muscles going slack, unable to support her, and she slumped over on him. The pain quickly subsided to a far more manageable level, but the moment of agony left her weak and shaking, collapsed on his chest, in his arms, her eyes closed as she tried to recover from the shock.

MacNeil gently turned so that she was flat on her back and he was half over her, one heavy, hairy, muscled leg thrown across her much slimmer ones, his arm under her neck, his broad shoulders blocking the light from her closed eyelids. One big hand covered her left breast, the contact brief and warm and electrifying, then moved up to her throat. She felt his fingers pressing against the artery there, then a soft sigh eased from him, and he briefly leaned down to press his forehead against hers, very gently, as if he were afraid the touch might hurt her. She swallowed, trying to control her breathing. That was the limit of her control, though, because there was nothing she could do about the speed at which her blood was thundering through her veins.

Only the thought of Sole Pleasure kept her focused. Maris gulped, opening her eyes and staring up at him. "They were going to *kill* him," she said in a stifled tone. "I remember. They were going to *kill* him!" Renewed rage bubbled in her bloodstream, giving force to the last sentence.

"So you stole him to save his life."

He said it much more as a statement than as a question, but Maris nodded anyway, remembering at the last second to limit herself to only a tiny movement of her head. The calmness of his voice again piqued her interest with its familiarity. Why wasn't he alarmed, indignant, or any number of other responses that could reasonably be expected? Maybe he'd already guessed, and she had only confirmed his suspicion.

He was a drifter, a man who routinely walked away from responsibility, but even though he'd guessed what she was doing, he had involved himself anyway. Their situation was highly precarious, because unless she could prove the charge she'd made, they would be arrested for stealing Sole Pleasure, the most valuable horse in the country. All she remembered now was the danger to the stallion, not who was behind it, so proving it could be a bit chancy.

Chancy...*Chance.* Chance and Zane. The thought of her brothers was like sunrise, bringing light to the darkness in her mind. No matter what was going on or who was behind it, all she had to do was call Zane, and he would get to the bottom of it. Maybe that had been her original plan, lost in the fog that obscured the past twelve hours. Get Sole Pleasure out of harm's way, contact Zane, and lay low until the danger was over.

She stared at the ceiling, trying to remember any other detail that would help clear up the situation. Nothing. "Did I call anyone last night?'' she asked. "Did I say anything about calling one of my brothers?''

"No. There was no time or opportunity to call anyone until we got here, and you were out like a light as soon as you hit the bed.''

That information didn't clear up the question of whether she had undressed herself or he had done it. She scowled a little, annoyed at how the physical intimacy of the situation kept distracting her from the business at hand.

He was still watching her closely; she felt as if his attention hadn't wavered from her for so much as a split second. She could sense him analyzing every nuance of her expressions, and the knowledge was unsettling. She was accustomed to people paying attention to her; she was, after all, the boss. But this was different, on an entirely different level, as if he missed nothing going on around him.

"Were you going to call your family for help?'' he asked when she didn't say anything else.

She pursed her lips. "That would have been the most logical thing to do. I should probably call them now.'' Since Zane had left the SEALs, he was much easier to contact; Barrie and the kids kept him closer to home. And he would know how to get in touch with Chance, though the odds of Chance even being in the country weren't good. It didn't matter; if she needed them, if she made the call, she knew her entire family would descend on Kentucky like the Vikings swooping down on a medieval coastal village—and heaven help those who were behind all this.

Maris tried to ease herself away from him so that she could sit up and reach the phone. To her amazement, he tightened his grip, holding her in place.

"I'm okay,'' she said in reassurance. "As long as I remember to move slowly and not jar my head, I can manage. I need to call my brother as soon as possible, so he can—''

"I can't let you do that,'' he said calmly.

She blinked, her dark eyes growing cool. "I beg your pardon?'' Her tone was polite, but she let him hear the steel underlying it.

His lips twitched, and a ruefully amused look entered his eyes. "I said I can't let you do that." The amusement spread to his mouth, turning the twitch into a smile. "What are you going to do, fire me?"

Maris ignored the taunt, because if she couldn't prove Sole Pleasure was in danger, neither of them would have to worry about a job for some time. She lay still, considering this sudden change in the situation, possibilities running through her mind. He was too damn sure of himself, and she wondered why. He didn't want her to call for help. The only reason she could come up with was that he must be involved, somehow, in the plot to kill Sole Pleasure. Maybe he was the one who'd been hired to do it. Suddenly, looking up into those blue eyes, Maris felt the danger in him again. It wasn't just a sensual danger, but the inherent danger of a man who had known violence. Yes, this man could kill.

Sole Pleasure might already be dead. She thought of that big, sleek, powerful body lying stiff, never to move again, and a nearly crippling grief brought the sheen of tears to her eyes. She couldn't control that response, but she allowed herself no other. Maybe she was wrong about MacNeil, but for Sole Pleasure's sake, she couldn't take the chance.

"Don't cry," he murmured, his voice dropping into a lower note. He lifted his hand to gently stroke her hair away from her temple. "I'll take care of things."

This was going to hurt. Maris knew it, and accepted the pain. Her father had taught her to go into a fight *expecting* to get hurt; people who didn't expect the pain were stunned by it, incapacitated and, ultimately, defeated. Wolf Mackenzie had taught his children to win fights.

MacNeil was too close; she was also lying flat on her back, which took away a lot of her leverage. She had to do it anyway. The first blow had to count.

She snapped her left arm up at him, striking for his nose with the heel of her palm.

He moved like lightning, his right forearm coming up to block the blow. Her palm slammed into his arm with enough force to jar her to the teeth. Instantly she recoiled and struck again, this time aiming lower, for his solar plexus. Again that muscular forearm blocked her way, and this time he twisted, catching both of her arms and pinning them to the pillow on each side of her head. With another smooth motion he levered himself atop her, his full weight crushing her into the bed.

The entire thing took three seconds, maybe less. There had been no explosion of movement; anyone watching might not even have realized a brief battle had taken place, so tight had been the movements of attack and response, then counterattack. Her head hadn't even been unduly jarred. But Maris knew. Not only had she been trained by her father, she had also watched Zane and Chance spar too often to have any doubts. She had just gone up against a highly trained professional—and lost.

His blue eyes were flinty, his expression cold and remote. His grip on her wrists didn't hurt, but when she tried to move her arms, she found that she couldn't.

"Now, what in hell was that about?" His voice was still calm, but edged with an icy sharpness.

Then it all fell together. His control, his utter self-confidence, the calmness that seemed so familiar. Of course it was familiar—she saw it constantly, in her brothers. Zane had just that way of speaking, as if he could handle anything that might happen. MacNeil hadn't hurt her, even when she had definitely tried to hurt *him*. She couldn't have expected such concern from a thug hired to kill a horse. The clues were there, even those sexy gray boxers. This was no drifter.

"My God," she blurted. "You're a cop."

Chapter 3

"Is that why you attacked?" If anything, those blue eyes were even colder.

"No," she said absently, staring up at his face as if she'd never seen a man before. She felt stunned, as if she really hadn't. Something had just happened, but she wasn't sure what. It was like the way she'd felt when she first saw him, only more intense, primally exciting. She frowned a little as she tried to pin down the exact thought, or sensation, or whatever it was. His hands tightened on her wrists, drawing her back to the question he'd asked and the answer he wanted, and reluctantly she gathered her thoughts. "I just now realized that you're a cop. The reason I tried to hit you was because you wouldn't let me call my family, and I was afraid you might be one of the bad guys."

"So you were going to try to take me out?" He looked furious at the idea. "You have a concussion. How in hell did you expect to fight me? And who taught you those moves, anyway?"

"My father. He taught all of us how to fight. And I could have won, against most men," she said simply. "But you—I know professional training when I see it."

"So the fact that I know how to fight makes you think I'm a cop?"

She could have told him about Zane and Chance, who, even though they weren't cops, had many of the same characteristics she'd noticed in him. She didn't, though, because she wasn't one hundred percent certain their organization or agency or whatever it was was exactly squared away with either the State or Justice Department. Instead, she gave MacNeil a secret little smile. "Actually, it was your shorts."

He was startled out of his control, his blue eyes widening. "My shorts?"

"They aren't briefs. They're not white. They're too sexy."

"And that's a dead giveaway for being a cop?" he asked incredulously, color staining his cheekbones.

"Drifters don't wear sexy gray boxers," she pointed out. She didn't mention the interest she could feel stirring in those sexy gray boxers. Perhaps, under the circumstances, she shouldn't have mentioned his underwear. Not that his reaction was unexpected, she thought. She was barely clothed, and he wore even less. She could feel the hard, hairy bareness of his legs against hers, the pressure of his hips. Just minutes before, she had thought his touch carefully controlled, so that there was no intimacy, despite his closeness. She didn't feel that way now. It wasn't just his arousal; there was something *very* intimate in the way he held her beneath him, as if their brief battle had startled him out of his careful control and provoked him into a heated, purely male response. She took a deep breath as an unfamiliar excitement made her heart beat faster, made every cell in her body tingle with life. The secret part of her, the wildness that she had always known was there but which no man had ever before managed to touch, shivered in fierce satisfaction at the way he held her.

"Cops don't necessarily wear them, either."

Her comment about his shorts had definitely disturbed him. She smiled again, her dark eyes half closing in sensual delight as she absorbed the novel sensation of having a hard male body on top of her—an extremely *aroused* male body. "If you say so. I've never seen one undressed before. What kind of cop are you, specifically?"

He was silent for a moment, studying her face. She didn't know what he saw there, but the set of his mouth eased, and if anything, he settled even more heavily against her. "Specifically, FBI. Special agent."

A *federal* agent? Startled out of her sensual preoccupation, she gave him a puzzled look. "I didn't think stealing a horse was a federal crime."

He almost smiled. "It isn't. Look, if I let go of your hands, are you going to try to kill me again?"

"No. I promise," she said. "Besides, I wasn't trying to kill you, and even if I had been, I'm not as good as you are, so you don't have to worry."

"I can't tell you how reassuring that is," he said dryly, but he released her hands and shifted his position a little, propping himself over her on his forearms. The change forced his hips more firmly against hers, forced her thighs slightly apart to accommodate the pressure. She caught her breath. His interest had grown, to the point that there was no politely ignoring it. But he *was* ignoring it, not in the least embarrassed by his body's response to her.

Maris took another deep breath, delighting in the way the simple action rubbed her breasts against the hard, muscled planes of his chest, making her nipples tingle. Oh, God, that felt so good. She would gladly lie in his arms and do nothing more than *breathe,* if they didn't have a stolen champion horse stashed somewhere and someone presumably on their trail, trying to kill both them and the stallion.

But they did have a stolen horse hidden away, and a big problem on their hands. She focused her thoughts, and despite the fact that she was lying helplessly pinned beneath him, she fixed him with a dark, penetrating gaze. "So why was a federal special agent mucking out my stables?"

"Trying to find out who's been killing horses and collecting the insurance money on them—boss." He added the last word in a dry tone, responding to her arrogant claiming of the Solomon Green stables as her own.

She ignored the not-so-subtle teasing, because she'd heard it so often from her family. What she loved, she claimed; it was as simple as that. She drew her head back deeper into the pillow and gave him a frankly skeptical look. "Insurance fraud rates a special agent?"

"It does when it involves kidnapping, crossing state lines and murder."

Murder. So she'd been right: Someone *was* trying to kill them. Had this someone hit her on the head, or had she gained the goose egg by a more mundane method, such as falling?

"What brought you to Solomon Green?"

"A tip." One corner of his mouth curved slightly. His face was so close to hers that she could see the tiny lines created by the movement, as if he smiled easily. "Law enforcement agencies couldn't operate without snitches."

"So you knew Sole Pleasure was in danger?" She didn't like that. Anger began to smolder in her dark eyes. "Why didn't you tell me? I could have been on guard without causing any suspicion. You didn't have a right to gamble with his life."

"All of the horses are insured. Any of them could have been targeted. Sole Pleasure should have been their least likely target, because he's so well-known. His death would raise a lot of questions, attract a lot of attention." He paused, watching her carefully. "And, until last night, you were on my list of suspects."

She absorbed that, her only reaction a slight tightening of her mouth. "How did last night change your mind? What happened?" It was both frustrating and frightening, not being able to remember.

"You came to me for help. You were so angry you could barely speak, and you were scared. You said we had to get Sole Pleasure out of there, and if I didn't want to help, you'd manage on your own."

"Did I say who was after him?"

He gave a slight shake of his head. "No. Like I said, you were barely speaking. You wouldn't answer any questions. I thought at the time you were too scared, and once we had the horse safe, I was going to give you a little time to settle down before I started questioning you. Then I noticed how pale and shaky you were, maybe a little shocky from the adrenaline crash. You wanted to go on, but I made you stop here. You conked out as soon as we got in the room."

That reminded her again of both the interesting question of whether she had undressed herself or he had done it for her and his rather irritating assumption that he could *make* her do anything. She frowned when she realized that he could back up that assumption with action; her current position proved it. He hadn't hurt her, but physically she was still very much under his control.

Her frown deepened as she grew more annoyed with herself than before. She was doing it again, letting her attention drift. She could keep letting herself get sidetracked by her undeniable attraction to him, or she could keep her mind on the problem at hand. Sole Pleasure's life, and perhaps her own, depended on doing whatever she could to help this man.

There was no question which was most important.

"The Stonichers," she said slowly. "They're the only ones who would benefit financially from Sole Pleasure's death, but they'd make more by syndicating him for stud, so killing him doesn't make sense."

"That's another reason I didn't think he was in danger. I was watching all the other horses. The insurance on them wouldn't be as much, but neither would their deaths cause much of a stir."

"How did I find you?" she asked. "Did I come to your room? Call you? Did anyone see us, or did you see anyone?" His room was one of ten, tiny but private, in a long, narrow block building the Stonichers had built specifically to house the employees who were transient and had no other quarters, as well as those who needed to be on-site. As the trainer, Maris was important enough to have her own small three-room cottage on the premises. The foaling man, Mr. Wyse, also had his own quarters, an upstairs apartment in the foaling barn, where he watched the mothers-to-be on video monitors. There were always people around; someone had to have seen them.

"I wasn't in my room. I'd been in the number two barn, checking around, and had just gone out the back door when you rode by on Sole Pleasure. It was dark, so I didn't think you'd seen me, but you stopped and told me I had to help you. The truck and trailer that brought in that little sorrel mare this afternoon were still sitting there, hooked up, so we loaded Sole Pleasure in and took off. If anyone saw us, I doubt they could even have seen there was a horse in the trailer, much less recognized it as Sole Pleasure."

It was possible, she thought. The number two barn was where the mares who had been sent to the farm for breeding were stabled. Night came early in December, and the horses were already settled down, the workers relaxing or at supper. The truck and trailer didn't belong to Solomon Green, and everyone knew they had brought in a mare that afternoon, so no one would think anything of the rig leaving, except the driver, who had decided to spend the night and start back at dawn the next day. And Sole Pleasure was exceptionally easy to load; he never made a fuss and, in fact, seemed to enjoy traveling. Loading him wouldn't have taken more than a minute, and then they would have been on their way.

"I didn't have a chance to call my family," she said, "but did you call anyone while I was asleep?"

"I went out to a pay phone and let my office know what was going on. They'll try to run interference for us, but they can't be too obvious without blowing the operation. We still don't know who's involved in the ring—unless you've remembered something else in the past few minutes?"

"No," she said regretfully. "My last clear memory is of walking down to the stables yesterday afternoon. I know it was after lunch, but I don't know the exact time. What little else I remember is just flashes of being angry, and scared, and running to Pleasure's stall."

"If you remember anything else, even the smallest detail, tell me immediately. By taking the horse, we've given them the perfect opportunity to kill him and blame it on us, or at least they'll see it that way, since they don't know I'm FBI. They'll be after us hot and heavy, and I need to know who to expect."

"Where's Pleasure now?" she asked in alarm, putting her hands on his shoulders and pushing. She squirmed under him, trying to slip free of his weight so that she could get up, get dressed and get to the horse. It wasn't like her to be so lax about a horse's comfort and security, and though she had watched MacNeil enough to know that he was conscientious with the animals, the final responsibility was hers.

"Calm down. He's all right." MacNeil caught her hands, once more holding them down on the pillow. "I've got him stashed in the woods. No one's going to find him. I couldn't make it easy for them. Leaving him in the parking lot, where anyone could get at him, would have made even a fool suspicious. They're going to have to come to us in order to find him."

She relaxed against the pillows, reassured about Pleasure's safety. "All right. What are we going to do now?"

He hesitated. "My original plan was to find out what you knew, then put you somewhere safe until we had everything settled."

"Where were you going to put me, in the trailer with Pleasure?" she asked, a slight caustic edge to her voice. "Well, too bad. I can't tell you what I know, and you need to keep me handy in case I do remember something. You're stuck with me, MacNeil, and you aren't putting me anywhere."

"There's only one place I'd like to put you," he said slowly. "And I already have you there."

Chapter 4

It wasn't a surprise, given all the evidence at hand.

Pure male possessiveness was in Alex MacNeil's attitude, in every line of his body, staring plainly down at her from those sharp blue eyes.

Maris knew she wasn't mistaken about that look. She had grown up seeing it in her father's eyes every time he looked at her mother, seen the way he stood so close to her, touched her, a subtle alertness in every muscle of his body. She had also seen it innumerable times in her five brothers, first with their girlfriends and later, for four of them, with their wives. It was a look of desire, heated and potent.

It was both scary and exhilarating, startling her, and yet at the same time it was as if she had known, from the moment she first saw him, that there was something between them and eventually she would have to deal with it.

That was why she'd been at such pains to avoid him, not wanting the complication of an involvement with him, or having to endure the resultant gossip among the other employees. She had dated, some, but she had instinctively shied away whenever a boy or man showed signs of becoming too involved, possessive. She'd never had much time or patience for anything that interfered with her concentration on her horses and her career, nor had she ever wanted to let anyone that close to her.

She had a strong private core that she'd never let anyone touch, except for her family. It seemed to be a Mackenzie trait, the ability to be alone and be perfectly content, and even though all her brothers except Chance had eventually married and were frighteningly in love with their wives, they had married *because* they were in love. Maris had always been content to wait until that once-in-a-lifetime love happened to her, too, rather than waste time by flinging herself without thought into a brief affair with any man who just happened to have the right physical chemistry with her.

The chemistry was there with MacNeil, all right. The proof of it, on his part, was pressing urgently against the soft notch of her legs, tempting her to open her thighs wider and allow herself to feel that rigid length full against her loins. The fact that she wanted to do so was proof of the right chemistry on her part. She should move away, she knew she should, but she didn't. There wasn't a cell in her body that wanted to move, unless it was closer into his embrace.

She stared up into his beard-stubbled face, into blue eyes that were hard and darkened by sharp desire, a desire he was ruthlessly containing. Her own eyes were dark, bottomless pools as she met that sharp gaze. "The question is," she said slowly, "what are you going to do about it?"

"Not very damn much," he muttered, shifting restlessly against her. His jaw tightened at the sensations resulting from that movement, and his breath sighed out between his teeth. "You have a concussion. You have a killer headache. We have an unknown number of unknown people looking for us, so I have to keep my mind on the situation, instead of thinking about getting into your little panties. And even if you said yes, damn it, I'd have to say no, because the concussion could be causing mental impairment!" The last sentence was raw with frustration, ground out as if every word hurt him.

She lay very still beneath him, though her instinct was to part her thighs and cradle him against her, pulling him into her soft heat. Her eyes went as dark as night, softening, something mysterious and eternal moving there. "My headache is better." Her voice was low, her gaze drawing him in. "And I'm not mentally impaired."

"Oh, God," he groaned, resting his forehead against hers and closing his eyes. "Two out of four."

Maris moved her hands, and he immediately freed them. She laid her palms against his shoulders, and he tensed, waiting for her to push him away, knowing it was for the best but dreading the loss of contact. She didn't push. Instead, she curved her hands over the powerful muscles that cushioned the balls of his shoulder joints, trailed her fingers over the curve of his collarbone and finally flattened her hands against the hard planes of his chest. His crisp black chest hair tickled her palms. His tiny flat nipples hardened to pinpoints, intriguing her. His heartbeat was hard and strong, throbbing beneath her touch.

She was amazed, a little taken aback, by the intensity of the desire that shook her. No, not just desire—*need*. Need, hot and strong. She had seen sexual attraction all her life, at the most basic level in her horses and the other animals on the ranch, and in her own family as something powerful and tender and somehow both straightforward and complicated at the same time. She didn't underestimate the compelling power of sex. She had seen it, but she'd never before *felt* it, not this heat and ache, this emptiness that could be filled only by him, this melting sensation deep inside. She had always thought that if she ever felt this way it would be associated with love, and love was impossible here, because she didn't know him, not really. She knew his name and his occupation, but nothing about the type of person he was, and it was impossible to love a stranger. Be attracted, yes, but not love.

But her sister-in-law Barrie had once said that within five minutes of meeting Zane she had known the kind of person he was, and loved him. They had been strangers, but extraordinary circumstances had forced them into an intimate situation and shown them facets of each other's characters that otherwise would have taken months for them to discover.

Maris considered her own situation and the stranger who was so intimately sharing it with her. What had she learned about him since awakening—or regaining consciousness—in his arms?

He wasn't pushing her. He wanted her, but he wasn't pushing. The circumstances weren't right, so he was waiting. He was a patient man, or at least a man who knew how to be patient when he had to be, something that was entirely different. He was intelligent; she would have seen that days—weeks—ago, if she had let herself study him. She wasn't certain, but she thought that an FBI special agent had to have a law degree. He had some working medical knowledge, at least about concussions. He was evidently strong-willed enough to have gotten her to do something she didn't want to do, though, of course, with a concussion she wouldn't have been at her best. He had taken care of her. And most of all, despite the fact that she had slept almost naked in his arms, he hadn't taken sexual advantage of her.

That was quite a list. He was patient, intelligent, educated, strong-willed, caring and honorable. And there was something else, the subtle quality of danger and controlled power. She remembered the quiet, authoritative tone of his voice, the utter confidence that he could take care of any problem that might arise. In that he was like her brothers, particularly Zane and Chance, and they were two of the most dangerous men she could imagine.

She had always known that one of the reasons she'd never fallen in love was that so few men could compare favorably with the men in her family. She had been content to dedicate herself to her career, unwilling to settle for less than what she knew a man could be. But Alex MacNeil was of that stamp, and her heart lurched. Suddenly, for the first time in her life, she was in danger of falling in love.

And then, looking into those eyes so blue it was like drowning in the ocean, she knew. She remembered the change inside herself, the quiet recognition of her mate.

"Oh, dear," she said softly. "I have a very important question to ask you."

"Shoot," he said, then gave a wry shrug of apology at his word choice.

"Are you married, or otherwise involved with anyone?"

He knew why she was asking the question. He would have had to be dead not to feel the electricity between them, and his state of arousal proved that he was far from it. "No. No involvements, period." He didn't ask the same question of her; the background check he'd run on all the employees at Solomon Green had given him the basic information that she was single and had no record of prior arrests. In the time he'd worked at the farm, from the questions he'd asked, he had also found out that she didn't date any one man on a steady basis. The other guys had kidded him about having the hots for the boss, and he'd gone along with the idea. Hell, it was true, so why not use it as part of his cover?

Maris took a deep breath. This was it, then. With the directness with which she faced life, and the fey quality with which she saw things so clearly, she gave him a tiny smile. "If you aren't already thinking of marrying me," she said, "you'd better get used to the idea."

Mac kept his expression still, not allowing it to betray the shock that was reverberating through him. *Marriage?* He hadn't even kissed her yet, and she was talking marriage!

A sane man would get up and get his mind back on the business at hand, which included keeping them alive through the next few hours. A sane man wouldn't continue to lie here with this woman in his arms, not if he wanted to preserve his enjoyable single state.

He wanted her, no doubt about that. He was familiar with desire, having indulged that particular urge since the age of fourteen, and knew how to ignore it when indulgence would interfere with work. The work was absorbing, and he'd thrown himself into it with the cool, incisive intelligence that he also used to govern his personal life. He'd always been the one in control in his relationships, the one who called an end to things whenever he thought a woman was beginning to cling, to expect more from him than he was willing to give. It wasn't fair to string a woman along and let her hope when there was no hope, so he always simply ended the affair before it got to the tears-and-recriminations stage.

But then, he'd never met Maris Mackenzie before.

He didn't get up. More disturbing, he didn't laugh and say the concussion must have impaired her mentally after all. She was small, delicately built, even fragile, so it was ridiculous for him to dread making her angry or, even worse, hurting her feelings. He wanted to continue holding her, wanted to cradle her close to him and protectively cover her, keep her safe from the danger that would erupt around them within the next couple of hours, shield her from everything—except himself. He wanted her open to him, vulnerable, naked, completely at his disposal. He wanted to sink into those beguiling, mysterious black eyes and forget everything but the feverish delight of thrusting into her.

The sharp turn of events had thrown him off balance, that was all. Until last night, she and everyone else at Solomon Green had been on his list of possible suspects, and he had refused to let himself dwell on the heat that ran through him every time her slight, disconcertingly female body came within sight. Hell, she hadn't even had to be in sight; the thought of her had slipped into his consciousness at odd times during the day and disturbed his sleep at night.

He had resented his inability to ignore her as easily as she ignored him. She had a very still, intense quality about her, a focus that bespoke a will of iron. She was as absorbed in her job as he was in his, to the point that he'd thought she didn't even know he existed as a person, much less as a man. The idea had been strangely disturbing. He'd needed to blend in, but instead he'd found himself wanting to stand out, so that she would look at him with recognition in her eyes instead of a blank stare. Night after night he'd lain alone and thought about her, resenting both the fact that he couldn't seem to stop and the fact that she was oblivious to him. He wanted her to be as aware of him as he was of her, wanted to know that she, too, twisted on lonely sheets and thought of him in bed with her.

He wanted her with an intensity that infuriated him. Everything about her appealed to him, and that was surprising in itself, because there was nothing overtly sexual about her manner. She was pure business; she never flirted, never played favorites with the men under her authority, never made a suggestive remark, didn't go out of her way to make herself more attractive. Not that she had to; he couldn't have been more aware of her than if she made a practice of parading naked in front of him.

He knew exactly how her jeans clung to her curvy little ass, had imagined more than once gripping those round cheeks in his hands and lifting her into his thrust. He'd studied the shape of her high, round breasts underneath the flannel shirts she wore and, considering the slightness of her build, driven himself crazy thinking about how tight she would be when he slid into her. He'd had all the normal, heated sexual thoughts. But he'd also found himself absorbed in the satiny texture of her skin, as flawless as if she didn't spend countless hours outdoors. No woman should have skin like that, as pure as a child's, and so translucent he could see the fragile blue veins in her temples. He would look at her pale brown hair, bleached by the sun into streaks of ashy blond, and think of how it would trail across his arm like a fall of silk. Her eyes were as black as night, fey and unfathomable, tempting a man to try to plumb those mysterious depths.

Desire, like heat, was measured in degrees, and ran the gamut from lukewarm to vaporization. She had long since turned him to steam, he thought; it was nothing short of a miracle that he'd held her in his arms all night and done nothing more than that, even though all she was wearing was a pair of skimpy, blood-pressure-raising panties and his own T-shirt, which was so large on her that it kept slipping down to reveal one silky shoulder.

This was desire, all right—and more. It was want carried to a higher degree than he'd ever before experienced, a fever that refused to cool, a need he hadn't let himself satisfy. Until last night, he hadn't even let himself talk to her, even though he'd known he should, to see what, if anything, he could find out from her. Oddly enough, she had seemed to avoid him, too, though he'd noticed immediately that Ms. Mackenzie was a hands-on trainer who knew everyone working under her and was on easy terms with them. She was pure magic with the horses and a tyrant when it came to their care, but a benevolent tyrant, and everyone from the stable hands to the riders seemed to treat her with varying degrees of respect and adoration. It was out of character for her to avoid him, but that was exactly what she'd done.

It had made him suspicious. It was his job to be suspicious, to notice anything out of the ordinary, and her behavior toward him had made him wonder if something about him had made *her* suspicious, put her on guard. With his background, he was familiar with horses, which had made him the logical choice for the job, and he'd tried to blend in. Still, he was always aware that his training had permanently changed him, and a sharp eye might be able to spot the little things that forever set him apart from others: the extraordinary alertness, so that he was aware of every little detail of the activity going on around him; his sharp, fast reflexes; his unconscious habit of placing himself in positions that could be defended.

And she had spotted those details, known what they meant. He didn't at all like the swiftness with which she had sized him up and said, "You're a cop," even if her actions of the night before had already convinced him that she wasn't involved in the ring that killed racehorses and collected the insurance money. She saw too much, with those black eyes of hers, and now she was looking at him as if she could see into his soul.

Honesty prodded at him. Even though every hormone in his body was roaring at him not to do anything to jeopardize his current position, to stay right where he was, on top of her and all but between her legs, he ground his teeth and said what he knew he had to say.

"Marriage? You must be hurt worse than I thought, since you're delirious."

She didn't take offense. Instead, she curled her arms around his neck and gave him that small, inscrutable, damnably *female* smile again. "I understand," she said gently. "You need time to get used to the idea, and you have a job to do. This can wait. Right now, you have to catch some damn horse killers."

Chapter 5

She needed to clear her head, needed some time away from him so that her nerves would settle down. Maris pushed lightly against his shoulders; he hesitated, but then rolled to the side, freeing her from his weight. The loss of that heavy pressure, the vital heat, was so unexpectedly painful that she almost reached out to pull him over her again. One glance at the straining fabric of his shorts told her that he might not be able to withstand any more temptation, and while her entire body yearned for him, she wanted to be able to fully enjoy their first time together. She had a concussion, and there were an unknown number of people after them who would likely try to kill them, as well as Sole Pleasure—powerful distractions, indeed.

Gingerly she sat up on the side of the bed, being very careful to hold her head as still as possible. The aspirin had helped; the pain was still there, but it didn't throb as sickeningly as it had before. She eased into a standing position and was relieved when the room remained stable.

Instantly he was on his feet beside her, his hand on her arm. "What are you doing? You need to rest as much as possible."

"I'm going to take a shower and get dressed. If I'm going to be shot at, I want to be on my feet and wearing clothes when it happens." God, he was big, and there was all that naked flesh right in front of her. She took a deep breath, fighting the urge to press herself against him, to find out exactly where her head would fit against his shoulder now that they were standing up. His body was so beautiful, his shoulders wide and powerful, his arms and legs thick with muscle. How silly she'd been to avoid him all these weeks, when she could have been getting to know him! Silently she mourned those wasted days. She should have realized sooner why her reaction to him had been so sharp, why she'd felt that odd sense of fright.

This was the man with whom she would spend the rest of her life. No matter where her career had taken her, home had always been a mountain in Wyoming, and Alex MacNeil was going to change that. Her home would be with him, wherever he was, and an FBI special agent could be assigned anywhere. Though her life would never be completely without horses, he might be assigned to a city, where she wouldn't be able to find a job as trainer. She had never before met a man whom she would even consider putting ahead of her horses—but she looked at him and instinctively thought, *No contest.*

He was hers. She was his. She recognized it at every level of her being, as if she were vibrating to a resonance that only he produced.

But danger surrounded them, and she had to be prepared.

He had been watching her face with that narrow-eyed, intensely focused way of his. He didn't release her, but drew her closer, his arm circling her narrow waist. "Forget whatever you're thinking You don't have to do anything but stay out of the way."

His nearness was too tempting. Maris leaned her head on his chest, rubbing her cheek against the hairy roughness as an almost painful tenderness filled her. "I won't let you do this alone." His nipple was right there, only a few inches from her mouth, and as irresistible as catnip to a kitten. She moved those few inches, and her tongue darted out, delicately licking the flat brown circle.

He shuddered, his arm tightening convulsively around her. But his gaze was grim and determined as he cupped her chin with his other hand and gently lifted her face. "It's my job," he said in the even, quietly implacable tone she had heard before. "You're a civilian, and you're hurt. The best way you can help me is by staying out of the way."

She smiled in wry amusement. "If you knew me better, you wouldn't say that." She was fiercely, instinctively, protective of those she loved, and the thought of letting him face danger alone made her blood freeze in horror. Unfortunately, fate had decreed that she love a man whose profession was putting himself between the lawless elements in society and those he had sworn to protect. She couldn't demand that he quit his job any more than her family had demanded that she quit the dangerous work of gentling unbroken horses. He was what he was, and loving him meant not trying to change him.

She straightened away from him. "I'm still going to shower and dress. I still don't want to face anyone in just my panties and a T-shirt...." She paused. "Except you."

He inhaled sharply, his nostrils flaring, and she saw his hand flex as if he wanted to reach for her again. Because time had to be growing short, she stepped away from him, away from temptation, and gathered up her clothes. Just as she reached the bathroom door a thought occurred to her, and she stopped, looking back at him. *Was* he alone? Though Zane and Chance never talked about their assignments, they had sometimes discussed techniques, back in their training days, and she had absorbed a lot. It would be very unusual for an FBI agent to be working without backup.

"Your partner should be close by," she said. "Am I right?"

His eyebrows lifted in faint surprise; then he smiled. "In the parking lot. He got into position an hour or so after we got here. No one's going to take us by surprise."

If his partner hadn't been on watch, Maris realized, MacNeil never would have relaxed his guard enough to be in bed with her or let himself be distracted by the sexual attraction between them. Still, she was certain he hadn't slept but had remained awake in case his partner signaled him.

"What's his name? What does he look like? I need to be able to tell the good guys from the bad."

"Dean Pearsall. He's five-eleven, skinny, dark hair and eyes, receding hairline. He's from Maine. You can't miss the accent."

"It's cold out there," she said. "He must be frozen."

"Like I said, he's from Maine. This is nothing new to him. He has a thermos of coffee, and he lets the car run enough to keep the frost off the windshield, so he can see.''

"Won't that be a dead giveaway, no frost on the car?''

"Only if someone knows how long the car has been there, and it isn't a detail most people notice.'' He picked up his jeans and stepped into them, never taking his eyes off her as he considered the somewhat startling workings of her nimble brain. "Why did *you* think of it?''

She gave him a sweet smile, her mother's smile. "You'll understand when you meet my family.'' Then she went into the bathroom and closed the door.

Her smile faded immediately once she was alone. Though she fully realized and accepted the wisdom of not interfering with a trained professional and his partner, she was also sharply aware that plans could go wrong and people could get hurt. It happened, no matter how good or careful someone was. Chance had been wounded several times; he always tried to keep it from their mother, but somehow Mary always sensed when he'd been hurt, and Maris did, too. She could feel it deep inside, in a secret place that only those she loved had managed to touch. She had been almost insane with fear that time when Zane was nearly killed rescuing Barrie from terrorists in Libya, until she saw him for herself and felt his steely life force undiminished.

It had happened to Zane, and he was the best planner in the business. In fact, expecting things to go wrong was one of the things that made Zane so good at what he did. There was always a wild card in the deck, he said, and she had to be prepared for it, no matter how it was played.

Her advantages were that she was trained in self-defense, was a very good shot, and knew more about battle tactics than anyone could expect. On the other hand, her pistol was in her cottage, so she was unarmed, unless she could talk MacNeil into giving her a weapon. Considering how implacable his expression had been, she didn't think she had much chance of that. She was also concussed, and though the headache had lessened and she was feeling better now, she wasn't certain how well she could function if the situation called for fast movement. The fact that her memory hadn't returned was worrisome;

the injury could be more severe than she'd initally thought, even though her other symptoms had lessened.

Who had hit her? Why was someone trying to kill Sole Pleasure? Damn it, if only she could remember!

She wrapped a towel around her head to keep her hair dry and stood under a lukewarm spray of water, going over and over the parts she remembered, as if she could badger her bruised brain into giving up its secrets. Everything had been normal when she went back to the stables after lunch. It had been after dark, say around six or six-thirty, when she stumbled across MacNeil. Sometime during those five hours she had learned that Sole Pleasure was in danger and either surprised someone trying to kill him or confronted the person beforehand and earned herself a knock on the head.

It didn't make sense, but the Stonichers had to be behind the threat to their prize stallion, because they were the only ones who could benefit financially from his death. Since they would make much more by syndicating him for stud, the only way killing him made any sense at all was if he had some problem that would prevent them from syndicating him.

It wasn't a question of health; Maris had grown up around horses, loved them with a passion and devotion that had consumed her life, and she knew every detail of the well-being of her charges. Sole Pleasure was in perfect health, an unusually strong, fast horse who was full of energy and good spirits. He was a big, cheerful athlete who ran for the sheer love of running, sometimes mischievous but remarkably free of bad habits. She loved all her horses, but Pleasure was special to her. It was unthinkable that anyone would want to kill him, destroy forever that big, good-natured heart and matchless physical ability.

The only thing she could think of that would interfere with his syndication, the only possible reason anyone would grab for insurance money rather than hold out for the much larger fortune to be gained from syndicating him, was if the fertility tests had proved him sterile.

If that was the case, the Stonichers might as well geld him and race him as long as he was healthy. But injuries happened to even the hardiest animals, and a racing career could be ended in a heartbeat

The great filly Ruffian had been on the way to victory, well ahead of her male opponent in a special match race, when an awkward step shattered her leg and she had to be put down. Given the uncertainties of winning purses on the track and the given of insurance money, if Sole Pleasure was sterile, the Stonichers could conceivably be going for the sure thing and have hired someone to kill him.

She didn't want to think it of them. Joan and Ronald Stonicher had always seemed like decent people to her, though not the kind with whom she would ever be close friends. They were Kentucky blue bloods, born into the life, but Ronald particularly seemed to be involved in raising horses only *because* he'd inherited the farm. While Joan knew the horses better and was a better rider than her husband, she was a cool, emotionally detached woman who paid more attention to social functions than she did to the earthy functions in the stables. The question was, could they deliberately kill a champion Thoroughbred for the insurance money?

No one else was in a position to collect, so it had to be them.

They wouldn't do it themselves, however. Maris couldn't imagine either one of them actually doing the deed. They had hired someone to kill Pleasure, but who? It had to be someone she saw every day, someone whose presence near the horses wouldn't attract attention. It was likely one of the temporary hands, but she couldn't rule out a longtime employee; a couple hundred thousand would be terribly tempting to someone who didn't care how he earned it.

She turned off the shower and stepped out, turning the situation around and around in her head. By the time she was dressed, one thought was clear: MacNeil knew who the killer was.

She opened the door and stepped out, almost stumbling over him. He was propped against the countertop in the small dressing area, his arms crossed and his long legs stretched out, patiently waiting in case she became dizzy and needed him. He, too, had dressed, and though he looked mouth-wateringly tough and sexy in jeans, flannel shirt and boots, she regretted no longer being able to see him in nothing more than tight-fitting boxers.

Maris jabbed a slender finger at his chest. "You know who it is, don't you?"

He looked down at the small hand so imperiously poking him, and one dark brow lifted in bemusement. He probably wasn't accustomed to being called to account by someone he could have picked up with one hand. "Why do you think that?" he asked in a mild voice, but even so he stood so that he towered over her, silently reestablishing his dominance.

It might have worked if she hadn't grown up watching her petite mother rule over a household populated by brawny males. She was very much her mother's daughter; it never occurred to her to be intimidated. Instead she poked him harder.

"You said a tip led you to Solomon Green. Obviously the FBI has been working on this for a while, so just as obviously you have to have a list of suspects you're watching. One of those suspects is now working at Solomon Green, isn't he? That's what tipped you off." She scowled up at him. "Why did you say I was a suspect, when you know darn good and well—"

"Hold it." He held up a staying hand, interrupting her. "You *were* a suspect. Everyone was. I know who my main suspect is, but he isn't working alone. This ring has to have the collusion of a lot of people. The owners are the main ones to profit, but any of the employees could also be in on it."

She didn't like to think any of her people would be involved in murdering a horse for profit, but she had to admit it was possible. "So you followed him there and you've been watching him, trying to catch him in the act so you'll have proof against him." Her dark eyes caught fire. "Were you going to let him actually kill a horse, so there would be no doubt?"

"That isn't the outcome we'd like," he said carefully, watching her. "But we're aware that could be the scenario."

Her eyes narrowed. She wasn't fooled by his formal "official speak," used by both the military and law-enforcement organizations. Reading between the lines, she knew that while he might not like letting a horse be harmed, he'd been willing to let it happen if that was what it took.

She wasn't thinking of slugging him; she was angry, but not foolish. He's already proven he was more than a match for her. Still, the expression on her face must have made him think she was about to try again to take him down, because his hand came up in one of those lightning-fast movements and caught her wrist, holding it against his chest.

She drew herself up to her full five feet almost three inches and lifted her chin. "I refuse to sacrifice a horse. Any horse."

"That isn't what I want, either." He gently cupped her stubborn chin, his fingertips tracing over the satiny skin of her jaw. "But we can't make our move until they do something conclusive, something we can make stick in the courts. We have to tie everything together in a knot some slick lawyer can't undo, or a murderer is going to walk. This isn't just about horses and insurance fraud. A stable hand was killed, a kid just sixteen years old. He must have stumbled across something the way you did, but he wasn't as lucky. The next morning there was a dead horse in the stall and the kid was missing. That was in Connecticut. A week later his body was found in Pennsylvania."

She stared at him, her dark eyes stark. The Stonichers might just be after the money, but they had aligned themselves with people who were truly evil. Any regret she might have felt for them vanished.

MacNeil's face was like stone. "I won't move too soon and blow the investigation. No matter what, I'm going to nail these bastards. Do you understand?"

She did. Completely. That left only one thing to do. "You refuse to compromise the case, and I won't let Pleasure be hurt. That means you'll have to use me as the bait."

Chapter 6

"Absolutely not." The words were flat and implacable. "No way in hell."

"You have to."

He looked down at her with mingled exasperation and amusement. "Sweetheart, you've been the boss for so long that you've forgotten how to take orders. I'm running this show, not you, and you'll damn well do what I tell you to do, when I tell you to do it, or you're going to find yourself handcuffed and gagged and your sweet little ass stuffed in a closet until this is over."

Maris batted her long eyelashes at him. "So you think my ass is sweet, huh?"

"So sweet I'll probably be biting it before too much longer." The concept appealed to him; she could tell by the way his eyes darkened. She was rather taken by it, herself. Then he shrugged the moment away and grinned. "But no matter how good you taste or how fast you flutter those eyelashes, you aren't going to change my mind about this."

She crossed her arms and offered him an irrefutable fact. "You need me. I don't know what I saw or who hit me. It could have been one of the Stonichers, or it could have been whoever they hired. But they don't know that I can't remember, and they don't know about *you,* so they think I'm the biggest threat to them.''

"That's exactly why you're staying out of sight. If it's one of the Stonichers holding the gun, I can't predict how he or she will act. Give me a professional killer any day, rather than an amateur, who's likely to panic and do something really stupid, like shooting you in front of a bunch of witnesses.''

"God forbid you should have to deal with anyone who would get rattled by committing murder,'' she said, sweetly sarcastic, and he gave her another of those patented narrow looks of his. She continued with her argument. "They're probably surprised that I haven't already called the cops on them. By now they're figuring I was either hurt more than they'd thought at first and I'm lying unconscious somewhere, or that I've realized I have no proof to take to the cops, so I have no excuse for stealing a priceless horse. Either way, they want me. I'm the perfect patsy. They can kill Pleasure, make it look like I did it, and then kill me. Everything's tied up nice and clean, and who knows, the insurance policy may even pay double indemnity, which is more money in everyone's pocket. Nothing will make them commit faster than seeing me.''

"Damn it, *no.*'' He shook his head in exasperation. "I can't believe the way your mind works. You must read a lot of thrillers.''

She glared at him, affronted. Her argument was perfectly logical, and he knew it. That didn't mean he liked it. It didn't even mean he would agree with it; she was fast learning that she could add *protective* to the list of his characteristics. And *stubborn.* God forbid she should forget stubborn.

"Sweetheart...'' He smoothed his hands over her shoulders, an unfamiliar, tender ache in his chest as he felt the delicacy of her bones. He tried to think of the words that would convince her to leave this business to him and Dean. It was their job; they were trained for it. She would be in the way, and worrying about her would drive him crazy. God, she evidently thought she was seven feet tall and made of pig iron, but he could see how pale she was, how carefully she moved. She wasn't normally fragile, despite the slightness of her build; he'd seen her ride, effortlessly controlling stallions that most men would have trouble handling, so he knew she was strong. She was also alarmingly valiant, and he didn't know if his nerves could stand the stress.

"Look at it this way," she said. "As long as they don't know where Pleasure is, I'm safe. They need me to get to him."

He didn't argue, didn't try to convince her. He just shook his head and said, "No."

She gave his forehead an experimental rap with her knuckles, a puzzled look on her face.

He drew back a little, blinking in surprise. "What are you doing?"

"Seeing if your head's made out of wood," she retorted, her exasperation showing through. "You're letting your emotions interfere with your job. I'm your best bet—so use me!"

Mac stood motionless. He couldn't have been more stunned if this delicate fire-eater had suddenly lifted him over her head and tossed him through the window. *He* was letting his emotions interfere with the job? That was the last thing he'd ever imagined anyone would say to him. What made him so good at his job was his ability to divorce himself from the emotions that could hamper his actions. He'd always been the one who kept his head, who remained cool no matter how tense the situation. He might have some sleepless nights afterward, he might sweat bullets, but while the job was going down he was an iceman.

He couldn't be emotional about her; it wasn't logical. Okay, so he'd had the hots for her since he'd first seen her. Chemistry happened. With her, it had happened in a big way. And he liked her; he'd learned a lot about her since she had practically commandeered him the night before. She was quick-thinking, had a sense of humor, and was too damned gutsy for his peace of mind. She also responded to his slightest touch, her soft body melting against him, with a sheer delight that went to his head faster than a hit of whiskey.

He frowned. Only the fact that she was concussed had kept him from taking her, and even then, it had been a near thing. Never mind that they were waiting for a killer to come after them, that he had deliberately left a trail that was just difficult enough to keep from being obvious. He never should have undressed last night; he knew that. But the fact was, he had wanted to feel her against his skin, and so he'd taken off everything but his shorts and slipped into bed with her. Dean would beep him when anyone showed up; if Mac had timed it right, he figured it would take another hour at least before anything happened, but still he should have been dressed and ready in case something went wrong. Instead, he had been on top of her, between her legs, and thinking that only two thin layers of cotton were keeping him from her. It would have taken him maybe five seconds to get those two layers out of the way, and then he would have been inside her and to hell with anything else.

But none of that was emotion. That was liking, and a powerful lust. So she had this crazy idea, after spending only a few hours with him— and being asleep most of that time—that they were going to get married. Just because she felt that way didn't mean he did, and he sure as hell wasn't going to let himself be buffaloed into something like marriage, no matter how hard he got whenever she was anywhere around.

The thought of using her as bait almost made the top of his head come off, but that wasn't emotion, it was common sense.

"You're concussed," he finally said. "You're moving like a snail, and you don't need to be moving at all. You'd be more of a hindrance than a help, because I'd have to watch you, as well as myself."

"Then give me a weapon," she replied, her tone so unruffled that he wasn't sure he'd heard right.

"A weapon?" he echoed incredulously. "Good God, you think I'm going to arm a *civilian?*"

She straightened away from his grasp, and his palms ached from the loss of contact. All of a sudden her black eyes weren't bottomless at all, they were cool and flat, and the recognition of what he was seeing jolted him.

"I can handle a pistol as well as you, maybe better."

She wasn't exaggerating. He'd seen that look in the eyes of snipers, and in the eyes of some fellow agents who had been there, done that, and had the guts to do it again. He had seen it in his own eyes, and he'd understood when some women had shied away from him, frightened by the dangerous edge they sensed in him.

Maris wouldn't shy away. She looked delicate, but she was pure steel.

He could use her. The thought flashed into his brain, and he couldn't dismiss it. Policy said that no civilians should be involved if it could be avoided, but too many times it *couldn't* be avoided. She was right; she was his best bet, and he would be a fool if he compromised the investigation by not using her. It wrenched every instinct he had to do it, but he had to put his feelings aside and concentrate on the job.

Damn it, he thought in surprise, he *had* been letting his emotions cloud his thinking. That wasn't a good sign, and he had to put a stop to that kind of idiocy right now.

"All right," he said swiftly, wheeling around to get their jackets. He jerked his on and began stuffing Maris into hers. "Time's short, so we have to move fast. First we need to get the stallion out of the trailer and hidden somewhere else, then position the trailer so that whoever comes can't see that he isn't in it. Then we come back here. You drive the truck, I'll be hidden in the truck bed, under some blankets or something." He turned out the bathroom light and began ushering her toward the door. "We'll post Dean down the road, where he can see them arrive. He'll leave then and get into position at the trailer. He'll give us warning. You leave by the back way just as they arrive, let them get a glimpse of the truck. They follow."

They reached the door. MacNeil turned out the lights and took a small radio out of his pocket, keying it. "Is everything clear?" he asked. "We're coming out."

"What?" His partner's voice was startled. "Yeah, everything's clear. What's up?"

"Tell you in a minute."

He slipped the radio back into his pocket and unchained the door. He paused then, looking down at her. "Are you sure you can do this? If your head is hurting too much, let me know now, before it goes any further."

"I can do it." Her voice was calm, matter-of-fact, and he gave a short nod.

"Okay, then." He opened the door, and cold air slapped her in the face. She shivered, even though she was wearing her thick down jacket. The weather bureau had been predicting the arrival of a cold front, she remembered. She had watched the noon news and weather yesterday; perhaps that was why she now had this thick jacket instead of the flannel-lined denim jacket she had been wearing yesterday morning. She was glad she had changed coats, because the temperature now had to be in the twenties.

She looked around as she left the cozy warmth of the motel room. The motel office and the highway were on her right. MacNeil took her arm and steered her to the left, circling her behind a late-model pickup truck that was covered over with frost. "Hold it a minute," he said, and left her hidden by the truck's bulk while he went around to the driver's side. He opened the door and leaned in. She caught the faint metallic jingle of keys; then the motor started and settled into a quiet idle. She noticed with approval that the interior light hadn't come on, which meant he had taken care of that little detail earlier.

Interior lights. As he closed the truck door with a barely audible click, the neon light from the motel sign slanted across his high cheekbones, and a door opened in her mind.

She remembered the way his face had looked last night as he drove, the grimness of his expression highlighted by the faint green glow from the dash.

She remembered the desperation with which she had hidden her condition from him. She had been afraid to let him know how weak she was, how terribly her head hurt, that she was vulnerable in any way. He hadn't said much, just driven in dark silence, but even through her pain she had felt the physical awareness running between them like a live electrical wire. If she showed any vulnerability, she'd thought, he would be on her. That was why he'd come with her, not because he was concerned about Sole Pleasure.

Her thinking had been muddled by the knock she'd taken on the head. She had been terrified for Pleasure's safety, trying to think of the best way to protect him, and she hadn't been certain she could trust MacNeil. She had taken a big chance in asking for his help; he had given it without question, but afterward she'd been too unbalanced by the concussion and the strength and unfamiliarity of her own sensual awareness of him to think straight.

She had wound up exactly where she was afraid she would, under him in bed. And he hadn't done a darn thing, except make her fall in love with him.

"Come on," he said softly, not looking at her. In fact, he was looking at everything except her, his head swiveling, restless eyes noting every detail of their surroundings.

The early morning was dark and silent, so cold that their breath fogged into ice crystals. No stars winked overhead, and she knew why when a few white flakes began drifting soundlessly to the ground. A cold breeze sliced through her jeans, freezing her legs.

He led her across to a nondescript tan Oldsmobile that was backed into a parking slot between a scraggly bush, the motel's attempt at landscaping, and a Volvo station wagon. She walked carefully, and her headache obliged by remaining bearable.

He opened the rear door of the four-door car and put her inside, then he got into the front, beside his partner. Dean Pearsall was exactly as MacNeil had described him, thin and dark, as well as definitely puzzled. "What the hell's going on?"

Briefly MacNeil outlined the plan. Pearsall's head swiveled, and he looked over the seat at Maris, doubt plain in his expression.

"I can do it," she said, not giving him time to voice that doubt.

"We have to work fast," MacNeil said. "Can you get the video equipment set up?"

"Yeah," Pearsall replied. "Maybe. We're cutting it damn close, though."

"Then let's not waste any more time." MacNeil popped open the glove box and removed a holstered pistol. He took it out, checked it, then slid it back into the holster before handing it back to Maris. "It's a .38 revolver, five shots, and there's a round under the hammer."

She nodded and checked the weapon herself. A faint smile eased the grim line of his mouth as he watched her; he wouldn't have taken someone else's word on the state of a weapon's readiness, either.

"There's a Kevlar vest on the seat beside you. It'll be way too big for you, but put it on anyway," he instructed.

"That's your vest," Pearsall said.

"Yeah, but she's going to wear it."

Maris slipped the revolver into her coat pocket and grabbed the vest. "I'll put it on in the truck," she said as she opened the door and slid out. "We have to hurry."

The snowflakes were still drifting down, ghostly in the predawn quiet. Their footsteps crunched on the gravel as she and MacNeil crossed the parking lot to the truck. The defroster had cleared the bottom half of the windshield, and that was enough for him to drive.

He didn't turn on the headlights until they were on the highway and he could tell there was nothing in sight in either direction except for the tan Oldsmobile, which had pulled out behind them. Then he hit the switch, and the green dash lights illuminated his face just as they had earlier.

Maris shrugged out of her coat and into the Kevlar vest. It was heavy and far too big, so big it covered her hips, but she didn't waste her time arguing about wearing the cumbersome garment, because she knew MacNeil would never give in on this.

"I remember driving with you last night," she said.

He glanced at her. "Your memory's back?"

"Not all of it. I still don't remember who hit me on the head, or taking Pleasure. By the way, don't you think you should tell me?"

He grunted. "I don't know who hit you. There's a choice between at least three people, maybe more."

"Ronald and Joan are two. Who's the one you followed to Solomon Green?"

"The new vet. Randy Yu."

Maris was silent. That name surprised her; she would have thought of a lot of other people before she would have come up with the vet's name. She'd been impressed with his skill, and he'd never shown anything but the utmost care for his four-legged patients. He was a quarter Chinese, in his middle thirties, and with the strength a veterinarian needed. If he was the one she'd tangled with, she was surprised she'd managed to get away from him with no more than a bump on the head. Of course, whoever she'd fought with wouldn't have expected her to know how to fight, much less fight hard and dirty.

"It makes sense," she said, thinking about it. "A quick injection, Pleasure dies of cardiac arrest, and it looks like natural causes. Not nearly as messy as a bullet."

"But you ruined that plan for them," MacNeil said, harshness underlying the calm of his tone. "Now they'll be planning to use bullets—for both you *and* the horse."

Chapter 7

Sole Pleasure wasn't happy. He didn't like being alone, he didn't like being cramped in a small trailer for so long, and he was both hungry and thirsty. MacNeil had backed the horse trailer deep into a section of woods, so deep she didn't know how he'd managed it, and Pleasure didn't like the unfamiliar surroundings, either. He was a horse accustomed to open pastures, roomy stalls, noise and people. As soon as they got out of the truck they heard his angry neighing and the thud of one of his rear hooves repeatedly kicking against the back of the trailer.

"He'll hurt himself!" Maris hurried to the trailer, moving faster than she should have for the sake of her head, but if Pleasure managed to break his leg, he would *have* to be put down. "Easy, baby, easy," she crooned as she unlatched the back gate, the special note she used for her horses entering her tone. The kicking stopped immediately, and she could almost see the alert black ears swiveling to catch her voice.

"Hold it." MacNeil's hand came down on top of hers as she started to open the gate. "I'll get him out. He's fractious, and I don't want him bumping you around. You stand over there and keep talking to him."

She gave him a considering look as she moved to the side. Really, the man was acting as if this were the first time she'd ever been hurt. Anyone who worked with horses could expect to be kicked, bitten, bruised and bucked off—though she hadn't been thrown since she'd been a kid. Still, she'd collected her share of injuries: Both arms had been broken, as well as her collarbone. She'd had a concussion before, too. What was the best way to handle an overprotective man, especially after you were married?

Exactly the way her mother handled her father, she thought, grinning. By standing her ground, talking rings around him, and distracting him with sex, and by choosing her battles and sometimes actually letting him have his way. This was one of the times to not kick up a fuss. She would ignore him later, when the stakes were greater.

MacNeil skillfully backed the big stallion out of the trailer; Pleasure came eagerly, happy to have company again, relieved to be unconfined. He showed his happiness by dancing around and playing, shoving MacNeil with his head and generally acting like any four-year-old. All things considered, Maris was just as happy not to be on the receiving end of those head butts, or to have to control all that power as he danced around. He would have been quieter for her—the horses found her especially soothing—but any jolt right now wasn't fun.

MacNeil led Pleasure away from the trailer, the stallion's hooves almost soundless on the thick pad of pine needles and decomposing leaves that carpeted the forest floor. He tied the reins to a sapling and patted the animal's glossy neck. "Okay, you can come over now," he called to Maris. "Keep him happy while I reposition the trailer."

She took control of the stallion, calming him with her voice and hands. He was still hungry and thirsty, but he was such a curious, gregarious horse that his interest in the proceedings kept him occupied. Dean Pearsall had stopped the Oldsmobile farther back, positioning the car so its headlights lit the area. MacNeil got in the truck and put it in reverse, leaning out the open door to check his position as he backed the truck up to the trailer. He was good at it; it took some people forever to get the trailer hitch in the right position, but MacNeil did it on the first try. Pretty good for an FBI agent, Maris thought. He was a fed now, but he'd obviously spent a lot of time around horses in the past.

It was snowing a little more heavily now, the headlight beams catching the drifting flakes as they sifted through the bare branches of the hardwoods. The pines were beginning to acquire a dusting of white. MacNeil maneuvered the trailer around, threading it through the trees, repositioning it so that it directly faced the narrow trail they'd made and anyone coming down it wouldn't be able to see that Pleasure wasn't inside. There were high, narrow side windows in the trailer, but none in front.

As soon as the trailer was in position and MacNeil had unhooked the truck and pulled away, Pearsall went to work, squirming underneath the trailer and setting up a video camera so that it couldn't easily be seen but would still have a good angle on anyone approaching the trailer.

MacNeil turned to Maris. "While Dean's working, let's get Pleasure tucked away back in the woods." He checked the luminous hands on his watch. "We need to be out of here in five minutes, ten tops."

The trailer contained blankets that had been used to cover the mare who had been brought to Solomon Green the day before. Maris got the darkest one and spread it across Pleasure's broad back. He liked that, swaying his muscular rump as if he were doing the hootchie-cootchie, and blowing in the particular way he did when he was pleased. She laughed, the sound quiet and loving, as she reached up to hug his big neck. He lipped her hair, but gently, as if he'd somehow realized by the way she moved that she wasn't quite up to speed.

"This way." MacNeil's voice held an odd note as he handed a flashlight to Maris, then untied the reins and began leading Pleasure deeper into the trees. He curved his other arm around Maris, holding her close to his side as they walked. Between the oversize Kevlar vest and her thick down jacket, he couldn't feel *her,* so he slipped his hand under the coat, under the vest, resting it on the swell of her hip. "How are you feeling?" he asked as they picked their way through the dark woods, stepping over fallen limbs and evading bushes that clutched at their clothes.

"Okay." She smiled up at him, letting herself lean closer into the heat and strength of his big body. "I've had a concussion before, and though this one isn't any fun, I don't think it's as bad as the first one

The pain is going away faster, so I don't understand why I can't remember what happened."

Her bewilderment was plain, and his fingers tightened on her hip. "A different part of your brain is affected, I guess. And parts of your memory are already coming back, so by tomorrow you'll probably remember everything."

She hoped so; these blank holes in her life were unsettling. It was just a matter of a few hours now, as she regained partial memory of things that had happened both before and after she was hit, but she didn't like not knowing everything that had happened. She remembered driving with MacNeil, but why couldn't she remember arriving at the motel?

Only one way to find out what she wanted to know. "Did I undress myself?"

Glancing up, she saw him smile at the abrupt change of subject. His voice deepened, evidence of the way the memory affected him. "It was a joint effort."

Maybe she would have been embarrassed an hour ago, but not now. Instead she felt a sort of aroused contentment fill her at the thought of him pulling off his T-shirt and putting it on her, the soft cotton still warm from his body.

"Did you touch me?" The whispered words were like heated honey, flowing over him, telling him how much she liked the idea.

"No, you were too out of it." But he'd wanted to, he thought. God, how he'd wanted to. He helped her over a fallen tree, supporting her so that she wouldn't stumble, but he was remembering how she'd looked sitting on the side of the bed, wearing nothing but her panties, her eyes closing, her pale hair floating around her delicate, satiny shoulders. Her breasts were high, firm, small but deliciously round, her nipples like dark pink little crowns. His right hand clenched on the reins; his palm was actually aching to touch her now, to fill his hand with that cool, richly resilient flesh and warm it with his loving.

"Well, darn," she said sedately, and in the glow of the flashlight he saw the welcome in her night-dark eyes.

He inhaled deeply, reaching for control. They had no time for any delay, much less one that would last an hour. An hour? He gave a mental snort. Who was he kidding? He was so worked up that five minutes was more like it, and that was only if his self-control turned out to be a lot stronger than it felt right now.

"Later," he promised, his voice a rough growl of need. Later, when this was settled and his job done. Later, when he could take the time with her that he wanted to take, behind a locked door and with the telephone off the hook. Later, when she felt better, damn it, and wasn't dealing with a concussion. He figured it would be two days, at least, before her headache was gone—two long, hellish days.

He stopped and looked back. They had gone far enough that he could no longer see the headlights through the trees. A small hollow dipped just ahead, and he led Sole Pleasure into it. The hollow blocked the wind, and tall trees leaning overhead protected him from the light snow. "You'll be okay here for a couple of hours," he told the horse as he tied the reins to a low, sturdy branch. Pleasure would be able to move around some, and if there were any edible leaves or stray blades of grass, he would be able to graze within a small area.

"Be good," Maris admonished the horse, stroking his forehead. "We won't be gone long. Then we'll take you back to your big, comfortable stall, and you can have your favorite feed, and an apple for dessert." He blew softly, then bobbed his head up and down in agreement. She didn't know how many actual words he understood, but he definitely understood the love in her voice, and he knew she was telling him good stuff.

MacNeil took the flashlight from her hand and settled his arm around her again as they walked back to the truck. Pleasure neighed his disapproval of being left alone, but soon the trees blotted out the sound and there was only the rustle of their feet in the leaves.

"You know what to do," he said. "They won't follow you too closely on the highway, because they won't want to make you suspicious. Let them see where you leave the road, but then drive as fast as you can, to give yourself as much time as possible. They'll be able to follow the tracks. Pull up to the trailer, get out of the truck and get into the trees. Don't waste time, don't look back to see what I'm doing. Get into a protected place and stay there until either Dean or I come for you. If anyone else shows up, use that pistol."

"You need the vest more than I do." Worry gnawed at her. He was sending her out of harm's way, while he would be right in the middle of it, without protection.

"They might pull in before you're completely out of sight and get a shot off at you. The only way I'll let you do this is if you're wearing the vest."

There that stubborn streak was again, she thought. Streak? Ha! He was permeated with it. She was beginning to think that if she scratched his skin, stubbornness would ooze out instead of blood. Living with him was going to be interesting; as he'd noted, she was used to being the boss, and so was he. She looked forward to the fights—and to the making up.

Pearsall was waiting for them when they got back. "Everything's ready," he said. "There's a six-hour tape in the camera, and the battery pack is fully charged. Now, if we can just get back into position before the bad guys show up, we're set."

MacNeil nodded. "You leave first. We'll let you get out of sight before we follow. Radio if you see anything suspicious."

"Give me an extra minute so I can swing through the motel parking lot to make sure there aren't any new arrivals. Then I'll pull back and take up position." Pearsall got into the car and backed out, his headlights bobbing through the trees.

Darkness settled around them as they listened to the sound of the car fading in the distance. MacNeil opened the passenger door of the truck and put his hands on Maris's waist, lifting her onto the seat. In the darkness, his face was only a pale blur. "Whatever happens, make sure you stay safe," he growled, and bent his head to her.

His lips were cold, and firm. Maris wound her arms around his neck and opened her mouth to him as he deepened the kiss, slanting his head for better contact. His tongue wasn't cold at all, but hot and strong, and her entire body tightened with excitement as she leaned closer to him. It wasn't enough; with the pleasure came frustration. She swiveled on the seat to face him, parting her legs so that he stood between them, pressed hard against her as the kiss changed yet again, into something fierce with need.

It was their first kiss, but there was no tentativeness, no searching.

They already knew each other, had already made the inner adjustment to the hot ache of physical desire, and accepted the hunger. They were already lovers, though their bodies hadn't yet been joined. The pact had been made. Invisible strands of attraction had been pulling them together from the first, and the web was almost complete.

He tore his mouth away from hers, breathing hard, his breath fogging in the cold air. "No more," he said, the words strained. "Not now. I'm as hard as a rock already, and if we—" He broke off. "We have to go. Now."

"Have we given Dean enough time?"

"Hell, I don't know! All I know is that I'm about ten seconds away from pulling your jeans off, and if we don't go now, the whole plan is blown."

She didn't want to let him go. Her arms didn't want to release their hold on him, her thighs didn't want to loosen from around his hips. But she did it, forced herself to open her embrace, because she could feel the truth pushing against her.

In silence he stepped back, and she turned in the seat so that she faced forward. He closed the door, then walked stiffly around the truck to climb in under the steering wheel, a look of acute discomfort on his face.

She wasn't good for his sanity, he thought as he started the truck and put it in gear. She made him forget about the job and think only about sex. Not sex in general, but sex in particular. Sex with her. Again and again, holding that slim body beneath him until he was satisfied.

He tried to imagine being sated with her, and he couldn't. Alarm tingled through him. He tried to think of some of the other women he'd slept with over the years, but their names wouldn't come to mind, their faces eluded him, and there was no concrete memory of how any of them had felt. There was only her mouth, her breasts, her legs. Her voice, her body in his arms, her hair spread across the pillow. He could imagine her in the shower with him, her face across the table from him every morning, her clothes hanging beside his in the closet.

The most frightening thing was that it was so damn easy to imagine it all. The only thing that frightened him more was the thought that it might not happen, that he was actually using her in a setup where she could be hurt, despite all the pains he was taking to keep her safe.

They left the cover of the woods, and he eased the truck across the rutted ditch and onto the highway. No headlights appeared in either direction. Fat snowflakes swirled and danced in the beams of their own headlights, and the low clouds blocked any hint of the approaching dawn.

The radio remained silent, meaning Dean hadn't seen anything suspicious. After several minutes the lights of the motel sign came into view, and a few seconds after that they passed the Oldsmobile, pulled off on the side of the road and were facing back the way they'd come. It looked unoccupied, but Mac knew Dean was there, watching everything. No vehicle could approach the motel without being seen.

He pulled into the parking lot and backed into a slot, so that she could get out faster. He left the engine running, though he killed the lights. He turned to face her. "You know what to do. Do exactly that and nothing else. Understand?"

"Yes."

"All right. I'm going to get into the back of the truck now. If the fools start shooting early, hit the floorboards and stay there."

"Yes, sir," she said, this time with a hint of dryness.

He paused with his hand on the door handle. He looked at her and muttered something under his breath. Then she was in his arms again, and his mouth was hard, urgent, as he kissed her. He let her go as abruptly as he'd grabbed her, and got out of the truck. Without another word, he closed the door, then vaulted lightly into the truck bed, where he lay down out of sight and waited for a killer to appear.

Chapter 8

The motel was located where a small side road entered the main highway. The highway ran in front of the motel, the secondary road along the right side. Dean had checked out the little road as soon as he arrived and found that it wandered aimlessly through the rural area. No one looking for them was likely to arrive by that route, because it went nowhere and took its time getting there. The Stonichers and/or their hired killer would be on the highway, checking motels, following the faint but deliberate trail Mac had left. The plan was for Maris to let their pursuers catch a glimpse of her as she drove around the back of the motel and onto the secondary road. She would turn left, then right, onto the highway. They would notice immediately that she wasn't pulling the horse trailer, so instead of trying to cut her off, they would hang back and follow her, expecting her to lead them to Sole Pleasure.

At least Mac hoped that was how it worked. If Yu was the only one following them, that was how it would go down. Yu was a professional; he would keep his head. If anyone else was with him, the unpredictability factor shot sky-high.

It was cold in the back of the truck. He had forgotten to get any blankets to cover himself, and the snow was still falling. Mac huddled deeper into his coat and tried to be thankful he was out of the wind. It wasn't working.

The minutes dragged by, drawn out agonizingly by his tension as he waited. Dawn finally began to penetrate the cloud cover, the darkness fading to a deep gray, though true daylight was at least an hour away. Traffic would begin picking up soon, making it difficult for Dean to spot their tail. People would begin leaving the motel, complicating the traffic pattern even more. And better light would make it more difficult for Maris to hide in the woods.

"Come on, come on," he muttered. Had he made the trail *too* difficult?

Right on cue, the radio clicked. Mac keyed it once in reply, then gave a single rap on the back of the cab to alert Maris, who had shifted into position behind the wheel.

The radio clicked again, twice this time. Quickly he rapped twice on the cab. Maris put the truck into gear and eased out of the parking slot. She was turning the corner behind the motel when headlights flashed across the cab as a vehicle pulled into the lot, and Mac knew the lure had been cast. In a few seconds they would know if the bait had been taken.

Maris kept the truck at an even pace. Her instinct was to hurry, but she didn't want whoever was following them to know they'd been spotted. The car hadn't turned the corner behind them by the time she pulled onto the secondary road, so if it *was* them, they were hanging back, not wanting her to spot them.

She stopped at the stop sign, then turned right onto the highway. Watching her rearview mirror as she turned, she saw the car easing out from behind the motel. Its lights were off now, and its gray color made it difficult to spot in the faint light; she wouldn't have noticed it at all if she hadn't been looking for it.

They were driving Ronald's gray Cadillac. Maris had only seen it once or twice, because she usually dealt with Joan, who drove a white BMW. The driveway wasn't visible from the stables, and she seldom paid attention to the comings and goings at the big house. All that interested her was at the stables.

Still, she wondered that they would drive one of their personal cars at all, until she realized that it didn't matter. Sole Pleasure was their horse, and no crime had been committed. If she had called the police, it would have been their word against hers that a crime had even been attempted, and no one in the world would believe the Stonichers were willing to kill a horse worth over twenty million dollars.

Dean's Oldsmobile was nowhere in sight. Maris hoped she was giving him the time he needed to drive the car deep enough into the woods that it couldn't be seen and to work his way into position on foot.

Watching the mirror, she saw the Cadillac turn onto the highway behind her. Without its headlights on, and with the swirling snow cutting visibility, she could barely make out the gray bulk. They would be able to see her much better than she could see them, though, because her lights were on; that was why they were hanging back so far, because they were unable to judge how visible they themselves were.

Their caution was working for her and against them. The distance would give her a few extra seconds to get out of the truck and hide, a few seconds longer for Dean to get set, a few seconds longer that Mac was safe. She tried not to think of him lying on the cold metal bed, unprotected from any stray bullets except by a thin sheet of metal that wouldn't even slow down a lead slug.

It was only a few miles to the place where she would leave the road and drive into the woods. A couple of times the snow became so heavy that she couldn't see the Cadillac behind her. The white flakes were beginning to dust the ground, but it was a dry, fluffy snow that swirled up with every breath of wind, and the passage of the truck blew it off the highway.

She maintained a steady speed, assuming they could see her, even though she couldn't see the Cadillac. She couldn't do anything that would make them suspicious. Finally she passed the mile marker that told her she was close, and she began braking, looking for the tire ruts where they'd driven before. *There.* She steered the truck off the highway, bouncing across the ditch faster than, for the sake of her head, she wanted to, but she didn't want to go any slower than she already was. Now that they had seen her leave the highway, she wanted to go as fast as she could, to gain a few more of those precious seconds.

Her headache, which had lessened but never disappeared, increased in severity with each bounce. She ignored it, gritting her teeth against the pain, concentrating on steering the truck on the narrow, winding path MacNeil had already blazed through the trees. She couldn't begin to imagine how difficult it must have been to do this with the trailer in tow, but it was a testament to both his stubbornness and skill that he had.

The Cadillac wouldn't be able to take the bumps and holes as fast as the truck did; it was too low to the ground. More seconds gained.

A bare limb scraped over the windshield, then her headlights caught the dark bulk of the trailer, almost concealed among the trees. Now. She parked the truck in the exact position MacNeil had decreed, killed the lights so the glare wouldn't blind the camera hidden under the trailer, then slipped out the door and walked swiftly to the trailer and then beyond it. She cut sharply to the left, stepping in places where the snow hadn't sifted down. She left no tracks as she removed herself from the scene so he could do his job without worrying about her.

She'd caught movement in her peripheral vision as she walked away, a big, dark shape silently rolling over the side of the truck bed to conceal himself behind one of the tires. At least he would have *some* protection, she thought, trying to console herself with that. His mind might be easier now, but hers certainly wasn't. He needed the vest she was wearing; she would never forgive herself if he was killed because she'd agreed to take his vest. It would have been better to remove herself entirely, even if it meant they wouldn't be able to get any solid evidence against the Stonichers. The FBI would get another crack at Randy Yu, but she would never find another MacNeil.

She'd gone far enough. She stopped, her back against a big oak. Snowflakes drifted silently down in the gray dawn, settling in a lacy cap on her unprotected head. She leaned her aching head against the tree and closed her eyes, listening, waiting, her breath almost halted, her heart barely beating, waiting.

Mac waited, his eyes never leaving the rutted trail. They might drive right up to the truck, but if Yu was in charge, they would probably get out of the car and come the rest of the way on foot. He and Dean were prepared for both circumstances. The underbrush was thick; if they tried to force their way through it, they would make a lot of noise. The best thing to do was to walk up the trail, staying close to the edges. Maris had parked the truck so that they could bypass it only on the driver's side; the tailgate on the passenger side was right up against the bushes. Anyone coming along that trail would be funneled into the camera's view and duly recorded on tape.

After what seemed an interminable length of time, he heard a twig snap. He didn't move. His position, crouched by the right front tire, was secure; he couldn't be seen until they walked in front of the truck, but by then they would have looked into the cab and seen it was empty, and wouldn't pay any more attention to the truck. They would be looking instead at the trailer, and at Maris's small footprints in the thin layer of snow, leading right up to it.

There were other sounds now, rustles from careless feet, more than one pair; the brushing sounds of clothing, the harshness of someone who was slightly winded trying to regulate their breathing. They were close, very close.

The footsteps stopped. "She isn't in the truck." The whisper was barely audible, sexless.

"Look! Her footprints go right up to the trailer." It was another whisper, excitement making it louder than the first.

"Shut...up." The two words were hissed between clenched teeth, as if they had already been said more than once.

"Don't tell me to shut up. We have her cornered. What are you waiting for?"

Though still whispering, the speaker's voice was so forceful that it was almost as audible as if he—or she—had spoken aloud. The mike might have caught it, Mac thought. With enhanced sound-extraction techniques, which the Bureau had, he was certain the words were now on tape. The only problem was, they hadn't exactly been damning.

"You hired me to do a job. Now stay out of my way and let me do it." There was fury evident now, in both words and tone.

"You're the one who bungled it the first time, so don't act as if you're Mr. Infallible. If you'd been half as smart as you seem to think you are, the horse would already be dead and Maris Mackenzie wouldn't suspect a thing. I didn't bargain on murder when I hired you.''

That should do it, Mac thought with grim satisfaction. They had just talked themselves into a prison sentence.

He tightened the muscles in his legs, preparing to step out and identify himself, pistol trained and ready. A crashing, thudding noise behind him made him freeze in place. He looked over his shoulder and almost groaned aloud. A big, black, graceful horse was prancing through the trees toward them, proudly shaking his head as if wanting them to admire his cleverness in getting free.

"There he is! Shoot him!" It was a shout. Pleasure's unexpected appearance had started them out of caution. Almost instantaneously there was the sharp crack of a shot, and bark exploded from the tree just behind the horse.

Damn amateurs! He silently cursed. Pleasure was behind him; if he stood up now, he would be looking straight down the barrel, caught between the shooter and the target. He couldn't do anything but wait for the next shot to hit the beautiful, friendly stallion, who had evidently caught their scent and pulled free so he could join the party.

Dean realized Mac's predicament and stepped from concealment, pistol braced in both hands. "FBI! Drop your weapons on the ground—*now*.''

Mac surged upward, bracing his arms across the hood of the truck. He saw Randy Yu, his hands already reaching upward as his pistol thudded to the ground. You could always trust a professional to know how to do things. But Joan Stonicher was startled by Mac's sudden movement, and she wheeled toward him, her eyes wide with panic and rage. She froze, the pistol in her hand and her finger on the trigger.

"Ease off, lady," Mac said softly. "Don't do anything stupid. If I don't get you, my partner will. Just take your finger off the trigger and let the gun drop. That's all you have to do, and we'll all be okay.''

She didn't move. From the excellent viewpoint he had, Mac could see her finger trembling.

"Do as he says," Randy Yu said wearily. The two agents had them caught in an excellent cross field. There was nothing they could do, and no sense in making things worse.

Pleasure had shied at the noise of the shot, neighing his alarm, but his life had been too secure for him to panic. He trotted closer, his scooped nostrils flaring as he examined their familiar scents, searching for the special one he could detect. He came straight for Mac.

Joan's eyes left Mac and fastened on the horse. He saw the exact instant when her control shattered, saw her pupils contract and her hand jerk.

A shrill whistle shattered the air a split second before the shot.

A lot of things happened simultaneously. Dean shouted. Randy Yu dropped to the ground, his hands covering his head. Pleasure screamed in pain, rearing. Joan's hand jerked again, back toward Mac.

And there was another whistle, this one earsplitting.

Maris stepped from behind a tree, her black eyes glittering with rage. The pistol was in her hand, trained on Joan. Joan wheeled back toward this new threat, and without hesitation Mac fired.

Chapter 9

He was mad enough to murder her, Maris thought.

She was still so enraged herself that it didn't matter. Fury burned through her. It was all she could do to keep from dismantling Joan Stonicher on the spot, and only the knowledge that Pleasure needed her kept her even remotely under control.

The woods were swarming with people, with medics and deputies and highway patrol officers, with onlookers, even some reporters already there. Pleasure was accustomed to crowds, but he'd never before been shot, and pain and shock were making him unruly. He'd wheeled at Maris's whistle, and his lightning reflexes had saved his life; Joan's bullet had gouged a deep furrow in his chest, tearing the muscle at an angle but not penetrating any internal organs. Now it took all of Maris's skill to keep him calm so she could stop the bleeding; he kept moving restlessly in circles, bumping her, trying to pay attention to her softly crooning voice but distracted by the pain.

Her head was throbbing, both from Pleasure's skittishness and from her own desperate run through the woods. She'd heard him moving through the trees, and in a flash she'd known exactly what had happened, what he would do. How he'd gotten free didn't matter; he had heard and smelled them, and pranced happily to greet them, sure of his welcome. She'd known he would catch her scent on MacNeil's clothes and go straight to him. It had been a toss-up which of them would be shot first, MacNeil or Pleasure. All she could do was try to get there in time to draw the horse's attention, as well as everyone else's.

For one awful, hellish moment, when Pleasure screamed and she saw Joan swing back toward MacNeil, she'd thought she'd lost everything. She had stepped out from the trees, moving in what felt like slow motion. She couldn't hear anything then, not even Pleasure; she hadn't been able to see anything except Joan, her vision narrowing to a tunnel with her target as the focus. She hadn't been aware of whistling again, or of taking the pistol from her pocket, but the weapon had been in her hand and her finger had been smoothly tightening on the trigger when Joan jerked yet again, panicked, this time aiming at Maris. That was when Mac had shot her. At such close range, just across the hood of the truck, his aim had been perfect. The bullet had shattered her upper arm.

Joan would probably never have use of that arm again, Maris thought dispassionately. She couldn't bring herself to care.

The entire scene had been recorded, complete with audio. The camera had playback capability and Dean had obliged the sheriff by playing the tape for him. Both Yu and Joan were nailed, and Yu, being the professional he was, was currently bargaining for all he was worth. He was willing to carry others down with him if it would lighten his sentence.

It had stopped snowing, though the day hadn't gotten any warmer. Her hands were icy, but she couldn't leave Pleasure to warm them. Blood glistened on his black chest and down his legs, staining his white stocking, splattering on the snow-frosted leaves and on Maris. She whispered to him, controlling him mostly with her voice, crooning reassurance and love to him while she held his bridle in one hand and with the other held some gauze the medics had given her to the wound on his chest. She had asked a deputy to contact a vet, but as yet no one had shown up.

Yu could have seen to the horse, but he hadn't offered, and Maris wouldn't have trusted him, anyway. It was he who had hit her on the head. As soon as she saw him again she had remembered that much, remembered his upraised arm, the cold, remorseless expression in his dark eyes. Other memories were still vague, and there were still blank spots, but they were gradually filling in.

She must have gone to the big house to see Joan about something. She didn't know why, but she remembered standing with her hand raised to knock, and freezing as Joan's voice filtered through the door.

"Randy's going to do it tonight. While everyone's eating will be a good time. I told him we couldn't wait any longer, the syndicates are pushing for a decision."

"Damn, I hate this," Ronald Stonicher had said. "Poor Pleasure's been a good horse. Are you certain the drug won't be detected?"

"Randy says it won't, and it's his can on the line," Joan had coolly replied.

Maris had backed away, so angry she could barely contain herself. Her first concern had been for Pleasure. It was the time when the stable hands would either be eating or have gone home for the night. She couldn't delay a moment.

Her next memory was of running down the aisle to his stall. She must have surprised Randy Yu there, though she didn't remember actually coming up on him. She remembered enough to testify, though, even if she never remembered anything else, and assuming her testimony was needed. The tape was solid evidence.

Another vehicle joined the tangle, and a roly-poly man in his late fifties, sporting a crew cut, got out of a battered pickup truck. He trudged wearily toward Maris, clutching a big black bag in his hand. Finally, the vet, she thought. Dark circles under his eyes told her that he'd probably been up late, possibly all night, with an ailing animal.

Tired or not, he knew horses. He stopped, taking in Pleasure's magnificent lines, the star on his forehead, the bloodstained white stocking. "That's Sole Pleasure," he said in astonishment.

"Yes, and he's been shot," Maris said tersely. Her head was throbbing; even her eyeballs ached. If Pleasure didn't settle down soon, her head would likely explode. "No internal organs affected, but some chest muscle torn. He won't settle down and let the bleeding stop."

"Let's take care of that problem, first off. I'm George Norton, the vet hereabouts." He was working as he spoke, setting down the bag and opening it. He prepared a hypodermic and stepped forward, smoothly injecting the sedative into one of the bulging veins in Pleasure's neck. The stallion danced nervously, his shoulder shoving her once again. She clenched her teeth, enduring.

"He'll quiet down in a minute." The vet gave her a sharp glance as he peeled away the blood-soaked gauze she'd been holding to the wound. "No offense, but even with the blood, the horse looks in better shape than you do. Are you all right?"

"Concussion."

"Then for God's sake stop letting him bump you around like that," he said sharply. "Sit down somewhere before you fall down."

Even in the midst of everything that was going on, as the medics readied Joan for transport, Mac somehow heard the vet. All of a sudden he was there, looming behind her, reaching over her shoulder for Pleasure's bridle. "I'll hold him." The words sounded as if he were spitting them out one at a time, like bullets. "Sit down."

"I—" She'd started to say "I think I will," but she didn't have a chance to finish the sentence.

He assumed she was about to mount an argument, and barked out one word. *"Sit!"*

"I wasn't going to argue," she snapped back. What did he think she was, a dog? Sit, indeed. She felt more like lying down.

She decided to do just that. Pleasure was going to be all right; as soon as he quieted and let the vet do his work, the bleeding would stop. The torn muscle would have to be stitched, antibiotics administered, a bandage secured, but the horse would heal. Even though the truck and trailer were stolen, under the circumstances she couldn't imagine that there would be any problem with using them to transport Pleasure back to Solomon Green. Until the vet was finished and Pleasure was loaded in the trailer, she intended to stretch out on the truck seat.

Wearily she climbed into the cab. The keys were still in the ignition, so she started the engine and turned on the heater. She took off her coat, removed the Kevlar vest and placed it in the floorboards, then lay down on the seat and pulled the coat over her.

She almost cried with relief as the pain immediately began easing now that she was still. She closed her eyes, letting the tension drain out of her, along with the terror and absolute rage. She might have killed Joan. If the woman had shot Mac, she would have done it. Enveloped in that strange vacuum of despair and rage, she had been going for a head shot. She hadn't even thought about Pleasure, not in that awful moment when Joan turned on Mac. She was glad she hadn't had to pull the trigger, but she knew she would have. Knowing her own fiercely protective nature was one thing, but this was the first time she had been faced with the true extent of it. The jolt of self-knowledge was searing.

Mac had already faced this; it was in his eyes. She had seen it in her father, in her brothers, the willingness to do what was necessary to protect those they loved and those who were weaker. It wasn't easy. It was gut-wrenching, and those who were willing to stand on the front lines paid for it in a thousand little ways she was only beginning to understand. She hadn't had to take that final, irrevocable step, but she knew how close it had been.

Her mother also had that willingness, and a couple of her sisters-in-law. Valiant Mary, intrepid Caroline, sweet Barrie. They had each, in different circumstances, faced death and seen the bottom line. They would understand the wrenching she felt. Well, maybe Caroline wouldn't. Caroline was so utterly straightforward, so focused, that Joe had once compared her to a guided missile.

The door by her head was wrenched open, and cold air poured in. "Maris! Wake up!" Mac barked, his voice right over her. His hand closed on her shoulder as if he intended to shake her.

"I am awake," she said, without opening her eyes. "The headache's better, now that I'm still. How much longer will it be before I can take Pleasure back?"

"*You* aren't taking him anywhere. You're going to a hospital to be checked out."

"We can't just leave him here."

"I've arranged for him to be driven back."

She could hear the effort he was making to be calm; it was evident in his careful tone.

"Are things about wrapped up here?"

"Close enough that I can leave it with Dean and take you to a hospital."

He wouldn't let it go until a doctor had told him she was all right, Maris realized, and with a sigh she opened her eyes and sat up. She understood. If their situations were reversed, she would be doing the same thing.

"All right," she said, slipping on her coat. She turned off the ignition and picked up the Kevlar vest. "I'm ready."

Her willingness scared him. She saw his eyes darken, saw his jaw clench. "I'll be okay," she said softly, touching his hand. "I'm going because I know you're worried, and I don't want you to be."

His expression changed, something achingly tender moving in his eyes. Gently he scooped her into his arms and lifted her from the truck.

Dean had brought the Oldsmobile out of its hiding place. Mac carried her to it and deposited her on the front seat as carefully as if she were made of the most fragile crystal. He got in on the driver's side and started the car; the milling crowd in front of them parted, allowing them through. She saw Pleasure, standing quietly now. The bandage was in place, and the wild look was gone from his eyes. He was watching the activity with his characteristic friendly curiosity.

As they drove by, Dean lifted his hand to wave. "What about Dean?" Maris asked.

"He'll get transport. It isn't a problem."

She paused. "What about you? When do you leave? Your job here is finished, isn't it?" She didn't intend to let him get away, but she wasn't sure exactly how much he understood of their situation.

"It's finished." The words were clipped. The look he gave her was one of restrained violence. "I'll have to do the paperwork, tie up some loose ends. I may have to leave tonight, tomorrow at the latest, but I'll be back, damn it!"

"You don't sound happy about it," she observed.

"Happy? You expect me to be *happy?*" His jaw clenched. "You didn't obey orders. You stepped right out into the open, instead of staying hidden the way you were supposed to. That idiot woman could have killed you!"

"I was wearing the vest." She pointed that out rather mildly, she thought.

"The damn vest only improves the odds, it isn't a guarantee! The issue here is that you didn't follow the plan. You risked your life for that damn horse! I didn't want him hurt, either, but—"

"It wasn't for Pleasure," she said, interrupting him. "It was for you." She looked out the window at the snow-dusted pastures they were passing.

It was quiet in the car for a moment.

"Me?" He was using that careful tone again.

"You. I knew he'd go straight to you, that he'd catch my scent on your clothes. At the very least he would distract you, bump you with his head. It was even possible he'd give away your position."

Mac was silent, absorbing the shock of the realization that she was willing to risk her own life to protect his. He did the same thing on a fairly regular basis, but it was his job to take risks and protect others. But he'd never before felt the terror he'd known when he saw Maris draw Joan's attention, and he hoped he never felt it again.

"I love you," she said quietly.

Damn. Sighing inwardly, Mac kissed his bachelorhood goodbye. Her courage stunned him, humbled him. No other woman he'd known would have put herself on the line the way Maris had done, both physically and emotionally. She didn't play games, didn't jockey for control. She simply knew, and accepted; he'd seen it in the soft depths of her black eyes, an instinctive inner knowledge that few people ever achieved. If he didn't snatch her up, it would be the biggest mistake of his life.

Mac didn't believe in making mistakes.

"How long does it take to get married in Kentucky?" he asked abruptly. "If we can't get it done tomorrow, we'll go to Las Vegas—assuming the doctor says you're all right."

He hadn't said he loved her, but she knew he did. She sat back, pleased with the situation. "I'm all right," she said, completely confident.

Chapter 10

"Getting married in Las Vegas seems to be a tradition in my family," she mused the next day as her new husband ushered her into their suite. "Two of my brothers have done it."

"Two? How many brothers do you have?"

"Five. All of them older." She smiled sweetly at him over her shoulder as she walked to the window to look out at the blazing red sunset. It was odd how completely connected to him she felt, when they hadn't had time to talk much, to share the details of their lives. Events had swept them along like gulls before a hurricane.

The emergency room doctor had pronounced her concussion mild and told her to take it easy for a day or so. He had agreed with her that, if she had been going to lapse into a coma, she would already have done so. Over the course of the day her memory had completely returned, filling in the blank spots, so she knew she was okay.

Reassured, Mac had driven her back to Solomon Green and turned his attention to the job, ruthlessly clearing up details and paperwork so he could concentrate on the business of getting married. While she slept, he and Dean had worked. He had arranged for time off, checked into the details of marriage in Kentucky, decided it couldn't be done fast enough to suit him and booked them on a flight to Las Vegas.

Ronald Stonicher had been arrested for conspiracy to commit fraud;

he'd had no idea his wife and Randy Yu planned to kill Maris, too, and was shattered by what had happened. Joan had undergone surgery on her arm, and according to the surgeon the nerve and tissue damage was extensive; he expected her to regain some use of the arm, but she would never again be able to write with her right hand, or eat, do or anything else requiring precise movements. Randy was spilling his guts to the feds, implicating a lot of people in the horse world in the scheme to kill off horses for the insurance money. He hadn't been charged with killing the sixteen-year-old boy. Evidently he had some information on it, though, and was holding that in reserve to bargain for an even bigger break on the charges.

Maris had called her mother, briefly filled her in on what had happened and told her she was getting married. "Have fun, baby," Mary had told her daughter. "You know your father will want to walk you down the aisle, so we'll plan another wedding for Christmas. That gives me three weeks. There shouldn't be any problem."

Most people would have screamed in panic at the thought of organizing a wedding in three weeks. Mary saw no problem, and from experience Maris knew that while other people might have problems accomplishing what her mother wanted, in the end she would have her way.

Mac had phoned his family, which consisted of his mother, step-father and two half-sisters. They would be joining the Mackenzies in Wyoming for the wedding at Christmas.

During the ceremony an hour before, Maris had learned that her husband's full name was William Alexander MacNeil. "A few people call me Will," he told her afterward, when she mentioned how difficult it was for her to think of him as Alex. "Most people call me Mac." Since in her mind she had already begun shortening MacNeil to Mac, that suited her fine.

"*Five* older brothers?" Mac asked now, walking up behind her and slipping his arm around her waist. He bent his head to nuzzle her pale hair.

"Five. Plus twelve nephews and one niece."

He chuckled. "Holidays must be lively."

"*Riotous* would be a better word. Wait until you see."

He turned her in his arms. "What I can't wait to see is my wife, in bed with me."

She clung to his neck as he lifted her and carried her into the bedroom. His mouth closed on hers as he lowered her to the bed, and the aching passion that had subsided but never vanished surged back at full force. He crushed her into the mattress in his need, but at the same time he tried not to be rough as he eased her out of her clothes.

She squirmed against him, pulling at his clothes, the roughness of the fabric against her nakedness driving her crazy. Mac drew back, staring down at her delicate body with open hunger. He was breathing hard, obviously struggling for control, his eyes hard and glittering with lust. Gently he shaped her breasts with his hand, each in turn, rubbing his thumb over her nipples and bringing them to aching hardness.

"Hurry," she whispered, reaching for his belt.

He laughed a little, though there was no humor in the sound; instead, it was raw with need. He shed his clothes, kicking them away, and rolled on top of her. A groan of deep satisfaction tore from her throat as his heavy weight settled on her, and she opened her legs to cradle him close. She wanted him with a ferocity that would brook no delay, wanted him as she had never wanted or needed anything else in her life.

Mac positioned himself, then framed her face with his hands and kissed her as he slowly pushed into her body. Her flesh resisted, and she gasped, surprised by the painful difficulty. She had expected all her riding to have eased the way, but the lack of a barrier had in no way prepared her for his size.

He lifted his mouth, staring down at her as realization dawned. He didn't say anything, didn't ask any questions, but something hot and primitive flared deep in his gaze. As gently as possible, he completed his penetration, and when he was fully home inside her he waited, waited until the tension left her and her body softened beneath him, around him. Then he began moving, a slight rocking at first that did no more than nudge him back and forth, but enough to make her gasp again, this time with sensual urgency, and lift herself to him.

He took exquisite care with her, restraining the power of his thrusts, maintaining a slow, easy pace even when anticipation clawed at him, making him groan aloud with each movement. She clung to him, desperately searching for her own ease, trying to take him as deep inside her as possible, because instinct led her to that satisfaction. She cried out, overwhelmed by the sheer glory of this dance and struggle they shared, by the generosity of his loving.

She surged upward, unable to bear it a moment longer, and everything inside her shattered with a burst of pleasure so intense that she lost herself, sucked down in the whirlpool of sensation, a mindless creature knowing only the feel of his body, and hers. And she felt him join her, convulsing, thrusting, hotly emptying.

He cradled her afterward, stroking her with shaking hands as if to reassure himself she was real, that both of them were still whole.

"How did this happen?" he asked roughly. He tilted her chin so he could look into her face, and she saw that the glitter in his eyes was wetness now, not lust. "How could I love you so much, so fast? What kind of magic did you use?"

Tears burned her own eyes. "I just loved you," she said, the words simple. "That's all. I just loved you."

The mountain was wreathed with snow, and her heart lifted when she saw it. "There," she said, pointing. "That's Mackenzie's Mountain."

Mac stared with interest at the massive bulk. He'd never known anyone before who owned an entire mountain, and he wondered about the people, and the way of life, that had nurtured this magical creature beside him. In the two days they had been married, he had come to wonder how he'd ever existed without her. Loving her was like becoming whole, when he hadn't even known anything was missing. She was so delicate and fairylike, with her pale hair streaming over her shoulders and her great black eyes that held all the knowledge of centuries of women, but he'd learned that she was strong, and that the heart of a lion beat beneath her lovely breasts.

His *wife!* The unexpected marvelousness of it kept waking him in the middle of the night to look at her, to wonder at how fast it had happened. Only three days before, she had awakened in his arms and politely said, "I'm sorry, but I don't remember your name," and the realization that she'd been hurt had jarred him down to his toes. Only three days, and yet now he couldn't imagine sleeping without her, or waking without seeing her sleepy urchin's grin as she curled into his arms.

He had only five days off, so they had to make the best of it. Yesterday they had made a fast trip to San Antonio, where he had introduced her to his family. Both of his sisters had arrived with their broods of kids, three each, husbands in tow, but after the crowd Maris was accustomed to, she hadn't turned a hair at any of it. His mother had been absolutely thrilled that he'd married at last, thrilled at the prospect of a Christmas wedding on top of a snow-covered mountain in Wyoming. Having gotten the telephone number from Maris, her mother had already called his mother, and they'd evidently become fast friends, judging from the number of times his mother referred to what Mary had said.

Today they were in Wyoming, and Mac wondered why he was getting a tight feeling in the pit of his stomach. "Tell me about your brothers," he murmured. "All five of them." He knew something about older brothers, being one himself.

She smiled, her eyes going soft. "Well, let's see. My oldest brother, Joe, is a general in the air force—on the Joint Chiefs of Staff, as a matter of fact. His wife, Caroline, has doctoral degrees in physics and computer science, and they have five sons.

"My next-oldest brother, Mike, owns one of the largest cattle ranches in the state. He and Shea have two sons.

"Next is Josh. He was a navy fighter pilot, aircraft carrier, until a crash stiffened his knee and the navy grounded him. Now he's a civilian test pilot. His wife, Loren, is an orthopedic surgeon. They have three sons."

"Do any of your brothers have anything but sons?" Mac asked, fascinated by the recital, and growing more worried by the minute. He tried to focus on the mundane. He thought he remembered Maris saying she had a niece, but perhaps he'd been mistaken.

"Zane has a daughter." There was a different note in Maris's voice and he raised his eyebrows in inquiry, but she ignored him. "He and Barrie also have twin sons, two months old. Zane was a Navy SEAL. Barrie's an ambassador's daughter."

A SEAL. He wondered how much worse this could get.

"Then there's Chance. He and Zane might as well be twins. They're the same age, and I think their brains are linked. Chance was in Naval Intelligence. He isn't married." She deliberately didn't mention what Zane and Chance did now, because it seemed safer not to.

"I wonder," Mac murmured to himself as he steered their rented four-wheel-drive up the mountain, "why I expected you to have a normal family."

She lifted delicate brows at him. "You're a special agent with the FBI," she pointed out. "There isn't one of those standing on every street corner, you know."

"Yeah, but my *family* is normal."

"Well, so is mine. We're just overachievers." Her smile turned into a grin, the urchin's grin that had laced itself around his heart and tightened the bonds every time he saw it. He stopped the Jeep in the middle of the road and reached for her. His kiss was hard, urgent with hunger. Her eyes were slumberous when he released her. "What was that for?" she murmured, her hand curling around his neck.

"Because I love you." He wanted to tell her one last time, in case he didn't survive the coming confrontation. She might think her family would welcome him with open arms, but he had a much better understanding of the male psyche and he knew better. He put the Jeep in gear again, and they resumed their drive up the snow-covered road.

When they topped the crest and saw the big ranch house sprawling in front of them, Maris said happily, "Oh, good, everyone's here," and Mac knew he was a dead man. Never mind that he'd married her before sleeping with her; he was an unknown quantity, and he was making love to their darling every night. She was the only daughter, the *baby,* for God's sake. He understood. If he lived, and he and Maris ever had a daughter, there was no way in hell he was going to let some horny teenage boy anywhere near his little girl.

He looked at the array of vehicles parked in front of the house, enough vehicles to form a good parade, and wondered if they would give chase if he turned around and headed back down the mountain.

Well, it had to be done. Resigned, he parked the Jeep and came around to open the door for Maris, clasping his hands around her narrow waist and lifting her to the ground. She took his hand and led him up the steps, all but running in her eagerness.

They stepped into warmth, into noise, into confusion. A very small person wearing red overalls suddenly exploded from the crowd, racing forward on chubby legs and shrieking, "Marwee, Marwee," at the top of her lungs. Maris laughed and dropped to her knees, holding out her arms in time to catch the tiny tornado as she launched herself forward. Mac looked down at the little girl, not much more than a baby, and fell in love. He lost his heart. It was that simple.

She was beautiful. She was perfect, from the silky black hair on her round little head to her crystal-blue eyes, dimpled cheeks, rosebud mouth and dainty, dimpled hands. She was so small she was like a doll, and his arms ached to hold her. Little kids and babies had never affected him like this before, and it shook him.

"This is Nick," Maris said, rising to her feet with her niece in her arms. "She's the one and only granddaughter."

Nick reached out a tiny hand and poked him in the chest, in a movement so exactly like Maris's that Mac couldn't help grinning. "Who dat?" the little angel asked.

"This is Mac," Maris said, and kissed the soft, chubby cheek. Nick solemnly regarded him for a moment, then stretched out her arms in the manner of someone who is absolutely sure of their welcome. Automatically he reached out and took her, sighing with pleasure as the little body nestled against his chest.

Mac became aware of a spreading silence in the room, of what looked like an entire football team of big men getting to their feet, menace in every movement, in the hard faces turned toward him.

Maris looked at them, her face radiant, and he saw her eyes widen with surprise at their militant stances.

He eyed the competition. His father-in-law had iron gray hair and the black eyes Maris had inherited, and looked as if he ate nails for breakfast. His brothers-in-law looked just as lethal. Expertly Mac assessed each one, trying to pick out the most dangerous one. They all looked like bad asses. The one with the graying temples and the laser blue eyes, that would be the general, and damn if he didn't look as if he went into combat every day. *That* one would be the rancher, whipcord lean, iron hard, a man who faced down Mother Nature every day. The test pilot...let's see, that would be the one standing with his feet apart in the instinctive cocky stance of someone who cooly gambled with death and never blinked an eye.

Then Mac's gaze met a pair of deadly, icy eyes. *That one,* he thought. That was the most dangerous one, the one with the quiet face and eyes like blue-gray frost. That one. He would bet a year's pay that was the SEAL. But the one who moved up to stand beside him looked just as lethal, despite the almost unearthly handsomeness of his face. That would be the one in naval intelligence.

He was in big trouble. Instinctively he moved, depositing Nick in Maris's arms and stepping in front of them both, shielding them with his body.

Six pairs of fierce eyes noted the action.

Maris peeked around his shoulder, assessing the situation. *"Mother!"* she called urgently, stressing both syllables as she brought in reinforcements.

"Maris!" There was utter delight in the soft voice that came from what Mac assumed was the kitchen, the cry followed by light, fast footsteps. A small, delicate woman, no bigger than Maris and with the same exquisite, translucent skin, burst into the room. She was laughing as she grabbed her daughter, hugging her and doing the same to him, even though he stood rigidly, not daring to take his eyes off the threat looming in front of them like a wall.

"Mom," Maris said, directing her mother's attention across the room. "What's wrong with them?"

Mary took one look at her husband and sons and put her hands on her hips. "Stop that right now," she ordered. "I refuse to have this, do you hear?"

Her voice was sweetly Southern, as light as a breeze, but Wolf Mackenzie's black eyes flickered to her. "We just want to know a little about him," he said in a voice as deep and dark as thunder.

"Maris chose him," Mary replied firmly. "What else could you possibly need to know?"

"A lot," the one with the quiet, lethal eyes said. "This happened too fast."

"Zane Mackenzie!" a pretty redhead exclaimed, stepping out of the kitchen and eyeing him in amazement. "I can't believe you said that! We got married after knowing each other for *one day!*" She crossed the no-man's-land between the two battle lines, hugged Maris and turned to glare at her husband.

So he'd been right, Mac thought. That was the SEAL. It would look good on his tombstone: He Was Right.

"This is different," said the general, a perfect clone of Wolf Mackenzie except for his light blue eyes. He, too, looked as if nails were a regular part of his diet.

"Different, how?" asked a crisp voice, and a stylish blonde stepped out of the kitchen. She pinned a sharp green gaze on the six men. "You're all suffering from an overdose of testosterone. The main symptom is an inability to think." Marching forward, she aligned herself on Mac's other side. Something that was both heated and amused lit the general's eyes as he looked at his wife.

Another bruiser, the test pilot, said, "Maris is—"

"A grown woman," another feminine voice said, interrupting. A tall, curvy woman with chestnut hair and serene blue eyes took up a position beside the blonde. "Hi, I'm Loren," she said to Mac. "The one who just spoke is Josh, my husband, who usually exhibits better sense."

"And I'm Shea, Mike's wife." Another reinforcement arrived. She was dark haired, and sweetly shy. She stood beside Loren, crossed her arms over her chest and calmly looked across at her husband.

The two sides looked at each other, the men glaring at their turncoat wives, the women lined up protectively beside Mac. He was a little stunned to find himself surrounded by this perfumed wall of femininity.

Caroline gave her husband glare for glare. "Every one of us was welcomed with open arms when we married into this family, and I expect you to extend the same courtesy to Maris's husband—or else!"

Joe considered the challenge, his pale blue eyes glittering as he cocked his head. "Or else, what?" he asked, his deep voice silky and full of something that might have been anticipation.

Silence fell in the room, even the kids were quiet as they watched their parents. Mac looked at the six women ranged on either side of him, and his face softened into tender amusement. "It's okay," he said. "I understand."

"I'm glad you do, because I don't," Maris growled.

"It's a—"

"Don't say it's a man thing," Mary warned, interrupting, and he bit back the words.

"No, ma'am," he said meekly.

Wolf's dark face lightened, and his lips twitched. Those two words were very familiar to him.

Nick squirmed to get down, and Maris leaned over to deposit her on her feet. The little girl patted Mac on the knee and said, "Mac," with great satisfaction in her tone. She trotted across to her father, holding up her arms to be picked up. Zane leaned down and lifted her, settling her on one brawny arm. "Dat's Mac," she said, pointing. "I wike him."

Suddenly that hard, deadly face softened into a smile, and a big hand smoothed a silky tendril of hair away from her face. "I noticed," he said dryly. "He took one look at you and turned into your slave, just like the rest of us. That's what you really like, isn't it?"

Her little head bobbed up and down, very definitely. Zane chuckled as he shot an amused glance across the room at her mother. "I thought you would."

From somewhere down the hall came a baby's wail. "Cam's awake," Barrie said, and immediately abandoned Mac to go to her baby.

"How does she *do* that?" Chance asked of the room in general. "They're only two months old. How do you tell twins apart by their cries?"

The females, Nick included, had won. The tension in the room dissipated, smiles breaking out as Chance followed his sister-in-law down the hall, intent on finding out if she'd been right. Before he walked out he winked at Mac, in a moment of male understanding. The crisis had come and gone, because when it came down to it, the Mackenzie men were unwilling to distress their women. The women had liked Mac on sight, and that was that.

Barrie was back in only a moment, a squirming bundle in her arms. Chance followed her, expertly holding another one. "She was right," he announced, shaking his head in bewilderment.

Mac looked at the two tiny faces, finding them as identical as if they were mirror images. It was impossible to tell them apart even by looking at them; how in hell did Chance know if she was right or not?

"Cameron," Barrie said, indicating her burden and smiling at his skeptical look. "Chance is holding Zack." She also carried two small, milk-filled bottles.

"How do you know?" He shook his head, still looking for any distinguishing difference in the babies.

"Cameron's the most impatient, but Zack is more determined."

"You can tell that in their *cries?*"

"Well, of course," she said, as if anyone should be able to do the same.

Nick was climbing up on her father's shoulder, gripping his hair for leverage. "Wook, Unca Dance," she exclaimed, standing upright and releasing her safety hold.

Zane reached up and snagged his daughter off his shoulder. "Here, swap with me," he said, and he and Chance exchanged kids. Zane settled the baby in the crook of his arm and took one of the bottles from Barrie, expertly slipping the nipple into the rapacious little mouth.

Chance balanced Nick on his hands, firmly holding her feet while she straightened and crowed with delight at her achievement. "Chance," he coaxed. "My name is Chance. *Chance.*"

Nick placed her little hands on each side of his face, leaning close to peer into his eyes and impress him with her seriousness. "No," she said with great finality. "*Dance.* Oo say it wong."

The room exploded with laughter at Chance's expression. He eyed the pint-size dictator in his hands, then shook his head and gave up. "Are you sure you want to marry into this family?" He directed the question at Mac.

Mac looked at Maris and winked. "Yeah," he said.

Zane was watching him while the baby took the bottle, his calm eyes measuring. "Maris said you're an FBI special agent," he said, and something in his tone must have alerted Maris.

"No," she said firmly, pushing Mac toward the kitchen. "You can't have him. Being in the FBI is enough. You absolutely can't have him."

Mac found himself borne along on the tide of women, because they all wanted to discuss the wedding, but before he left the room he looked back. His gaze met Zane's...and Zane Mackenzie smiled.

"Welcome to the family," he said.

Epilogue

"You so *pwetty*," Nick sighed, her big blue eyes rapt as she propped her elbows on Maris's knee and stared at her aunt. The entire process of preparing for a wedding had fascinated the little girl. She had intently scrutinized everything as the women of the household had painstakingly made hundreds of tiny net bags, filled them with bird seed and tied them with ribbons. She had stood on her tiptoes, clinging to the table's edge, and watched as Shea, who made wonderful cakes, practiced making dozens of roses from icing before decorating Maris's wedding cake. Before long the practice roses had all borne evidence of a tiny, investigative finger. Once Nick had determined they were edible, they'd gradually disappeared, and her little face wore telltale smears.

Maris's gown held her absolutely enthralled. The long skirt, the lace, the veil, everything about it entranced her. When Maris had tried it on for the final fitting, Nick had clasped her hands under her chin and with shining eyes had said, "Oo a *pwincess!*"

"You're pretty, too, darling," Maris said. Nick was her flower girl. Zane had muttered about inviting disaster, and since Nick wasn't quite three years old, Maris was prepared for anything, including an outright refusal to perform her role. At the rehearsal the night before, however, Nick had strutted down the aisle with her little basket of rose petals and proudly strewn them, aware that every eye was on her. Whether she would do so when watched by a huge crowd was another question, but she was undeniably adorable in her long, blush pink dress, with ribbons and flowers in her silky black hair.

"I know," Nick replied matter-of-factly, and left her post at Maris's knee to return to the mirror to admire herself. It was something she had done every five minutes since Barrie had dressed her.

Barrie and Caroline were the acknowledged fashion mavens of the Mackenzie family, and they had taken over the arrangement of Maris's hair and the application of her makeup. They were astute enough to keep things simple, rather than overwhelming Maris's dainty face and frame with big hair and layers of makeup. Barrie had finished her hair and retired to a rocking chair to nurse the twins before the ceremony started. She supplemented their feedings with a bottle, but breast milk kept them contented longer, and she didn't want to have to feed them again in the middle of the reception.

Mary had quickly realized that the Mackenzie house, as large as it was, simply couldn't hold the crowd that was invited to the wedding. Because Christmas was on a Wednesday, the church in Ruth had held its Christmas service on Sunday, freeing it for the ceremony. The nine-foot-tall Christmas tree still stood in the corner, its multitude of white lights twinkling. Holly and evergreen needles still decorated the windowsills, filling the church with a wonderful aroma. White lights outlined the arched doorway, the windows, the sanctuary and the steps leading up to it. Rows of white candles lent their mellow glow to the church. None of the overhead lights would be on, but the tree, the Christmas lights and the candles combined to give the setting a magical aura.

This was Christmas Eve, a time when most of the occupants of Ruth would normally have been at home either having their private celebrations or preparing for them the next day. This year they were attending a wedding. From the private room off the vestibule Maris could hear the swell of noise as more and more people arrived.

Mary stood quietly, a sheen of tears in her slate blue eyes as she watched her daughter prepare for her wedding. It didn't matter that Maris and Mac were already married; this was the wedding that counted. This was her beloved daughter who looked so delicate and beautiful in her silvery white gown, a color that turned Maris's pale, ash brown hair to a darker shade of silver. She remembered the first time she had seen her daughter, only seconds old, so tiny and lovely and already staring around with big, solemn black eyes, her father's eyes. She remembered the tears that had sheened Wolf's own black eyes as he'd taken Maris in his arms and hugged the little scrap to his chest as if she were the most precious thing he'd ever seen.

There were thousands of other memories. Her first tooth, her first step, her first word—predictably, "horsie." Maris sitting on a pony for the first time, her eyes huge with delight while Wolf kept a protective arm around her. Maris, a little shadow dogging her father's footsteps just as her older brothers had done. Maris in school, fiercely joining in any fight the boys had gotten into, her little fists flying as she rushed to their defense, utterly ignoring the fact that the boys were twice her size. Maris sobbing when her old pony had died, and her radiant joy when, the next Christmas, Wolf had given her her first "real" horse.

There had been Maris's first date, and Wolf's scowling, prowling nervousness until his baby was safely back under his roof. One of Mary's favorite memories was of Zane and Josh and Chance pacing along with their father; if Joe and Mike had been there, they would have been pacing, too. As it was, the poor boy who had been so brave as to take Maris out had been terrified when the four Mackenzie males met them on the front porch on their return and had never asked her out again. They had gotten better about it over the years, but Maris must have forgotten her first date or she wouldn't have been so surprised at their reaction to Mac when she'd brought him home. *Men.* Mary loved her men, but really, they could be so overbearing. Why, they *liked* Mac, once they'd gotten over their bristly protectiveness. If Maris didn't watch out, Zane would have Mac recruited into whatever it was he and Chance—

Zane. Mary stopped short in her thoughts, looking around the room. All three of his children were here, with Barrie. Usually he was tending to at least one of the babies, or riding herd on Nick. That meant

Zane was free and unencumbered, and she was sure it wasn't by accident.

"Zane's free," she announced, because she thought Maris really ought to know.

Her daughter's head snapped up, and her lovely eyes caught fire. "I'll skin him alive," she said wrathfully. "I will *not* have Mac gone for months on end the way Chance is. I just got him, and I'm not letting him go."

Barrie looked startled; then she, too, realized the significance of having all three children with her. She shook her head in rueful acknowledgment of her husband's canniness. "It's too late to do anything about it now. He's had plenty of time to have a private talk with Mac, and you know Zane—he planned it perfectly."

Maris scowled, and Caroline drew back with the eye shadow brush in her hand. "I can't do this with your eyebrows all scrunched up," she admonished. Maris smoothed her expression, and Caroline went back to work. "I don't believe in letting hormone-driven men interfere in a woman's wedding. You can skin him alive tomorrow. Ambush him when he least expects it."

"Zane always expects everything," Barrie said, grinning. Then she looked at her daughter, who was twirling and dancing in front of the mirror, admiring herself. "Except Nick," she added. "He wasn't prepared for her."

"Was anyone?" Loren murmured, smiling fondly down at the little girl. Nick, hearing her name, stopped her pirouetting to favor them all with an angelic smile that didn't fool them for one second.

"Mac's besotted with her," Maris said. "He didn't turn a hair even when she polished his boots with the Magic Marker."

"An indication of true love if I've ever seen it," Caroline said dryly. She touched the mascara wand to Maris's already dark lashes, then stood back to admire her handiwork. "There! Mac would be crazy to leave you and go running around half-civilized countries where there's no sanitation and no shopping." Caroline's philosophy in life was to be comfortable, and she went to extraordinary lengths to accomplish it. She would gladly walk miles to find the perfect *comfortable* pair of shoes. It made perfect sense to her, since her work often required her to be on her feet for hours; how could she possibly concentrate if her toes were cramped?

"I don't think Mac would care about the shopping," Shea said. She picked Nick up and whirled around the room with the giggling little girl, humming a lively tune.

There was a knock on the door, and John poked his head inside. "It's time," he said. His pale blue gaze fell on Caroline. "Wow, Mom, you look great."

"Smart guy," she said approvingly. "I'll let you stay in my will."

He grinned and ducked out again. Maris stood, sucking in a deep breath. It was time. Never mind that they'd been married for three weeks already; this was a *production,* and practically the entire town was on hand to witness it.

Shea set Nick on her feet and got the basket of rose petals from the top of the closet, where they'd put it to keep Nick from scattering the flowers around the room. They'd already picked up the velvety petals once, and once was enough.

Barrie laid Zack beside Cameron. Both babies were sleeping peacefully, their little bellies full. Right on time, one of Shea's teenaged nieces arrived to watch them while Barrie attended the wedding.

The music began, their cue to begin entering the sanctuary.

One by one they began filing out, escorted by the Mackenzie men to their reserved seats. Zane's big form filled the doorway. Maris said, *"No,"* and he grinned as he held his hand out to Barrie.

"Just a minute." Barrie stooped in front of Nick, straightening the ribbons in her hair and at last placing the basket of flower petals in the eager, dimpled little hands. "Do the flowers just the way you did them last night, okay? Do you remember?"

Nick nodded. "I fwow dem aroun' on de fwoor."

"That's right, sweetheart." Having done all she could, Barrie stood and went to Zane, who slipped his arm around her waist and briefly hugged her close before they left to take their places.

Wolf came to the door, severely elegant in a black tuxedo. "It's time, honey," he said to Maris. His black eyes were tender as he wrapped his arms around her and rocked her back and forth, the way he had done all her life. Maris laid her head on her father's chest, almost overwhelmed by the sudden rush of love for him. She'd been so lucky in her parents!

"I was beginning to wonder if you'd ever forget about horses long enough to fall in love," he said, "but now that you have, I feel like we haven't had you long enough."

She chuckled against his chest. "That's exactly how I knew." She lifted her head, her eyes shining with both tears and laughter. "I kept forgetting about Sole Pleasure and thinking only about Mac. It had to be love."

He kissed her forehead. "In that case, I'll forgive him."

"Poppy!"

The imperious small voice came from the vicinity of his knee. They looked down. Nick was tugging on Wolf's pant leg. "We dotta *huwwy.* I dotta fwow fwowers."

As usual, her mangled English made him laugh. "All right, cupcake." He leaned down and took her free hand, to keep her from darting ahead of them and "fwowing fwowers" before they were ready.

He and Maris and Nick made their way into the vestibule, and Maris leaned down to kiss Nick's cheek. "Are you ready?" she asked.

Nick nodded, her slanted blue eyes wide and shining with excitement, and she clutched the flower basket with both hands.

"Here you go, then." Gently Maris urged Nick forward, into the center aisle. The church glowed with candlelight, and hundreds of smiling faces were turned toward them, it seemed.

Nick stepped out into the limelight like a Miss America taking her victory walk. She bestowed smiles to the left and the right, and she daintily reached into the basket for a rose petal. One. She held it out and let it drift downward. Then she reached for another. One by one she distributed the rose petals on the carpet with dainty precision, taking her time, even stooping once to adjust a petal that had fallen too close to another one.

"Oh, God." Beside her, Maris could feel Wolf shaking with laughter. "She's enjoying this too much. At this rate, you won't get to walk down the aisle until midnight."

People were turning and looking, and laughing at Nick's concentration on the task. Barrie buried her head in Zane's shoulder, lost in a helpless fit of giggling. Zane was grinning, and Chance was laughing out loud. Mac, standing at the altar, was beaming at the little imp who had so won his heart. The pianist, looking around, saw what was taking so long and gamely continued playing.

Tickled to be the center of attention, Nick began improvising. The next rose petal was tossed backward, over her shoulder. The minister choked, and his face turned red as he tried to hold back his guffaws.

She twirled on her tiptoes, flinging rose petals in a circle. Several flew out of the basket, and she frowned, stooping to pick them up and return them to the basket.

I can't laugh, Maris thought, feeling it bubbling inexorably upward. *If I laugh, I'll laugh until I cry, and it'll ruin my makeup.* She put her hand over her mouth to hold the mirth inside, but it didn't work. Her chest constricted, her throat worked and suddenly laughter burst joyously out of control.

Nick stopped and turned to look, beaming at them, waiting for them to tell her what a good job she was doing.

"*Fwow*—I mean, *throw* them," Maris managed to say between whoops.

The little head tilted to one side. "Wike dis?" she asked, taking a handful of petals from the basket and flinging them upward.

At least it was a handful, and not just one. "Like that," Maris said in approval, hoping it would speed the procedure.

It did. Another handful followed the first one, and Nick's progress down the aisle picked up speed. At last she reached the end, and bestowed an absolutely radiant smile on Mac. "I fwowed dem all," she told him.

"You did it just right," he said, barely able to speak for laughing. Her mission accomplished, she strutted to the pew where Zane and Barrie sat, and held up her arms to be lifted to the seat.

Relieved, the pianist launched into the familiar strains of "Here Comes the Bride," and at last Wolf and Maris began their stately walk down the aisle. Everyone rose to their feet and turned to watch, smiling.

Because time had been so short, there were no bridesmaids or groomsmen, no maid of honor or best man, so only Mac awaited Maris at the altar. He watched her approach, his hard face relaxed in a tender expression, his blue eyes still shining from his laughter. As soon as she stopped beside him, he gently took her hand in his, and behind them, they heard his mother give a teary, joyful little gasp.

Because Maris and Mac were already married, they had decided to skip the part about "who gives this woman." Wolf leaned down and kissed his daughter's cheek, hugged her tenderly, then shook hands with Mac and took a seat beside Mary.

"Dearly beloved," the minister began; then there was another gasp behind them. Recognizing Barrie's voice, Maris wasn't surprised when a little body slithered between her and Mac, taking a stance directly in front of them.

"I do it, too," Nick chirped, her little voice audible in every corner of the church.

Glancing over her shoulder, Maris saw Zane start to rise to retrieve his errant offspring. She shook her head, smiling. He winked and sank back into his seat.

So Nick stood pressed against their legs while the minister performed the service. They could feel her quivering with excitement, and Mac subtly gathered her closer to him so he would have a better chance of grabbing her if she started to do something startling, such as peek under the minister's cassock. She was already eyeing the garment with some curiosity. But she was content for the moment, completely taken with the ceremony, the candles, the twinkling Christmas tree, the beautiful clothes. When the minister said, "You may now kiss the bride," and Mac did so, Nick merely tilted her head back to watch.

"What's the best way to handle her when we leave?" Mac whispered against Maris's lips.

"Pick her up and hand her to Zane as we pass," she whispered back. "He'll be expecting it."

The pianist launched into the familiar stirring strains. Mac swooped Nick up with one arm, put the other around Maris, and they hurried up the aisle to the accompaniment of music, laughter, tears and a round of applause. As they passed the second pew, a tiny girl in a long dress was deftly passed from one pair of strong arms to another.

The reception was a long, glorious party. Maris danced endlessly with her husband, her father, all her brothers, several of her nephews, her brothers-in-law and an assortment of old friends. She danced with the sheriff, Clay Armstrong. She danced with Ambassador Lovejoy, Barrie's father. She danced with Shea's father and grandfather, with the ranchers and merchants and gas station attendants. Finally Mac claimed her again, holding her close and swaying to the music as he rested his cheek against hers.

"What did Zane say to you?" she demanded suddenly.

She felt him grin, though he didn't lift his head. "He said you'd know."

"Never mind that. What did he say?"

"You already know what he said."

"Then what did *you* say?"

"That I'm interested."

She growled. "I don't want you to spend months out of the country. I'm willing—barely—to let the FBI use you on investigations, but I don't like it. I want you with me every night, not thousands of miles away."

"That's exactly what I told Zane. Remember, I don't have to do what Chance does." He held her closer, dropping his voice to an intimate murmur. "Has your period started yet?"

"No." She was only two days late—but two days was two days, and she was normally very regular. It was possible her system had been disrupted by the concussion and the stress of everything that had happened, so she wasn't making any announcements yet. "Would you mind if I am pregnant so soon?"

"Mind?" He kissed her ear. "When we might get our own Nick?" His shoulders quivered under her embrace. "I didn't think she was *ever* going to get rid of those damn flower petals."

"She's one of a kind, I hope." But she leaned against him, feeling her breasts, her entire body, tighten with desire. If she wasn't already pregnant, she likely would be soon, given how often he made love to her.

They danced in silence for a moment, then Mac said, "Pleasure should have arrived by now."

She had to blink back tears, because Mac had given her the most wonderful gift for Christmas. With Sole Pleasure's worth hugely reduced now that the racing world had been rocked with news of his very low sperm count, the syndication offers had evaporated. It was *possible* Pleasure could sire a foal, but it was such a small possibility as to be negligible. He still had worth as a racehorse, and Ronald Stonicher might have gotten more for him than Mac had offered, but huge legal expenses had been staring him in the eye, and he'd jumped at the chance to sell the horse. Maris had worried so about Pleasure's future that Mac had made the offer for him without telling her, because he didn't want her to be disappointed in case the deal fell through.

"Dad can hardly wait to ride him," she said. "He's said several times that he envied me because I got to work with Pleasure."

They fell silent, simply enjoying the feel of being in each other's arms. Their wedding hadn't been a stately, solemn affair—Nick had seen to that—but it had been perfect. People had laughed and enjoyed themselves, and everyone for years would smile whenever they thought of Maris Mackenzie's wedding.

"It's time to throw the bouquet!"

The cry went up, and they swung around to see a crowd of giggling teenage girls gathering for the tradition, flipping back their hair, throwing sidelong glances at the older Mackenzie boys. There were more mature women there, too, giving Chance measuring looks.

"I thought you were supposed to throw it when we're ready to leave?" Mac said, amused.

"Evidently they can't wait."

She didn't mind hurrying things up a little; after that dance, she was ready to be alone with her husband.

Nick had been having the time of her short life, stuffing herself with cake and mints, and being whirled around the dance floor in the arms of her father, her grandfather and all her uncles and cousins.

When she saw Maris get the bouquet that had so fascinated her earlier, with all the "pwetty" flowers and lace and ribbons, she squirmed away from Sam's grip on her hand and moved to where she had a better view of the situation, her little head cocked to the side as she intently watched.

Maris climbed on the dais, turned her back and threw the bouquet high over her shoulder. Cries of "Catch it! Catch it!" filled the reception hall.

Almost immediately there was a collective cry of alarm. Maris whirled. The crowd of girls and women was rushing forward, eyes lifted, intent on the bouquet sailing toward them. And directly in front of them, also concentrating on the bouquet as she darted forward, was a tiny figure in pale pink.

There was a surge of black-clad bodies moving forward as seventeen males, one MacNeil and sixteen Mackenzies, from six-year-old Benjy up to Wolf, all leapt for the little girl. Maris caught a glimpse of Zane's face, utterly white as he tried to reach his baby before she was trampled, and somehow she, too, was running, leaping from the dais, heedless of her dress.

Two crowds of people were moving toward each other at breakneck speed, with Nick caught in the middle. One of the teenage girls looked down, saw Nick and emitted a shrill scream of panic as she tried to stop, only to be shoved forward by the girl behind her.

Chance had been standing back, avoiding any contact with that wedding bouquet business, but as a result, his movements were less impeded. He reached Nick two steps ahead of Zane, scooping her up, enfolding her in his arms and rolling with her out of harm's way. Zane veered, putting himself between Chance and anyone who might stumble over him, and in another second there was practically a wall of boys and men protecting the two on the floor.

The bouquet hit Chance in the middle of the back.

Carefully he rolled over, and Nick's head popped out of the shield he'd made with his arms. "Wook!" she said, spying the bouquet. "Oo caught de fwowers, Unca Dance!"

Maris skidded to a stop beside them. Chance lay very still on the floor, with Nick on his chest. He glared up at Maris, his light, golden-hazel eyes narrow with suspicion. "You did that on purpose," he accused.

The MacNeils and the Mackenzies moved forward, smiles tugging at stern mouths. Maris crossed her arms. "There's no way I could have arranged this." She had to bite her lip to keep from laughing at his outraged expression.

"Hah. You've been doing spooky stuff all your life."

Nick leaned over and grasped one of the ribbons of the bouquet, pulling it toward her. Triumphantly she deposited it on Chance's chest. "Dere," she said with satisfaction, and patted it.

Zane rubbed the side of his nose, but he was less successful than Maris at hiding his grin. "You caught the bouquet," he said.

"I did not," Chance growled. "She hit me in the back with it!"

Mary walked up and stood beside Wolf, who automatically put his arm around her. Slowly a radiant smile spread across her face. "Why, Chance!" she exclaimed. "This means you're next."

"I—am—not—next." He ground the words out, sitting up with Nick in his arms. Carefully he put her on her feet, then climbed to his own. "Trickery doesn't count. I don't have time for a wife. I like what I do, and a wife would just get in the way." He was backing away as he talked. "I'm not good husband material, anyway. I—"

A little hand tugged on his pant leg. He stopped and looked down.

Nick stretched on tiptoe, holding the bouquet up to him with both hands. "Don't fordet oor fwowers," she said, beaming.

* * * * *

Sizzling, Sexy, Sun-drenched...

SUMMER SENSATIONS

Three short stories by *New York Times* bestselling authors will heat up your summer!

LINDA HOWARD
LINDA LAEL MILLER
HEATHER GRAHAM POZZESSERE

Experience the passion today!

Available at your favorite retail outlet.

Silhouette®

The World's Most Eligible Bachelors are about to be named! And Silhouette Books brings them to you in an all-new, original series....

World's Most
Eligible Bachelors

Twelve of the sexiest, most sought-after men share every intimate detail of their lives in twelve never-before-published novels by the genre's top authors.

Don't miss these unforgettable stories by:

Dixie Browning

MARIE FERRARELLA

Jackie Merritt

Tracy Sinclair

BJ James

RACHEL LEE

Suzanne Carey

Gina Wilkins

VICTORIA PADE

MAGGIE SHAYNE

Anne McAllister

Susan Mallery

Look for one new book each month in the **World's Most Eligible Bachelors** series beginning September 1998 from Silhouette Books.

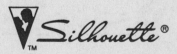

Silhouette®

Available at your favorite retail outlet.

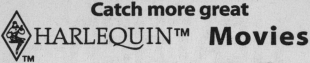

 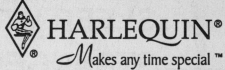

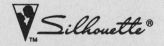

MATERNITY LEAVE

Coming September 1998

Three delightful stories about the blessings and surprises of "Labor" Day.

TABLOID BABY by Candace Camp

She was whisked to the hospital in the nick of time...

THE NINE-MONTH KNIGHT
by Cait London

A down-on-her-luck secretary is experiencing odd little midnight cravings....

THE PATERNITY TEST by Sherryl Woods

The stick turned blue before her biological clock struck twelve....

These three special women are very pregnant...and very single, although they won't be either for too much longer, because baby— and Daddy—are on their way!

Available at your favorite retail outlet.

Look us up on-line at: http://www.romance.net   PSMATLEV-M

MEN at WORK

All work and no play?
Not these men!

July 1998
MACKENZIE'S LADY by Dallas Schulze

Undercover agent Mackenzie Donahue's
lazy smile and deep blue eyes were his best
weapons. But after rescuing—and kissing!—
damsel in distress Holly Reynolds, how could
he betray her by spying on her brother?

August 1998
MISS LIZ'S PASSION by Sherryl Woods

Todd Lewis could put up a building with ease,
but quailed at the sight of a classroom! Still,
Liz Gentry, his son's teacher, was no battle-ax,
and soon Todd started planning some
extracurricular activities of his own....

September 1998
A CLASSIC ENCOUNTER
by Emilie Richards

Doctor Chris Matthews was intelligent, sexy
and *very* good with his hands—which made
him all the more dangerous to single mom
Lizette St. Hilaire. So how long could she resist
Chris's special brand of TLC?

Available at your favorite retail outlet!

MEN AT WORK™

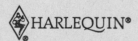

SILHOUETTE·INTIMATE·MOMENTS®

commemorates its

15th Anniversary

15 years of rugged, irresistible heroes!

15 years of warm, wonderful heroines!

15 years of exciting, emotion-filled romance!

In May, June and July 1998 join the celebration as Intimate Moments brings you new stories from some of your favorite authors—authors like:

Marie Ferrarella
Maggie Shayne
Sharon Sala
Beverly Barton
Rachel Lee
Merline Lovelace
and many more!

Don't miss this special event! Look for our distinctive anniversary covers during all three celebration months. Only from Silhouette Intimate Moments, committed to bringing you the best in romance fiction, today, tomorrow—always.

Available at your favorite retail outlet.